PRAISE FOR *ALL THAT RISES*

"I first met Alma García at the Bread Loaf Writers' Conference. I knew her work would be important, and now *All That Rises* proves it. Alma brings it and gives it all. Enhorabuena, novelista. An auspicious debut."
—LUIS ALBERTO URREA, author of *Good Night, Irene*

"Expansive and well grounded, *All That Rises* shines as a novel willing to trace its fingers into the highest and darkest branches of the family tree. García gives us an astounding panoply of characters—funny, wounded, smart, and proud—all of them striving to understand how families can nurture the strength of their roots only through hard-won honesty. An immersive and compassionate first novel."
—MANUEL MUÑOZ, author of *The Consequences*

"Beautiful, outrageous, and beguiling."
—HELENA MARÍA VIRAMONTES, author of *Their Dogs Came with Them*

"*All That Rises* introduces us to a refreshing new voice in Latinx literature. With empathy and grace, Alma García has mapped the borderlands in a bold new way. The result is a novel of stark originality populated by characters whose lives readers won't easily forget."
—ALEX ESPINOZA, author of *Still Water Saints*

ALL THAT RISES

ALMA GARCÍA

ALL THAT RISES

A NOVEL

THE UNIVERSITY OF
ARIZONA PRESS
TUCSON

The University of Arizona Press
www.uapress.arizona.edu

We respectfully acknowledge the University of Arizona is on the land and territories of Indigenous peoples. Today, Arizona is home to twenty-two federally recognized tribes, with Tucson being home to the O'odham and the Yaqui. Committed to diversity and inclusion, the University strives to build sustainable relationships with sovereign Native Nations and Indigenous communities through education offerings, partnerships, and community service.

ISBN-13: 978-0-8165-4915-3 (paperback)
ISBN-13: 978-0-8165-4916-0 (ebook)

Cover design by Leigh McDonald
Designed and typeset by Leigh McDonald in Calluna 10/14, Iva WF and Tallow Sans (display)

Publication of this book is made possible in part by the proceeds of a permanent endowment created with the assistance of a Challenge Grant from the National Endowment for the Humanities, a federal agency.

Library of Congress Cataloging-in-Publication Data are available at the Library of Congress.

Printed in the United States of America
♾ This paper meets the requirements of ANSI/NISO Z39.48-1992 (Permanence of Paper).

For my father

and

for my mother

FOREWORD

EL PASO, TEXAS, IS ONE of the most compelling settings in Chicano literature. From John Rechy's queer novel *City of Night* (1963) to Estela Portillo Trambley's novella *Rain of Scorpions* (1975) to Alma García's stunning debut novel set in recent times, the border city continues to hold its place as a premier landscape of the literary imagination. Credit its groundbreaking writers who refresh our eyes by paving unexplored pathways into the heart of El Paso's vibrant life. Such is the case with *All That Rises*, a multivalent narrative that journeys through the range of experiences of the Mexican labor force and Texan professionals—both Chicano and white—shattering demarcations that we have long believed separate people by class, ethnicity, language, and nationality.

García's novel, populated by a notably large cast of characters whose stories pulse with secrets and deceptions, unearths the uncomfortable truths of familial and community relationships, the precariousness of imposed hierarchies and economic dependencies, and the brittleness of borders. Though readers will encounter protagonists who work as sweatshop managers and border patrol guards—arguably two of the most embattled occupations in the borderlands—García's nuanced characterizations will trouble both prejudice and assumption, eschewing reactionary politics by privileging a communal portrait over individual headshots. It's the greater, more complex history that counts. Yet even that pronouncement is unsettled by García's intricate and clever storytelling.

The word *history* cascades down the pages of this novel, situated not as a fixed concept or definition, but one that is subject to question. "*History*," one characters quips. "What good is it anyway?" And then elaborates, "Well, that's the thing about history, ain't it? All you got is somebody's memory. No one can prove anything ever happened." *All That Rises* showcases the collision between knowledge and belief—what took place and how it is remembered. And, most consequentially, how a view of the self (and others) changes with the discovery of new insights or information.

If all of this sounds weighty, rest assured that the narrative you are about to enter is buttressed by humor and scenes that wallop with emotional punches and surprises. The dust only begins to settle after one revelation when another one starts to come to light, which makes for quite an unpredictable reading experience.

The late Chicano author and El Paso native Arturo Islas once pointed out that "the 2,000-mile-long Mexican–United States border has a cultural identity that is unique." That condition, he observed, is what fueled the energy in his novel *The Rain God* (1984). García, too, draws inspiration from this magical and conflicted place, and without question has written a great novel destined to become another classic set in la gran frontera.

—*Rigoberto González*

ALL THAT RISES

What's past is prologue.
—SHAKESPEARE, THE TEMPEST

El amor es ciego, pero los vecinos no.
Love is blind, but the neighbors aren't.
—MEXICAN PROVERB

ANTES

BEFORE

EVERY LIGHT IN THE HOUSE is off. The neighboring houses too. Below lies the sloping curve of the street, the carpet of city lights, the highway bending through the desert and streaked with sparse trails of red and white. Farther still, a river, the divide between *here* and *over there*.

Her shoulder cramps. In her duffel bag, the necessities, stuffed in without folding: sundresses, sleeveless blouses, swimsuit, underwear of a certain quality—in particular, a silk slip, its hem stained with coffee. No time for washing. Or maybe she would fly it like a flag. Her hand slides to the bag's outer pocket. The envelope crinkles at her touch.

She holds whatever breath she's still able to breathe as she skims down the driveway. There is who she once was and who she is now, but nothing holds them apart anymore. She is permeable, thinner than air, except for the great weight certain people have left on her heart. She thinks of those sleeping behind her, the shapes they each make in their beds, the arc of their breath. Her hand shakes. Key instead of the beeper, so she won't make a sound.

Her slippery thumb sets off the car alarm.

She hisses "Shh, shh, shh, shh!" to the horn that announces her, over and over, as she hot-potatoes the fob.

The alarm chokes off. Her heart pounds, eyes spinning wild toward the house. She waits, with despair and relief, for the lights to turn on. For everyone to wake up.

She waits until the crickets resume their rasping in the hedges. The lights do not come on.

Hmmmph.

She aims the key fob like a gun. Allows the door to slam shut behind her. As she pivots out of the driveway, she forces a squeal from the tires.

Yet she idles in the street, listening to her own slowing breath. Her hands grow heavy and warm on the steering wheel as the darkness opens around her. It can't keep her out. Her eyes almost close.

"Wake up," she whispers. "You've been dreaming."

And she's off.

AL TIEMPO, TIEMPO LE PIDO

FROM TIME, I ASK TIME

2005

1

SHALLOW WATERS

HUCK DUPRE FINDS THE NOTE taped to the toilet.

What if, Huck? What if there was someone else?
What if I was on my way to meet him right now?
While you're chewing on that, here are some ideas
for explaining my absence: I've lost my mind. I'm
going on a world tour. I've gone off to find myself.
I'm trying to rediscover my youth. I've joined a
convent. The Peace Corps. A cult. I'm a secret
alcoholic or prescription drug addict. Tell the girls
at the country club I dropped dead. Tell the kids I'll
be back in a couple of weeks. Probably. It depends on
how things go. We could all just use a damned break
from each other, don't you think?

Rose Marie's Lexus is not in the garage. And no one has made any coffee. Outside, the kid he pays to manage the lawn applies pruning shears to the rosebushes.

"I see someone's up early."

Jordan, his nine-year-old, screws her fists into the waistband of her pajamas, a cowlick tenting her hair. Huck slots the coffeepot back to its burner. Jordan yanks open the refrigerator. Out come the eggs, a package of bacon, bread loaf, oranges.

"How do you want your eggs?" she demands.

"Make some hash browns," Quinn calls out from the den. He's seventeen. Both TV and stereo jabber behind him. In the window-framed distance that is unannexed Ciudad Juárez, a van plows a dirt cloud up a hill.

The tap spurts.

"Jesus!" Skyler, Quinn's twin, holds her hair as she spits in the sink. "This coffee sucks!"

"Dad made it." Jordan turns an egg end over end in her hand.

Huck sets down his mug with a slosh. Outside, the kid who takes care of the lawn—Miguel, his name is Miguel—lifts his baseball cap from his head to fan himself as he casts a brazen glance into the dining room.

The river gleams brown, far below.

"No eggs," Huck announces. "We're going to Western Playland."

On the lawn, Miguel, head bowed now and bronze forearms taut, adds gas to the lawn mower with the intensity of a man who knows exactly what should be done.

It had been only the night before last that Rose Marie, leg-lifting in her bathrobe, had asked what Huck thought about the idea of her taking a separate vacation.

"So? How would it make you feel?" Her kneecap cracked as she brought her knee to her chest.

He lifted a copy of the quarterly report from the bedside table. Always, he had found it advantageous to read something or watch television when a careful answer to a question was called for. Whenever things were behind schedule at the maquiladora, or the manufacturer discovered a design flaw, or the workers installed the letters on a batch of keyboards upside down, or a foreman quit, or any of the problems associated with operating a Mexican factory with American money reared their treacherous heads, it was best to create an impenetrable bubble inside which he could assess his situation, dismiss what could've been or should be, and move on. In that moment, though, the answer had been simple enough.

"If it would make you happy," he'd said to her, "then go ahead."

"But how does it make you *feel*?"

He studied the profit/loss column. "I'd have to think about that."

"What do you mean you have to think about it?"

"It means I haven't thought about it. So it doesn't really make me feel anything in particular."

"But what's your gut reaction? What does it make you feel *right now?*"

What he'd felt was the heaviness of his eyelids. It had always been Rose Marie's habit, as a first-class, grade A insomniac, to wait until just before bed to drop the conversation bombs, but the truth of the matter was that arguments after a certain hour of the day made him sleepy.

Even now, as he hoofs up from the parking lot to the gates of Western Playland, he's still damned tired. The air tastes of burnt sugar and hot dogs and crude oil from the refinery upwind. Everything under the mid-morning light sears the eye—the Ferris wheel, the half shells of the Tilt-a-Whirl, the roller coaster with its familiar metallic silhouette of a grinning, sombreroed, pistol-wielding Mexican.

He tugs down the brim of his Stetson and trails the kids to the carnival games, where Skyler is already rupturing a balloon with a dart.

"Yes!" he shouts, projecting cheer.

Quinn sidles up on Skyler's next pass, probing his hoop-studded ear, and knocks his elbow into hers.

"Asshole," she hisses.

"What?" Quinn knee-nudges Jordan, who sits in a meditating posture on the lip of a cement planter. Failing to get a response, he leaves a footprint on the back of her T-shirt. "Did you hear that? She just called me an asshole."

"Quit," Jordan says with her eyes shut.

Quinn bumps Skyler's arm again. She shoves him back.

"Kids." Huck bites into a grin. "For Chrissakes."

Jordan sighs. "Dad. Why are we *here?*"

"Hello? Why does *anybody* come to an amusement park?"

The kids roll their eyes as one, as though they were communicating by radio signal. Then they walk off.

Rose Marie once said to him during one of their fights, "Kids *need* to question things. Trouble is you don't want them to think for themselves. Do you just want them to be obedient little drones? Is that what you want?"

He answered in jest, in refusal of guilt, in defense, with a wounding he wouldn't admit to, "Hell yes."

Who was she in league with now?

He considers Joe Chandler at the Rodríguezes' barbecue, the way his eyes trailed her to the buffet table. Richard Martínez at the country-club bar, holding court after his divorce like a big-game hunter freshly returned from safari. These were the known quantities. In the distant, weekday world of her charity work, he had only ever imagined Rose Marie in the company of other women with clipboards and a brisk way of walking. Not a man who might be good looking, who jogged, who ate sushi on trips to California and bought the right kind of birthday gifts and could talk about art, and—

Who the hell cares! If, in fact, there's someone else, the son of a bitch wouldn't be impervious to scrutiny. Or punishment.

The kids slouch in line for the roller coaster. Huck pushes toward them through a moist clot of bodies, strollers, tethered balloons that lurch out to rap him on the head. A load of passengers crests the ride's first summit above him. Would he be able to bear watching the secret videotapes? How much lip-lock could he handle, how much chest pressing chest? What would he do when the unbuttoning and flinging of clothing began? The passengers shriek as they hurtle to earth.

He turns heel on a hot wave of nausea. "Let's go," he says, nudging them out of line. "I don't want to go on El Bandita."

"Dad," Skyler says. "it's Ban*dido*."

"That's what I said."

He scans the perimeter as he shepherds them forward. The whiplash temptation of the bumper cars is off limits when the familial mood is precarious. A ride through the Golden Nugget would get them out of the heat—he had always enjoyed the piano-playing skeleton in Old West garb—but it would come at the cost of ten minutes of strobe lighting and a face-to-face meeting with the honking front end of a semi.

Was it possible to sue your own wife?

"No." Skyler strains away from the rudder of his hand. "You said 'El Bandita.' It's supposed to be '*El* Ban*dido*,' '*La* Ban*dida*.'"

"Whichever. Now look at that." Just ahead, a load of cheering passengers splash-lands at the base of the log ride. "That was you and your brother's favorite ride when you were Jordan's age."

"What do you mean 'whichever'?"

Huck turns to her. He's in no mood. He's lived in El Paso for fourteen years—they all have—and this is where he belongs. He knows
the difference between a mesa and a vista. He knows which restaurants offer the hottest chile con carne and the chiles rellenos containing real cheese instead of Velveeta. He could trace the khaki contours
of the Franklin Mountains with his eyes closed, name every major
intersection in the gray grid visible from the edge of his lawn, identify by odor the manufactured substances that foul up the air. He has
traveled the pulsing cord of this city's east–west freeway five thousand times over, Mexico on its far side like a suggestion that hadn't
been taken—the patchwork of cinder block houses and scrap metal
roofs, dirt roads that wrap the hills and seem to go nowhere, the huge
Mexican flag rippling in the distance, Jesus watching both sides from
the white crucifix atop the mountain that is actually a sliver of New
Mexico, as though the state had stepped on the back of Old Mexico to
elbow Texas in the ribs. In between worlds, the Rio Grande, eternally
at his shoulder whether he was coming or going, brown and slack as
dropped rope.

This land is his land.

"I mean," he says, "whichever."

"Do you not care at all about how ignorant you sound?"

He bristles. "I'm not stupid."

"Dad." Jordan appears at his side in the log ride line, Mary Janes dug
into the ground, fists rammed under her armpits. "We don't want this
ride. We want to go on the roller coaster."

He bores his gaze into hers—her brows hard set beneath the shag of
her carroty hair, cheeks spattered with freckles, eyes as fierce and inky
brown as Rose Marie's—but his fury seeps suddenly away. He kneels
beside his youngest and says, "Honey."

Jordan doesn't blink. "Dad, get up. You're not proposing to me."

He laughs.

"All right. Have it your way."

He scoops Jordan up, flinging her over one shoulder, arm pressing
against the scissors of her legs. Then, up to the dock. She makes a soft
whump as he drops her into the hollow log bobbing beside them, then
another as she throws herself against the far side to glare. He extends

a hand toward the rear bench as if to say, *After you*, and knows, even before the moment they dart eyes to each other, that the twins will obey. Skyler steps in before Quinn. Birth order. The water is a cheerful shade of aqua, like the painted channel beneath it and the brilliant sky above. The attendant, a pretty, camel-eyed Mexican girl, even offers him a smile as she reaches for the safety bar over his head.

He twists around in his seat to look back. The log jerks them all toward the sky. Below, people on burlap bags whoosh with joy down the hump of the potato-sack slide. Skyler sways in the seat beside him. In profile, the girl's all Rose Marie—the nose with its exotic arch, the generous lips, the point of the chin—even with the sharp blue-gray eyes he gave her and her matted pile of blond sausages. Libertarian or not, Rose Marie once told him she fantasized about slipping into Skyler's room at night and snipping her dreads off with Miguel's pruning shears.

"Stop staring at me," she mutters now.

He straightens forward as they lurch into a covered chute, the sunlight disappearing, the water reeking of chlorine. His thighs begin to buzz numbly—the safety bar is set too low for him. "Don't get your undies in a bunch."

Skyler's seat creaks. "Where's Mom?"

"I wouldn't know."

"Naturally."

"What's that supposed to mean?"

"It means you never seem to know the important things."

The log makes a short whoosh downward, and they smack against an incline, water slopping over the sides.

"Guess what?" Huck strains against the bar. "I'm not the only one in this family who—"

"She left you, didn't she." Quinn's voice rings in the tunnel.

Huck's heart pounds in his neck, in his teeth. Honestly, he's not sure.

"So." Quinn laughs through his nose. "Were you screwing around on her or what?"

The log levitates as Huck wrenches himself around. The front of Quinn's shirt puckers in his fist. The log falls. A hand—whose?—is squashed between Huck's body and his backrest, and they crash back onto the down ramp with a slosh. Jordan tumbles against him, and as he stiff-arms her back to her seat, rolling onto one butt cheek, he tenses against the sudden, stomach-lifting pull of gravity, and the safety bar pops open over his thighs. He teeters over the side of the log, but before he can correct anything, decide anything, finish anything, stop anything, he's pushed. He doesn't know whose hands do it, but there it is—one hard, quick shove. Then he tumbles through a bright burst of sunlight and smacks into the water.

He's going under. Under the thick, aqua-blue water smelling of toilet bowl cleaner. He's drinking it, choking on it. He kicks, fighting his way back to the surface, but his Tony Lamas are soggy bricks on his feet, and he knows in a wordless, paralyzed moment that this is how he will meet his doom.

"Dad!" his children shout. Hands grasp his slippery wrists and shirt-sleeves. He's dragged by the armpits, cheek pressing the slime-slick side of the car.

He realizes then that the bottom of this pool meets his feet. The water is only chest high.

On shore, pandemonium. Brakes squealing, the electric decrescendo of lost power. Onlookers clog the dock area, shouting words he can't understand.

The last thing he sees before passing out is Jordan, standing back from the crowd as she clutches his dripping hat.

III

The truth of the matter is that Rose Marie had always confused order with oppression. It defied all natural law. She'd once been one of those creatures who make Texas college sororities possible—Dallas girls, extravagantly hair-sprayed and manicured, who go to church on Sundays after Saturday-night beer benders, leaving the alarms of their sports cars to howl in the dormitory parking lots.

Pre-wed is what you called a girl like that, not to mention seriously out of his league—this was the oil money–lubricated playing field of Southern Methodist University, after all—though as he passed her on the lawn of Northrup Hall, he couldn't resist the challenge he saw in the well-groomed arch of her eyebrow. She'd snorted at his introduction and asked whether he was planning an epic rafting trip down the Mississippi. He'd cackled with the pleasure of his surprise. Still, he didn't reveal his real name—Harold—until he paid his first visit to the house that made him think, *Plantation*, as he passed between its two white pillars.

By that time, though, he'd removed his shoes in the foyer and received the stiff parental handshakes and the appraising glances of the two Black women who served them a roast beef dinner followed by a bourbon pecan pie. Of course, he was embarrassed by the way they all watched him handle the silverware, but he looked his future in-laws in the eye, managing *Yes, sir* and *Yes, ma'am.* Yes sir, he had a scholarship. He had a game plan. Rose Marie grinned like a cat.

That was back when she was still part of his team. Even in the blur of the twins' first months, all she had to do was meet his eyes in the dim light of the nursery as she nursed one baby and he bottle-fed the other, and he would be overcome by a terrifying sense of cheer, as though together they made up a task force forged expressly for the purpose of fighting desperation.

They came to El Paso, the glory of NAFTA paving his way at last toward the stock portfolio of his dreams. Then Jordan. Jordan, Jordan, accidental Jordan, who from her first moment had been a force with which none of them was prepared to reckon.

The morning she was born, he'd taken the long way home from the hospital on the frontage road beside the river and pulled over. He'd been light-headed as he shuffled from his vehicle to the chain-link fence, uncertain of what he was looking for. A wide, dusty incline of creosote-pimpled rock rose up at his back to where the railroad tracks lay. Above that, the freeway rumbling with early traffic and the university looming at mountainside, its red roofs like square hats. Before him, the river was free of the concrete bed that bound it for much of the length of the city, and it was running muddy and low.

He released an unsteady breath. Eight years out on the open highway of parenthood, only to find himself now back on the doorstep of that soul-fracturing, gutted sleep; the mountains of diapers and snot wipers; the long, long tantrum-filled march toward kindergarten, already item-ized with expenses and delays for the next eighteen to twenty-five years.

His new child had smelled of blood as she squalled in his arms, and had felt like a very ripe peach.

It was then that he noticed a man in the distance. A boy, actually. He stood almost opposite Huck on the Mexican side, at river's edge—no barbwire on his side, of course—pitching stones into the murk. Behind him, a low, graffiti-slicked cinder block wall held back the familiar clumped shacks, which seemed to be trying but not quite managing to arrange themselves in straight lines. Huck watched the boy leaning, his arm slicing the air again and again, the explosive splash of each rock. He watched until the boy lowered his arm and looked up.

The boy raised his hand to wave.

Huck raised his hand in return, a swift current of optimism rising within him before the sun flashed against a tin roof and everything was lost in the glare.

If only he could have gotten Rose Marie's attention the same way. It was as though she, too, had vaporized in the dazzle of the weeks that followed. Of course, she was busy with the baby. With only one to wrangle this time around, she was brilliant with the care and feeding—it was only natural. But still he would wake in the night, as though yanked by a cord summoning him to a task he could no longer define. He'd stumble out to find the baby already fed and asleep, and Rose Marie, hair brushed and in her pink silk robe, poring through a volume of the *Encyclopaedia Britannica*. He once asked her groggily, "You studying for a test on the letter *p*?" She didn't look up. She only muttered, "I'm trying to learn something I don't already know."

"Huck," Rose Marie had said to him night before last. "I would like to know, right this instant, right stinking now, what your feelings are on the matter of a separate vacation."

Then she put down her leg until he knew he had to look.

All right. Here was his wife of nineteen years, a woman who was definitely still good to look at. Her hair lay in a damp, gold slick against her neck; the freckles on the part of her chest she referred to as her décolletage peeked from the lacy thing under her bathrobe. The skin at her temples was pinched; her dark eyes glowed electrically. Want rose from her in an almost palpable cloud.

What he couldn't stand, from where he hunkered at his center, was his implication in that want. Nor his sudden thought—similar to the way he might regard a suspiciously dated carton of milk—of what it would be like to open the door of that want this time, just a crack.

"Huck?"

"S'talk about it in the morning," he mumbled into his pillow.

"Huck!"

He awakened the next morning with the pressing opinion that what she needed was a hobby, not a vacation, though she should still go if she wanted. She appeared to receive this diagnosis well. In fact, she released an abrupt, throaty laugh, as though she had discovered something perfectly absurd, which—of course—all of this was. With relief seeping through him, he joined her.

Whatever the laugh meant wasn't the point. If she knew what she wanted, she should say what it was. What does it mean when everyone you know is harboring some kind of hidden agenda, and what the hell is that thing looming over him? He can feel it now, slithering under his chin and his armpits, and as it opens its vast, sucking maw, he understands that it is stronger than he is. He lunges for it. He tries to throttle it, but it squirts through his fingers, everywhere and nowhere at once, and then he's jerked from the water and laid out on a warm slab of pavement.

"Dad!" Quinn leans in with wrinkled forehead. "Holy crap."

Skyler and Jordan lift their necks like gophers.

His lungs seize in his chest. He hacks, rolls onto his side.

"Dad," Jordan says, "you've got some algae on your face."

He probes his numb cheek.

"Harold, don't get up, okay?"

At Huck's feet, someone kneels—a damp park employee with a goatee that tickles the collar of his polo shirt. *Llama*, Huck thinks distantly. He pushes against the ground with one hand and rises unsteadily.

"Whoa! Harold! Don't move. The paramedics are on their way."

"It's Huck." His voice sounds hoarse and far away. He reaches for his hat and tugs it free of Jordan's grip. "I go by Huck."

"Okay, Huck. Please just lie back down."

Huck motions the kids onto their feet. It's strange, the way the crowd parts silently to let them pass, the self-conscious way the kids carry themselves like movie stars past the whirling swings of the Yo-Yo. The llama calls after them. When the guy himself steps up to clap a hand on his shoulder—an act that should call for violence—Huck feels only a slow throb at the core of his head. He detaches the hand. The voice recedes behind him. *Please. Come back. Lie down.*

Huck's silence piles around him in the back seat of the Cherokee. It thickens as Quinn maneuvers the vehicle out of the parking lot, past the inexplicable statue of blind Lady Justice hoisting her scales at the park entrance, past the oil refinery belching its chemical tang. The silence swells all the way home and up to the front door, where Huck realizes his house keys lie somewhere at the bottom of the log ride.

He jiggles the doorknob. None of the kids have house keys on them—that's clear from the sag of their shoulders. The drone of cicadas grates the air. Across the street, a pickup truck laden with lawn equipment blazes in the brassy afternoon light. Huck's clothes hang on him damply; a purple bruise blooms like a Rorschach test on his forearm. He angles himself out of street view behind a juniper hedge, tries the doorbell—just in case—and offers the swift tip of his boot to the door.

First, a starburst of pain. Then, at pain's center, a perfect, gleaming nugget of clarity.

"I'm going to go find a locksmith," he announces. His big toe throbs, but his voice is surprising to him in its strength.

Jordan exhales. "Dad. Let's make this easy." She extracts a cell phone—pink and bearing the Hello Kitty logo—from her purse.

Huck almost laughs. "Where did you get that thing?"

"Shh." She flaps her hand at him as she punches buttons with a thumb. "The reception here is terrible."

His mirth slips. "Did your mother buy it for you?"

She makes for the thorny pyracantha at the edge of the yard.

"Hey!" He steps forward onto his toe and winces. A radio blasts to life from the bowels of the lawn truck just as the music dissolves to a haranguing blur of Spanish. "I'm talking to you!"

She slips away as he lurches, clawing but missing her shirt collar, until a swift object smears between them.

Skyler. Her hands make fists at her sides.

"Leave her alone!"

He blinks. "Are you talking to *me*?"

"I said, leave her alone!"

"Just what is the problem here?"

"Hello? Mom's gone and you didn't even tell us?"

"Goddammit! All I wanted . . ." What he wants in this moment is to gather his children into the crush of his arms. "Would it have killed you all to try to have a little fun?"

"You almost drowned!"

Because one of you pushed me, he almost retorts, but the taste of humiliation rises simultaneously at the back of his throat, so he rolls his eyes.

"This is stupid," Quinn announces from the curb. "I'm waiting in the car."

Jordan is the only one to offer Huck a fleeting backward glance before the passenger door groans open and seals the three of them in with a slam.

The radio across the street resumes with excitable Mexican music, the bass line *oompah-ing* with tubas. The beat pounds in Huck's big toe. Someone turns over the Cherokee's engine for the sake of the air-conditioning, and he lurches like a train, part of him going forward before the rest of him is ready, until he finds his palm pressed to the window.

"You know," he tells his children through the glass, "sooner or later, y'all are going to have to decide whose side you're on."

They don't answer. They all look away.

He wishes he knew who they'd choose.

He turns and retreats to the porch. Lowers himself to the steps, leans back on a post. His skin tightens in the sun, as though he was covered in clay.

He feels the clamp of an unfamiliar hand on his shoulder. His eyes spring open to the shadow that leans over him. It's a brown-skinned man, unsmiling, and Huck releases a weird bark and cocks back his fist to his ear.

Miguel snatches his hand away and steps back.

"Chingado! Mr. DuPre, sorry! Sorry, sorry, sorry."

"Jesus Christ!"

"Sorry!" Miguel backs up. "I thought something was wrong with you, man."

"Wait." Huck rubs his face. He hoists himself dizzily onto his feet. "Miguel. It's okay."

Miguel pauses. He lifts the coil of the garden hose. "You want water?"

Huck drinks in slow, lolloping gulps until his throat aches. He runs the warm stream under his hat and over his face. It tastes of sun, rubber, metal, grass, earth.

"Thank you," he says afterward, dripping.

Miguel shuts off the valve. The pickup—Miguel's, of course—thumps now with some kind of Latin-beat rap music. Huck swipes the water from his eyes. He wonders whether Miguel overheard them. Whether he watched.

Miguel winds the hose onto its hook. He's a good-looking young man, on the small side but with wiry, quick limbs. He doesn't meet Huck's eye. Rose Marie has always been the one who makes the arrangements with him. Who pays him.

"How's life treating you?" Huck asks anyway.

The kid pulls down his thumb until it touches his wrist. "Pues, all right, I guess."

"Hot out here."

The kid links pinkies and turns his arms inside out. "Pues, sí."

"God*damn*, Stretch. You made of rubber?"

Miguel laughs at his palms. It's just a chuckle—the sort born of nerves, or maybe bewilderment—but Huck sees the relief in his face, and he feels it too and joins him. He laughs in reassurance. He laughs because they are laughing together.

He laughs until he realizes Miguel has stopped, and that he's laughing alone.

"I better finish," Miguel tells the lawn soberly. He turns away.

"For God's sake," Huck snaps. "Am I invisible?"

Miguel straightens. "No."

"Then look me in the eye."

It's a long moment before Miguel turns, but when he does, his hand slips to his shirt pocket to retrieve a pair of eyeglasses, which he unfolds with self-conscious care. They're big ones, with gray plastic frames and lenses that magnify his eyes to the size of Oreo cookies, and through them he beholds Huck with an unmistakable gleam of contempt. Then he turns away and stoops to examine the sprinkler head, leaning with the resolve of a man who doesn't know what to do, but will do something anyway.

Huck's head sags. The river catches the sun below, mirror-bright.

"Miguel," he says, gently now, because it seems to him that finally he's found the right question. "Are you happy?"

Miguel tightens, just for an instant. Then, an odd chuckle. "Am I what?"

Huck squats beside him. "What makes you happy?"

Miguel uproots the sprinkler with so much force that he stumbles. Huck shoots his hand out, meaning to steady him. But Miguel flinches out of his reach.

Huck reaches for him again—a conciliatory gesture, a reflex.

Miguel sloughs off his hand and steps back. Huck means to say "what?" but hears only the sound of his breath. His words have flown elsewhere. In fact, it seems to him that everything's receding from him now—his lawn, the brown hills below, the cinder block shacks, the horizon itself. Nothing more than a ribbon of river to hold it all at the seams. He could still step up to grasp Miguel's slight shoulder, tell him it's all right, it's going to be fine. But the look in his eye says he's already gone, so Huck stays his hand, trying not to look like a man who didn't know how deep the water was, who was farther than he knew from shore.

2

THE BROWN INVASION

IN THE BRONZE LIGHT OF late afternoon, as Jerry Gonzales stands at the french doors overlooking his deck, Chavela gives her orders.

The coffee table, she says. Make sure you use two tablespoons of wax, just two, only two. Top to bottom. Never in circles. It's an antique.

"Sí, señora," is the response.

Jerry glides to the landing at the top of the stairs and peeks over. The heavyset woman whom Chavela addresses stands with her back to him in the kitchen, her black bun drooping, the waistband of her pants bunching beneath her T-shirt. She shifts between feet in bread loaf–sized athletic shoes.

Chavela with her pixie cut, her pink blouse, her pantsuit the color of ashes.

"También las ventanas, por favor," she adds, tapping the bottle of Windex on the kitchen island.

The woman nods.

For she is the maid. The *maid*.

There's no way in hell he's addressing this woman as "tú."

"Dad," calls a voice behind him, "can I take one of the cars?"

Adam, their son, pokes his head from his bedroom. Black attire, as ever. Orange stripes in his hair. Eyebrow with ring inserted without permission and which he is required to remove in the presence of his grandmother.

"Where?"

Adam shrugs. He has developed a theory that matriculated seniors shouldn't have to explain everything. He is focused mostly on packing things into duct-taped boxes in anticipation of the day his parents will drive the seven hundred miles to San Diego to deposit him at a dormitory's doorstep—God forbid he should attend El Paso's serviceable university, where, it so happens, his father recently achieved tenure. But Adam desires new experiences and opportunities; he wants to see more of the world. Of course, Jerry has encouraged this curiosity. Of course, both he and Chavela want only what's best for him.

Although if this were completely true, Chavela wouldn't have spent the past two weekends angrily cleaning out the garage.

"Take the Volvo," Jerry says now. "Return by midnight."

Adam grins. "Thanks, viejo." He disappears.

Jerry returns to his desk, his embossed tomes. *Popé's Dream: A New View of the Pueblo Revolt of 1680. Sons of Oñate: Modern Colonialism in the American Southwest.*

From downstairs comes a surprised female gasp, followed by the yapping of a small dog. He oozes back out of the room. Chavela's Pomeranian dances on its hind legs.

"Ay, Paquito."

Chavela stoops down and tickles him under the chin. She extracts a dog biscuit. Her voice rises an octave—"Who's my good boy, are you my good boy, yes you are"—and the biscuit is snapped up in midair.

She looks up from the floor. "¿Te gustan los perros?"

The maid is practically standing with one foot on top of the other. "Sí, señora."

Adam breezes into the room, car keys jingling.

"Hi, sweetheart," Chavela says, rising. "Say hello to Lourdes."

"What's up, Lourdes?"

Chavela gives him a narrow look.

"Hola," he says. Then to his mother, "What's for dinner?"

"Chicken."

Chavela shakes her head as Adam snatches a Coke from the refrigerator and slips out.

"Y tú . . ." She glances over her shoulder. "¿Tienes hijos?"

Lourdes nods.

The coffee table, Chavela says. Top to bottom, not in circles. Never. It streaks. It's an antique, and by the way, there is a sandwich in the refrigerator for you.

"Muy bien, señora. Gracias."

Chavela makes her gathering sounds—papers, keys, sunglasses.

Señor Gonzales is upstairs, she says. He'll be home for the summer, researching. Writing. In any case, he knows you're here—she pauses, as though to let this information sink in—and I myself will be back in a few hours. Goodbye.

Jerry cracks opens *Sons of Oñate*. He whaps it shut.

He descends through a rising aroma of Pine-Sol into the kitchen, where he comes upon the maid herself, a dowdy vision in rubber gloves and seventies-era headphones, from which are emanating the sounds of a soccer game at tremendous volume.

She stands at the sink with her back to him, filling a bucket with hot water. Welcome back, booms the announcer, to the midseason game of the Primera División, and it's shaping up to be the biggest game yet of 2005! Chivas have the ball!

He watches coolly as she moves the bucket to the floor and scrubs the sink. Foul on Bautista! Monarcas get the penalty kick! Chivas take possession at midfield. Medina passes to Ávila. Ávila to Agüayo—but no, Chivas recapture and Vermeulen, the Belgian, takes the ball, he's closing in, he shoots—

"Sí, sí, sí," she chants at the ceiling.

"GOOOLLLLLLLpe de poste!"

She hisses through her teeth. "¡Me lleva!"

"Buenas tardes," he calls out.

She startles and whirls around to face him.

"Ay, perdón." She shuts off her headphones and removes them, blushing. "Buenas tardes, señor."

He forces a smile. "¿Usted se llama Lourdes, no?"

Her dark complexion mottles as she nods at the window over the sink. Does she think he's making fun of her by speaking to her as an equal? He has no idea. He removes a casserole dish of macaroni and cheese from the refrigerator and inserts it into the microwave, then snatches up the remote from the kitchen island.

The TV squawks to life in the den. The news is nattering on again about the fence. Every bit of disconnected chain link and barbwire along the border converted into a seven-hundred-mile wall of concrete and steel. Brownsville to San Diego. In theory.

Also, the war in Iraq. Some new mid-occupation iteration of the United States invading somebody, bombing somebody, installing somebody, evading somebody.

He zaps the TV off.

Remind me of how often will we be seeing you, Lourdes?

Twice a month, señor.

The microwave beeps. She mops.

Well, he says. He locates a Diet Coke and fills a glass with ice. Have . . . fun.

The mop never pauses as he climbs the stairs to the deck.

From above, he contemplates the rocky, blasted-away flank of the mountain beside him, the long-defunct twin smokestacks of the Asarco copper smeltery in the distance, the haze smoking upward from Mexico. He firms his feet. For the Gonzales name entered the local register even before the 1848 Treaty of Guadalupe Hidalgo and the annexation of Texas to the United States—which is, as he enjoys clarifying for his students, before its inhabitants were invaded by white settlers but after said inhabitants invaded the Indians and, one could say, intermarried, though you wouldn't want to bring that latter point up in polite company—and those who are descended from this stock are rooted here like the most ancient trees.

On the street below, three houses away, the back gate of the DuPre home whaps open.

It's Miguel, the neighborhood lawn guy, shoving his mower as though fleeing a bank heist.

The door of the DuPre household slams open behind him. Here appears Huck himself, minus his ever-present cowboy hat. His shirt is torn. His hair plasters his head, as though he'd hatched recently from an egg. A toolbox-wielding man in coveralls nudges past him. Huck smashes the door with the side of his fist and retreats back inside.

Something tingles distantly in Jerry's veins. He looks about for other DuPres, but none are in evidence.

Out the side door of Jerry's own house scuttles another human form, round and low to the ground.

Lourdes.

She calls out to Miguel—for apparently, they know one another—a question in her voice. Miguel shakes his head like a weary old man. Is that a puff of laughter escaping Lourdes's lips? Did she really just say, "Pues, *todos* son locos"?

And then Huck's at the door again, calling out to *her*.

When she approaches, he talks at her in English. She supplies some halting English in return. She breaks free and hurries back to the house, dabbing at the valley in her bra with a paper towel she extracts from the waistband of her pants.

A flock of grackles swoops down to the telephone wires above him, arguing, heckling.

He finds Lourdes in the den. Already she's got her headphones on, this time with music cranked to an impossible volume as she swishes the duster. He watches as she pops open the can of wax, swirls a rag into the brown ointment, leans over the rough grain of the tabletop to rub in circles. Around and around and around.

The guitar inside her headphones makes a dirty-sounding shimmy.

"Good grief," he pipes, loudly enough to be heard. "¿Está escuchando a Creedence Clearwater Revival?"

She jumps, clutching the smeared rag to her chest, and fumbles for the off switch. "¿Mande?"

"Es nada," he says. "¿Le gusta classic rock?"

"No sé." Her face is on fire. She turns a quick eye toward the table, where the brown-orange circles of wax cut across the grain of its surface.

He doesn't care about the table. He tries for a conspiratorial smile.

So. What's all the excitement about over at the DuPres?

She shifts from foot to foot.

Oh, come on, Jerry presses.

She tries to shrug and darts another glance at the table, where the wax darkens.

I guess I'll ask Miguel, he teases. You can stay here with the table.

Señor DuPre has asked me to come every week from now on, she bursts out.

Jerry raises an eyebrow. "Oh?"

Señora DuPre, she tells him, seems to have left señor DuPre.

She sinks, as though something has punctured a hole in her.

His smile feels stuck to his face.

"¿Le dijo Huck? ¿Señor DuPre?"

"Sí." She looks as though she might cry.

He chuckles to himself. "Que la chingada." For her benefit he adds, "Perdón."

Then he sets down his glass, carelessly and too close to the edge of the table beside the recliner, where it topples and crashes to the hardwood floor.

She moves even before he can exclaim his surprise. He laughs his embarrassed laugh, turning in circles, his hands massaging the air as though the necessary implements will somehow appear. But she has already returned with dustpan and whisk broom, wastebasket, rags. He reaches for the wet shards with a crumple of newspaper, but she says, "No, no," takes the paper from his hand, shoos him back.

From the front door comes the sound of a key turning in the lock.

"Hola-hola," Chavela calls out breezily. Her heels click-clack on the tiles.

"Gracias," Jerry says hastily and backs out of the room.

"De nada," Lourdes murmurs without looking at him. She snatches up the table wax.

"Rose Marie DuPre just left her husband," he blurts into the kitchen.

Chavela looks up over the screen of her laptop. "You're kidding. Where did you hear *that*?"

"From our exceptionally efficient new maid."

It is with a cooling horror that he hears, seconds too late, the burr of resentment in his voice.

And yet he finds himself unable to speak—to clarify, to calibrate—as Chavela freezes in her pose.

"I am sorry," she says with a final, deadly calm, "to hear about our neighbors' marital problems. We've already discussed the fact that I'm done with housework. Forever. But because our maid also happens to work for the DuPres, not to mention a dozen other neighbors"—glancing toward the den, she lowers her voice—"que quiero saber is where she gets off being so indiscreet. The first time she meets you, no less."

"There's no need to be so hard on her."

He's not sure from what part of his body these words have been dislodged. Or why his resentment has been replaced with a rippling offense.

"So now you're defending her?"

"I am not defending the maid in any shape or form. I'm saying to leave her alone."

She slides off her stool. Without shoes, she's the same height as he. "Would you defend her if she gossiped about us to Huck and Rose Marie?"

"Tranquilo." He pats the air. The doorbell rings. "Son," he calls up the stairs, because he has yet to hear the car backing out of the driveway, "get the door."

Chavela examines the backs of her hands. "Too bad she had so much to say."

"Perhaps we ourselves could stop talking about it."

"I'm getting another maid. This one isn't going to work out."

"No!" he sputters. "We're keeping this one!"

Again, the doorbell.

Chavela fumes at the ceiling. "Adam, answer the door. Right now!"

She is answered by the flushing of the upstairs toilet.

For the briefest of instants, Jerry's eyes meet his wife's in a shared consternation. But it is not enough to provide counterbalance. He stalks to the door.

A woman waits on the other side. Like Jerry, she is at midlife, though perhaps slightly older, dark and weather worn in complexion, with a long, woolly, gray-streaked braid tossed forward onto her shoulder. Her face is creased with the half curl of a smile.

A sudden wooziness softens his knees.

"Madre de Dios," he says to his sister.

And she cackles and asks, "Did you miss me?"

Inez.

She's thinner than he remembers, but still sturdy enough, still the same short, hawk-eyed woman who has always tossed back her head in laughter to show all her square Indian teeth. Only now, she is missing an eyetooth.

The screen door creaks. He feels his arms lift, enfold. He detects a faint odor of gasoline. Strange, he thinks from some place outside of himself, the things you come to believe with the passage of time.

For starters, that Inez was most likely dead.

"Come in," he warbles.

The thundering at the top of the stairs is Adam. Inez turns in Jerry's hands, and as she registers the young man descending upon her, she breaks free, her face blooming with joy.

"Well, hello!" she exclaims when he reaches ground level, and then she throws her arms around him.

Adam startles inside her grasp. His face is so blank that, to Jerry, its meaning is instantly clear. He hasn't recognized his aunt. At all.

And Inez steps back with a very cool countenance, indeed.

"Surprise!" Jerry announces. "It's Inez! Let's all sit down!"

He herds the lot of them into the kitchen, counseling himself: *Tranquilo*. For he is not afraid of his sister. Not the way he'd been when they were kids and she, still a full head taller than he, could be moved to de-trouser him publicly unless he offered up a cut of his paperboy's wages. No. He is a different creature now, and Inez is merely a woman seated at his kitchen table in dirt-streaked jeans and a man's plaid button-down shirt, drumming her calloused fingers as though wait-ing for a slow bus. Even Chavela, who has been as stiff in this eternity of minutes as a mannequin whose eyes follow you at the store, bends enough to remove a set of drinking glasses from a cabinet.

"¿Algo de tomar?" she inquires.

"Tequila," Inez answers with a slap to the tabletop.

Chavela runs her tongue over her teeth.

"And what are *you* up to these days, young man?" Inez continues across the table.

"Well," Adam begins, "I just graduated from high school."

"I see. College?"

Adam picks at his eyebrow ring. "Uh-huh."

Inez gives him an impatient look and stirs the air with her hand.

"UC San Diego?" Adam responds.

Jerry gathers warm fistfuls of silverware from the dishwasher. For he who moves last is more likely to win the game—isn't that what their father always said?

"¿Y tú, Inez?" Chavela interjects. "Where are *you* living these days?"

"At the moment, I suppose I live in El Paso."

Chavela draws a breath of great patience. "Were you living somewhere else in the previous moment?"

Inez laughs. "What is this, the Spanish Inquisition?"

Chavela responds with a grunt of amusement. Perhaps time, friend that it is, has blunted the darker emotions. Inez, for her part, extracts a small packet from the vinyl fanny pack at her waist and tears it open. Pop Rocks. Por Dios. As though she were still ten years old. She offers some to Adam, who declines, and tips the packet to her mouth.

"Now that all these pleasantries are out of the way," she says through a mouthful of sizzle, "what does a person have to do to get something to drink around here?"

Chavela pastes her smile onto her face. "You know, Inez, your appearance is a bit of a surprise."

"Pues, claro. I'm sure it is."

"I'm sure"—Chavela pauses aridly—"everyone will be relieved to hear of your return."

"I'm not here to please them. Or anyone, really." An evil smile pricks Inez's lips.

The pounding in Jerry's ears is almost physically painful. In fact, he's uncertain whether he's imagining the commotion he hears at the front of the house—an enthusiastic rattling, a fumbling with a lock.

"What's going on at the door?" he barks.

"I'll check it out." Adam leaps from his chair.

"I forgot," Chavela says as she follows him out of the room. "It's Marcus."

And then Jerry is alone with Inez.

There is neither fury nor glee on his sister's face. Only an aging woman in work clothes who looks, frankly, tired.

He releases his forks into the silverware drawer. "It's been a very long time," he begins.

She offers a half smile. "Claro que sí."

"It's good to see you."

She inclines her head. "Likewise, Momito."

He cringes. "God. Don't call me Momo."

"It's your *name*."

"Por favor. 'Geronimo,' if you must." He sighs. "Have you been to see anyone else?"

"Certainly not. Who else but you would be my first choice?"

He smiles faintly, achingly, into the silence that follows.

Now, from the region of the front door, comes Chavela's low voice: "You're not going to believe who's here."

Yet the elder of his two sons blows in like a believer. Here's Marcus in the kitchen on his way to work, in an olive-green uniform, muscular and brimming with youth, throwing his arms open wide. "Tía!" he calls.

Inez spreads her wings. "M'ijo!"

Then they meet in a joyous embrace that looks as though it could end in the breaking of Inez's ribs.

"You're huge!" she says.

"You're . . . little!"

"So you remember your old tía, do you?"

"How could I forget my favorite aunt?"

Jerry offers a look of pure wonder to his wife. But she only lifts her eyes to the ceiling before she opens the refrigerator and removes a six-pack of 7UP, a six-pack of Sunkist, and a liter of Diet Mountain Dew and clacks them down on the table.

"Does anyone want a Coke? We've got three kinds."

"Tequila," Inez says, dropping back into her chair.

"I didn't know you were coming, Son," Jerry says.

"Didn't Mom tell you?" Marcus digs with a thumbnail into an orange. "She's making me take home a bunch of old stuff she cleaned out of the garage."

"Ah." Only now does he notice the stack of boxes resting beside the back door.

Chavela nudges forward two cans of Sunkist. Inez gives Marcus a look that says, *Can you believe this?*

Marcus cracks one open. "So where have you been keeping yourself?"

"Bozeman, Montana. At least for the last couple of months."

"Doing what? Herding goats?"

She smacks him on the side of the head. "¿Cómo que 'goats'? I was working at a Dairy Queen." She eyes Marcus's uniform. "So. You're Border Patrol now too."

Marcus leans back in his chair and offers the toothy grin he uses in self-defense. "Yup."

"Well. *That's* interesting. I thought the line would end with my brother."

Jerry stills his hand. The trouble with history, he reminds himself, is that by the time you notice it repeating, it's already happened. Especially when Number-One Son, who certainly could have finished college, who has an excellent aptitude for earth sciences, is now a two-year veteran of the United States Border Patrol.

"Is there something the matter," he says very calmly, "with my son's choice of vocation?"

A great stillness seems to overcome Inez. Then she smirks.

"I dunno. *Is* there?"

Jerry runs his tongue over his teeth. He will not take the same bait she habitually offered for her own amusement thirty years ago. He will only offer a few clarifications.

"Has the border been secured yet?" he responds.

"Do you want the cynical response or the philosophical one?"

"What odds are you putting on a border wall ever being built in our lifetime?"

"I thought we were discussing bloodlines, not bureaucracy. And anyway, does anyone really believe that thing could stop the Brown Invasion?"

"It's not like he has to be an agent forever," he adds hotly, "if he doesn't want to. Especially if he ever decides to go back to *school*." He gives Marcus a pointed look.

"You guys," Marcus interrupts, laughing. "Look. I'm not cut out for an office job. I like being outside. I like figuring people out. And it's not like I don't have plenty to do, you know?"

A glow of approval warms Inez's face. "Ah. A student at the University of Life."

"That's right," Jerry says. "One who has decent health insurance."

Adam, for his part, gives his brother the sort of look that means, *You make me want to vomit*. Chavela sips Diet Mountain Dew.

"So, m'ijo," Inez continues. "Has your father ever told you about the prank he used to pull when he was an agent?"

Jerry's breath leaves him. As surely he knew it would.

"Inez," he warns, croaking.

Marcus scoots to the front of his seat. "This I've got to hear."

"Totally," Adam adds.

Inez leans onto her elbow. "Okay, so on slow nights, he would wrap himself up in an old sheet and a wig and wade out into the river, see?"

"Inez."

"And his partner would be the lookout, and if anybody approached, he'd give the signal, and your father would start moaning and wailing and calling out in this high, ghostly voice for his drowned children."

Jerry grinds his heels to the floor. "Inez!"

She turns to him. "What? Are you saying it's not true? If we're to believe the stories you told, you used to play spook all the time."

Marcus snorts. "You pretended to be La Llorona?"

Jerry feels his mustache bunching under his nose. "That was a long time ago."

"He always said it was for purposes of morale," Inez continues. "And that half the time the detainees were cracking up too."

"Dad," Adam says, in a tone that conveys both shock and approval.

Marcus shakes his head. "Oh man."

Chavela, who already knows, rolls her eyes.

Jerry looks away. "We always apologized after we cuffed them."

"Of course you did," Inez says, her voice suddenly gentling. "You were hardly more than a kid. Like this youngster here."

She smacks Marcus on the thigh.

"Of course," Inez adds, "they did have to pry that woman off you when she ripped your wig off."

"Inez, por Dios!"

"Seriously?" Adam pipes. "You know this is Mister Moral High Ground himself, right?"

Marcus grins. "So, what other dirt have you got?"

"Ever hear about the time I took your father to the circus? This was before anyone knew about his clown phobia."

Marcus rises. "Hold that thought. I gotta see a man about a horse." He exits, laughing, toward the powder room at the front of the house.

And at the opposite entry to the kitchen appears a short, dark, rounded form, whose eyes pin themselves to the floor as Jerry leaps from his chair to cover the molasses-thick distance in the hope, the hope beyond hope, that he might somehow block the view before Inez can turn in her seat, who peels off her rubber gloves to announce meekly, "He terminado, señores."

Inez sits up, electrified.

"¡A la verga!" she crows. "¿Eres la criada?"

Lourdes turns the color of a tomato.

And you work for my *brother*!

Lourdes steps back like a spooked horse.

"My God," Inez continues, grinning at Jerry. "She's not even legal, is she?"

Jerry, gritting his teeth, swoops in on his maid and escorts her outside.

He bids her adiós on the front lawn after handing over the last of the cash in his wallet. Then he removes himself to the deck.

The sun squats on the horizon now as he leans against the railing, Asarco's smokestacks going dark against a drift of neon-pink clouds. The mountain peaks of Juárez steep in shadow; the buildings of downtown El Paso have begun to wink on. He rubs his dry lips. Any drier out here and it all might spontaneously combust—two inches of rain with the year half over, news reports of starving desert animals creeping into the city, little gray foxes and coyotes and even, if one is to believe the sighting, a mountain lion. When the boys were still small, you could sometimes see a lone figure or two clambering up out of the Mexican side of the foothills in these cooling hours and hurling themselves across the freeway. Now, on the access road near the boundary-marking chain link, he can just make out the glow of a parked white-and-green Border Patrol vehicle.

Inez. Whose fault had it ultimately been that she'd gone flaming out of their lives? As far as he's concerned, the ancient Swiss Army knife in the shoebox at the back of his closet still belongs to her.

Adam once told him the local water supply is doped up with a naturally occurring solution of lithium. "Everybody's drugged," he said. "Why else would anyone stay here?"

Perhaps the more salient question was *How does anyone escape?*

Below, in the kitchen, Chavela. Who hates it when he calls her by her proper name, Isabel. Who was once so unsure of herself—having not yet grasped in their college days that she was actually a very sure person trapped inside the life of someone expected to marry young, have babies immediately, and cook gallons of frijoles for everyone involved—that Jerry had to pick her up daily to ensure she would make it to class. And how glorious it was, pulling up to the curb in front of her parents' house in that first car of his—an exploding Ford Pinto with a bright-orange paint job—to honk, windows down, 8-track cranked and Freddy Fender "hey-baby-que-pasó"-ing into the still morning air, her father angrily whisking aside the curtains to receive his cheerful wave as Chavela dashed to him with delighted terror from her front door.

Now, somewhere else in the world, Mrs. Rose Marie DuPre makes her getaway. His eyes light on the relevant house. Lingering.

At ground level, on the other side of the rear wall, a stand of creosote bends and snaps back.

He frowns into the encroaching darkness. The response is the chirping of a lone cricket.

Another snap, down on the ground.

In silence, with great care, he descends and crosses the dry, crunching grass to his rear wall.

It's just a rodent, he tells himself. A horny toad. A house cat. Or who knows—maybe a fox. Coyote. Semimythical mountain lion.

A stone's throw away, a prickly pear cactus drops its rotten, half-eaten fruits.

He slips sideways along the length of the wall. Lights streak along the distant highway now, a soft whoosh behind every passing. The great dome of sky lofts like a black silk blanket with its hem on fire. In the air is something animal, rank. He leans over the side wall, searching his neighbor's patio furniture.

He should get back inside.

He steps silently through the gate. Past the trash cans. Down the driveway. To the asphalted street, still radiating warmth. Inez had *paid* those clowns that time at the circus. Gave them two weeks of babysitting earnings to snatch him and shake him upside down in front of a hooting crowd of children until his pockets emptied.

He could go for a walk. A lap or two around the block, just to clear his head. He could go for a drive.

He skims back up the driveway.

"Where have you been?" Chavela hisses when he returns to the kitchen.

It's a predictable response. He is glad of it. In fact, the mood in the room itself is somehow lighter than before, as though it had been buoyed by his absence. His sons arrange themselves in their chairs in loose-limbed positions. Inez offers a pleasant face, her hands laced over a knee. It's as though they've been waiting for a parade.

"I thought I saw a flat on the Volvo," he says.

Adam grins. "We've been learning all kinds of things about you, Dad."

"I see." Jerry turns to his sister. "Have you eaten?"

Inez regards him with an innocent look. "Me? No."

"Then I suppose we should all go to dinner." He pauses. "Do you have a place to stay?"

Inez shrugs.

"You can stay with us a few days, if you'd like."

Inez beams. "I thought you'd never ask!"

He's not sure whether to be grateful that Marcus chooses this moment to announce that he's got to get going. Still, everyone rises. Embraces. The boxes pile into his son's arms. Chavela sighs, and Jerry claps a fortifying hand around her shoulder. For Inez would always be Inez.

The past he will banish to the past. Where it belongs.

He shores up the world—flipping off the air conditioner and the lights in the hallway, the bathroom, the den—as his family shuffles to the opened garage.

And stops short, his heart suddenly pounding in his throat. For something is behind him in the dark.

Por Dios, he tells himself as the small hairs on the back of his neck rise. *Don't be ridiculous.* The window on the far side of the den has been opened, just a crack, he can see that now, but nothing could slip through. The only thing he feels is the breeze. He crosses the room and cranks the window shut. But as he stands beneath the skewed curtains, he hears something on the other side of the window. A rustle. A rasp. A scratch and a rattle, though surely it's only the creak of the mulberry trees in the yard. He peers again into the dark, and a shapeless shadow looms abruptly on the wall beside him. But what the hell? The moment he whirls to it, it's gone.

3

KEYS TO THE KINGDOM

P IS FOR *PRIVATE INVESTIGATOR*.

At his dining room table, Huck cracks open the yellow pages—to hell with the internet, he needs a material object in his grasp. It has been a week since Rose Marie's exit, a week of cloudless skies and deepening heat, awkward phone inquiries to in-laws and friends. Inconclusive examinations of bank account activity. Girl Scouts at the door, demanding payment for cookies in off-putting flavors. A brief discussion with an attorney acquaintance he'd run into this week at a Texaco had clarified that he couldn't petition for abandonment until a certain amount of time had elapsed—a few months, a year.

Still, if Rose Marie thought she could waltz right back home when she was done with her little fling, or pout session, or "separate vacation," or whatever the hell this was, she had another thing coming. There would be a period of atonement before he would allow her back inside to begin with, an amortization of goodwill that she would need to accumulate before this stunt could be paid down. *If* it could be paid down.

When he tried calling her cell, he followed the ring he heard back to her bedside table, where her phone had been tucked into a Kleenex box.

Physicians. Pianos. Pizza. Pottery. Maybe he should change the locks.

For the rest of his household, the week has brought an unspoken truce. Last weekend, when he'd debriefed the kids at the kitchen table— damp and bruised, gripping an overripe banana because he needed something, anything, in his hand—they had each, in their own way, regarded him with calm. True, Quinn had frowned hard at the tabletop and Skyler had twisted her rings as though she were tightening screws. But Jordan had acted as she almost always did, studying his face with the dispassionate eye of a scientist, and even when he ran out of words and offered his upturned palms, no one had risen to slam a door or to hurl something. He poured himself a whiskey and retreated to the sofa to watch an infomercial for vegetable juicers starring an ancient and heavily rouged Jack LaLanne.

Printers. Private Investigators.

"Here," announces a voice at his elbow, and then Jordan deposits before him a raisin-ringed inferno of oatmeal crowned with an upright half banana.

"Thanks, darlin'." He nudges the bowl away. The temperature outside is ninety-five and rising.

"What are you doing?"

"Just thought I'd let it cool a little."

She eyes the phone book. "Are you and Mom getting a divorce?"

A small piece of motorized equipment snarls to life across the street. There, at the yucca-studded curb—Miguel. With a chain saw and stepladder.

He reaches for his cell phone. "We'll talk later."

"But *are* you?"

With great heaving motions, Miguel slices through the bottommost branches of the Radoseviches' weeping willow. They crash to earth.

"Honey. Look. It depends."

His cell phone rings in his hand.

It's Mendoza. AltaVista wants the contract signed on Monday, wants it signed yesterday, actually, they want product by July, and by the way, HR sent a memo regarding some organization with questions about "workers' rights" that would like to tour the main building first thing on Tuesday.

"Tell them we'll overnight the terms on Tuesday, end of story, and let the HR folks know I'll gladly lead the tour myself."

By the time he hangs up, Jordan's gone.

He locates her in the recliner in the den, watching cartoons, eating toast. On the sofa, Quinn punches buttons on his game thing with his painted-black thumbs.

"So." Huck lets out his breath. "What's new with you two anyway?"
Both of them shrug.

"How about you?" he calls out to Skyler, who is unloading potted plants into the kitchen sink. "You got a job this summer?"

"Dad. I've been waiting tables for a *week*."

Jordan pulls the recliner's footrest lever in a solemn rhythm as Wile E. Coyote opens a gift box and is smashed by a spring-loaded sledgehammer from the ACME Corporation.

Let it be said he's never tried to force this kid to be someone she wasn't. That's always been Rose Marie's area of expertise—the mandatory playdates, the unwanted ballet lessons, the irritation during curriculum-night visits to Jordan's school for "gifted" children, when Jordan drifts off to a table in a corner of the classroom to study bacteria while the other kids pretend to be Supreme Court justices or play Pancho Villa and the Incident at Columbus. Personally, he'd taken Jordan's most recent birthday party refusal in stride. So what if it was the fourth year running she'd declined? Was it the worst thing ever, to have to eat another chocolate cake in your pajamas in front of *Good Morning America*? There was no point in dwelling on last year's disastrous birthday trip to Carlsbad Caverns.

Rose Marie pestered anyway. Ground her teeth and begged until Jordan uncharacteristically relented and allowed herself to be taken to Farrell's, where you could order a twelve-scoop sundae that was set on fire before a waitress extinguished it with an aerosol can of whipped cream. But while the rest of the family—himself included—had actually wrung some enjoyment from this gluttony, Jordan had made her true feelings clear. She looked furious even as she scraped every last rivulet from her bowl.

Who was going to take her to summer school now? Rose Marie had the damned Lexus.

What if Rose Marie didn't come back at all?

"Y'all," he begins, and then he notices the furniture is wrong. It's as though someone had borrowed it all while they slept, then returned it without realigning to the carpet indentations. He sets down his oatmeal. Slurpee cups and granola bar wrappers blanket the photography books on the coffee table, which is coated with the fine dust the air conditioner deposits on everything. A handprint smears the window facing Mexico.

When Jordan reaches across her lap to drop a balled-up napkin into the wastebasket, the napkin topples off the towering mound within.

He grips the back of the love seat, sweating, heart hammering.

"Why don't we all go out to lunch?" he croaks before his throat can close up.

"Can't," Skyler says. "Carlos is picking me up in half an hour."

That damned hippie. "Bring him along." He gulps air. "How about you guys? Grab some chow?"

"You're not seriously suggesting a family outing, are you?" Quinn asks.

Skyler opens and slams shut the refrigerator. "Nobody wants to go, Dad."

"Jordan does," Huck says, though her eyes glaze in front of the TV. "Jordan and I are going for burgers at Lucky Boy. Or pizza, if she'd rather. But later, all of us could—"

Skyler snatches open the back door. He lunges after her, unable to spit out *Wait!*

She's not escaping. She's letting the dog in.

And the dog is so very glad to see them all.

The dog acts, in fact, like he hasn't seen them for months instead of just one night, but then again, Ripley has never been the sharpest spine on the cholla. He scarfs up Huck's oatmeal before Huck can yank him away by the collar. When Ripley licks Jordan's toes, she giggles like an actual child.

The swipe of a tongue meets Huck's lips as he stoops to rub the dog's head. He spits. "When was the last time anyone walked this dog?"

He is answered with shrugs as everyone stretches, rising.

"Forget lunch!" he hollers. "What we need is a vacation. Jordan, you can skip the end of summer school and Quinn, you don't have a job, and Skyler, they'll find another waitress. We're going on a road trip."

The kids stare.

"I haven't figured out where," he adds, "but I'm taking suggestions."

And like an answer to a prayer to delay or avoid this conversation altogether, the doorbell rings.

"I'll get it," he says, springing forward.

As he whips open the door, he entertains a fantasy wherein Rose Marie returns home only to find them gone. Gone, gone, gone.

Lourdes waits on the doorstep.

"Hey," he says. Her round face seems to mirror his surprise. "I didn't know you were coming today."

She furrows her brow, as though struggling to read words on his forehead. "Saturday. You say."

"Right," he says, ushering her in as though he hadn't forgotten. He glances at the den. "Lourdes, have you . . . been here this week?"

She tilts her head.

"Wednesday," he says, a little more loudly. "Did you come on Wednesday? Isn't that your regular day?"

"Wednesday I come," she says. "Pero"—she looks around the entryway, harried, lifting the palms of her hands—"nadie en casa. Nobody."

"Don't you have a key?" He pantomimes the jiggling of the lock.

She shakes her head.

"I'll make you one."

She furrows.

"A key," he says, straining to keep his voice even. "Skyler," he calls out. "Honey, would you please tell Lourdes I'm going to make a key for her, and that she can come in if we're not home?"

"What?"

It's clear from her annoyed tone that she's heard him. "Go talk to my daughter." He offers Lourdes what he hopes is an encouraging smile. "She knows Spanish."

Lourdes peers into the den with a marveling horror.

The chain saw rips through the air.

Miguel is in the Radoseviches' mulberry tree on one foot, gripping an overhead branch with one hand, thrusting the saw with the other.

He can handle things, Huck tells himself as he cuts the warm sidewalk on the diagonal. Everything. Every*one*.

"Hey, Miguel," he calls from the Radoseviches' mailbox.

A mulberry branch falls.

III

"Una llave," Skyler tells Lourdes in the kitchen. She turns an invisible key in the air. "Mi papá le dará usted una llave."

Lourdes lifts her eyebrows. "Bueno."

"Bueno." She bites her lip as Lourdes bustles toward the broom closet. Even with three years of accelerated Spanish under her belt, it's embarrassing to open her mouth. Or maybe she's just embarrassed that Lourdes works for her parents to begin with.

She seats herself at the kitchen table, across from Quinn. "Do you *want* to go on this stupid trip?"

He twirls a pair of rubber bands. "*Hell* no."

"I'm not listening to country music for a week."

"Jesus, who could?"

"But what are we going to *do*?"

"What's *he* gonna do, ground us for refusing to go on vacation?" He shoots the overhead light fixture.

She bites her lip. What she had actually meant was *Mom is gone and that's really fucked up and we don't even know when she's coming back and nobody's talking about it and did anyone even see this coming and what do we do now?* But somehow he didn't hear her.

Or maybe, she thinks as he plucks up three avocados and starts juggling them, he did.

At the breakfast bar, Jordan is only pretending to read *Twenty Thousand Leagues Under the Sea*. She gnaws her thumbnail. If their dad got someone to investigate their mom, and the investigator found her and maybe even brought her home—Jordan isn't sure whether the procedure involves an arrest, but her heart races suddenly with longing—their mom and dad would have to start talking, which meant they would have to start fighting. And the faster their mom could be found, the faster they could fight. Once that started, they all would probably never go anywhere ever again.

Not that the trip to Carlsbad Caverns was a bad idea. There was just what happened on the way.

Quinn catches the avocados. "Anyway, I have a plan. We're launching a Campaign of Sabotage. All passive resistance—you know, like Gandhi?"

Skyler snorts.

"The first rule is, nobody picks up anything around the house. Ever. Then when Dad freaks out, you just smile and nod and continue not doing anything. Got it?"

Jordan turns over her book. "You guys," she says, "I have some other ideas."

Skyler huffs. "Oh, *now* you've got something to say."

"We should—"

"Jo-Jo, chill," Quinn says. "Are you in?"

"Okay, *fine*. But don't call me Jo-Jo."

"Now you." He thrusts his hand out to Skyler. "Shake on it and look happy."

Skyler rolls her eyes in surrender. She tugs his hand with a fake, Barbie-doll smile.

Something surges up in Quinn, faster than he can think. Jordan sees it. "That looked like Mom," he says nastily.

Skyler yanks her hand away, looking like she's standing on a teeter-totter and on one side is her feelings hurt and the other is *I know*.

"You guys," Jordan says. "I have some *ideas*."

"Jo-Jo."

"Chill."

"DON'T CALL ME JO-JO." She snatches up her book and fumes her way back into the submarine, toward the giant squid.

III

"Well," Huck begins. He braces his hand on a freshly amputated tree branch, the blunt stub oozing with sap. "Things are looking pretty good up there."

Miguel balances on a branch overhead, the inert saw blade beside the tip of his sneaker. Huck suppresses the urge to yank the saw away from him.

"Of course," he continues, "without a safety harness, you'll want to make sure you're holding on with both hands."

A crease forms behind the bridge of Miguel's glasses.

"Problem is," Huck continues, "you need two hands to operate this thing."

Miguel nods. Maybe it's an encouraging sign. He has in no way forgotten the look Miguel gave him on the day of the Western Playland incident.

He adds, "Maybe Eugene can get you a *real* ladder. A twelve-footer. You think?" There's just enough arch in his voice to indicate a friendly ribbing.

Miguel nods again, his saucer eyes meeting Huck's for an instant before they slide away. He follows Miguel's gaze. On the rooftop of the Gonzales home, a woman leans against the air-conditioning unit.

He turns back to Miguel. "Incidentally. You might have noticed my wife's been . . . out of town for a while. And I was just wondering, since I know you're in the neighborhood a lot—you ever see any visitors at our place?"

Miguel blinks. "No."

"I mean, anyone who might have been visiting my wife. On a week-day. Other than Lourdes."

"I haven't seen nobody."

"Will you let me know if you see her?"

"Okay."

Huck paws the yellow grass. The woman on the roof is still there. A tiny, dark little thing with a long braid, looming, leaning in their direction.

"The hell's *that* woman doing?" he says. "Is she *watching* us?"

The chain saw kicks on abruptly when Miguel twists to look.

Huck flinches as the saw comes somersaulting down. It launches a plug of grass into the air. When another blur the size of a floor lamp follows, Huck flings his arms open, his rear leg bracing the earth; a thud knocks the wind from his lungs. He jerks the whole load in his arms backward as his leg collapses.

His head cracks against the ground. Miguel slides off him with a great, shuddering wheeze.

They lie side by side in the dry grass, their feet in shade, the tree's remaining branches swaying gently above them.

"You all right?" Huck's body is a throbbing bag of pain.

Miguel coughs. "Chingado."

The desire to say "I told you so" pounds in Huck's chest. "No worries," he says. He rolls toward him, forcing a chuckle. "Guess we're even now."

Miguel twitches—a shrug, but maybe a nod—before he rolls away.

III

"Dad and Miguel fell out of a tree," Jordan announces.

From nearby comes the sound of water rushing through the plumbing, and also the jaunty ringtone of a cell phone.

"Just *now*?" Skyler's bracelets jangle.

"Kids."

Their father stands in the doorway covering the mouthpiece of his cell phone, a smear of medicated ointment across his cheek.

"I want you guys to consider the following possibilities. A road trip to San Antonio to see the Alamo and all that, a guided camping trip to the Gila Wilderness—I've heard of this place that uses llamas to pack in supplies—or a hike down the Grand Canyon with a side trip to see the meteor crater. I've got to stop in at work. Put in a load of laundry, all right? And make sure you walk that dog."

"Whatever you say." Quinn laces his hands behind his head, smiling as his dad heads out.

Outside, a car horn honks.

"It's Carlos," Skyler yelps, prairie-dogging toward the window.

"Jesus." Quinn casts a conspiratorial, sidelong glance at Jordan, whose nose is back in the book. In the driveway, the boy toy in question—goateed, ponytailed, tie-dyed, the reek of his Marlboros almost visibly rising above him—leans against the hood of his mother's station wagon, kissing the air at his sister.

"Shut up," Skyler says as Quinn snorts.

He waits until the station wagon has pulled out of the driveway to lean his elbows on his knees, rubbing his forehead. His little sister gives him one of her thousand-yard stares from the doorway.

Before he can find a wisecrack that will annoy her, he says, "You okay?"

Jordan seems to hold her breath. But her expression stays exactly the same as she nods. He wishes that, for once, she wouldn't be weird.

He messes up her hair on his way out of the room, failing to elude the slap of her hand on his arm.

And then Jordan is alone with the anxious blob that has throbbed in her chest all week.

In the living room, Lourdes skims the vacuum over the Oriental rug, head nodding to her secret music. Jordan breathes in the entryway. The sound of vacuuming has always been calming to her, like an electronic *om*. She slinks in and sits crisscross on one of the beige, velveteen high-backed chairs. Her mother's knickknacks line the bookshelves—the iron sculpture of the drooping Indian on horseback, the gold leaf piano-shaped music box, the hand-painted Santa Claus figurines from thirty-two different countries, including the ones that don't even have Santas, as Skyler once pointed out, like Nigeria.

Lourdes turns, startling, and hits the off switch. "Ay, m'ija," she scolds as she pushes her headphones onto her neck.

Jordan looks Lourdes in the eye.

"My mom and dad are probably getting divorced."

Lourdes lifts her eyebrows. Jordan feels a crackle of satisfaction. She likes to report things, to be the first to know them, even if she's not yet sure what she thinks about this maybe divorce. Whether it's good. Whether it's bad.

"Un divorcio." Lourdes clucks her tongue and wraps the vacuum cord back around its prongs.

Jordan creeps onto the ottoman. "Also, my dad is taking us on vacation."

Lourdes pauses. "Vacaciones? You go vacation? When?"

Jordan shrugs. Lourdes purses her lips. "I ask you daddy." A hank of black hair slips out of the silvery net encasing her bun as she turns to swat the drapes with the lint brush.

If she stares long enough, eventually Lourdes will look at her.

And sure enough, Lourdes's hand slows. She turns and folds the brush into the cross of her arms. Jordan holds steady. Now that Lourdes is looking, the point is to make her look away, like all adults do if you just wait them out long enough.

But Lourdes doesn't look away. She only sinks more firmly into her Reeboks.

Jordan forces her eyes open wider, crushing the rug with her toes.

If her mom were to walk in on this moment, she would probably say, *Young lady, you can stop that right now.* Or *For God's sake, leave that woman alone.* Then Jordan would have to say, *What?* and start staring at her mother, which would either make her furious or flabbergasted, depending on her mood, and would likely result in Jordan being sent to her room, where all her books are.

Except for Saturday night before last, when she'd found her mother in the kitchen, sculpting a pedestaled bowl from a pile of modeling clay with a Popsicle stick.

An incomplete cooking project sat on the countertop behind her—buttered casserole dish, cutting board heaped with chopped onion. Beside her, a spiral notebook filled with her handwriting splayed open. She'd left off in the middle of a sentence.

Jordan scratched her calf with a toe. "What are you doing?"

"I'm trying to make something."

Her mother jabbed with her stick. Her ponytail bobbed. Her freckles were showing because she'd already taken off her makeup.

"Make what?"

Her mother's gaze drifted to the notebook.

"Something that makes sense." She closed the notebook.

Jordan climbed onto the stool across from her. She had just finished watching a cable movie about piranhas that ate people every time they stupidly set foot in the river until only this one scientist survived. She was awake. "Why?"

Her mother plucked a slim object from beside the newspaper that was her work surface and slipped it into the waistband of her yoga pants. An envelope. Jordan glimpsed the folded yellow notepad paper under the flap.

"It's almost birthday time," her mother said.

Jordan's gaze lingered on her mother's midsection. "What's—"

"The big nine."

Jordan felt a prickling behind her ears.

Her mother twiddled her Popsicle stick. "I have an idea."

Jordan buried her thumb in a piece of clay.

"My idea," her mother continued, with a strange light in her eye, "is that this year we give you a birthday party."

Jordan smeared the clay between her palms. "I don't want a party."

"We could keep it small—maybe just a few kids from your class. Dad and I might invite a couple of people too."

"I don't want a couple of people."

"Decorations," her mother was saying, and her whole body rose, as though she were attached to a bicycle pump. "We could put up balloons."

Jordan shook her head. Her hair whipped her eyebrows.

Her mother put down her stick. "Why? Why won't you ever?"

What she wanted to ask her mother was why she always wanted a party so bad. But then it occurred to her that maybe her mother was thinking about Carlsbad Caverns.

She met her mother's waiting gaze and locked down.

Her mother's long nostrils inflated. She was going to say, *Oh no you don't.*

Except, instead, the top half of her collapsed. Her elbow dropped to the counter. Head in her hand. "Jordan."

Jordan's head felt watery. Inside of her was a question she couldn't put into words. She wanted to say something like "sorry." But she didn't, so her mother returned, in silence, to her sculpture. Jordan watched until her eyes burned and blurred and her mother lifted her, with effort, from the breakfast bar, where she had fallen asleep.

Now Lourdes makes a shooing motion. "Jovencita. Ándale pues."

Jordan drills with her eyes.

Lightning quick, Lourdes pokes her in the ticklish spot under her ribs.

Jordan squeals and falls off the ottoman. She scrambles up when Lourdes feints with the feather duster, snatching her book from the chair to flee, uncertain whether this maneuver represents a retreat. Yet her limbs feel quick and light.

She's got an idea.

III

"I know," Huck tells Mendoza from the dining room. The cell phone is warm against his ear. "I know. But I'm not shipping to Gateway if we've got a QA rating under sixty percent. Now give me some options."

The voice in his earpiece buzzes on the verge of hysteria. Ask for a third production extension, it says. Send the circuit boards back to assembly with two weeks of required overtime. Sell at a loss to Malaysia and start over. Also, the workers are making noise again about unionizing.

Huck runs his thumb along the flaking paint on the window sill. Lourdes and Miguel are having some kind of powwow at the curb. She dabs at the back of his head with a dish towel.

"Here's the other thing," the voice continues. "There's some question of whether the parts have been . . . tampered with. In-house."

Huck clamps down on the raw edge of his mood. "Get them back into assembly." He takes hold of the window frame and hangs up.

The frame breaks away from the wall.

He stumbles backward. The break is a clean one, as though long ago the plank had been glued rather than nailed into place. He throws it down. He'd made his case for functionality, those years ago—two-car garage, storm windows, up-to-date plumbing and electrical. Rose Marie had wanted character—the so-called charm of dust-collecting crown moldings and glass doorknobs and creaking staircases. A sense of history, she'd called it. And he thought of the mansion she'd hated and fled, even as he saw how happy it made her to get it all back again.

He sweeps the whole mess of ugly, nubby, gold drapes into his arms, wraps them in the white sheers underneath, and yanks them from the rod.

Light engulfs the room, revealing all. The walls need fresh paint. Above the liquor cabinet, the painting of farmers threshing wheat is dull with age; the cut-glass vase on the sideboard has clearly been broken and glued back together. Scratches mar the dining room table and the floors. The whole room, in fact, is on the small side. Cramped. He's not sure why he never noticed it before. Maybe he should extend the west wall. Open the whole thing up and turn it into an alcove. A sun porch. Another wing altogether.

"Dad."

Jordan, in the doorway again. She sets upon the still-open phone book.

"When the private investigator finds out where Mom is, let's go get her."

From the center of his chest comes a great swelling of hope.

This one's mine, he thinks. He claps a hand to her shoulder, beholding her in the bright room.

SHE DRIVES THROUGH THE DESERT.

Desert after desert and more desert still, as though this is the world's only topography, little nopal cacti encroaching on the cracked two-lane highway. Hours smearing into hours, elongating. She slips from one nation to the next. Over her shoulder, the massive, aquamarine stretch of the Pacific. She is the mirage on the blacktop that appears just ahead and then, before she reaches it, disappears.

4

IN THE BEGINNING

ON THE DAY INEZ APPEARED on his doorstep, after Jerry had taken everyone out to dinner at a serviceable Italian restaurant embellished with plastic grapes (Inez ordered a meal big enough for two linebackers and shoveled it in like she hadn't seen food in a week), then decamped homeward (she fell asleep in the car), Inez announced, "I need to get my things." Then she disappeared for two hours and returned with three duffel bags full of possessions and a detectable stagger.

Since then, she has awakened him more than once as she paces the stairs in the night. She has watched pay-per-view movies. She asked to borrow money a good three days or so before he had planned to ask her delicately whether she needed any, and so he found himself spluttering and handing her a twenty out of his wallet while she grinned.

Should he have been in any way surprised? He only wondered what kind of dupe he was.

Now, on the deck, he finds her reading a monograph on the Navajo Code Talkers of World War II and chewing on the end of her braid.

She looks up from under her satirical cowboy hat—the kind that curls up on the sides like a taco—and says, "What?"

He untucks two glasses and a soda can from the crook of his arm. "Do you want a Coke?"

"I don't drink the brown ones. Only the orange ones."

Down in the yard, a pair of men in jumpsuits unload a stack of folding tables under the portable canopy. Jerry lowers himself to the seat opposite hers.

"Did you tell me the other night," he begins, cracking open his beverage, "that you worked at a Dairy Queen?"

"Oh yes. In Montana. I wore a polo shirt. And a hairnet! My teenage coworker and I used to open our mouths under the ice-cream taps when the customers weren't looking."

He grins. "You didn't!"

"And then there was a stretch I spent in the kitchen of this Hare Krishna commune in Oregon. The other guy in there would chant while chopping vegetables, so I'd stir the lentils with my wooden spoon and mutter, 'Double, double toil and trouble.'"

He grins wider. "Did you tell him you were practicing *your* religion?"

She tips back her hat. All week long he has pushed his research notes around and around on his desk, unable to concentrate. Now he only nods, sipping his Coke and chuckling at appropriate intervals, for he has managed to start her outboard motor, which has always been the best possible indicator that her internal barometer is registering low pressure, cool temperatures, a good mood.

"But El Paso, hermano," she says now. "Dios mío. Coming back to El Paso is like running into an old flame at a high school reunion. The flame in question looks almost exactly the same. But he's wearing clothes that are two sizes too small and is sweating profusely at the armpits."

"And to think I've never left this armpit at all."

Their laughter rattles the chairs.

"Chavela has really outdone herself, hasn't she?" he adds, looking over the railing.

Inez leans back. "You guys definitely shelled out."

"It's turning out to be quite an event. *Everyone* is coming."

"I guess this is what passes for entertainment around here."

"Please tell me," he says, still chuckling, "that all things considered, you'll to do your best to behave." He swirls the ice in his cola.

Inez folds her hands on the book. Then she smiles a strange smile at his ice cubes.

"Exactly what the hell," she says, "do you mean by 'behave'?"

"Surely, you don't need me to explain."

"Por favor, sí." Her smile evaporates.

He releases his breath. "Bueno. I only mean that there are certain rules of conduct, certain standards of behavior which make it possible for disparate humans to exist in the same—"

The book thumps to the tabletop.

"Geronimo," she says, "you're so full of shit, los ojos son marrones. If you're going to insult my intelligence, if you're going to assault my dignity, if you intend on treating me as a child—and may I remind you that *I* am the elder—then I clearly made a mistake in believing I could—"

"Oh God." He lowers his forehead into his hand.

"My bags." She rises. "Where are my bags?"

She leaves the french doors flung open. He can hear her from his seat on the deck as she stomps around in the guest room, stuffing and zipping things. Eight days she's been there among them. Eight days of restlessness and torment and secrecy, the sum total of fifteen years' absence amounting only to a series of accusations that seemed, even after all this time, insurmountably familiar. Would it really be so terrible if she left?

He follows her down the stairs, then circles around to block her path. Inez thumps to a stop. Here before him is a small, furious woman with an unraveling braid who teeters under the hump of the bags slung over her shoulder, and although he can nearly taste the sigh of relief that would pass through his body once she was gone, he is overtaken by an unexpected sensation.

He has missed her.

"Hermana," he says as she wobbles past him. "Siéntate. Por favor."

She allows for a hitch in her step before she continues out the door, out of his house and his life with the two rolls of stolen toilet paper he can see bulging from her topmost bag. Then she turns to him with a deadly look on her face that means, *Well?*

"I'm sorry," he begins. "I was out of line. I might have chosen a better word than 'behave.' But do you think we could set aside our differences for the time being? There's a party about to start out there, for heaven's sake. Are you going to miss your own party?"

She shrugs.

"I've missed worse." She drops her bags. "If you people want to have a party, that's fine by me. But right now I'm going for a walk."

He watches, through the screen door, as she saunters around the corner at the end of the block.

"Is Inez ready?" Chavela asks him in the kitchen.

Jerry moves to the window. A human form atop his backyard wall hacks at the juniper bushes with the hand clippers. "You told Miguel to come? *Now?*"

Chavela clacks on her laptop. "He was supposed to come this morning, but he just showed up a little while ago."

"Why didn't you tell him to come back tomorrow?"

"With the hedges looking like *that*? Anyway, who knows when we'd get him back again? You know how these people are."

"Señora," says Lourdes, materializing. I'm finished with the bathrooms.

Good. Please mop before the guests arrive. You're still available for cleaning up afterward?

"Sí, señora."

"Bueno, bueno."

"By the way," Chavela continues, swiveling to align with the periscope at the back of her head. "Who told Adam he could invite Quinn, and would you please stop them from what we know they're going to do?"

Adam's companion enters behind him at the gate, resplendent in black, the top of his head as blue as a gas flame.

He turns to her. "You do remember that you're the one who wanted to give Inez a welcome-home party. Right?"

"It wasn't meant to be a move-in party."

"There didn't need to be any party at *all*."

"Yes, yes, Mr. I Hate Parties." She calls Paquito as he *click-click-clicks* into the room, and lifts him onto her lap. "So is she ready or not?"

In the den, the boys have managed to set up a video game on TV with such speed that they appear to have been already poured onto the floor for hours.

"Hey, Dr. G," says Quinn, punching buttons. His voice seems much too deep for such a gangly kid. His father's voice, of course.

Something about his profile, though, the way he tips his chin—that's his mother.

Jerry looks away. "Young Master DuPre."

"Yes!" Adam explodes a small moon, rippling the indistinct legend on his T-shirt. "Uh-oh. Did Mom send you?"

"Don't let her catch you."

Inez's bags are still heaped beside the front door.

Jerry stoops to retrieve them. Grunts under their weight as he ascends the stairs. Kicks open the door to the guest room and drops the bags with a thump just over the threshold, marveling that such a tiny woman could lift them at all.

He stops short just before he pulls the door shut behind him. *No*, he tells himself. *You couldn't.* Still, he turns back to the room behind him—its unmade bed, the nightstand heaped with used tissues. If anyone was to ask him what he was doing, he could answer truthfully, *I'm looking for my sister.*

But no one would know. And who would it hurt then?

Silent as a shadow, he slips into the lair.

III

"You're dead, gabacho," Adam announces.

Quinn turns back from the window to the TV screen. He's been vaporized. He snorts and dumps the joystick to the floor.

"So, what's this party about again? Awesome shirt, by the way."

"Thanks." Adam straightens against the sofa, still firing. "It's my parents' attempt to reintroduce my aunt to civilization." This despite the fact that Inez had awakened them all yesterday morning by putting on a mariachi record and replaying the same track four times with the volume cranked up to nine. "Personally, I think they'd have an easier time rehabilitating a feral cat."

"Tell me this, mojado," Quinn pipes suddenly. "How good would you be at making crank calls to my house?"

Adam looks at him sideways. Dude's been like this all week, all non sequiturs and thousand-yard stares.

"Who's the benefactor?"

"My dad. I need to make him think he shouldn't leave town. Otherwise me and my sisters are going to have to go on a really stupid vacation."

Adam shrugs. "I can do that." He blows up a weather satellite.

The doorbell rings.

"Uh-oh," Quinn says. "Should I leave?"

The front door opens, the hallway filling with voices. Adam leans and catches sight of his tía Flavia and tío Lester and a trio of cousins in the hallway just before his mother shepherds them through to the back. The opening track of one of his dad's god-awful Vikki Carr CDs thunders in the air.

He shrugs and rolls onto his stomach. "Nah. Anyway, it's just a matter of time before my mom busts us. We might as well keep going as long as we can."

He finds it promising that Quinn chuckles without any lag time at all.

III

"Hello!" Chavela exclaims at the door. "Hello, hello!"

On the porch step, Jerry's sister Ofelia awaits, her husband Nati and the two nephews who are still at home pulling up the rear.

"How are . . . things?" Ofelia begins, lifting her penciled-in eyebrows once Chavela has collected the purse and massaged them into the living room.

"Things are fine," Chavela coos.

Ofelia turns her attention to the buffet. "Oh! Everything looks so good!"

Chavela glows and excuses herself to open the door to the heavily powdered, perpetually startled face of Jerry's sister Hortensia.

"Tencha! Come in! Are you hungry?"

For sure, as she relieves her sister-in-law of her personal effects and nods through her commentary about refusing to carpool with her children—she's prided herself on arriving everywhere alone ever since her annulment—Chavela tingles with joy over the way the room has begun to fill, how the voices crowd each other and fight the music. True, Flavia had asked if she was crazy for allowing Inez to stay with them, and even Tencha, lifting the lid of each steaming chafing dish, says something now about how she wasn't sure she had a single thing to say to her sister, not even after all this time. And okay, more than once this week, as Chavela cooked Inez's meals and washed her clothes and drove her to Juárez to get her teeth repaired and from discount outlet to discount outlet to replenish, on her own dime, her wardrobe ("Brassieres from Sears!" Inez hooted. "Who could ask for more?"), she'd asked herself why she was bothering, when what she really wanted to do was tell Inez to shut *up* once and for all and then point her in the direction of the nearest Greyhound station.

For now, however, the tide is rising. Marisa, daughter of Lalo the Accident Prone, comes up the walk with her new baby. At the curb across the street, Salomé's son Robert pulls on the hand of his two little girls—Chavela can't remember their names. Paloma, eldest of the clan, emerges from a car, her husband, Gil, rummaging in the trunk as a herd of their grandchildren shove each other in the street. Chavela props open the front door, even though it's going to screw up the air conditioner. She will welcome them all, there is room for each of them plus one more plus one more after that, there is plenty of food and drink.

But today, no booze. Not with Inez in the house. No way.

Now there's a collie loose in her backyard. She scans the lawn for Paquito from the edge of the oven-hot patio. He's tearing up the yellowing grass as he races behind the bigger dog, yapping with joy. She extracts a bottled iced tea from the cooler and presses it to her neck, an exquisite wave of frozen needles moving through her. She has triumphed over her past. If her parents were ex–migrant workers born in Mexico during the Depression, if her father had been furious when she refused to drop out of high school to find work and apoplectic when she landed a college scholarship (But you're a *girl*, m'ija! her mother had wailed. Who is going to listen to anything you have to say?), if she'd spent every damned summer of her youth picking chiles and pecans—¿y qué? Now she could throw her own parties.

Now, at the back gate, comes Jerry's sister Delfina, constant evoker of the will of God. As her husband, Roger, plods in through the gate behind her, she eyes the crowd sorrowfully, her double-football bosom heaving up, then down.

Leave it to Inez to turn a simple visit into a game of hide-and-seek. Chavela waves and takes her tea to the living room, where Inez is not in the crowd. Ditto the front yard. Chavela elbows her way gently to the hallway. The bathroom is unoccupied, the door open.

Where, for that matter, is her husband?

She turns toward the den. On the floor, awash in the bellowing of Jerry's Lola Beltrán CD, her son and his friend sprawl before their electronic feast.

"Hey, Mom," Adam says after a very long moment in which she stands in the doorway breathing with fury.

"Didn't your father tell you to stop playing?"

"Uh," Adam says, grinning, "not exactly."

"Off," she says. "Out. Right now. Quinn, you can stay if you like, but Adam needs to interact with his relatives. The two of you will be gone from this room the next time I pass it."

"Okay, Mom. We'll be done in a minute."

She fixes him with a final murderous eye and turns back to the hall. Toward her party.

Which she is hosting because it is the right thing to do. Because when black sheep return to the pasture, someone has to serve as the shepherd, whether the sheep want to be shepherded or not.

She whisks open the screen door to a square, shadowy form that lumbers up the walk.

Tavo. Her brother-in-law. Sporting his habitual sour expression and a six-pack of Budweiser.

She summons another breath and produces her best no-nonsense smile. "Cuñado. ¿Como estás?"

He snorts. "Como de costumbre. So where is she?"

"Around here somewhere. Upstairs maybe." She eyes his armful. "Who told you to bring beer?"

"Beto called and said you people were running a dry county over here. So are you ringleading this circus or what?"

"All three rings."

Tavo looks over each shoulder.

"Who else is here?" he whispers.

She glances into the crowd. The collie gallops past with a paper plate in its mouth. She can discern the wails of three separate children.

But no Jerry. Who, as is so often the case at the moment he is needed, is elsewhere.

She forces down the knot that rises in her throat.

"Everyone," she answers crisply. She steps aside and takes her brother-in-law by the arm, the better to sling him toward the patio.

III

As Marcus plods up the sidewalk, the cicadas scream in every tree he passes. Already it's hot enough that he's sweating under the bridge of his sunglasses, beneath his baseball cap, into the footbed of his sandals, in the crease of the elbow where he carries his folded uniform. The last time he left it in the car before work, he felt like he was putting on a microwaved oven mitt.

Still, he tells himself as he slips into the crowd in front of his parents' house, he might consider putting it on early if Ashley Gutierrez called him today and wanted him to stop by her place before work. She hadn't yet seen him in uniform. Last week when they'd had dinner at a sports bar near his apartment and she'd kept her bright eyes on his face instead of on the basketball game on the widescreen TV—he knew she followed the Miners—and then let him take her hand over the tabletop and laughed at his jokes, he'd wondered if it had been the second pint of beer at work. In the days before that, they'd exchanged a couple of promisingly lengthy kisses in his car, his hand sliding onto her warm midriff. But then she'd bid him good night. So it was pretty clear she hadn't made up her mind about him. Which therefore meant that maybe he hadn't made up his mind about *her.*

He finds himself in the midst of a brief fantasy wherein Ashley leans up against him to trace his name on the placard over his breast pocket.

Inside he's greeted by a cresting wave of Linda Ronstadt. He scans for his mother—the definite source of this musical selection—but as he bobs in a sea of dark heads he only manages to trip over Paquito, to whom he offers a brief knuckle rub. Then, in the living room, an unnatural sight—a pair of blond college girls in green aprons, leaning over a draped and laden table. Absent are the usual Velveeta-drenched casseroles in disposable tins, the supersize pies from Costco, the two-liter bottles of RC Cola.

He emits a long, low whistle. So this is the kind of party his parents throw these days.

He drops his uniform into an armchair.

"Where's the guest of honor?" he asks the line at the buffet.

His tío Beto swipes a broccoli spear into a bowl of dip. "Nobody knows."

Tía Salomé lifts her eyes to the ceiling. Tía Delfina crosses her arms over her pointy bra with a great, heaving sigh.

Marcus suppresses a cough and thinks, *Uh-oh.* "She's probably still getting ready." He cracks a grin. "Where's the beer?"

A disgruntled vibe ripples across the room.

"There *is* no beer, m'ijo," tía Paloma clarifies. "Gil and Roger just went out to get some."

"*I* think," tía Flavia says sharply to Tencha in the food line, "that it's none of your business who I go on vacation with."

Tencha levels her gaze. "Even if your girlfriend has been running around with your other girlfriend's husband?"

"It's an insult to God!" Delfina adds.

Paloma shakes her head at her enchiladas. "Still bossy, still nosy, still acting like a teenager."

Marcus encircles his aunts with his arms.

"Break it up, everybody." He throttles them gently. "Don't make me confiscate your lunch."

Beto gives him a dry and long-suffering look. "M'ijo, do you carry a Taser?"

"Of course, I told Geronimo not to expect Inez to cooperate," Delfina tells Flavia.

"You told *Momo*?"

"Relax. I told Chavela to tell Momo."

He slips out into the hall, just ahead of a creeping, familiar sense of exhaustion. Little wonder Inez is taking her time.

Of course, it had to be said that his father—wherever he is—wasn't exactly helping.

"She's crazy," his father had frothed when they'd spoken on the phone earlier this week. "Unbalanced, insane, loca."

"So?" he'd answered, laughing. When he was a kid and Inez quizzed him in spelling and math and essay topics like "Describe a perfect society" and "Name a few of the conditions that can lead to the collapse of a civilization," he understood—though he doubts he ever gave a satisfactory answer—that the point was to be game. This was sport. His father would inevitably snarl, "Por Dios, leave him alone," but Inez would only come up with a question that was even more outrageous for a second grader ("What are some of the ways a religious skeptic might disprove the existence of God?"), and then she would rough up his hair and tell him hilarious jokes that his father categorized as "scatological," and later she would toss him a Nerf football on the front lawn.

Now he watches—in the steamy semi-dark between drawn window shades, in front of a sofa completely occupied by rapt eight-to-fifteen-year-old boys he cannot identify—as his brother plays *Grand Theft Auto*. The room exudes a perceptible animal stink.

Adam boosts the controls in Marcus's direction. "Wanna play?"

"Nah," he answers, though, in fact, he does. "So, what's the plan for when Inez gets here? Is there a cake or something?"

Adam shrugs. "Maybe she's going to jump out of one."

"You just gonna keep playing all day or what?"

"What are you, my manager?"

The ceiling fan makes hypnotic revolutions in the muggy air.

"Chill." Marcus looks at his watch. Two hours until he reports for work. Time to get this show on the road.

With a rising sense of duty, he heads for the stairs.

III

On his knees before the lumpy trio of Inez's duffel bags, with one eye turned toward the cracked-open door, Jerry roots.

It is an exercise that perhaps would be best undertaken while wearing rubber gloves. For what does he find? Clothes emanating the scent of a gym locker. Hole-ridden undergarments that he refuses to so much as brush with a hand. Basic toiletries. A small camping lantern and a bedroll consisting of a rubber mat and a tightly rolled sleeping bag. Matches. A transistor radio. Canned tuna. A handful of geriatric, water-damaged *National Geographics*. Two library books, apparently stolen from the Yuma, Arizona, public library, on the philosophies of Kant and

Schopenhauer. A pint of whiskey, two-thirds empty, which he tosses back to the bag.

He sits on his heels. Perhaps Inez is recovering from a broken-off love affair. Or seeking the job that will enable her to fund the next leg of her travels. Maybe she has been ill. Bankrupt. In trouble with the law. In trouble with the mental health system.

Or the most obvious possibility: she simply has nowhere else to go.

He stoops before the unmade bed, panic thrilling in his blood. Beneath the bed lies a cardboard box whose markings—in addition to featuring the letters *DQ* inside of a red, eye-shaped logo—indicate that it once contained 150 hamburger buns.

It holds photos now. Dozens of them.

He scoops a tattered black-and-white print from the depths and beholds Inez, in some long-ago era in which girls did not wear pants, dressed as Zorro. What if *he* had been the elder, he asks himself now—the one who administered the head slappings and Indian burns, who commanded performances of scripted, pay-per-view puppet shows and unfavorably critiqued his sibling's rhyming poems about cats and otherwise shaped her impressionable mind?

¿Quién sabe? She was number five, he was number seven, and since their parents saw no reason to stop until they got to ten, they were stuck in the middle together, destined either to sink into amiable anonymity or else do everything in their power to distinguish themselves. The date on the back of the photo indicates it was not even close to Halloween.

Also, as a five-year-old, she'd won a local talent competition by singing "Ol' Man River" at the top of her lungs while wearing a platinum Monroe-style wig. He lifts the yellowed news clipping from the box. Here, too, is news of the elementary school state spelling bee championships. A story from the late fifties, headlined, "Girl Wins Science Fair Prize with Moon Travel Hypothesis." The sparkling high school–era reviews of her starring roles in adult productions of *The Sound of Music*, *West Side Story*, *Macbeth*, the singing and acting lessons paid for with an after-school laundromat attendant job. All the while, as evidenced by the slim, sixties-era biography he extracts from between the newsprint, she'd been developing an almost unhealthy interest in Sor Juana Inés de la Cruz, "the greatest intellect of the sixteenth century," as she used to put it. "And a friggin' nun!" Of course, no one was surprised when she became the first in the family to attend college, on full scholarship, albeit after a long stint working concessions full time at the city zoo.

When he himself had graduated from high school, the first thing he did was join the Border Patrol. It was the most respectable job he could think of that required no further education, and in those days, they still took anyone whose draft number hadn't come up and who wasn't blind or crippled (as they put it back then) or flat-footed.

It wasn't bad. It beat being in Vietnam, and he still got to wear a uniform and carry a gun. He stood around at the border crossing, checking IDs and liberating baggies of marijuana from glove compartments, giving chase occasionally to the hardy souls who surfaced damply on the American side of the Rio Grande following the five-hundred-meter crawl stroke. His colleagues waited beneath the Stanton Street "Friendship Bridge," catching five or six of the hundreds who came galloping through during their morning commute—you could apparently set your watch to it. Those days seem so impossibly distant now, what with all the agents lining up every couple hundred yards or so now in their SUVs, so that your average border crosser, looking at the massive, bored line of uniforms arrayed the whole length of the city, either gives up and goes home or, if they have a job to report to on the other side, merely procures the basic ID that allows them to cross the bridge in a more conventional fashion but in no manner actually permits them to work. The people from parts farther south had yet to start paying someone their life savings to seal them into the produce crate in the cargo hold of a semi, or to push out farther west, on foot, on a death march into the desert. These were the days before an agent could get his ass shot off out in the field by heroin smugglers, or the Mexican army, or both of them working in cahoots.

It was serious work. Respectable work. And yet the moment finally came, as he sat in the station's lunchroom one particularly torpid day, engrossed in a biography of Pancho Villa someone had left in the men's room, when it occurred to him that he was bored with his life. And he hadn't a clue what to do about it.

College, said his friend Chuy, a third-year who was on the GI Bill. "I absolutely guarantee you will attract better-quality chicks."

The suggestion gave him pause. On the one hand, college was the province of Inez—Inez the Great Brain, the showstopper, the one in whose shadow he had lived so completely throughout his childhood that he had never seen reason to cast much of one of his own. When not involved in university theatrical productions, she was by now so heavy into philosophy and religious studies that it would have been easier for him to make an appointment with Joan of Arc. Chuy, conversely, had flunked the library aide elective in high school and still liked to crush beer cans under his armpit. If he, of all people, could transform into a studious being with long-term employment prospects in sports medicine, and with quality chicks besides, then couldn't he, Geronimo, reinvent himself?

Naturally, this moment of his life coincided with what he had come to think of as Inez's First Notorious Incident. Not that this event had surprised him in any way. After all, the guy in the diner booth beside hers apparently had quipped to his companion, "What's with all the Mexicans in this place? I thought they were supposed to be in the kitchen." Then he'd laughed. And Inez had risen up from the table beside his, where she had been enjoying breakfast with friends, and—turning with the bearing of someone balancing a large plate on her head—seated herself across from the perpetrator. "I guess you're not from around here," she began. "Cabrón." The response, Jerry was told, had not been favorable. And yet who else but Inez would have swept his plates from the table? Who else would have threatened him with a butter knife, continuing her harassment until both she and her nemesis had to be physically restrained by their companions, until the authorities were called? Until she was the one who was marched out of the joint by an amused pair of Anglo police officers, while the other guy made lewd gestures through the window. "Do you know what he *said*?" she snarled as she twisted in their indifferent grip.

Of course, he was the one she had called, afterward. "Hermana," he told her as she drank a bottled Fanta on his sofa with a shaking hand. "Tranquilo. Forget that pendejo. You're going to burn up all your fuel."

It was weeks—months, even—before she was the same again. As though she were dipping into the supply of rage that had fueled her in an earlier era.

But that was another matter altogether.

And in any case, by the time he'd made his own college entrance, Inez had seemingly regained her equilibrium. In fact, despite his own best efforts to slide in unnoticed as a freshman well past the drinking age, she made a point of detaching from her activities long enough to shepherd him in—no matter what the size of his vocabulary, she informed him, he knew nothing about university life. And so he allowed her to introduce him to a circle of friends whose primary activity was making religious and political arguments while swilling Bonny Doon wine. He'd felt an embarrassed sort of gratitude to her for a very long time, at least whenever they weren't bickering over who owed money to whom.

But then there was Chavela, who from the beginning had been convinced he held the key to something she wanted.

She had developed this notion only because, at the party where they'd met, he'd been arguing for the merits of an anarchic society versus government by benevolent dictatorship with some members of the philosophy club when someone shoved her in front of him.

That person had been Inez. Having seen the rapt expression on the face of the young stranger who was eavesdropping on their conversation, she'd figured that they—ingenue and know-it-all—were clearly a match made in heaven.

Indeed, weeks later, when Chavela's pursuit had begun in earnest, he'd been flattered, of course, and flabbergasted, and completely charmed by the combination of her awkward grammar and agile mind, and therefore did everything possible to sustain a confident charade wherein he took her—seven years his junior—under what he came to describe as his "tutelage."

He walked her through the steps of purchasing and reselling used text books. Applying for a job. Opening a bank account. Then he taught her the rules of logic, as used in formal debate. He encouraged her not to use the word "put" when what she meant was "give." He demonstrated the proper way to take a shot of tequila and introduced her to the intricacies of progressive rock.

It wasn't the last thing he had to fake his way through. When his junior year arrived and he still had no idea what direction his great reconstruction plan should take, he made an appointment with a guidance counselor who eyed the wavy line of his grade point average, cross-referenced it against the array of night-class offerings, and suggested further studies in a subject for which Jerry would eventually show a surprising aptitude. The rest of his life, as they say, is history.

"Dad."

Jerry startles and whaps shut the box.

"Hello, Son," he says brightly. "What brings you up to your old room?"

Marcus eyes the box, then the print on the wall that Chavela has added—pink watercolor flowers in a vase—and makes a sound through his nose. "I was *wondering* where you were."

"I had some things to put away."

"Actually, I was hoping I'd find Inez. The natives are getting restless."

"She's somewhere. She's . . ." Jerry sighs. "Several hours ago, she went 'for a walk.'"

"How long do these walks usually last?"

"The last one took fifteen years."

A phlegmy throat clears itself across the room. "Is this the hideout or what?"

Jerry turns. "I'm not hiding. Why does everyone think I'm hiding?"

"Well, hello to you too," Tavo says, and then he guzzles his beer.

Jerry exhales. "Pues, ¿cómo estás, hermano?"

Tavo shrugs, sour faced, and turns to his nephew. "¿Y tú? ¿Qué tal, hombre?"

Marcus offers his uncle a handshake. "Not bad, tío."

"¿Qué tal de trabajo? Hey, if they build that wall, it might put you out of a job."

"*If* they build it."

"I know, right?" Tavo snorts in Jerry's direction. "Pues, nothing changes, I guess."

Jerry resists the impulse to straighten. For Tavo has always been bigger than he, broader in shoulder and a good three inches taller, with the kind of strength that once lent itself to holding down a younger brother with a single hand while applying titty twisters with the other. Only now, his knuckles bear the scars of the various trades he's practiced since the seventies—plumbing, sheet metal punching, auto body work. Tavo, whose number had in fact come up and who had come home from Vietnam after two tours of duty with a medal he'd flushed down a public toilet. Tavo, who was number six. Not so much the bridge between him and Inez as the filling of the incongruent sandwich they made around him, oozing contempt at their points of contact.

Jerry folds the box closed. "Who wants to join me out on the deck?"

"¿Pues, qué piensas de esta fiesta?" Tavo adds wryly, still addressing his nephew. "¿Están tus padres haciendo miel para la boca del asno?"

"Uh," Marcus says, and then he breaks into his widest grin of self-defense. "*What* about the party?"

A pause, and then Tavo smirks, rolling eyes. "Sorry. I forgot."

Jerry steps up. "So ask him in English if you want to know if he thinks we're casting our pearls before swine."

"This is how you teach your son?"

"¿Cómo que how *I* teach him? This is how the *world* teaches him."

"Dad. Tío." Marcus claps both father and uncle around their shoulders, like a football coach. "Tranquilo."

"Well," Tavo continues once Marcus has sauntered out of the room, "if that's the legacy you want to leave or whatever, that's cool."

How, Jerry asks himself now with a shiver of fury and greed, would his life have been different if he had been an only child?

"Don't start," he growls.

III

As Marcus leans on the side wall beside the trash cans, the parental soundtrack cuts out. He inflates with relief.

Yet from the house now comes the loud and confident strumming of a live guitar. He recognizes the opening chords even before he hears the words, feels the throbbing in his DNA of the old-fashioned *oompah-pah* rhythm. Then the voices of man, woman, and child all join together, their pitch and rhythm out of sync, until all at once, they lift together into a perfect and triumphant chorus:

"Ay, ay, ay, ay . . . Canta y no llores."

"Oh God," he mutters.

At the base of the driveway, a little girl with rust-colored hair hops the sidewalk on one foot, then comes to a standstill. She drills holes at him with her eyes.

He smiles, making claw hands. "*Boo.*"

The girl stares until he looks away. Then she lifts her arms into the cresting vocal strains of the All-Mariachi Review, flapping away in slow motion, like a manta ray.

The back gate squeaks. Behind him, a guy his age he's never seen before freezes with one foot on the grass.

Marcus straightens. "Hey."

The guy readjusts a sweaty baseball cap, as though uncertain about whether to pass or go back the way he came. "Hey."

"I'm Marcus." He extends his hand. "Jerry's son. You're going to have to tell me how we're related, though, because I have no idea."

"I . . ." The guy shuts the gate. He wipes his hand quickly on his shirt-tail and gives Marcus's hand a single tug. "I didn't know anybody was back here, man. I'm the lawn guy."

"Oh." Marcus processes the guy's grass-stained jeans and tennis shoes, the plaid work shirt rolled all the way down to his wrists. "You work for my parents?"

"Gonzales?"

"That would be them." He chuckles, wondering, *Who are these people, and when did they stop doing their own yard work?* "Kind of a weird time to be doing the lawn, isn't it?"

The lawn guy shrugs. "I just finished. First here, and then next door. I had to come late."

Marcus nods, as though in complete understanding. He eyes the guy's getup.

"Dude, aren't you roasting?"

The guy offers a shy grin. "No, man. I feel good."

His accent is that of a person who learned Spanish first.

The little redheaded girl sails back up the sidewalk on a single Rollerblade, turning her head as she rolls past.

"Did you see that?" Marcus rushes back up to the wall. "That girl has been totally mad-dogging me."

The guy squints. He closes one lid, then the other, then the first one again.

"Oh, *her.* She's weird. Lives over there." He tips his chin. "Los DuPre."

Which meant she was probably Quinn DuPre's sister. Jesus. "You work for them too?"

"I work for everybody on this street."

Of course you do, Marcus says to himself. "What's your name, dude?"

"Miguel."

Marcus traces his teeth with his tongue. He asks himself what he wants to know. What he doesn't.

"Good to meet you, Miguel."

Miguel nods. He shuffles his feet and slips one arm behind his head, so that his elbow is pointing skyward, then bends the other behind himself to join his hands somewhere in the middle of his back.

Marcus's toes tap inside his sandals. "Something the matter?"

"Pues, mira . . ." Miguel releases his pose. "Could you ask your viejos to pay me?"

It's a beat before Marcus grasps of the essence of the moment. Then he almost laughs.

"Right," he says. "Right. Actually, both of them are inside. You could just—"

Miguel, studying his shoes with intensity now, bends one thumb against his wrist at an impossible angle. He is not going anywhere.

Marcus bites the inside of his lips. He extracts his wallet.

"How much do they owe you?"

Miguel mumbles a number, and then, "Pues, gracias," as he folds the bills Marcus passes into his hand. "Thanks a lot."

"No problem."

"Thanks."

And with that, his parents' gardener quicksteps toward a dented pickup truck parked at the corner.

At least the dude knows where he's supposed to go. Marcus pushes away from the wall. Before him, the redheaded girl skates past. In the living room, they sing.

III

Tavo refolds his thick arms. "She's not even here, is she?"

Jerry tucks in a box flap. "Nope."

"Are you going through her stuff?"

Jerry slides the box under the bed. "Yup."

"Find anything good?"

What Tavo cannot see is his hand as it retracts from the box, the object he slips swiftly into his waistband.

"Not yet."

"Why you letting her stay with you, man?"

Jerry looks his brother in the eye. He knew what happened, so long ago. He was there.

Tavo doesn't blink. "You're still a sucker, you know that?"

"I cannot be held responsible," Jerry says, as he zips shut Inez's duffel bags, "for any of Inez's comings or goings."

He can sense the knowing look Tavo gives him, the smirk, the shaking of his head as he moves for the door.

"You're no good at parties either. You never were."

III

"Can I have a beer?" Adam pipes.

Marcus slugs from his Budweiser, his free thumb a blur on the joystick button. "You wish."

Tavo lumbers in from the hallway. "You kids are all hypnotized. This crap is corporate mind control. You got a bottle opener?"

"Sure thing, tío." Marcus gropes the floor.

"I don't know why I came here today." Tavo uncaps and drops onto the sofa. "I'm the black sheep of the family. But I'm sure you knew that already."

"What are you boys still *doing* in here?" demands a brittle female voice from the doorway. "Why are *you* allowing this?"

"Allowing what?" says his father's voice in an offended tone. "I was just walking by."

"Mom," Adam says, stretching, turning to face her. "Don't worry. We only need like ten more—"

But this is when he realizes his mistake. For his mother has zeroed in on the front of his T-shirt, and as she takes in the words printed there, her eyes grow wide and darken.

"Take it off," she hisses through her teeth.

"Mom," he says, pressing down his palm in a soothing motion.

"Take it OFF."

He can feel all the eyes in the room upon him as he glances down at the legend—"1 Only *Look* Illegal"—and grins.

Marcus finishes his turn. Then he looks at the shirt.

"HAhahahaaa!"

In the doorway, his father chokes on his Diet Coke, then smiles despite himself.

"I'll drink to that," Tavo says, lifting his beer.

Quinn sets down his joystick and scoots away.

"Out," his mother says threateningly. "All of you. You're making my den smell like a locker room!"

"Everybody take cover!" Tavo calls out as he rises. "Madame Hussein is gonna bust out the weapons of mass destruction!"

"She doesn't *have* any weapons of mass destruction," his father grouses on his way out of the room.

The rest of the gallery rises unevenly and shuffles out, gazes averted from the finger pointing into the hallway.

"Mom," Adam says, slowing before his mother's outstretched arm. "It's just a shirt."

His mother presses her lips with fury.

"I've got news for you. We're us. They're them. And don't you ever forget it."

Then she's gone, like a string of firecrackers trying to keep ahead of its own explosions.

"Wow," Adam murmurs to Quinn out in the hallway as the crowd clears. He mock-wipes his forehead with the back of his hand. Then, with a backward glance, he grabs Quinn's arm and pulls him back to the den.

"I don't know about this," Quinn says, tensing.

"No, no. We're not gonna play." Adam spies the cordless phone submerged halfway between sofa cushions. "Okay. Your dad. What's something he can't stand having go wrong? What's most important to him?"

Quinn snorts. "Work."

Adam extracts the phone. "He's home right now?"

Quinn nods.

"Am I allowed to go for it? Like, really go for it? No caller ID, right?"

Quinn shrugs, then nods, then shakes his head.

Adam punches the number with his thumb.

"Yello?" says a deep voice after the third ring.

Adam clears his throat, to deepen his own voice. "Harold DuPre?"

With the accent he's laid on, it comes out sounding like "Harol."

First, a pause, followed by a vague rustling. "Speaking."

"You think you a big, good boss?" Adam blurts. "You make us too much work. Cuidado, pendejo—we give you a big surprise."

"Who is this?" the voice says, with a rising edge of belligerence.

But of course, by now, Adam has hung up, his pulse trilling with adrenaline.

"How's *that*, gabacho?"

Quinn gives Adam a slow smile. Thumbs up.

III

"Son," Jerry says as he pauses with Marcus outside the patio's sliding glass door, "*I* am the black sheep of the family. But I'm sure you've realized that by now."

"Dad, just so you know, a little while ago I ended up paying your—"

"She stole the Seat of History from me," Jerry blurts, his blood welling up from unknown places.

"The *what*?"

"When your mother and I got married, on the day I moved out of my apartment? Inez strode into my living room as my friends were preparing to deadlift the sofa, gave them all high fives, approached my favorite armchair—and mind you, it belonged to your grandfather until he bought his first recliner, and it was ugly and of zero value but comfortable as hell and *I claimed it first*—and wrestled it out the door and into a borrowed pickup truck. Or so I was told."

Marcus snorts, laughing. "And you're still mad about it?"

"Some people never change."

"Oh, come on. How bad could she possibly be?"

"Son. Do you remember the last time we saw her? Her birthday gift to you was a *knife*."

"I know. It was awesome. At least until you took it away."

"Do you remember what happened next?" Jerry heads to the back wall for the view. "No. You were outside, pinning the tail on the burro."

"Dad. Maybe you shouldn't get so worked up about—"

"Chingado!" A clutch of thorns snags Jerry's pants as he climbs into the rose bed, then gouges his palm as he tries to extricate them.

Marcus smiles lightly. "Maybe you should get your *gardener* to cut those back."

Jerry raises a warning eyebrow.

But the music has cut out again. A commotion has erupted inside the house. It ripples into the yard behind them, through the crowd, growing in strength and volume and, like a dust devil, sucking everything into its orbit. Jerry looks over his shoulder at the same moment Marcus does, though there's hardly a need. They already know who is here.

III

Chavela faces her raccoon self in the bathroom mirror, clutching a hand towel smeared with mascara. She should've known no one would appreciate this party.

Out in the yard, a male voice bellows, "Well, it's about damned time."

She steps into the bathtub and forces open the frosted window. It opens only an inch, as usual, but she presses an eye to the bright crack. Nothing but a sliver view of rear wall and shrub. Yet above the twittering of the crowd rises an all-too-familiar voice, soaring into a single-note aria: "Ta-daaa!"

She shoves the window closed. From the moment of her sister-in-law's return, she'd felt the old alarm in her gut, pero como una pendeja, she'd ignored it. Guess what else? It would be just as foolish to believe that whatever was in the past would stay in the past. And to assume that history wouldn't somehow repeat itself.

Now, wouldn't Jerry love to hear her say *that*? A familiar clicking of nails sounds against the tiles, followed by a cheerful "arf," as she tidies her makeup with a wad of toilet tissue. She bends to sweep up the puff-ball at her feet.

"Enough of this pity party," she tells Paquito with her nose in his fur. "Right?"

Downstairs, on the kitchen counter, four empty cardboard cases of beer sit askew. She turns to the refrigerator, a prickling beneath her skin. Inside lies a treasury of beer. Beer in the vegetable crisper. Beer on the Tupperware. Beer in the meat drawer, in the butter compartment, wedged between milk and juice jugs.

Flavia's girl, Danielle, slinks in through the sliding door in her short-shorts.

Chavela looks up her brightly. "How are you, m'ija?" The cans make a satisfying crack as she opens them. Into the sink they glug-glug-glug. "Did I hear you're starting high school next year?"

III

At least four dozen empty beer cans await Lourdes beside the kitchen sink.

She sets her bucket of mop water in the sink. Lifts a can, rattles it. It hasn't even been properly rinsed. Outside, everyone is raising some kind of big fuss—she's surprised they aren't passed out on the grass.

"Rrrrraf!" says a red blur near her feet, and then it jumps up on her shin.

She gasps, whirling, and hurls the bucket's contents onto her tormentor.

She turns to find señora Inez in the doorway, her head tipped at a quizzical angle as the dog yips and scrambles away.

The blood pounds in her ears. She spins back to refill the bucket.

Still here? señora Inez asks, grinning.

Lourdes nods faintly and turns off the tap, praying that Inez has seen nothing.

Inez glides to the pantry and emerges with a stick of beef jerky.

Too many vegetables out there, she clarifies. She yanks off a hunk with her teeth. Look at this. All of it just for me.

Lourdes retrieves a fresh trash bag from the cabinet. "Sí, señora."

I assume you also come from a large family?

Lourdes rinses a pair of cans and tosses them in. "Sí."

Well then, you know what it's like. Children?

"Sí, señora." The cans tinkle as they land.

Stop calling me "señora"! This isn't a hacienda and I'm not the landowner.

Lourdes tosses. The heat rises in her cheeks.

Look, Inez adds, if you happen to enjoy working for my brother for slave wages, I'm not going to stand in your way. But haven't you ever wondered just how much you're actually worth to these people?

Lourdes attacks the countertop with a sponge. She's definitely not stupid enough to answer that question.

Inez cackles and oozes toward the back door.

Maybe someday you'll decide to find out. Until then, I'll see you later, Lourdes. It seems I'll be staying a while. I've got some business with the neighbors. What's the name—DuPre?

She turns back just before she slips out.

By the way, I can't stand that damned dog either.

And Lourdes is left to her own palpitating heart, her hand quivering on the sponge. The air-conditioning whistles through the door. Inez pauses outside at the side wall. As though she saw a shape in the distance and would fly over and snatch it up if she could.

Jesus y Maria. Lourdes pushes the door closed.

The dog is waiting for her when she turns around. It heads right for her with its soggy red coat, tongue hanging, its grin crazed. She snatches up a beer can and hurls it, swallowing a shriek.

III

"Have a beer, bro," Lalo tells Jerry as he stuffs a damp can into his hand. For Inez has returned in her cowboy hat and a fresh plaid shirt. Inez dispenses hug after hug after hug to her adoring fans. Inez ascends a lawn chair like a podium.

Jerry pops the top and allows himself a very long swallow. Where has Marcus gone? He does not know. Beneath the mulberry trees, Inez elicits a laugh from her fan club—nephews and nieces and cousins, though

Flavia and Ofelia wait nearby with polite expressions ironed onto their faces. When Beto approaches and Inez pauses to raise her voice with sarcasm—"What, have you come to pay homage to me too?"—Jerry braces for collapse. But Beto only administers an impertinent tug of her braid before moving on, and Inez returns to her story, something about a man escaping her bedroom window with his pants on fire.

And they say *he's* no good at parties? Por Dios.

His thumb rings with pain. When he peels it away from his beer can, an entire constellation of tiny red pricks rise from his palm, welling over.

He looks to Château DuPre. One open window, curtains fluttering.

No. Enough. Ya. He chugs from his beer and trains his hard gaze on his sister. For it is Inez who inhabits his untidy nest. Inez with her secret agendas, with her own sense of timing, who couldn't be trusted, fork of the root that connects him to earth. Who pulls him back to the muck again and again. In this much, Chavela is right: she must leave.

For in the waistband of his pants is the switchblade he snatched from her box.

He studies the glad ease with which Inez now inhabits her stage, how she reaches to greet her guests. She shakes the arm of the one who carries the guitar, lifts her hands to the sky, throws back her head, and—at long last—looses from her lips the opening notes of the Trio Los Panchos song with which, a few days ago, she'd awakened them.

How she had always loved arriving. Every entrance was a chance to be new.

BESIDE THE POOL, AS THE waiter glides past in his white madras shirt, she marvels about what she has done.

She spends entire days marveling. Sipping palomas. Thinking. She thinks about the notes—the one she left for Huck, the other that came in the mail.

She is here to do some reckoning, to imagine her way into an inhabitable future—and okay, fine, also to punish her family, just a little and only temporarily—but it's the other note she's stuck on, the past, her choices, the choices someone else had once made. For her. Which is something she hasn't allowed herself to think about for a very long time.

Maybe she'll write.

Except that she hasn't. She opens books but allows them to fall unread to her lap. She looks out across the water, to the blue-on-blue horizon. She paces. She grows weary of being trailed by truckloads of men who call out "güera güera güera" as she walks the dusty road into town, until they get close enough to see that she isn't as young as they hoped.

5

OH, THE PLACES THEY'LL GO

IN THE LITTLE WORLD THAT lies below Huck's desk, the human machinery is humming, making its revolutions, generating heat and the sweet-burnt smell of product—except for the workers in the plastics injection module, who are in the middle of some kind of heavy conversation with his shift managers.

Huck clicks his pen. "I take it Sanders and Armijo are giving some kind of motivational talk."

Mendoza shifts his rear on the edge of the two-drawer filing cabinet. "We've had some discussions about retraining. And also about the male workers showing more respect to the female managers."

The ringleader crosses his arms.

Is he the one? The one who called him last weekend? Huck leans on his elbows. For each of the past three nights, he's reared up out of the black density of his sleep in a rage that not even rocky road ice cream and reruns of *Hawaii Five-O* can flatten. He wants to know how any of them could have gotten his phone number. His *unlisted* phone number. What kills him is that he was too furious at the time to remember to hit *69, though it probably doesn't work for calls originating from Mexico. If the guy calls again, he'll be ready with the third degree: *What kind of "surprise" are we talking about here, and how about you show me your face when you say that?*

Down in the assembly area, the workers in their bright-blue uniform shirts and rubber gloves have begun to lift their heads beneath the noise-canceling headphones. They elbow their neighbors, nodding in the direction of the motivation convention, the testing wands stilling in their hands. One guy even calls out to them. The half row of teenage girls behind him dissolves into giggles.

Huck swivels his chair. "How much more overtime do we need to make this deadline?"

"Maybe a week." Mendoza bounces his knee under his hand. His fingertips are yellowed with nicotine. "We've got QA rating of seventy-six percent at this point, by the way."

Huck glances at his watch. He's got a conference call with the CEO and two reps from Sanyo in twelve minutes.

"Make the announcement."

Of course, he tells himself as he downs his second cup of sour, tepid coffee, he was going to have to put this whole production run to bed before he went anywhere with the kids. Mendoza, for all his worry, could handle whatever might come down in the short term. If anything got *really* woolly, he could even temporarily divert the attentions of Laurence Villalobos, PI, with whom he'd already made an appointment to discuss the matter of a certain woman who had now been gone now for two and a half weeks, which some people might consider as still being within a certain grace period, but who had in any case clearly applied for a separate credit card at some point in order to stay off the financial radar.

Oh, he's going on vacation, all right. Just let anyone try to stop him.

He makes it as far as the top of the stairs that lead to the warehouse floor before he feels the cool grip of a familiar hand on his arm. Carmen, his admin, pressing a clipboard under his nose with forms for him to sign and her usual grim expression as she starts up with one of her lectures. He nods. Initials. Down below, to his relief, Sanders and Armijo and their pal have disappeared.

"So are we good?" Carmen calls out as he descends.

He lifts a hand without turning around. "We're good."

"I left them in the break room."

"Left what?"

"The observers," Carmen hollers. "From Fair Labor International."

He turns back. "What are *they* doing here?"

"You gave the okay on this last week. What did you think you were initialing just now?" She looks at her watch. "Your call from Sanyo should be coming through in ten minutes."

He allows her to escort him to the break room, where a trio of women in blazers and jeans, who clearly haven't been out of college for long, are loitering over the complimentary magazines.

"So," he begins once the handshaking is behind them. "What can I do for y'all?"

One of the young women offers him a sunny smile. "Basically, we're here to gather information about working conditions at the maquilas."

"Ours or theirs?" he jokes.

"We're interested in worker impressions. About hiring and firing policies, for starters."

"What exactly can I clear up for you here?"

"We wouldn't mind having a look at your workers' employment files," says the one holding the clipboard. "Just to confirm everyone is of legal working age."

"Every worker here has presented the proper documents."

"Have you verified their authenticity?"

Huck forces a smile. "I'm running a busy, high-volume, high-turnover, multinational factory here. We don't have the resources to do background checks on everyone who comes through. The law here doesn't even require it. We have to trust what they show us."

"We understand that female applicants are required to take pregnancy tests before they can be hired," the sunny one says. "And that pregnant workers are let go?"

The woman who stands behind them takes silent notes in a little flip pad.

Huck glances at the coffeepot. It's turned off, though a couple inches of some viscous substance remain.

"I'm not the one who does the hiring," he says. "But obviously, I have a doctor on staff, which not every maquila can say, and he has to make some decisions about who's fit for duty and all that. But we take care of them. We give them TB shots. Hell, some of these people have never had immunizations in their lives until they get them from us."

"We'd still like to have a look around," the sunny one says apologetically, and only now does he see the strap of the video recorder on her shoulder.

"Fine by me," he says. "Knock yourself out. But I won't allow interviews during working hours. We're on a deadline here. Talk to them after work, if you can get them interested."

"Could we get some more detailed information about your overtime policy?" the clipboard asks. "And also about the rate of pay?"

He looks her in the eye. "You know—right?—that this maquila is one of the biggest employers in the area? And that the maquilas have brought down the unemployment rate on the border from the highest in Mexico to the lowest?"

"Well, yes, but—"

"You can thank NAFTA for that. I know *I* do."

The intercom above the refrigerator buzzes.

"Huck," says Carmen's voice in a tone that makes it clear she has never, not for a moment, been on his side, "I've got Mr. Nagao from Sanyo on the line."

"Incidentally," he adds, reaching for the coffeepot, "we've got no hazardous waste complaints on record."

"Actually, we've received some preliminary reports about—"

"I said *on record*. Now if you ladies will excuse me."

He tosses back his whole sludge-laden cup before he's even all the way out the door.

For Chrissakes, though, he's not oblivious. Any fool can calculate the volume of American money the maquiladoras invest in payroll versus its value in pesos in a Second World economy, and by the way, he's a manager, not the corporate shelter that hired him. He crosses the floor back to the stairs. Half of these people were going to quit in the next few months and hop to some other maquila anyway—it's what you do when you're juggling a second job in the "comercio informal" sector, possibly as a last stop on the route north, or so the exit interviewers said. He tries to discern what he sees on their faces now, what level of resentment, boredom, acceptance. Is that the clench of stress he detects in their postures? Rose Marie had always told him this was something he was no good at, this business of "reading people emotionally," because apparently he was supposed to be watching their "body language" to determine whether it matched whatever was coming out of their mouths, which was, in his opinion, a load of horse crap.

Rose Marie, for her part, had still been relatively happy when they left Dallas. Of that much, he feels certain. Not that he hadn't tried to prepare her for what was to come—he'd been inside her sorority mansion plenty of times, most often for those god-awful formals that she enlivened by secretly imitating her sorority sisters and slipping him a whiskey flask out of her purse, occasionally after hours for a sneak-in—until he'd said to her dryly after their engagement, "Honey, I do hope you are not expecting me to be able to support the lifestyle to which you have become accustomed."

She snorted. "Soon," she said, "very soon, my parents are going to try to give us enough money to ensure that we'll live in a so-called presentable neighborhood, and we are going to turn it down."

"Damn straight we are."

She planted a lipstick print on him that he didn't find until someone pointed it out at dinner.

Nevertheless, after they returned from an upbeat five-day honeymoon at a motel in San Antonio that was an uncomfortably long walk from the River Walk itself, after he brought her to the doorstep of the apartment he'd rented but she hadn't yet seen, after he'd jokingly thrown her over his shoulder and she'd shrieked with delight as he hefted her backside-first over the threshold, he planted her back on her feet and watched as she took in the mismatched furniture in two different patterns of plaid, the thin gray carpet, the dizzying pattern of the orange-and-brown kitchen tiles, the television with its antennae wrapped in aluminum foil, the translucent light fixtures spotted with flies, all the textures of what was no longer some kitschy adventure but officially her life to come.

She swallowed and said, "Wow," looking as though some layer beneath the surface of her face was melting.

In the grander scheme of things, she couldn't cook. At all. Not that he was any expert, but he could at least make a grilled cheese sandwich and scramble an egg. Also, she wasn't entirely clear on how to operate the vacuum cleaner, or use a washing machine, or wash dishes by hand.

Sometimes he teased her. Sometimes he tried, but didn't quite manage, to conceal the rolling of his eyes.

Sometimes she spat back at him bitterly, "Nobody taught me how to do this stuff!" But in the end, she made a decision that had surprised him. "I would like," she said quietly one evening as they watched the tin-foiled TV, "to learn how to be a real person."

And by God, she'd done it. She'd bought two secondhand cookbooks and taught herself to burn a number of dishes, until one morning she finally served three successful pancakes. She figured out the schedule for replenishing their supply of clean underwear, and at the Laundromat, asked a formidable-looking woman with five kids how much soap she should add and in what slot and what would happen if she mixed the colors and whites together. She landed a job with the alumni magazine even though she still had one more semester to go with her English degree, and she proofread and fetched lunch for the editors until they let her try her hand at stories on newly installed sculptures and faculty members' New Year's resolutions and homecoming queens who were studying law.

Huck, for his part, business diploma already in hand, had seen the future and knew it was in manufacturing. An entry-level manage-ment position had been ridiculously easy to land, and furthermore, it was solid—the world was not going to stop needing electric motors for restaurant, medical, and packaging equipment.

And so it might be said that the two of them were functioning pretty damned well by the time the twins arrived—Rose Marie's departure from the magazine notwithstanding—so well that whenever her parents came to the apartment to jiggle the babies on their knees (which was rarely; they preferred to issue commands to visit the mansion), they still managed to look sour and furious at the lack of misery they observed. It took only seconds after closing the door behind Jarvis and Francine for either him or Rose Marie to start imitating them, which never failed to crack both of them up—although occasionally, her laughter would explode without warning into tears.

Of course, the motors could only hold him for so long. Sure, he liked a dependable situation as much as the next guy, but there was more to life than just getting by. The border was where the real action was—international business at the crossroads of worlds, now tariff free and with an unlimited workforce. Suddenly there they were, headed to a land of promise and adventure, even if was still located within the state of Texas. It might as well have been Timbuktu. And if the landscape was strange to them, if people smirked at their accents, if they joked about the fairness of their skin and laughed outright at his hat, he would smile back and learn the customs of this place and, eventually, blend in. However things would turn out, he already knew they would suit him just fine.

Rose Marie seemed to share this perspective. Hadn't she been the one who wanted to prove to her parents that he could make something of himself? The days leading up to their departure were infused with the fierceness of her cheer, a sense of determination that, though by now familiar to him, was unnerving in its focus. She packed quickly, without lingering over unnecessary items, which she stuffed unsentimentally into the trash. She disconnected the utilities a day early, resulting in a somewhat amusing dinner of take-out hamburgers illuminated by camping lantern. When the twins developed last-minute runny noses and stomach aches and weird skin rashes, she fed them Jell-O and Benadryl and otherwise prepared to press on.

And yet over the course of the long weekend, as they'd driven ahead of the moving van to their new home, the twins sleeping narcotically in their car seats as Dairy Queen after Dairy Queen whizzed past on the prairie, the great green, grassy expanses giving way to the desert's cracked hide, raptors circling overhead in a cloudless sky so enormous and curved it seemed almost to breathe, he'd watched as Rose Marie gnawed her manicured thumbnails to the quick. When he'd finally pulled into the driveway of the rental house he'd secured, she'd stepped silently from their station wagon into the moistureless air to survey the brick box with wrought iron barring the windows, the chimneys of the cement factory visible over the rooftop and the scent of oil refinery in the air, her eyes glittering with tears that never fell.

He had assured her all along that these arrangements were to be temporary. She had assured him she understood and accepted this plan—even if, just as they arrived, the peso was devalued and every maquila in Juárez was locked down into a labor strike; it was six weeks before he could get to work, and not even then without danger of his car getting tipped over by a street mob. Hadn't he put his arms around her anyway? Rubbed her back and put his nose in her hair (which she had lightened with some sort of Clairol product)? Had she lifted her arms in return?

Or had she already become a target he circled without any place to land, just as he circles the room now, grazing a row of workers who regard him with a ripple of eyebrows, glances, elbows, side nods.

Carmen stands at the window beside his desk, waving and pointing at his phone.

He hustles upstairs.

III

At her desk at the back of the classroom, Jordan draws up formulas for a series of flavored toothpastes. One part baking soda to two parts vanilla. Two parts baking soda to one part coconut extract, mashed with one-half packet of NutraSweet. One and a half parts baking soda compounded with six and a half sugar-free lemon-flavored Certs, the kind that spark when you chew them with your mouth open in the dark. Up at the dry-erase board, Mrs. Tomlinson is reviewing the law of cosines, which Jordan already knows. She sits between a rocker chick and a mouth breather who either erase violently or crumple paper just before they ask her for the answer.

She doesn't give answers. She stares. Then the breather begs and offers her pieces of candy and the rocker calls her "you little shit."

Why is she here? Because when her father read the letter from her school announcing summer accelerated class cancellations—renovations gone wrong, it said, staff compensation disputes, the "high percentage of students requiring time off for overseas vacations"—his hands had trembled with rage. Then he got on the phone with the enrollment office at her brother and sister's public high school.

On the first day, Mrs. Tomlinson glided up to her desk in the front row and said, "Now, honey, if you need any help at all, you just let me know."

She didn't need help. She knew the answers. And she knew them first. She raised her hand relentlessly, straining in her seat in the long silences that followed Mrs. Tomlinson's questions. Sometimes, if she saw the tentative lifting of other peoples' hands, she blurted her answer out before they could get any further. She corrected other people's incorrect answers.

By the second week of school, Mrs. Tomlinson had taken her aside and asked if she would please consider not answering every single question so that other people might have a chance to do so, and when Jordan countered that most of them didn't *know* the answers, Mrs. Tomlinson had said that they needed to be given a chance to think about the questions, and when Jordan told her that she didn't think they were thinking about the questions, Mrs. Tomlinson had asked her to please stop thinking about them herself. Now it took absolutely forever to get through any lesson, and whereas before, people gave her dirty looks for answering everything, now they gave her dirty looks because she didn't.

Now she traces her finger over the top of her desk, carved with the message "Take more bong hits!" Maybe she should be taking classes at UTEP. She straightens. If her mother were here, she would love this idea. She would get on the phone to the university immediately, using her most flirtatious, insistent voice.

But her mother's not here. She was *supposed* to be here, by now.

Maybe she should ask her dad when the investigator is coming, in case he'd forgotten about hiring him. Maybe she'll tape up a sign on his bedroom door that says "Investigate!" Then she'll get everyone's suitcases out of the garage. Once the investigator figures out where her mom is, they'll need to be ready for departure. Who knows how much time they'll have before she moves on to her next secret locale? They'll have to pack ahead of time, and what they bring will depend on where they're going. California or Maine or Alaska or Ecuador. Whether they'll be traveling by car or by plane or by boat or by snowmobile.

She pictures her mother wrapped in white robes and veils, trekking across sand dunes on a camel, alone. Their mother would turn to them in her saddle as they trudged to her. She would throw her leg over the hump and slide to the ground, waiting until they all stood an arm's length away, and they would look at her and she would look at them and she would smile and say, *I knew you'd find me.*

She would also say, *I got rid of that other guy.*

In the meantime, Jordan finishes all the assigned homework for the week.

Beside her, the hand of the breather creeps slowly onto her desk, deposits a caramel, and withdraws. One of the white perforated ceiling tiles above her head is ajar in its metal frame, opening into a dark world. She wouldn't mind climbing onto her desk and sticking her head in to have a look around.

Instead, she scans the empty parking lot after class as the shade under the math building recedes. The street traffic whooshes. Carlos's dented station wagon with her sister's woolly head in shotgun position does not appear; the buses stopping at the corner do not produce her brother.

She considers her watch. Paws through her purse, pulls out her cell phone, and shoves it back in. Someone unplugged her phone before it could charge.

She lies back on the warm concrete step and rolls over until she lands with a thunk on the next step. It doesn't hurt much. So she does it again. She lifts her head just enough not to conk it against the cement until she reaches the bottom of the steps. Then she climbs back up to the top and starts over.

"Young lady."

Jordan pauses midroll. It's a moment before she can focus her eyes through the glare on the woman who is standing over her.

"Are you waiting for someone to get out of class?"

"No."

"Are you waiting for someone to pick you up?"

"Yes."

The woman adjusts the satchel on her shoulder. "I see. And how long have you been waiting?"

"Since one thirty."

The woman looks over the top of her glasses. "Come with me."

III

Quinn jerks his head from his pillow.

The stereo downstairs. It blasts a steel guitar twang. Then hip-hop. If his cheesy-hits-of-the-eighties detector is functioning properly, Pat Benatar bellows next at the top of her lungs. He squints at his clock. Jesus. Ten forty-two. He'd rather it was noon. But who the hell is home anyway? Skyler, off from work early?

No. Not in any universe would Skyler tolerate "Hit Me with Your Best Shot."

He tugs himself into a pair of sweats he retrieves from the floor and opens his door with care. He pads down the hallway, peeks over the stairs railing. What if he's awakened to a robbery in progress? Someone is trying out the stereo to see if it's worth ripping off. He needs a weapon. A hammer or ski pole or X-acto knife.

He descends the stairs wielding the globe that sits on the corner of Jordan's desk, his vision tunneling as he sidles to the den, from which issues a rustling, scuffing sound, and also the baritone surfer-guitar riff from the B-52s' "Rock Lobster." He rounds the corner, globe cocked behind his ear. What if it's his mother? The thought of this seizes up something in his chest and freezes his brain, so his arms are operating without him as he swings the heavy globe toward the robust human form swaying its hips in front of the stereo, who drops the heavy book in her hands and shrieks. He squawks and pulls the globe up short.

Lourdes. She clutches her chest at him. On the floor between them, *Merriam-Webster's Collegiate Dictionary*, a pile of raked-together shoes, and an overflowing garbage bag.

"Jesus, Lourdes." He hugs the globe, the spindle gouging his ribs. "I thought someone was robbing us."

"I think you no home!" she sputters over the spastic chords of the organ. She lurches for the dictionary and stuffs it back onto the shelf. "I think very, very much quiet!"

"It's cool." He locates the stereo remote and lowers the volume, then eyes the dictionary, jutting slightly forward on its shelf. "What—"

"¿Qué pasó?" Her fists meet her hips. She tips her chin at the shoes, at the room around them, at the whole house.

In the kitchen, the phone rings. Lourdes waits with light-sucking eyes.

"I'm . . . gonna answer that," he says, backing away.

At first, he hears only breathing.

"Jo-Jo. Is that you?"

"Nobody got me. I need a ride home from school."

"Crap." Quinn chews a black-polished nail. "Jo-Jo, I hate to tell you this, but no can do."

"Why?"

Lourdes has decamped to the other side of the den, where she scrubs a milky handprint from the window with crumpled newspaper. "Well, for starters, Dad's got the truck. And I totally do not have any bus money. Can somebody give you some?"

"No. You should just come get me."

The newspaper squeaks against the windowpane. "Hang on."

He sets down the phone and slips back to the den. Lourdes douses the window with Formula 409. He watches for as long as he dares. Then, silently, while her back is still turned, he gathers up two and a half pairs of high-tops from the shoe pile, opens the cabinet of the entertainment center, and shoves the shoes on top of the TV. He shuts the door.

"Jo-Jo," he continues back in the kitchen, "even if I could, it would interfere with the Sabotage Campaign. How are we supposed to make things harder for Dad if we take care of everything for him?"

"Oh." And then, after a pause, "Don't call me Jo-Jo."

"Just do your homework or something until Dad comes home. I'll make it up to you later." Lourdes balls up a new paper wad, pricking her ears in his direction. "I've gotta go."

He hangs up and slinks back to the den, offering Lourdes a sweet smile before she turns to spritz the window again. He gathers the rest of his shoes into his arms. He's sorry for what he's going to have to do to her, but in war, there are often civilian casualties.

One shoe pair he drops in the doorway to the downstairs bathroom. Another he stuffs under the sink. He trails the rest behind him up the stairs, like breadcrumbs.

III

"It's for you, güera," the voice of management says. She holds out the cordless. "A *kid*."

Skyler presses the phone to her ear.

"Who's coming to get me?"

"Jo-Jo?" Skyler wipes a mist of kitchen grease from her forehead. "Where are you?"

"I'm at school. Don't call me Jo-Jo."

"What? Quinn was supposed to come get you!"

"Come get me."

In the adjacent dining room, under the piped-in mariachi music, the other waitresses—Raquel, Josefina—gossip out of view out of the closed-circuit cameras. If she were to walk in on them, they would immediately stop talking and glare at her.

"Jo-Jo, I'm not getting off until nine. Plus, Carlos is picking me up."

"Come get me."

She leans toward the inadequate ceiling fan, sweating. Whenever they finally hear from their mom, Skyler is going to have a few things to say. Like, thanks a lot for taking the car, and how long has she been living this sleazy double life, and did she know how totally lame she was when she practiced good posture, or used two different forks in her table settings, or spoke French in public, or wore pantyhose and heels just to go shopping at the mall, and shopped at malls to begin with, and offered people fake smiles just before turning away and saying something sly about them behind their backs, and did she have some whole other family somewhere else that she liked better or what?

Maybe she didn't even feel bad about the time she laughed at her mother's poem. If her mother didn't want anyone to see it, she shouldn't have written it on the grocery list.

"Güera." At the register, management tallies up receipts with a calculator, using the tip of a Lee Press-On Nail. "If you're going to keep blocking up my phone line with your personal conversation, you have to clock out."

"I have to go. Call Quinn."

Raquel pokes her head out of the dining room, narrows her eyes, and retreats, hissing offstage, "She's so *skinny*."

"Güera! Are you a zombie or what? Get a move on!"

Maybe she will. Right after she scoops up the wooden toothpick holder from table five and, with her back to the security camera, stuffs it into her bra. *Sabotage*.

III

Behind the recliner in the den, Lourdes finds a naked Barbie stuffed headfirst into a box of crackers.

The TV's remote control awaits her in the pantry, on top of a jar of peanut butter.

When she opens the TV cabinet, out tumbles a small pile of shoes.

She plucks up each shoe by its heel, except one—a black high-top sneaker, which she kicks to the edge of the area rug—and carries them up the stairs, to el hombrecito's bedroom door. He's inside, clickety-clicking away on his computer. She lines up his shoes, save for one, beside his doorway. Does she only imagine she hears a pause of the fingers on the keyboard? She's already on her way back down the stairs, to the kitchen, where she drops the remaining shoe into the trash.

She stuffs the knotted trash bag into the can on the side of the house and stands at the top of the driveway, hands on her hips, the sun singeing the part in her hair and a righteousness inflating her heart.

"Órale." Miguel stands in his truck bed as she strides up. "¿Que pasó?"

Lourdes wipes her hands on the dishrag tucked into her waistband. She has just kidnapped a *shoe*.

What would they do if we just disappeared one day? she spits out.

He shrugs and climbs down. I'm pretty sure they would find someone else.

Have you ever imagined doing it anyway?

Have *you*? he asks, grinning.

III

"Mr. DuPre," says the woman on the other line. "This is the school secretary at Coronado High. Your daughter—who, am I understanding this correctly, is one of our students?—has been waiting for a ride home for most of the afternoon. How soon can we expect you?"

A film of blood descends over Huck's eyes.

"Get Mendoza to initial the addendum to the AltaVista contract by the end of the day," he tells Carmen as he stuffs the contents of his inbox into his briefcase. "I need progress reports from Armijo and Yee. If the gals with the cameras start talking to the workers before close of business, kick 'em out. And for God's sake," he says, coughing as he crunches down on the miniature marshmallows from a packet of dry

hot chocolate mix he has emptied into his mouth, "get some more coffee into the break room."

It's only as he hits the stairs that he slows, his eye catching on a row
near the center of the assembly area. Two neighboring workers have
fallen into sync with each other. He watches the tandem motions of
their hands, the sweep of the wands, their upward glances at the pass-
or-fail designation on the monitors. As though by silent, mutual agreement, their neighbors fall into step with them. And then, suddenly,
impossibly, the whole row takes up the components in unison, a chore-
ography of hands, arms, eyes transmitting and repeating in a silent language, rolling now across the room like an ocean's wave, beautiful and
enormous and unstoppable, until a knot of workers breaks off at the far
side of the room and beckons the closest portable camera-bearing member of Fair Labor International.

He drives away from the building with a numbness behind his eyes.
Collects Jordan in silence from school. She wants to know when they're
going on vacation.

"Don't know yet," he tells her as he pulls into their driveway and kills
the engine. He reaches behind the seat for his briefcase.

"How about after you meet the investigator?"

"There could be a certain cause and effect there, yes."

"*When* are you meeting the investigator?"

He opens his door to the inferno outside. "Soon enough. Do we know
what our dinner situation is for tonight?"

"But when is he going to start *investigating*?"

He stops with one foot on the driveway and twists back. Jordan's dark
eyes blaze bright as headlights. Her mother's eyes. But somehow, at the
same time, he is gripped with the sensation that he is looking into the
eyes of a stranger.

His blood whomps in his ears. "I'm going inside."

"We should go on vacation as soon as possible," Jordan continues as
she follows him up the walk.

Farther down the street, Miguel fiddles with something over the
rear tire of his pickup. If he's not mistaken, the female form beside him
is Lourdes, though it's a little hard to tell, considering the way she's
crouched behind the opened passenger door.

Maybe they're working. Who knows?

"Dad," Jordan says as he plants his hat on the coatrack. The open bag of dog food has been removed from the entryway, though the pile of unwanted religious pamphlets remains. "Maybe the investigator should use bloodhounds."

"Son," he calls up the stairs. "I'd like a word."

It's a moment before Quinn emerges with an innocent expression. "Yeah, Dad?"

"You," Huck begins, "have caused me some *considerable* trouble today. What's the big idea in refusing to pick up your sister?"

"Dad. I had no car. I had no money. The change jar was empty. Skyler's at work. What could I possibly do?"

"Come on! You're old enough to figure this out. Why didn't you get a ride from Adam?"

Quinn shrugs. "He's at work too."

"Why didn't you get a ride from *any* of your friends?"

"They're *all* at work."

"Which explains why you're the only one without any money."

"You realize—right?—that it's impossible for me to look for a job if you expect me to be a bus chauffeur all summer."

"Of course, I didn't hear word one about this before I left this morning."

"Dad," Quinn continues, with an air of great patience, "you know, this whole situation could have easily been avoided if you would just get us another car."

"That's it! You're—" Huck sputters, on the cusp of the word *grounded*.

The ceiling seems to be much lower than he remembered. Also, the floor stretches away, like the lane of a bowling alley.

"This is not the end of the conversation," Huck wheezes, lunging into the kitchen, where Lourdes furiously mops up a fresh, grass-stained set of adolescent-sized footprints.

He leans on the doorjamb, gulping air. Maybe he never saw Lourdes outside at all. Maybe she's avoiding his gaze out of politeness, having just overheard an argument in the next room. Maybe this loyal and dependable employee—who has never been any trouble to him, even if she didn't belong here, whose daily trek was likely only marginally worth it to her bottom line—is the most reasonable person in the house.

"Lourdes," he says, finding his voice somewhere at the back of his throat. "¿Como está?"

She breaks no stride with her mop. "Bien, bien, señor. ¿Y usted?"

"Dad." Jordan swivels on her stool at the breakfast bar. "Where's your suitcase? I didn't see it in the garage."

A lawn mower's engine rips the air outside. Lourdes flexes her substantial biceps, squeezing the dirty mop water back into the bucket.

If he could, he would pay her to come every day.

"Lourdes," he hears himself saying, "just how available *are* you during the week?"

The look she gives him makes him think of a mouse caught in a pantry.

"We'll talk later," he says in a soothing tone, calculating the next time he might be able to get her into a room with Skyler.

"If you want," Jordan continues at his elbow, "I can pack for you."

He turns to his daughter. Somehow he's got to get her home from school for the rest of the summer. She meets his gaze with firmness and gravity. As ever. How could he think her anyone else?

Lourdes squeezes the mop. Outside, Miguel pushes his mower in concentric ovals on the Iversons' pool of crabgrass, then cuts the motor.

Squirrelly, ever-present, potentially trustworthy Miguel. Who, quite frankly, owes him one.

He drops a hand onto Jordan's shoulder as he slips out the door.

"Knock yourself out."

THE LEXUS DROPS SOME PART of its undercarriage onto the pavement as she clears the return point of entry. This, after the guard eyes her tourist card and birth certificate with the usual puzzlement and then gives her a spiel about the upcoming change in passport requirements, whatever whatever. She limps to the first mechanic she finds at the side of the freeway, an octogenarian who employs no helpers. He gives her a prescription of two weeks.

What to stinking do *now*? A room at a San Diego Motel 6 costs more than a suite at the El Paso Hilton. She paces the boulevards lined with fast-food joints. She paces, and around the next corner is a sign swinging from a splintery post in front of the Seaside Manor: Weekly Rentals Available.

"I can give you a better rate if you take the whole month," the sleepy-eyed manager tells her.

It shocks her, the way her heart leaps toward *yes*.

6

ALL THE TIME IN THE WORLD

"THAT'S DISGUSTING," CHAVELA SAYS.

Inez extracts her paw from a box of bran flakes. "What?"

Chavela tightens her bathrobe belt. "Incidentally, I was chatting with Mr. Benavidez—"

Inez crunches. "Who?"

"Our mail carrier. And I think he would appreciate it if you would stop trying to make him have those theological discussions."

"Ah, but ignorance is the curse of God; knowledge, the wing wherewith we fly to heaven."

"Is that from the Bible?"

"No, dummy. Shakespeare."

"Could you at *least* put your things away?"

"Sure." Inez oozes to the kitchen table, tugs a single pair of underpants from the stack Chavela has folded, topples a tower of bras, and pours herself upstairs.

Chavela knocks the remaining pile to the floor. Then she, too, ascends.

Jerry sags over his breakfast burrito.

When he finds Chavela at her vanity table upstairs, he says, "I've been thinking." He palms her bare shoulders. "What if we made Adam's school drop-off into a family vacation? We could go somewhere ridiculous. Like Disneyland. Afterward, you and I could stay in San Diego for a few days. We could even swing through Cloudcroft on the way back and see if there are any enticing vacation properties on the market and—"

"Could you take Paquito for his walk tonight?" Chavela sears her hair with a curling iron. "I won't be home before ten."

He pauses. "Sure."

"You'll remember?"

"Of *course*."

The doors to the deck make a sucking sound as they are opened from the outside against the air conditioner. Inez drifts past the cracked-open bedroom door.

Jerry pulls a smile. "So. What do you think?"

Chavela sets down the iron. "Would that mean *she's* going with us?"

"Presumably not."

"Pues entonces, I guess she'd be staying behind in the house. Unsupervised. What are her plans for the day, by the way?"

He retracts his hands. "I'm not sure."

"Does she have plans for the month?" She stirs something in a compact with a brush. "For any time in the future?"

The creak of footsteps in the hall. A whoosh as the doors to the deck are pushed open again.

"Can you at least consider the original question?"

She reaches for a wide-tooth comb and scrapes at her bangs. "What about a Fourth of July party instead?"

"No! No parties!"

She slaps her comb on the tabletop and turns to him. He straightens to full height.

"Arf!" says a creature in the doorway.

Chavela softens her body. "Well, hello to *you*." She lifts Paquito—grinning, tongue lolling—into her arms. "Are you coming to work with me? Hmm? Or do you want to stay and laze around with these people?"

"You think I'm *not working*?"

Chavela scoops up the outfit laid out on the bed, takes her armfuls into the bathroom, and shuts the door.

On the deck, Inez slumps in a patio chair, nose in the newspaper. The half-smoked cigar in her hatband smells of ash.

He takes a breath and seats himself lightly beside her.

"Would you care to join me on a Walmart safari today?" He reaches for the Home and Garden section. "I'm told we need toilet paper and shampoo and a twenty-pound bag of Pomeranian chow."

"They're going to move Western Playland! The whole damned thing. All the way out to some godforsaken stretch of desert near Sunland Park."

Home and Garden settles onto his lap. "Why on earth—"

"Political skullduggery. And back taxes. By the way, Asarco just filed bankruptcy."

The familiar smokestacks wait below, like two sentries who have fallen asleep on their feet.

"Isn't it a little late for that?" he goads.

"Somehow, it's supposed to get them back into business, which will be good for the local economy. If they don't, the Feds are going to make them demolish everything and then clean it all up. The whole site is contaminated as shit, as I'm sure you know."

"A moot point," he scoffs. "Neither of those things will ever happen."

She sighs. "It's true. Nothing ever happens here." She pushes back into her chair, dimming, and slides down. Only her eyebrows are visible when she lifts the paper again.

He scans the headlines with desperation.

"Chupacabra!" he blurts.

Her face brightens. "Where?"

He flips over her page.

"Juárez locals attribute the attacks," she reads, "mostly of goats and sheep, to the mythical creature known as El Chupacabra—the Goatsucker—which earns its name from its habit of attacking and draining the blood of livestock." She skips ahead. "It seems there was evidence of the 'signature three-point fang marks the creature purportedly leaves behind on the bodies of its victims.' In the shape of an upside-down triangle, naturally."

Jerry chortles. "How long has that thing been lurking now? Ten years?"

"Most likely since the dawn of time. It was just in hibernation for a couple of centuries."

"Unless it's a mutant," he adds.

"Or a flesh-eating parasite that lives inside the host."

He leans back in his chair. "It's the work of pranksters, of course."

"Satanists."

"Mass hysteria."

"Hallucinogens in the food supply."

"Media hoax."

"Top-secret U.S. government operation conducted via black helicopter."

"Mountain lions."

"Don't be absurd."

"There's a monograph to be had in this," he says dreamily. "Psychohistorical-Cultural Origins of the Modern Spooks of the U.S.-Mexico Border." He allows for a pleasant pause. "So. Have you come here to survey the ghosts of El Paso?"

"Who's the cowboy?"

He offers a deadpan glance to her own headgear and follows her gaze across the yards.

"That's Huck."

Who, under the brim of his Stetson, appears to be removing the stucco from the back of his house with some sort of power tool while throwing a rubber ball for his dog.

"Looks like a bit of an overachiever," she says. "He's the only one I ever see outside."

The dog scrambles to the rear wall, gulping up the ball and swaggering back. It looks overweight enough to be in danger of heart attack.

Jerry shifts in his seat. "I suppose that's one word for him."

"Oh? Do tell."

"He's probably got some energy to vent. His wife left him last month."

Her chair creaks abruptly. "*Left* him?"

A hunk of stucco drops to the ground. Huck revs the device in his hand and turns to receive the slobbery ball.

"Left him with a Dear John note and no forwarding address," he continues. "Or so the rumor mill goes."

He waits for the inevitable snarky yet witty remark. But none comes.

A tide begins to rise within him. A strange anxiety.

"Personally," he says. "I never found the lives of my neighbors to be all that interesting."

"No?" Her eyes remain on Huck and the dog. "Why not?"

He turns toward the desert. "Why *should* I?"

He can sense her eyes sliding sideways to him. "Is she beautiful?"

"*What?*"

"Well," she begins with what strikes him as a false nonchalance, "it's always interesting to ponder the story behind someone's disappearance. Don't you think?"

His pulse thumps suddenly in his neck. Would there ever be a day when she wouldn't be able to read him like a book? He hardens his gaze on Château DuPre. Okay. Fine. After all these years, even in her absence, he still finds his neighbor's wife smoking hot. ¿Y qué? For God's sake, he's only human. A man. Who isn't blind.

"No," he answers sharply. "No, I *don't* think. I don't think it's interesting. At all. In fact, why should I even care?"

He senses, too late, the shift in the barometric pressure between them.

"I dunno." Her voice is sweet venom. "I guess it's just interesting when someone chooses to leave, as opposed to, say, being thrown out." The venom spreads. "Or forcibly removed."

What he sees in the black pool of Inez's gaze now are the hands. Those big hands on her thin arms. The way she twisted within them as she was forced into the car. Thrashed. Begged.

He rises, his chair clattering beneath him. "So are you coming to Walmart with me or not?"

Some part of her recedes. "Not today."

He storms past the den. Adam is eating a peanut butter and jelly sandwich on the sofa.

"Want to get some lunch?" Jerry calls from the doorway.

Adam pops out an earbud. "What?"

"Movie," he counters. "Let's go to the movies!"

"Dad. It's like ten in the morning."

"Maybe we should go to Western Playland. Did you know it's moving?"

Adam gives him a lingering *What the hell?* look.

He waves his son off and backs out of the room, bumping against the well-padded rear of Lourdes as she empties a wastebasket into a trash bag.

She gasps and straightens.

He steps on his own foot as he moves to the side of a new outrage. He hadn't even known she was *here*. "Perdón."

She murmurs her own apologies.

Have you heard about the Chupacabra attacks this week? he demands before she can scuttle down the hall.

Lourdes holds very still. Then she nods.

Do you think it's the work of the supernatural? He makes a sharp gesture at his neck with three hooked fingers.

"No."

Satanic cult? he presses. United States government? Mountain lions?

"No sé, señor."

Are you saying it's all in people's imaginations? Nothing happened?

She knots the trash bag and beelines for the back door. "No sé."

Inez is still in her patio chair on the deck. From the doorway he notes the slow rise and fall of her shoulders. She makes no move to acknowledge his presence as he steps around her. Where to start? With what words? He lays his hands on the railing. The sun sets its sear upon his head.

"I suppose we all have stories to tell," he begins quietly.

Then, a plume of motion. Dust stirring on the mountain's brown flank. A small rockslide, perhaps.

No. Not dust. Smoke.

He leans out over the railing, squinting hard. "Is that a brush fire?"

Inez doesn't respond, not even when he looks back at her. She only looks past him, over the yard where his neighbor blows the dust off his power tool, to some place so far away that the only parts of her remaining are her hands, crumpling the comics section.

From low to the ground comes a *click-click-click-click*. The reddish blur that approaches through the double doors rears up to dance at Inez's side.

With no change in expression, Inez hurls her newspaper wad. Paquito dodges. He's wagging his curly tail when he jumps up on Jerry's shin.

Jerry does not lean to scratch the dog's head. The land is on fire. Inez jiggles her foot—slowly at first, then faster, until he feels the vibration of it in the soles of his own feet. It's like sensing the rumble of a distant locomotive, he tells himself. It's like looking down to find that he's standing on the tracks.

III

Now what? Miguel wants to know, fumbling on his glasses as Lourdes barrels up.

Señor Gonzales wants me to say I believe in the Chupacabra. He's got spirals in his eyes.

Miguel tosses rakes into the back of his pickup.

Órale. Guess where I'm going right now. To go pick up the little DuPre girl.

You're *driving* her?

To school. And back. During the summer.

Jesús and Maria. Are you the chauffeur now too?

I am as long as DuPre wants to pay me for it. He shrugs and adds with a titter, The *Chupacabra*?

Have you met señor Gonzales's sister?

A few days ago, he says, hoisting the mower onto the tailgate, she called me over from across the street and asked me about—crap, how do you even say it in Spanish?—"post-9/11 immigration policies," and also if I knew where to find a good pawnshop. And she was smoking a *cigar*!

I've been cleaning her butts out of the flowerpots for a month.

Listen, he continues, lowering his voice, I was working over there for the Andersons last week, and the whole backyard smelled like weed. I thought it was the kids, but then I looked up, and who was smoking a joint at the kitchen table? Señora Anderson herself!

Lourdes looks over her shoulder.

A señora I used to work for kept naked pictures of herself on her nightstand.

This one guy tried to pay me once in frozen fish, he says. Nine boxes from Costco.

Señora Davis and I have this routine now. Whenever I'm scrubbing in the bathroom, she sits on the toilet lid in her yoga clothes and tells me her problems. She says, "You are the only one who listens to me, I am so depressed, I am so . . ." What is the word? "Unfulfilled." What does that mean?

That pendejo Schuster, he says, tipping his chin toward the end of the block, one time I knocked so I could talk to la señora, and he came to the door with a gun. He had a cold and stayed home from work. It was the first time he ever saw me.

For a moment, they regard the sky together in silence. Then, with a mutual glance, they collapse, laughing, until they run out of breath.

And señora DuPre? she says, still chuckling as she regards the pillared white house. What do you think was the matter with *her*?

For a moment, she could swear it, Miguel's body tenses.

"No sé," he says finally. He takes off his glasses and cleans them on his shirttail.

Well, she says into the silence that follows, I guess we should go earn that dollar.

He flips up the tailgate. Or *something*, he says.

But something else about this moment is not right. Lourdes feels it like she feels the hot morning sun on her arms. Even the air seems thicker somehow, and it tastes funny. She looks over her shoulder, then back at Miguel.

Do you smell something? she says.

III

"What?" Chavela says sharply, the cap of her nail polish hovering over her toenails. "What do you mean 'Something's on fire'?"

Jerry grips the bedroom doorway. "There's a fire."

"Where?" She lowers one foot from the nightstand with alarm. "Something in the yard? What?"

"On the mountain," he says. "Come have a look. And by the way, I just had a chat with Inez."

She waddles behind him in her pantsuit, toes splayed, to the french doors. Inez has vacated the deck, though the rumpled newspaper remains.

Chavela frowns. "I don't see anything."

"Over there. Smoke." He takes a fortifying breath. "You know, I think we're all letting our nerves get the best of us today. I know how my sister works. If we can keep things low key, if we can all just work together a little bit longer, she'll come around and tell us what's going on. She's almost there, I'm sure of it."

Chavela squints into the distance. "It's probably someone burning tires."

"Tires?" He follows her into the bedroom again. Outside, the greasy haze has begun to actually billow. "It's coming from this side, not Júarez. Besides, who's cold? It's June."

"Look." She retrieves her laptop from the nightstand and seats herself on the edge of the bed. "I have to leave in five minutes. I don't care anymore *why* Inez is here. If you're worried about whatever you think you see out there, call the fire department. And you *will* remember to walk the dog tonight, right?"

"I said that I would walk the dog!" he snaps. "And so I'll walk him! Right now I'm going to Walmart!"

He's scraping the car keys from the change bowl downstairs when his ears catch the purring timbre of a certain voice emanating from the den.

"Pero, ¿por qué no?"

A pause follows, during which comes a weary release of breath. "No puedo, señora."

Inez laughs. "Not this again. ¿Por qué?"

He flattens himself against the hallway wall.

Lourdes murmurs some kind of dissent.

But I've got plenty of time, Inez tells her with a great, sudden energy. All the time in the *world*, it would seem. Don't you want to improve your lot?

Señora, Lourdes responds, I, personally, do not have any time on my hands.

We can make arrangements, Inez tells her. Before work. After. At lunch. On days when you don't even work here. I can speak to my brother, if it makes you feel better. Knowing him, he will like the idea.

"La otra señora," Lourdes says, and he can hear the beginnings of real desperation in her voice. The other señora would not like it.

This is the moment to intervene, Jerry tells himself.

Never mind whether you like me or not, Inez continues. The most important thing is that someone is offering you something for free. You have children, don't you?

Four girls.

And your husband?

A contemptuous sound follows.

Well then, Inez continues. It's even more important, no? To do something that will help them get ahead in life? Especially because they are girls. Things are what they are. It's a simple fact.

Jerry frowns into the wall. Could this be altruism? From Inez?

And so. Shall I speak to my brother?

A long silence follows. "Bueno, señora."

Then it's settled. We'll start this week. But stop calling me señora! My name is Inez.

"Sí, señora."

"*Inez!*"

"Sí, señora . . ." A pause, as though for a swallow. "Inez."

There's something faintly stubborn about the way she says it. Under different circumstances, he might find it promising.

In a different climate, whatever is torching the mountainside wouldn't be irritating his sinus passages so much. He sneezes before he can stop himself.

The voices in the next room go silent. He jerks away from the wall, meaning to act as though he was just passing by, when Inez leans out into the hallway.

She cocks her head at him. Then she laughs.

"Are you eavesdropping on us?"

Jerry summons his most offended look, meaning for it to speak for itself.

"What are you planning on 'asking' me?" he blurts instead. "What the devil are you promising *her*?"

"What else?" Inez responds. The way she draws herself to full height is the very definition of *imperious*. "English lessons."

"English lessons?" he says, tossing his head as though he hasn't heard right.

She shrugs, her limbs loose. She looks nothing so much as refreshed. "I need a project."

When she sees the alarm apparently flooding his face, she adds, "Oh, don't worry. I assure you that Chavela's floors will still be spotless."

In the room beyond, Lourdes whips the blinds with her feather duster, her headphones pressed to her ears like two enormous hamburger patties.

A project. Something to keep Inez occupied, something that might distract her long enough to keep her out of trouble.

Which implies that she's settling in for the long haul.

"Well then," she says. "I guess that's that." She smiles, pats his cheek, brushes past him, and sashays back up the stairs. The sun blasts hot stripes through the den's blinds.

A great icy wave crests in his veins. His wife's voice drifts down from above.

"So I'll get you some more," he hears Inez retort just before he hits the half turn on the stairs. "Por Dios, mujer—it's just an empty bottle of shampoo!"

"That's what you said about the grapefruit juice," Chavela mutters. "And the hand lotion. And the ice cream."

"You want *more* banana-marshmallow surprise? Now *that* was one nasty flavor."

Jerry moves for the stairs. The first step groans beneath him.

"The point," Chavela says, her voice rising, "es que es una cuestión de being considerate."

"¿Y qué te dije? That I'd take care of your shampoo. Are you running around como una greñuda with filthy, unmanageable hair in the meantime? Mira, the problem with you is that you are seriously uptight. Sobre *todo*."

Jerry ascends, slowly, and stands on his toes to glimpse the two of them in the upper hallway. Chavela tucks her laptop under one arm as she retrieves a wadded towel from the floor.

"Además," she responds, holding out the towel to Inez, "creo que esta es tuyo."

"You know, you would be a whole lot happier if you didn't worry so much about whose towel ended up where."

"You," Chavela says, "are slamming the door every time you come in at two in the morning from your middle-of-the-night walks, and you are waking me up. Have you ever considered . . . pues, no sé . . . making up . . . putting up"—she huffs, as though to clear a path toward the right phrase—"getting up a hobby?"

"A hobby?" Inez's voice trails behind him as he creeps backward down the stairs. "Now *that* is a capital idea."

Chavela makes the sound of a cat trapped under a blanket.

He slips back into the kitchen and braces his hands against the sink. Then he reaches for the phone and hits speed dial.

"H'lo?" says Marcus's groggy voice after several rings.

Jerry pops open a Diet Coke with the phone tucked under his chin. "Did I wake you, Son?"

He hears a rolling-over sound in the receiver. "Mmmp."

On the refrigerator is a note in Chavela's hand: "Jerry, walk dog in PM!" He yanks off the note and stuffs it into his pants pocket. "I need a favor from you."

A violent female shriek blasts from the top of the stairs.

Marcus rustles. "Whoa. What the—?"

"Can you talk to Inez?" Jerry zaps the TV with the remote as he falls into his recliner. The movie that appears features a seventies-era Yul Brynner, in Western duds and with electronic circuity protruding from his head, turning robotically to plug his pursuers with a six-shooter. "Like, ASAP?"

It's quite marvelous, Jerry tells himself once he hangs up the phone— the quality of patience that marks his elder son's impatience. Even Adam, whom he now spies surveying the contents of the refrigerator, has always been the kind of boy who grinned and shrugged through calamity. From whom did either son inherit these traits? Not from him. Certainly not from Chavela. Neither did they inherit his dislike of electronic devices. He roots through the drawer beneath the phone, dislodging a pristine, unused volume of the yellow pages.

He flips the crisp pages until he finds the M section. An engine turns over down the street. What, he asks himself as Huck backs his truck out of his driveway, would he do if he were in Huck's situation? Vacuum out the cars before settling in to watch all three *Godfather* movies with a bucket of fried chicken and the bottle of tequila he's hiding from Inez in the trunk of the Volvo?

Mobile homes. Mortuaries. Motels.

Motels. His finger slides down the columns of listings, searching the alphabet within the alphabet, for some kind of shelter—offered from the bowels of his own wallet—that would appeal to Inez.

Hadn't he once believed, long ago, that were something to go wrong with his marriage, he would likely be the one who left first?

He doesn't realize until he reaches the Ys that he's looking for the word *yes.*

III

Las señoras are still yelling at each other. The smoke outside is a dark plume against the mountain.

Lourdes descends on the already clean sink with Comet. English lessons. For free. From Inez. The whole thing is clearly both a punishment and a gift horse whose teeth she shouldn't be counting. Not when the girls are always pestering her for whatever she knows, and she knows half of what she tells them is wrong.

Whatever Inez thinks she can pry from her, she can't have it.

Outside, something is burning. Las señoras argue. None of it is any of her business.

She thinks of her flimsy words in English, forever knotted together with an unraveling string, and she scrubs and scrubs and scrubs.

III

Marcus stares at the phone in his hand after he punches the off button. Is this another domestic meltdown? Is that what it is? He rises to guzzle his morning Coke. The year he was fourteen, his parents had argued like opera divas. None of the arguments was the real argument—he understood that much, even when they switched to Spanish, and then his mom yanked him and Adam out of summer camp and put the three of them on a bus to L.A. The soundtrack of his tía Silvia's house? Audible, adult tears in Spanish at the kitchen table after bedtime, the nonstop squealing of his girl cousins, Adam whispering to him from his adjacent cot to ask whether he thought they were going back, like ever. The question was moot. It was only two weeks until they all bused back home, where his father flung open the door. And his arms. *There was a party while you were gone*, he blurted, *a block party to end them all, it was great, you should've been here.* An olive branch, if ever there was one. And then all was forgiven, and his parents went back to their usual benign routines, to their coffee and toast and padded slippers, their television shows, their toothbrushes lying on the sink. Most things pass if you let them. The sun, as he exits the freeway, hangs like a gong in the afternoon sky. He pulls into the graveled parking lot and maneuvers into place beside the fleet of white-and-green vehicles, his eyes stinging as he steps from his car into the bright slant of the light. The world smells of dust and creosote and gasoline fumes. The desert stretches around him in every direction, mountains and mesas in the distance where the sky will purple and blister to gold soon enough. His gun and baton make a solid weight on his hips. His uniform chafes as he walks.

He enters the familiar, homely white portable building, moving into a rush of air-conditioning, a flash of fluorescent lighting and linoleum.

"¡Órale!" Peña calls out.

He beckons Marcus over from a spot by the bulletin board where their colleagues have gathered.

"Dude," Peña says, grinning. "New Chupacabra attack. Nine dead sheep with fang marks."

Marcus folds his sunglasses into his shirt pocket. "You get the tank filled up?"

"Also," Peña answers, "last night, Lerner and Mendez hauled in these dudes from Oaxaca who—I shit you not—were totally wearing wreaths of garlic around their necks. They said something had been following them all the way from Puebla."

Marcus rubs his nose. "I brought back your CD."

"We should get a sheep and bait it," Peña continues with glee. "Watch for it with the night vision, and hey, we could employ some wets to wait out there with a big net, and then . . ."

None of the various pieces of paper on the bulletin board have been tacked on straight. Truck for sale. Memo about dirty dishes in the sink.

The latest official notices: "Operation Hold the Line Deemed a Success." "Plans for Enhanced Border Fence Still On Track." "Effective October 2005, a Passport Will Be Required to Enter or Exit Mexico—Prepare Now!"

How should he prepare to deal with his parents? In a house where *three* adults are going nuts?

". . . and then we could sell it to a museum, although probably it's invisible, and even if we recorded it, all we'd see is some bushes moving and then a cow falling over . . ."

Marcus jingles the keys in his pocket. Really, when you think about it, silence is a fairly effective way of dealing with an undesirable or annoying situation. The crucial element, however, is to simultaneously take action. Move forward. In that way, he is different from his father. Oh yes.

He turns from the bulletin board. "So you ready or what?"

"Yo," Peña says.

"Watch your back," Barelas calls out from the watercooler. "I mean your neck."

Marcus waves from the door, wondering whether he's a fool for entering the big top when all he can see are the clowns.

III

Upstairs, somebody throws something. It thumps against a wall; a metallic object clatters to the ground. Señora Gonzales screams.

Lourdes looks out the window. Then she hurls her scrubber into the sink.

III

Jerry slams shut the phone book and tosses it into the recliner. From behind him comes a flurry of footsteps. His drink slops over his hand as he whirls, his toes colliding with a huge pair of white athletic shoes.

"¿Qué le pasa?" he snaps.

Lourdes stutter-steps back and looks at the spattered floor in dismay, clutching the hem of her "I Heart the Bahamas" T-shirt.

He shakes out his damp hand, considering the way he might apologize to his wife's maid.

Well? he demands instead.

Señor, she tells him soberly, I think something is on fire.

He gazes upon her a moment, gripping his half-empty glass, enthralled by the squaring of her round shoulders and the tranquility of her expression.

Yes, he responds with a kind of astonishment. A fire. There's a fire.

Everything suddenly feels very slow. Still, he hurries. He crams his feet into sandals. Pats his pockets for keys. He makes for the phone, but it is no longer in its cradle and he has no idea where he left it.

"Lourdes," he calls when he turns back at the rear door. He means to tell her to tell Adam to call 911, or Chavela, or even Inez.

Lourdes is already looking his way, her black eyes meeting his now with a strange intensity, a film of perspiration on her nose. It gives him the unsettling sense that she's studying him. Or appraising him. But he's surely imagining it, and he has no time to ponder her pondering. He breaks away, out the door.

The plume billows up from the brown mountainside, its source just out of view from the vantage point of the backyard. Jerry braces his hands against the rear wall and hoists himself over. He lands with a thump, a great poof of dust kicking up around him. A stalk of cholla catches on his pant leg. Small, unseen creatures scurry into their burrows.

He sweats as he catches his breath. How much, he asks himself, does he actually want to know? He looks back over his shoulder. He could slip back inside his house and pretend he never saw any of this. He could wait for things to die down, or for someone else to put an end to it all, or for the world to flame out around him.

But the smoke is growing darker, and so he hurries to close the gap.

7

DRY AS HELL

"WHY IS IT ALL SMOKY out here?" Jordan hollers over the radio. "Why does it smell weird?"

The truck sputters and chugs as Miguel pulls to the curb. "Don't know."

She studies his dirty fingernails and the red birthmark that peeks from behind his right ear. It's shaped like France.

He shifts in his seat. "What?"

She stares, still unclear about whether Miguel is supposed to hang out with her after school. Would he eat Pop-Tarts and watch old-generation *Star Trek* reruns if she offered?

"See you tomorrow," she says experimentally.

He chugs away and parks at the end of the block.

The house, inside, is a dark reverse of the day. Quiet in the kitchen as she pours Lucky Charms into a bowl. Quiet as she discovers no milk in the fridge, just the empty gallon jug.

Quiet, quiet, quiet. Nobody to bug her or boss her around.

She settles in cozily at the breakfast bar with her copy of *Moby-Dick*, her cereal drizzled with the last of the OJ and topped off with water from the tap.

The phone rings, but before she can lift her hand, the doorbell bongs in the hallway.

The man on the other side looks much too happy. Around his big wrists and wide neck his gray blazer might be a size too small.

"Hello, m'ija." He shifts his accordion folder from one arm to another. "I have an appointment with your father."

Jordan wipes her mouth on the back of her hand. Nobody told her about any appointments this morning.

"I'd appreciate it if you wouldn't call me m'ija."

"All right. What would you like to be called?" Perspiration gathers at the man's curly hairline.

"Are you a friend of my dad's?"

"You could say that. I work for him."

"At the maquila?"

"No, no." He shifts on his feet. "My name's Larry Villalobos. I'm a private investigator. Is your dad home?"

Jordan straightens, a sudden tingle in her spine. If someone had told her the investigator was coming, she would have prepared a list of questions.

"No."

His brow creases. "Do you expect him back soon?"

She leans against the doorjamb. "I have no idea."

"Well, young lady." He sounds like a preschool teacher, or a librarian about to start story hour. "I'm pretty sure he's expecting me. Is there anyone here who could let me come in and wait?"

In the quiet, quiet house, Jordan raises an eyebrow. It's the kind of eyebrow her mother raises in any questionable situation. She wonders whether her mother would raise an eyebrow to know that someone had come to investigate her. She doesn't even know if Larry Villalobos is who he says he is, or if he's just pretending.

Neither is she clear about whether her father meant for her to conduct this meeting in his absence.

The phone has stopped ringing. Skyler's still at work. Quinn is wherever he is. Not that either of them is the boss of her.

"You can come in."

He takes the screen door handle gingerly from her.

"There's someone home?"

"Well, *duh*."

He peers down the hallway. "Who's—"

"Come with me."

Larry Villalobos follows Jordan into the kitchen with long, halting steps, waiting while she tips the still-open box of Lucky Charms into her cereal bowl again and fills it at the tap. "So," he begins again, "where's your—"

"I have an IQ of 154," she answers.

Larry Villalobos rams his free hand into his pocket and leans against the refrigerator. "Good," he says in a big Santa Claus voice. "Good for you."

"You might not realize that's a very high score. I'm only nine years old."

"I'm impressed. I am." He eyes her cereal bowl. "That's a very interesting snack you're having there, young lady."

She tips the bowl to slurp the last dregs. "Are *you* my mom's boyfriend?"

"No!" he sputters.

"How are you going to investigate her?"

"That's something your father and I are going to discuss."

"He's not here."

"No," he admits. "He's not."

She deposits her cereal bowl in the sink and settles back in at the breakfast bar, lacing her hands together so that she can lean forward in a meaningful way.

"What clues have you found so far?"

Again, he smiles. "I'm not really at liberty to say."

"Are you going to have a stakeout when you find her?"

"Well . . . possibly."

"Will you plant listening devices?"

"Prrr-obably not."

"How are you even going to find her in the first place?"

"Generally, I just start by asking people questions."

"What questions?"

"Jesus Christ." He sets down his file folder in front of the Mixmaster. "Okay, fine. Have you talked to your mother lately?"

She raises another eyebrow at him. "No."

"Would you happen to know if she had any special friends? Any . . . gentleman friends?"

"No."

"Did anyone ever call the house for her that you didn't recognize?"

"Not really." She wonders whether he's ever even heard of *corroborating evidence.* "When we find out where my mom is, we're going to go on vacation there."

"You're . . . what?"

"My dad said we could."

"He *what?*"

"We're already packing." Jordan leans over her tented hands. "So. How long is it going to take you to find her?"

The front door crashes open. Here's her father, cheeks flushed, hat crooked, charging into the kitchen with a cardboard box full of groceries that he drops on the newspaper-piled table.

"Sorry I'm late," he tells Larry Villalobos. "Let's get started." He herds him toward the living room, and without breaking stride, calls over his shoulder to Jordan, "Honey, tell Quinn to bring in the rest of the groceries."

She scowls. "He's not here."

Her dad digs into his pants pocket for his keys and tosses them. "Do me the favor, will you?"

She doesn't want to catch them, but she does. Then he's gone.

She scoots up close to the wall separating the kitchen from the living room, pressing her ear.

"Get the milk," her dad suddenly hollers, as though he knows what she's doing. "The milk's gonna go bad."

She huffs, then stomps outside.

Larry Villalobos pivots in his wingback chair to face Huck. "She's . . . really something," he says pleasantly.

Huck drops into the opposite wingback. "So's her mother."

"Right," says Larry Villalobos, opening his accordion folder on the coffee table. "Let's talk about your wife."

Huck sits back. He'd remembered his appointment with the PI in the paper products aisle at Costco as he was hoisting a supersize pack of toilet paper into his cart. He'd punched his home number into his phone, scraped a raft of cocktail napkins into his cart, and plowed toward the canned goods, grabbing six pairs of men's tube socks in the correct size as the phone rang and rang.

Then the voice mail kicked in.

"Crap," said Rose Marie's barely audible voice, concurrent with the sound of some metallic object falling. Next came a rustling, and the loud sniff of composure that signaled the rallying of a forced display of cheer. "Hello! You've reached the DuPres!"

His feet slowed beneath the cart. They stopped. An ache welled in his chest and the blood in his legs turned gelatinous.

It had been more than a month since he'd heard the sound of her voice.

". . . would probably be a good idea," he hears Villalobos say now. "Anyone who you think might not have been exactly forthcoming with you."

Huck pulls his eyes from the window. "Say that again?"

"Sometimes the friends and relatives are hesitant to talk to the spouse left behind. They withhold information." He taps his pencil against a mini-notepad. "What's your relationship like with the in-laws?"

Huck snorts. As though Jarvis had ever stopped squinting at the middling quality of Huck's shoes, Huck's belt, Huck's watch. He and Francine had taken to staying in hotels during their visits, after the time Francine complained that the sheets on the guest bed, freshly applied by Lourdes, just didn't smell "fresh," and heavens, but there were just so many *Mexicans* in this city. She whispered the word "Mexicans."

"I can handle those two."

"Siblings?"

"Only child," Huck counters, and he can barely hold back another snort. It had long been his opinion—particularly during marital arguments—that Rose Marie would have been a different person if she'd had to share things when she grew up, or fight with anyone bigger or smaller, or just hadn't been at the center of attention or gotten her way in almost every situation, having had no competition. "It's a lot more complicated than that," she always snarled back.

Villalobos leans back. "How about her friends?"

He jots down the names—Erica Swanson and Suzie Gallegos and Misty Fontaine, the country-club girls Rose Marie volunteers with, drinks fruity cocktails with, who accompany her to symphony performances. The ones Huck has always tried to spend as little time with as possible. Outside, the sky looks like it's been wiped with a dirty rag.

In fact, he can smell the smoke from here—the greasy, chemical stench of a melting artificial substance. He rises and moves to the window. "Damn," he murmurs. "Look at that."

"I noticed that on the way in. You think something's on fire?"

Huck peers into the distance. "Wouldn't be out of the question. It's dry as hell out there."

"Feel free to, you know, call the fire department, if you want."

If I want. This house that he'd never wanted, that was becoming a relic before his very eyes—if it burned to the ground, would he care? Even if their kids had played in the yard, and the shelves were still full of Rose Marie's books, and the afternoon sun warmed the breakfast nook in which the five of them had eaten countless sandwiches and the carpet was balding in the living room corner where the white-flocked Christmas tree stood every year, and upstairs, Rose Marie's expensive scalloped-edged sheets still lay on their bed, the very ones she'd last slept in, in fact; he can't explain to himself why he's been keeping the door of his bedroom locked to Lourdes, and—

A phone rings in a distant room.

He remembers the time Rose Marie lost her bikini top in the country-club swimming pool, and how—despite the mortified, averted gazes of the pool bunnies—both of them had laughed as he waded out in his chinos to retrieve it.

"Huck?" intrudes the voice of Larry Villalobos. Someone in the kitchen picks up the phone on the second ring. "Should we talk about her financial records?"

Villalobos's face bears the strain of politeness.

"She's adopted," Huck snaps. "All of this to-do in her family about breeding and bloodlines, and yet they raised a woman who's technically got no roots at all."

There. He said it. She didn't like thinking about it, and she didn't like anyone else thinking about it—heck, her parents didn't even like *acknowledging* it—and therefore he'd never earned more than the barest details. He feels a ripple of satisfaction at the thought of her *exposed.*

"Now *this* is some news I can use." Villalobos leans forward. "And what do we know about—"

"Dad."

Jordan. In the doorway with a bottle of Formula 409 in one hand and the cordless outstretched in the other.

"It's for you."

For a moment, Huck thinks he might try to stare her down. "Who is it?"

"Mrs. Fontaine."

He exchanges a glance with Larry Villalobos and excuses himself to the den.

"Misty?" he says into the phone.

"Huck," says the brisk voice on the other end. "How's things?"

He paces to the side of the sofa. "Things are good!" He digs his nails into the backrest of the love seat. "What's up?"

"Actually, I'm calling about Jordan. We'd like to invite her to Clarissa's birthday party weekend after next."

"That's all?"

"Beg pardon?"

He paces to the entertainment center and looks at all the little dials and lights. "I thought maybe you'd . . . heard something."

"I haven't," she says after a careful pause. "Have *you*?"

"Nope," he says cheerfully. "Nothing new here."

"Well then," she continues, "we'd love to see Jordan at the party, if she's available."

He pushes play on the DVD player, even though it's empty. What drives Rose Marie crazier—that Jordan refuses birthday parties for herself, or that she refuses to attend anyone else's? Misty Fontaine surely already knew that. She surely knew a lot of things.

"You would, would you?" A faint belligerence creeps into his voice.

"It's about me," Jordan calls from the doorway, "isn't it?"

"Do you want to go to Clarissa Fontaine's birthday party two weeks from now?" he asks pointlessly, his palm over the receiver.

Misty remains silent. He imagines her curled up on a leather sofa with a cocktail, picking at hors d'oeuvres with the tips of her salon fingernails. She probably had Rose Marie on speed dial. Maybe she was looking for recruits. These were sorority girls, after all. But the joke was on Misty if she thought Jordan was going to join their little club—she obviously didn't have the slightest clue about what kind of kid she was dealing with.

"Well?" he prompts Jordan. He hopes he sounds conspiratorial.

She lights up. "I'll need to check my calendar."

He chokes a little over his sweaty palm.

"Fine then." He wipes his hand on his jeans. "Get the details and we'll take care of it." To Misty he adds, "I'll be keeping a close eye on this business."

"Excuse me?"

"I'm not stupid."

He's pretty sure he hears a sound like "ha!" emanating from the receiver just before he presses it back into Jordan's hand.

In the hallway, he pauses to catch his breath. It seems to be in short supply. He leans against the wall as Jordan addresses the phone in the kitchen in a secretarial voice. Larry Villalobos waits in the living room, tapping his pencil.

He's relieved to find the dining room empty. He could use a few moments of peace.

Outside, the smoke thickens. He imagines Misty Fontaine's nails softly tapping the phone receiver as she and Jordan make their plans.

The wall offers hardly any resistance as he puts his fist right through it.

III

Everything is in flames.

Jerry beholds the conflagration from the top of the view-blocking slope, his breath caught in his throat. A garbage heap the size of a queen-size mattress crackles and seethes, releasing toxic blue clouds.

He runs down the hill. And yet, as he skids and finally stops against the hard earth, a fierce calm descends upon him—a particular professional, hard-nosed calm, though it has been a very long time since it had occasion to visit him. He assesses the perimeter. A quickly disintegrating black tarp determines the fire's border, but the dead grasses and twigs underneath have already begun to smolder; the dehydrated stands of creosote encircling it are only a gust of breeze away. He hastens to scrape up a pile of sand with the side of his foot, then stops, his scalp tingling. For there are no footprints other than his own. No tire tracks. No scorch mark of an object lit and dropped, no depressions indicating the drip of flammable substances, no broken bottles or shards that might serve as magnifying lenses for the sun. No evidence of human involvement at all.

No involvement, that is, other than the tableau itself that blazes before him. He wipes the sweat from his eyes. Here lies an upside-down grocery cart, crowned by a slightly crushed microwave lacking a door but containing a pink rubber duck. The oven is tied down with the flaming, precisely fanned lengths of a plastic float–studded pool divider. Inside the cart melts the upright half shell of an infant's bathtub. And inside of the bathtub, a lawn statue of the Virgen de Guadalupe, now slumped and dripping paint, her shrine faced by a semicircle of naked Barbie dolls with singed hair, arms lifted skyward. Also bookending this stage: a pair of empty plastic water jugs. Or, almost empty. An inch or so of water remains in each one, boiling.

Like the gallon jugs he used to stumble across in the middle-of-desert nowhere. Long ago.

The plastic duck explodes. He flinches with rage. What is this tableau anyway? Religious shrine? Anti-religious shrine? Art project? Transient's hoard? Plaything of a very strange child? It hardly matters. This is an act of God. Or nature. Nature at war with God. Nature, destroying what is unnatural.

When he glances down, the hair on his forearm is singed off.

He kicks sand. Piles of it, right into the face of the Virgen—he pauses to mutter "Sorry," then kicks down the bathtub from behind, so that it encloses her and her naked audience in a melting tomb. He tosses the last sizzling droplets from the water jugs into the interior of the microwave, from which has begun to emanate a stinking, black plume. He stomps on the pool divider.

There, he tells himself as he smothers the worst of it. *There.* He leans and braces his hands to his knees, coughing, panting, his shirt soaked through.

But the breeze finds an ember, and it lifts it into the air—he sees it, a bright pinpoint lofting in arcs overhead—just before it drops onto the nearest creosote bush, like a match.

III

Señor Gonzales crashes back into the kitchen.

Do you have another bucket? he demands as he snatches up the mop water. Or two?

Lourdes digs quickly in the cabinet under the sink.

Help me, he adds when she emerges.

"¿Mande?" What she really means is *Oh no.*

And then she is straddling the yard's rear wall, the sun branding her head as el señor helps her down and hands back her bucketful of dirty water. He hoists his own two buckets, and they waddle, at high speed, into the desert.

The smoke burns her eyes even before they crest the final hill. Then, there it is—a nasty, smelly, smoldering trash heap, its edges licked by flames. The bushes behind it are fully on fire.

"Híjole," she says.

El señor draws a breath. "De veras." He lurches the rest of the way down the hill to hurl his bucket of water.

The bushes sizzle and smoke. She hurries up beside him when he empties his second bucket, offering her own. Then she rushes back to the house, this time with two empties, as el señor claws handfuls of sand into the remaining container.

To the house. Back. To the house. Back. Her chichis flop and her hair sticks to her forehead, but her legs are strong, her lungs full of air as she boosts herself each time, dropping the buckets and rolling over the wall. Splash and sizzle and dump. The water almost evaporates before it even hits the ground.

Then, all of a sudden, they're done.

She frowns with her boss into the steaming, pulpy gray mess, a stitch like a dagger in her side.

What's under the shopping cart? she asks finally, catching her breath.

He glances at the crucifix dangling from her neck.

Best not to think about it.

Yet even he can't look away from the mess.

She gathers up the buckets behind him, turning each one upside down and pounding, then stacking them one inside the other. Sweat drips under her bra; prickly things stick to the little pom-poms on the heels of her socks.

What could have started this? he asks next, though she isn't sure he's talking to her. He says, Is this what they mean by "the work of the devil"? ¿Quién sabe? She's already walking away.

III

A hole. A chest-level opening, large enough to fit a human torso, yawning behind a white veil of dust.

Huck sticks his head in.

It's dark, of course, save for the neon outlines of sunshine seeping through the unsealed walls. The air is musty and cool. And then, as his eyes adjust, he apprehends that he is looking into a small chamber of sorts, a weird, sealed-over dead space in the heart of his home. As though once there was a room here that had been remodeled out of existence.

"Goddamn," he murmurs.

Faint wisps of insulation slump from the outer walls, which look termitey.

He calls out, "Be right back."

Kneeling in the front flower bed on top of Rose Marie's petunias, sneezing out soot, he wonders what would happen, structurally speaking, if he were to take down the entire front wall of his house. The stucco, as he probes with a spade he finds within reach, comes off in hand-sized chunks.

In the middle distance, someone is watching.

Jerry Gonzales. Planted at the end of his driveway, his comb-over plastered with sweat, looking like he's been dragged through a campfire.

Huck rises and brushes the dirt from his knees. Is Jerry glowering? Or just appraising him? At the mountainside, the smoke is clearing, though the scent of fried electronic circuitry lingers on.

But now his gaze is diverted by the sudden appearance at Jerry's back gate of Lourdes, moving like someone recovering from a blow to the head. She wipes down her arms and face with a wad of paper towels and stuffs it all into the garbage can.

It bothers him, seeing her over there at Jerry's. He likes to think of her as *his* maid.

Neither can he help but notice the woman on the roof above her.

Her again. She leans against the air-conditioning unit in a red plaid work shirt like an aging gangbanger, watching. She's also smoking a cigar.

She blows a malevolent puff of smoke at him.

Jesus Christ. He's going inside.

In the entryway, the blast of air-conditioning makes clear to Huck what parts of him have been sweating. He reaches for a windbreaker that he's pretty sure is his on the coatrack beside him and uses it as a towel—head, neck, pits.

"Huck?" calls Larry Villalobos's voice.

"Just a minute!"

The hole in the dining room hasn't gone anywhere. It waits at shoulder level, a jagged outline of ancient lathe and plaster. Huck stoops, looking into the void, and is buoyed on the waves of a sudden, ineffable calm.

"Dad," says a voice behind him. "I have one more idea about vacation."

"Later, honey." He rips a chunk from the edge of the hole with both hands.

Larry Villalobos pokes his head out into the hallway. "Everything all right?"

Jordan looks to her father—half-squatting, head in a hole in the wall. His boots are dusted with a fine white powder.

"Everything's swell," his muffled voice calls back. "Out in a sec."

She looks over her shoulder at Larry Villalobos. He looks back.

"That sounded dramatic," he says in a thin voice.

She suddenly hates him even more than she already did.

"I bet my mom will come back before you can find her."

Larry Villalobos stares. He gives her a stiff smile and whips out a little notepad. "What did you say your name is, young lady?"

"Jordan."

"I thought that was a boy's name."

He's back in ho-ho-ho mode. His pencil makes an irritating scratch.

What, was she supposed to tell him where her name came from? Anyway, the phone is ringing. She tries to lift an eyebrow at him in exactly the way her mother would—deadly and cool—but it feels like she's lifting them both. She throws herself toward the kitchen.

"This is Jordan."

"Hello? Do I have . . . wait a minute. Jordan? Hi, sweetie. This is Brittany's mom. Is your father in?"

The last time she saw Brittany Gallegos was at a country-club picnic. All Jordan wanted was to be left alone on her folding chair with her copy of *Stranger in a Strange Land,* but Brittany loomed over her with claw hands, flexing her pretzel-stick fangs and swinging her shiny hair, until Jordan asked her why she was such a moronic ding-dong.

"Just a minute, please," she says into the phone.

In the dining room, her father has removed his head from the hole. His face has a weird sheen to it, as though it's an exact replica of his original face, like in a sci-fi movie about body-snatching clones.

She finds this invigorating.

"It's for you," she says, holding out the phone.

He reaches for it, still studying his hole. "Yello?" He nods. "Birthday party. Right. So you *say.*"

She hands him the message pad and pen. "Tell her I can come."

Huck returns to the living room once he's hung up. "Sorry, where were we?"

Villalobos, at the window, chuckles as he lowers himself back to his seat. "We were talking—I *think*—about your wife's personal history."

Huck takes the window spot. "She's got the Lexus, you know. I want the Lexus back."

"There might not be much I can do about that." Villalobos leans on his armrest. "Both of your names are on the registration. But sooner or later, she's going to run out of cash and then, of course, your credit card statements will show us where she's been gassing up. Unless she's using somebody else's card. But assuming she's not, and that she visits the same station more than once, I'll be watching for her."

"Anything you find out about the boyfriend, I want to know about it."

Villalobos jots on his notepad. "Of course. Any evidence I find is going to shift the divorce proceedings in your favor. Big time." He pauses. "Can I ask, is there something else you're planning to do with that information?"

Huck rubs an eyebrow, releasing white dust. Before he gets this remodel started in earnest, he'll have to speak to an architect. And a contractor. At the very least, he could do the demolition himself. He could probably get started before he and the kids go wherever it is he's going to take them, which he figures should be about a month from now, tops. And if this PI got wind of Rose Marie's location before then, if it was farther than any of them had anticipated, if Huck had only been humoring Jordan before, well, maybe he should consider the possibility that she was on to something. Because what could be more righteous than watching someone come face-to-face with the consequences of their actions, then checking in to a beach resort afterward?

Outside, the lingering smoke. A cold current rises suddenly within him. "Excuse me for a minute."

He reaches Mendoza on his direct line.

"Everything okay over there?"

Mendoza's chair squeaks. "As okay as things ever are. Something the matter?"

"Have you heard about anything going on with the peso?"

"The peso? God, no. Have *you*?"

"No." He eyes the haze and hangs up.

Back in the living room, Larry Villalobos lifts his head from the back of his chair.

"Huck," he says. "Seriously, man. Are you okay?"

Huck pauses in the doorway. Is he going to tell him? That the real plan—the plan inside of the plan—is to take back *everything* that's his?

He smiles a dark smile. "Everything's fine."

III

Before she goes back inside, Lourdes just wants to breathe.

Only the thinnest streaks of smoke drift now near the horizon. From somewhere above her comes a scraping crunch.

She steps away from the house. There, up on the flat roof, Inez. Lourdes can just make out the edge of the patio table on the deck behind her, on top of which a lawn chair has been stacked.

Inez watches from above. Lourdes holds her gaze, steady. Inez acknowledges her with the slight raise of an eyebrow, a solemn nod. Then she looks away, over the rooftops, and takes a slow drag from her cigar.

A sudden chill creeps over Lourdes's bones. Even in this heat. She watches the red embers of Inez's cigar as they fall, the breeze catching each one and buoying them back into the air. They circle above Inez's head, like thoughts that tumble over themselves again and again, and then they sail out toward the mountain.

III

Jerry, alone, looks out toward the dark land from his deck. He's not going to walk the fucking dog.

He sips from his whiskey-laced soda. In the yard below, Paquito gnaws and crunches a drumstick-sized rawhide bone.

Chavela, of course, is still at work. Tomorrow, he tells himself. Tomorrow he will approach her, and offer apologies, and share with her what has transpired on this day with Inez. And Lourdes. And everyone.

Paquito gnaws and slobbers. He'll chew all night, Jerry knows. He'll chew to the point of exhaustion, until he has no idea what or why he's chewing, until nothing's left.

The horizon glows atop the unrisen moon, under a cathedral of stars. If Jerry were to lose all he holds dear, this piece of earth would be the last thing left to him. Wall or no wall. A lone cricket chirps. *The land*, it says, *the land, the land*. Ancient and immovable. The dust in his veins. Place of his ancestors' ancestors.

But here, on the far side of the yard, in the invisible space just behind his own stretch of rock-and-cement, comes a strange sound. A scratching.

Over the wall leaps a sinewy shape.

Madre de Dios.

It's a mountain lion.

From below comes a short, sharp squeal. And then silence.

Jerry shouts, a wordless noise of protest that echoes and then is no more. The cricket goes silent. The shadows shift. The shape in the yard morphs into its true form: coyote. It turns its head and marks him, light reflected in its yellow eyes. Then, with the prize in its mouth, it vaults the wall back out into the great beyond.

SHE WALKS THE BREEZY BEACHES with her jacket zipped, past the bikini-clad babes, the volleyball games, the longhaired surfers with guitars. She plays house. Puts her name on the mailbox, patronizes public libraries, seeks the aid of dental school students when she cracks a crown, plays an occasional game of hearts with her neighbor, Mrs. Kim. She does not check her email. She intends to call. But first she settles in with a very large ATM withdrawal—the best money management is often hands-on management, as Huck always says. She thinks. Or doesn't think, because the best problem management is often hands-off management.

And yet she wakes in the night, over and over, a slick dread rising up within her to wrap itself around her heart, pulsing with all the ways in which her absence now amounts to something appalling, until the morning she rises and says, "For God's sake."

She drops her apartment key into the after-hours mail slot.

On the outskirts of El Paso, well after midnight, she swerves into the parking lane and stops. Rests her had on the steering wheel as she steadies her breath.

She could go back. She could go forward. She could undo the strings that bind her together and see which way she flies.

AL TIEMPO, TIEMPO LE DOY

TO TIME, I GIVE TIME

8

ASK AGAIN LATER

THERE IS SO MUCH TO do. Homework, for starters, precalc and physics and suburban wildlife surveys and essays about the influence of Texas pioneer women on frontier government, and on TV the blond woman in the blazer and the Mexican guy in a tie face the round-table of experts to explain the NAFTA-dominated Mexican economy is tanking. The drug lords have taken over Juárez (executions, kidnappings, extortions) and just this week, four more young women were found dead in the desert—is it the work of one perpetrator or many? Grocery lists. Meal plans. The tracking of four separate schedules on a wall-mounted day planner. Unloading the dishwasher, but only if the cupboards are totally empty of dishes, and laundry, but only if underwear is in short supply or the towels smell like wet dogs. Feeding the actual dog. Not forgetting to turn on the sprinklers. Not forgetting to turn them off. People are nervous. Border traffic is down, businesses on both sides are suffering, is it really a good idea to be introducing these restrictive new regulations—the passports and so forth? Blah-blah-blah, post-9/11 security measures, blah-blah-blah, illegal crossing out of control, blah-blah, do you blame anyone for trying to escape a sinking ship, when the waiting list for citizenship is fifteen to twenty years long? Look, we obviously can't absorb the excess, a border fence needs to be built. No, no—Border Patrol needs more agents. No, no, no—Border Patrol is out of its league, there will come a day when the president will have to call in the National Guard. Except they're not available at the moment—most of them have been sent to Iraq.

Anyway, the future hasn't happened yet. The future is unclear. If we consulted a Magic 8 Ball about the whole mess, the advice would be "Ask again later." Also, a cake labeled Triple Chocolate Fudge Explosion has appeared on the kitchen counter, along with a note scrawled on the back of a torn envelope: "Troops: Make sure the garbage gets out before pickup. Going to Costco after work."

The cake rests under a plastic cover, its glossy frosting crowned with a maraschino cherry. Jordan clicks off the TV. She lifts the cover and inhales the chocolate cloud underneath. The question is who this cake is for. Whether an occasion is involved. Whether somebody, by neglecting to consult her or notate the day planner, has thrown the entire system into disarray.

She glances over her shoulder and, with a palpitating heart, stuffs a chocolate lump into her mouth with a butter knife.

"Where'd *this* come from?" Quinn shuffles in to poke the cake cover, looking crazy around the eyes. Maybe it's because of his eyeliner.

Jordan shrugs and sucks on her knife. Somewhere, in other kitchens, her classmates are eating Raisin Bran and drinking protein smoothies.

Quinn shears off a cake hunk and drains the milk she's poured him.

"Jesus Christ." Skyler enters with her head wrapped in an enormous towel. "Is that *cake* you're eating?"

Quinn tosses his fork into the sink. "Want some?"

"Oh my God." Skyler holds up her hand to the glass of milk Jordan slides toward her. "You've got to be kidding me. For *breakfast*?"

Jordan shrugs. "Have some cake." The phone is ringing. She snaps up the receiver.

"This is Jordan."

"Hello . . . ? Jordan, is that you? Sweetie, it's Mrs. Gallegos. Brittany has strep. We're rescheduling the party for weekend after next. May I let your father know?"

"I already know I can go," Jordan says, and hangs up.

She finds her father at the dining room table. Behind him gapes the hole, like a door-sized mouth.

She lowers her backpack to the floor. "How come you're not at work?"

"Oh, I'll be leaving shortly." With a pen, he makes a series of checkmarks in a pair of three-ring binders.

She eyes the supersize box of Cheerios that crowds him at the table, the array of canned chilis, the vacuum-sealed rotisserie chickens, the instant mashed potatoes. A very large lever-armed orange juicer has been bolted to the lip of the china hutch behind him.

"When did you go to the store? You didn't take my list!"

"I woke up early."

She digs her short nails into the plastic sheath on a flat of macaroni and cheese—it makes a satisfying pop—and crinkles the plastic in her fist. He doesn't look up. Last week, he discontinued her cell phone service. "That goddamned thing was your mother's idea!" he said when she stormed up to him. "You can have a phone when you can afford to pay for it!"

"Has Larry Villalobos found out who Mom's boyfriend is yet?" she countered.

He didn't answer.

Now, glaring, she opens the lower cabinet of the buffet thing against the far wall, retrieves a glass cup that goes with the punch bowl, and pours herself a coffee from her father's pot with deliberate flourish. She slurps and thinks, *Blech*. No turn of the blocky head. She whaps the cup down. Yesterday their father skipped dinner altogether, turned on *Jeopardy!* without volume and, immobile in his armchair, listened consecutively to George Jones and Roy Orbison CDs, followed by an extravagant wail that turned out to be Beethoven's *Eroica* Symphony No. 5.

He spent the night in the hole.

Outside, the clouds. Maybe her mother is at some faraway beach, in the sun, with a floppy hat on. Suddenly, her throat aches. She imagines driving through the night, sleeping against her siblings' warm shoulders, arriving in the cold, white morning, their breath fogging the glass. Jordan looks at her father. Would her mother get in the car? What would he do if she wouldn't?

Her father looks up to find Quinn testing the juicer on a tennis ball. "Jesus Christ!" he barks. "You think that's a toy? Go get that makeup off your face!"

Back in the kitchen, Jordan roots in the vegetable crisper. No oranges, no fruit of any variety. When she slams shut the fridge door, her father is studying her through the archway, sharp eyed.

"What?" she says.

He shrugs and looks away. "Nothing."

"You were looking at me."

"No I wasn't."

"Yes you were."

His cell phone rings in his rear pocket. "You best get ready for school, don't you think?" To Quinn, he adds, "You look like a vampire." He downs his coffee, collects his binders and keys. "Yello?" he says into the phone on his way out the door.

Quinn extracts the frozen miniature cream puffs from the freezer and offers Jordan the tub. Skyler slouches past, eating cake.

"Hey!" Jordan stomps with both feet.

The two of them turn to look at her, placid and free of rancor. "What?"

Sometimes, when she awakens in the middle of the night, she hears Quinn and Skyler speaking their secret twin language. When she staggers up to where they hunker in one of their rooms, they sound like they're speaking Spanish. Or maybe Tigua, like on the Indian reservation. Or possibly Vietnamese. It doesn't matter how many times she pipes at them, *Hey, you guys*—they never answer. In fact, she's pretty sure they're not even awake. They just stare through her with glassy eyes, as though she were a window with an invisible view. The next day, when she asks them what they were talking about in the middle of the night, they look at her like she's totally wacko and say, *What? What do you mean?*

It was exasperating, how she could never prove anything.

"We're having frozen lasagna for dinner," she announces. "With ice-cream sundaes. And I need a ride to Brittany Gallegos's birthday party weekend after next."

She rams the chickens and a supersize box of Otter Pops into the freezer and heads outside to the curb, where Miguel is waiting.

"Can somebody else take you to school next week?" he asks her at the first stoplight.

She looks up from her copy of *Moby-Dick*.

He says, "I got to take some time off."

A group of Mexican guys hurries out from beneath the overpass to brandish Windex and old rags at the cars idling on either side of them. They do not approach Miguel's truck.

"Why?"

Miguel pulls down a thumb until it touches his wrist. "I'm getting married, man."

"Why?"

"Why am I getting married?"

"How old are you?"

"Twenty-two."

"Is that old enough to get married?"

He laughs and stomps on the gas.

"You're not supposed to," she says.

"I'm not supposed to get married?"

She throws down her book. "You're not supposed to *go anywhere.*"

He gives her a wary side-eye.

III

"That's absurd! It was a freak event! A once-in-a-lifetime sort of thing!"

"You can't prove that! Things happen, whether they already happened or not!"

Marcus clears his throat in the kitchen. "Hi, guys."

His parents—braced behind their usual plates of scrambled-egg substitute and turkey bacon, still in their pajamas—startle and whip their heads.

"Son," his father says finally, offering a curt nod. "Inez is upstairs." He turns back to his newspaper, which he raises to eyebrow level. "The assumption that any freak event will happen again is completely irrational."

"Hi, m'ijo." His mother glares at the newspaper. "All I know is that, for months now, I haven't felt safe in my own home. And I refuse to live that way anymore."

"No one in this world can be safe from everything," the newspaper responds. "Nadie."

His mother turns to him. "We're getting an electric fence."

His father crushes the newspaper into his lap. "We're not. We've already got an alarm."

"You usually forget to turn it on. And it doesn't extend to the yard. Something in the backyard could be left on all the time."

"So why don't we just get some kind of wrought iron railing?"

His mother's eyes are two spinning drills. "Because that would look trashy."

"Por Dios." His father rattles the newspaper. "I feel bad about Paquito too, but we're talking about *coyotes*. They aren't wolves. Are you concerned for the safety of our garbage?"

His mother flares her nostrils, then rises to deliver the contents of her plate to the garbage disposal.

His brother plods in to extract a Coke from the refrigerator.

"Have some eggs, m'ijo," his mother trills.

His brother snorts. "Those aren't eggs." He toasts Marcus on his way back out of the room.

His mother gazes longingly after him, then turns her googly eyes on Marcus. "Do *you* want some breakfast, m'ijo?"

No one could accuse his mother of going soft, exactly, but the closer it gets to Adam's college departure, the squishier she gets. He glances at his father's plate.

"No thanks."

"Suit yourself." She attacks her plate with the sprayer hose. "Además," she continues over the hiss of the water, "security systems increase the value of a house."

His father slaps the newspaper to the tabletop. "We are not livestock, and we will not," he says, swiping his index finger sideways through the air, "not ever"—swipe—"I repeat, *ever*"—swipe—"install an electric fence around this house. Punto final." The finger stabs into the tabletop.

Marcus waits for Inez on the deck, a hot breeze ruffling his hair. The two sets of mountains make a wide beige bowl cupping the cities below him, new-construction houses creeping up the foothills on his side toward the old neighborhoods. It's enough to make you wonder where a coyote would even go out here.

A finger pokes into his ribs.

He grabs the finger, flinching. "Hi, tía."

Inez grins at him, revealing her new gold eyetooth. "Ready?"

"Yup. You hungry?"

"If you're paying, I'm eating. But might you assist me with something before we go?"

She leads him by the arm to the guest room.

A teetering wall of stacked, duct-taped boxes greets them there. Also, attire in bold colors, hanging from a portable clothes rack, and book stacks that rise to the ceiling. In the opposite corner, frozen in an everlasting hiss, a medium-sized taxidermy animal rears on its hind legs.

"Tía," he says, laughing in the doorway, "what *is* all this crap?"

She tosses her head. "That's the problem with coming out of the underground. People hear you're around and want you to take back your stuff." She huffs. "Anyway, your mother wants it out of here. And your father allegedly has bum knees and a bad back. And your brother generally is either packing or sleeping. Can you help me get it into the garage?"

His eyes return to the corner. "Is that a badger?"

"Wombat," she says. "That stays."

"Find out anything you can about what her plans are," his father had instructed earlier. "Just be cool about it. She's got a police dog's sense of smell." Marcus snorted into the phone. "Am I the FBI now?"

In the garage, he drops his load of boxes with a whump. "So, what are you up to this week?"

His parents' voices echo through the floor like the volleys of a tennis match.

Inez shoves her load against a shelving unit. "Just getting my affairs in order. One never knows when one will be called into action."

"Are you awaiting the orders for your next mission?"

She gives him a sharp, steely look that stops his heart for a moment, then turns to rip a strip of duct tape from a box lid. "I take orders from no one. But I do have some bird-watching to do today; I've given myself a thirty-bird challenge this month. Tomorrow, it's the university philosophy club meeting—I've been crashing them."

So she's bored. And probably broke, though not looking for a job. "Sounds . . . stimulating."

"Also, I've been teaching English to your parents' illegal maid."

"Their *what?*"

"When do I get to meet this girlfriend of yours?"

Really, it was hard not to think of how, if you leave an intelligent animal alone and cooped up in a house for too long, it will destroy the furniture.

"Well, Ashley's not exactly my girlfriend. But maybe, you know, sometime. Depending on how long you think you'll be around."

"Ah," she responds mildly.

The voices above raise themselves by a half tone.

"They want to meet her too," he adds. "Though maybe I should avoid that for the time being."

"Indeed." She rips open another box and digs.

He glances up before he lowers his voice. "Is this seriously about an electric fence?"

Inez frowns at a pamphlet she unearths. "Well, there's no question that things have been measurably worse since the dog got eaten."

He thumbs at the hanging clothes. White minidress against yellow jumpsuit against hot-pink ball gown. "How are *you* getting along?" he ventures. "I mean, with *them?*"

She gives him another sharp look. "As well as I ever do. So I suppose that's in the eye of the beholder." She turns back to her papers. "Are you working tonight?"

"Yup. My other date is with a dude in a green uniform."

"Your father doesn't always like how well I know him, you know," she adds abruptly. "He doesn't always want to admit to the dirt I've got on him."

He removes the ball gown from the rack and measures it for size against himself. "You mean, like, the Llorona thing? That *was* some pretty excellent dirt."

"Coyote, my ass." She paws through her box. "Like any bona fide Mexican, your father has always been fixated on the supernatural, though he will never admit it. Therefore, he is a spook magnet. It was actually the Chupacabra that ate the dog."

He lowers the gown. "The Chupacabra? I think it was your wombat."

"Of course, only your father knows for sure what happened." She smirks. "Even if he never liked that dog."

He studies her for signs of fatigue, sallowness of skin, yellowed eyes. Anything that might be terminal. "So, like, your health is pretty good, right?"

She pauses. "I am here because there's someone I'm trying to get in touch with. But it's no one you know, so I wouldn't worry about it."

Busted.

"Okay, I won't."

He surveys the contents of the garage instead. The stacked boxes and books jut out, blocking passage; the clothes rack cuts the rest of the space in two. Nothing is squared away around the dust-coated camping gear and gardening tools and sports equipment. Nothing is settled.

He can live with that.

"Let's get the hell out of here," he adds, moving to open the garage door.

Inez claps a hand on his back. "That's my boy."

III

Skyler—in the mild fog of a recently smoked joint, bra sticking damply to her chest—turns on her hip, ruffling the drawn venetian blinds. The air conditioner stirs the warm air overhead. She studies the sweatered Kleenex box beside her, the vases of plastic flowers, the decade-old JCPenney studio family photos and portraits of miserable-looking Jesuses and Virgins with yellowed Palm Sunday fronds tucked into their frames, the afghans—afghans wrapping every seating surface in view, in zigzag patterns, in the colors of impossible rainbows, as though someone were knitting a house-sized cocoon.

She loves it here.

"I need the car," barks a voice across the room.

Her head swivels, as though joined by a string to Carlos's head. In the doorway waits his older sister, Monica, her bag already on her shoulder.

"I'm taking her to work." He nods sideways at Skyler. "I'll drop you off."

"Yo, precious man-child—why is it that the only person here without a job has first dibs on the car?"

He flips her off as she exits, then points the remote at the TV until he stalls out on *Antiques Roadshow*. A man in a suit fondles a stained glass lamp.

"Oye, greñudo."

That, Carlos has told her, is what his mom calls anything that looks like a hippie. She appears now in the doorway. "Hi, m'ija," she adds.

"Oh, hi." As usual, Skyler avoids the pronouns. Calling Carlos's mom Mrs. O'Toole seems too formal at this point, but neither does she have the guts to call her Maribel.

"Is anyone hungry?" his mom asks. "I've got tacos de lengua."

"Ew." Carlos shudders.

"But lengua is *good*," Skyler responds earnestly, before she can stop herself.

"Exactly," his mother says, yanking his ponytail. "I'll fix you a plate, m'ija."

She disappears into the kitchen. Carlos's younger sisters—all three— are fighting in the backyard about which nail polish bottle belongs to whom. On the other side of the screen door, under the green plastic carport, Mr. O'Toole nods into *Psychology Today* magazine with a beer can in his free hand, soaking to the ankles in a children's plastic swimming pool.

Carlos sighs. "We should have gone to your place instead."

God, those eyelashes of his—black and double-fringed, like an Incan supermodel's.

She bursts into tears.

His hands clutch her shoulders. His hands stroke her dreads. He chants, "Baby, what's wrong, baby, it's okay," or something like that, she can't really hear him, because she's blubbering now, God, she's stupid, she's such an easy sobber, she has no idea why she should be upset about much of anything at the moment, it's not like anything is any different than it was yesterday or the day before or the day before that. Even if she had, without premeditation, cornered Quinn in the kitchen this morning to ask whether he thought their mom was actually ever coming back.

He'd stirred his iced coffee with a finger. "You're asking *me*?"

"I'm asking . . . I'm just asking. I don't know who to ask."

"Do you really even *want* her to at this point?"

This gave her pause. Because who was always after her to "Comb your hair out! Cut it! Get rid of it and start over, for the love of God, you look like a woolly mammoth"? Who once, during a scolding about Skyler's lack of quantifiable and defining interests, said, "Young lady, how do you expect to take the wheel of your life if you can't even get out of first gear?"

"Maybe we shouldn't have crank-called Mom that one time," she said. Quinn slurped coffee. "That's possible."

Now she wipes her eyes on Carlos's shirtsleeve. It smells comfortingly of Marlboros and deodorant. On-screen, an elderly woman sits stroking a life-size ceramic ram affixed to a wheeled, leashed platform. An appraiser palpates the ram. "Do you have any idea how much this piece is worth?" he teases.

"Do you want to call in sick to work?" Carlos's voice lilts with concern.

She sniffles. "Did you ever turn in that research paper from last year? The one you have to finish to graduate?"

He shrugs. "I'll figure something out."

She adds in a rush of breath, "If you applied to community college, you and Monica could carpool."

He laughs and kisses her neck, then her hand, so freckled and pale against his brown cheek. "Baby, the only thing that matters is that we'll be together."

Meaning that she's going to stay here and go to UTEP. Which she guesses is the plan. Right?

On-screen, the camera pans over a collection of Bavarian beer steins. Off-screen is a world very far away from El Paso. The East Coast maybe. Someplace where Christmas means snow on the ground and fireplaces put to actual use, where people speak with aristocratic-sounding accents and eat maple syrup and clam chowder. The kind of people you only see on TV.

III

Quinn oozes through his open bedroom window. His feet meeting the patio roof triggers a heart-stopping cascade of pebbles. He crouches, scuttles, lowers himself from the roof's lip into empty air. His arms shake and a sour scum of fear coats his tongue. He lets go.

His landing below is solid, like a sofa dropped to the floor from one end.

He lurches along the paving stones of the courtyard, a mulberry leaf crackling under his sneaker. He holds his breath and slips to the other side of the gate.

Minutes ago, he woke abruptly in the muffled dark of his room wanting to know what happened to his black high-top sneaker. Is it in his dirty laundry pile? Under somebody else's bed? He threw off his hot sheet and stepped into some pants.

This is how it goes now. He wakes in the night—long before birds, hours before paperboys—the gears in his head grinding on pointless questions and what-ifs. He lurches downstairs, watches TV. He eats cereal by lamplight and waits for the world to wake up.

Or he walks. He treads now past the familiar two-story houses of stucco and brick, half-circle driveways, curbside mailboxes ringed with yucca and blunted swords of agave. His feet make a rhythmic scuff on the asphalt. He wonders what would happen if he started a new bad habit, like cigarettes. Or how long he could get away with not going to class once school starts. Maybe Lourdes took his shoe. She glowers at him these days, then looks away when he catches her, in a way that makes him think of a pot of boiling water with a very tight-fitting lid. Would she admit to taking it if he asked? What if he acted all tough? How long could he fake that?

He walks, the crickets in the shrubs beside him falling silent when he passes, then croaking again to life behind him. Streetlights halo the cars parked in driveways. Maybe, whenever the details of this so-called vacation finally emerge, he should stage a sit-in. He could do it alone, if he had to. And he would have to. His sisters were not on board with the Campaign of Sabotage in the way that they'd promised. Maybe it was time to say, *Fuck passive resistance.* What if he faced down the old man for once and for all? What if he stood nose to nose and said, *Make me?*

A silver gleam draws his eye below curbside. A hubcap. Fallen from the car tire beside it and reminiscent, somehow, of a turtle's shell. He picks it up, turns it around in his hands, and tucks it under his arm.

He walks, veering off the sidewalk where the street dead-ends against the haunch of the mountain. He slips halfway up a driveway, squeezing against a cement-and-rock wall, toward a window. The shade is drawn. Every time Quinn comes over lately, Adam says, "Wish I could go out, gabacho, but I can't," and then he stuffs something else into a cardboard box. He's going to UC San Diego on a scholarship. For Quinn, there's senior year. He pictures this year as an enormous cardboard box inside a dark room. He has a hard time fixing on its shape. He just knows he's supposed to spend the next nine months wandering around inside of it.

Last night when he went out to walk, something stopped him at the curb. A sense that someone was watching. He looked back over his shoulder to find Jordan at her bedroom window. He didn't know why she woke up. He didn't know what made her look outside. But there she was, swaying in her blue pajamas with the cartoon sheep on them, and when they beheld each other across the dark lawn, she'd raised her hand to wave. He drew his finger to his lips. She didn't call after him when he walked away.

He looks up at the window before him and thinks, *Mojado, I could totally toilet paper your house right now.*

His eye snags at ground level just before he rounds the corner of the property. A patch of pink, bright even under the dim streetlight, peeks from the base of the big, puffy Spanish broom that borders Adam's yard and the one next door. He stoops and lifts an armful of leaves to find a smiling ceramic goose—the sort of thing an old lady would keep in her yard. Its eyelashes are batted, its head tilted coyly, as though urging, *Go on.*

That crank call had been Skyler's idea. Hers, after their mom had flipped out over Skyler's armpit hair at the city symphony boosters' picnic. Even if the day before, his mother spied his eyeliner as he was on the way out the door to school, yanked him into the bathroom, and shoved a jar of Pond's at him.

Even if he was the one who made the call. His voice high and officious, unrecognizable on the second line as he informed her that he was calling from Career Finders International, it had come to their attention that she had no life; would she like some assistance with reversing the atrophy of her mind?

He palmed the receiver as he and Skyler choked on their hilarity, as their mother rounded the corner with the cordless to pin them with eyes of flame. The look beneath her face trembled with something far worse.

Now he pries the goose loose from the dirt. At the far side of the house, he jumps the wall into the desert.

He walks. He tastes the dust he kicks up. His jeans brush brittle branches and prickly things, and invisible creatures scurry away from him. The haze of city light fuzzes up the edges of the night. He shuffles and rises and dips over the foothills.

There's just enough light for him to see the silhouettes of the things he has begun to fit again into place. Broken tree branches. A bicycle horn. An old syringe with no needle. A wrench and an assortment of LEGOs and jacks and an empty wrapper of Bimbo-brand bread. Melted tarp scraps darken the sand. He still smells the char in the air.

When he'd found everything burnt, he'd kicked the blackened shrubs and stomped on the plastic bathtub until it collapsed, then scooped the whole stinking mess into the shopping cart and wheeled down the mountain to heave it in the dumpster behind Circuit City. Even now he can't explain to himself why any of it mattered. Or why he's been making these weird little monuments to nothing to begin with. All he knows is that they're never complete, each time there's something missing, and this absence feels like an ache in some part of his body that doesn't exist. He digs with his heel in the ground in front of the teepee he has made of the tree branches and fits the hubcap into place, the circumference of its concave side flush with the earth. He sets the goose within.

A hot breeze lifts his hair. He straightens and tilts his head back to take in the sky. It's not dark enough, and the city haze swallows the stars, but it's still endless. Fucking endless.

What if he decided to leave. What if he went somewhere far away and didn't tell anyone where. What if he didn't come back. He hears his own deepening breath. Streaks of red and white light trace the curve of the highway. The houses that crowd the flank of the mountain loom in their unnatural glow.

9

DEEP WATER

IN THE DRIVEWAY, BEFORE JERRY'S eyes, the electric fence unfolds. The Volvo idles beneath him. He taps the gas pedal to lower its growl. The requisite all-Mexican work crew bustles in and out of his backyard, unraveling coils of wire, applying drills and other noisy tools to the rock and cement. He digs his thumbnail into the steering wheel's gummy crud. Here comes Chavela, all business in her Bermuda shorts, shading her eyes from the sun. A worker nods as she gives direction. Jerry cranks the air-conditioning to nine. He considers how long he might wait here, like a crocodile with only its eyes and nostrils above the water.

A whine emanates from his back seat.

He turns. The creature in the plastic crate behind him labeled "Dog Taxi" circles and claws at its gridded metal door.

"Relájete, perro," he mutters. "You've got a good life ahead of you."

A series of earsplitting yelps is the response, as though someone had dropped a heavy frying pan on a little rat tail.

He kills the engine and lugs out the taxi.

"Oye," he calls out to a worker as he approaches.

The worker, a tattooed, anvil-shaped fellow with a shaved head and a coil of wire looped over his shoulder, turns his head. So does Chavela.

The controls, Jerry continues, setting the crate down. Will they be inside or outside the house?

He lifts a staying hand as Chavela opens her mouth. He has further questions for this worker, questions about safety, health hazards, electric bills, the technical details of installation. He nods thoughtfully when the responses come.

"Bueno," he says at last, with a friendly but authoritative nod. "A trabajar."

Chavela flares her nostrils when the worker has gone. Her gaze dips to the crate.

"What," she says, "is *that?*"

He looks to the brilliant, cloudless sky. He could have responded to the "AKC Pomeranian pups" ads in the paper, of course, could have made the rounds at the puppy mills of Juárez. Instead, after a fruitless morning in which he scoured the kibble-scented pet supply warehouses of the city for a certain small, fluffy breed of dog, he found himself standing before a glass enclosure containing a litter of beagles. They struck him as attractive dogs, actually, floppy eared and muscular, surely inclined to flush out prairie dogs and other vermin.

In the pet store, in the farthest corner of a very small cage, huddled a trembling rat whose eyes looked as though they were about to pop out of its head.

He turned to the employee on duty. "How much," he asked with difficulty, "for the Chihuahua?"

Now he faces his wife. "That's your new dog."

He meets his sister descending the outside stairs as he climbs to the deck.

"So," says Inez when they meet halfway. She leans, with languor, against the handrail and takes in the bustle below. "Here it comes."

He says nothing. He only looks in the direction of the view that awaits him from his deck.

Inez leans, the better to take note of Chavela, kneeling now before the cage as she extracts the Chihuahua and lifts it into the air. It whimpers. "*That's* what you got her?"

He shrugs. His wife has always been drawn to that which is pitiful and small.

Inez adjusts the brim of her cowboy hat. "Well, if the other one was dinner, this one's going to be a midnight snack. I hope you're prepared."

He looks at her as his foot creeps onto the next step.

"Nothing's getting in once that thing is turned on," he says. "You know that, right?"

She offers him a bitter smile. "I guess I'd better be on the right side when you flip the switch."

The heat bakes the top of his head. A week ago, when Inez and Lourdes were installed for the umpteenth time with their notebooks at the patio table at exactly the moment Chavela wished to occupy the same space, when Chavela turned to him from the kitchen window and said, "I'm done with this. I want her out, and if you won't take matters into your hands, then I will," the words that rushed from his mouth surprised even him.

"You're not throwing her out like garbage," he said. "¿Me entiendes?"

She met his spiraling gaze with a terrifying calm. "Que entiendo is that you'd better give me a good reason not to."

He looks past Inez's shoulder now, toward the deck. "None of us wants to admit that putting up this fence is probably for the best."

Another snort. "For who? Chavela's dog?"

If he leans to one side, he can see partway over the back wall. If he told Inez that he traded the fence for her, would she find it amusing? Or would she abandon them for once and for all, out of spite?

"Eventually, we'll forget that things were ever any other way." The taste in his mouth is sour.

She pushes back from the railing to stretch. "It's not natural, you know," she adds just before she turns to ascend again. "It screws up the electromagnetic field. This is going to put you on Mother Nature's shit list." She regards the Chihuahua once more as it shivers in the crook of Chavela's arm. "Seriously, though, is that a dog or a rodent? I'm going to call it Speedy Gonzales."

He looks toward the deck with a fierce longing as Inez settles herself there in a chair. Then, feeling leaden, he descends.

A vehicle roars into a driveway farther down the street. It's Huck DuPre.

Jerry's feet brace against the sidewalk, but it's too late to turn away. Huck is already squinting in the direction of Jerry's lawn. His hat casts a shadow on his face as he lumbers up the walk.

"Hey, Jerry," he says as he steps up beside him. He nods and looks solemn.

Jerry nods in return. "Huck."

"What you got going on there? Rewiring the house?"

Jerry's hands find his pockets. "Electric fence." Something about being around Huck reduces the number of syllables he can use.

"You have a break-in?"

"No," Jerry says. "A fucking coyote ate my dog."

"A *coyote*?" He says it in two syllables: "*kai*yoat." "You serious?" He waits for Jerry's nod. "Well, it must have been damn near starving to death. What kind of dog was it?"

"Pit bull," Jerry says, just to test him.

"Christ almighty!"

Huck seems not to know what to say next. Nor does he consider the possibility that he should leave. Instead, he turns his attention back toward the installers of fence. Jerry stands beside him doing the same. For a brief moment, he has the discomfiting sensation that they are two men bonding in the silent appraisal of other men's handiwork.

"Firmese, por favor." The workman at Jerry's elbow extends a clipboard and pen.

Jerry signs. The doors of the service vehicle slam. He is free to move toward his fortress.

And yet, as Huck's lean shadow stretches across the pavement, as his own shadow makes a shape beside it disturbingly reminiscent of Sancho Panza's, he can't help but wonder what Huck is thinking, now that Rose Marie is gone.

In fact, he feels sorry for him.

But he doesn't want to feel sorry for *anyone*. He waves away the pickup truck with Mexican plates that veers to the curb to offer a load of low-cost citrus fruit. Perhaps Chavela was right after all. Better to erect a division than to live with a membrane.

And yet. He suddenly wishes he could ask Huck whether, when reviewing his life in order to determine how he ended up where he is, he ever becomes aware of a certain pervasive sense of dread.

Huck turns to go. "Sorry about your dog," he says, but what Jerry imagines him saying is, "Dread of what?"

"Nature," Jerry blurts. "The inexorable cycle of life." The late-summer sky is so blue and blazing it could burn holes in somebody's brain.

III

Chavela loves the Chihuahua. She names it Kiko. In the evenings, with the electric fence set on low fry, she sets the dog outside like a windup toy and watches him deposit his miniature turds in the yard, then leaves him there, reassured, while she readies herself for bed.

Mornings, she spoons into his bowl a serving of ALPO half the size of his body, then stoops to rub his knobby head as he buries it in the bowl. A calm descends upon her. Not that Jerry would describe her as relenting. No. But they have begun to communicate in a language of silence. If they brush up against each other while passing in the hallway, they no longer stiffen. They set each other's places at the table. Their eyes meet in mirrors and do not look away.

They dress together. In the yellow light of midmorning, Jerry turns back and forth in his gray blazer, sucking in his gut behind Chavela at her vanity mirror.

She of the caramel-colored skin and sturdy white bras. She who is, still, his wife.

"So," he says to her reflection, "have you given any further thought to a vacation? After we take Adam to school?"

The smile on Chavela's face shifts, as though she is diving deeper into the available supply of her kindness. She looks back down at her makeup. "I really just want to come back home afterward."

He almost touches her shoulder. "We'll already have the time off."

"No. Thanks." She sounds like she's declining a cup of coffee.

"It'll be fun!"

From farther down the hall, in the guest room, comes a sudden explosion of symphonic music.

"No," says Chavela. This is less polite. She reaches for the chocolate-brown dress suit laid out on the bed.

He resists the impulse to look in the direction of the operatic soprano that rips through the air. "So this is still about Inez."

She moves to the dresser to rummage through her underwear drawer. "Could we maybe not talk about Inez for five minutes? Our son is about to leave us."

"Do you mean to tell me," he says as something slows and reverses within him, "that you're just going to feel sorry for yourself? Adam has to go. It's a fact of life. We *want* him to go."

"Maybe *you* want him to go." She pops open an unopened pantyhose egg.

"Right," he says. "That's exactly what I want. Madre de Dios."

"I need to mourn this. ¿Por qué no puedes respetarlo?"

"Lo respeto. I just don't think I should overindulge it. Don't you remember como se comportó tu papá when *you* went to college?"

"No tienes corazón."

"Right." He rolls his eyes, so that she can't see she's stabbed him in exactly the spot where he's supposed to have nothing. "I should have known this would happen," he adds.

Her toe hovers over a waiting sheath of hose. "And just what exactly is that supposed to mean?"

"Forget it." He turns to the mirror above his dresser and chokes himself slightly as he knots his first-week-of-class tie. "What's for dinner tonight?"

She snaps the waistband of her pantyhose and does a deep knee bend to snug it into place. "Order a pizza if you want."

"Fine."

In the hallway, outside the open guest room door, sits the boom box from which emanates their soundtrack—a selection from *Carmen*, if he's not mistaken. Bracing himself, he shuts it off.

Inez's room is empty.

Adam's room, however, resembles the loading dock of a small aircraft. The boy himself sprawls sideways across his bed with his earbuds on, head resting on a plastic storage tub containing shoes and what appears to be a plastic lawn flamingo.

"Want to go for a drive?" Jerry calls out from the doorway.

Adam lifts his head. "Where to?"

"I'm not sure. I suppose we'll know when we get there."

Adam laughs. "Maybe later, Dad."

"Any later and someone will have to scrape our melted bodies off the blacktop. Take a break from packing. Or relaxing. Whatever it is you're doing."

"Dad, I've got some plans in a little while."

"Me too."

"*Dad.*" Adam lets out his breath. "We don't need to do a bonding ritual, okay? It's cool."

It's cool, Jerry says to himself once he's standing alone at the edge of his patio. The mountainside slopes at his shoulder, its stubby foliage looking brittle and gray. A subtle but ominous hum—so low that he feels it more than he hears it—envelops the perimeter of his yard.

He looks past the top of his wall, to the rooftops beyond. Huck DuPre's house looks like it could use a new roof. And some stucco under the eaves. And a new gutter. On the second floor, the same window has been cranked open once again, the gauzy curtains pushed aside, rippling over gusts of hot wind.

If all the logic that holds the world together dissolved, a particular woman would be the one responsible, and here she would step into the frame.

He feels his throat tighten. Because she would be stunning, framed in the window like that, her wheat-colored hair lit up with sun, chingada madre, she *would*, even if she had the wild, disheveled look of a madwoman locked in a tower.

The world around him smells of burning rubber. He turns away and heaves open the sliding glass door. Speedy Gonzales races up to his feet, eyes bulging, grinning and tap-dancing in the hope that it's time for a second breakfast. His bowl has been licked to a shine.

Jerry looks to the window again, still expecting some phantom to appear there. Still wanting one.

He's alone, it occurs to him now. In all of this. With a Chihuahua.

III

"You mean to tell me you still don't have any solid leads?"

On the other end of the line, Larry Villalobos, PI, clears his throat.

"What I mean, Huck, is that Rose Marie probably has been very lucky or very clever. She's done a good job of staying off the radar. However, and I hate to say it, we do have to consider the possibility that something has happened to—"

"Go back to 'off the radar.'"

Villalobos lets out his breath. "She hasn't left many traces. If she's contacted anyone, they're not talking. And obviously, she still hasn't used your credit card."

Huck resists the urge to say, *No shit, Sherlock.* Also, maybe he should have looked at the memo Mendoza slipped him yesterday, before now. The demands, in translation: Pay raises, of course. Better food. Unionizing rights.

"However," Villalobos continues, "did you catch the fifteen-hundred-dollar withdrawal she made from your checking account the week after she left? From an ATM in Mexico?"

That first week had been hazy. "Mexico?"

"Mexico. In a town near a small, out-of-the-way resort."

"Mexico." For Chrissakes. "Who was she with?"

"I don't know yet."

"Didn't you talk to anybody?"

"I spoke to the hotel's front desk, but no one could remember her specifically. All they said was 'We get a lot of güeras around here.'"

"So you're just going to leave it at that?"

"No. But I do want to warn you that, if she's left the country—or if she leaves it again—she could be hard to find. Mexico can be a good place to hide."

"If she wanted a divorce, why the hell didn't she just ask for one?"

"Can't answer that," Villalobos says. "Now, the thing is—"

"Where, exactly?" Huck presses. "Where in Mexico?"

"A little beach town called San Carlos. On the Baja peninsula."

At the dining room table, Huck folds the memo's stiff corner. Outside, the trees Miguel pruned in the spring now look like candied green apples on sticks. Once he cornered the lovebirds in their little nest, he was going to have to take the boyfriend aside and have a private word with him and then punch him in the face. But then he'd tell Rose Marie to pack her things, because she's going to come home with them. He hasn't signed the divorce papers. They're cooling in a manila envelope on top of his bedroom chest of drawers. Would he call this an act of love? Of spite? He's not sure. The point is that she's his wife. *His.*

As for the memo, there are two courses of action he could take— forward it to the board, who would ignore it, thus absolving him of any responsibility, or take care of it himself by holding some sort of unofficial powwow after work, listening to the concerns, promoting goodwill, et cetera. Whether or not he could do anything about these demands was beside the point.

He wonders what it will cost him to set up a Mexican vacation for four. Whether they'd have to fly into Mazatlán or some other tourist trap and then drive a pockmarked highway where everything was marked in kilometers.

Larry Villalobos clears his throat. "I doubt she's still there."

From somewhere within Huck's cordless phone connection comes the faintest perceptible click. A poorly concealed breath.

Huck sits up in his chair. "Who's on the line?" he barks.

"I beg your pardon?" Villalobos asks.

"Not you!" He puts some extra bass in his voice. "Whichever of you kids that is, you'll have to wait your turn. This is a private call. So get off."

He waits for the reverse click but doesn't hear one.

"I'm warning you," he continues.

Villalobos clears his throat. "Do you want to call me back?"

Quinn sidles into the doorway and waits.

Huck clanks his glass down onto the table. "What I want—*after somebody gets off this phone*—is for you to keep doing what I'm paying you to be doing, only better."

He takes a breath in the stiff silence that follows and adds, in a conversational tone, "If you wouldn't mind. Hold on for a minute."

He palms the receiver. "Was that you on the line?"

Quinn is wearing a dog collar with spikes on it. "No."

"Where's your sisters?"

"Skyler's in the kitchen. Jordan, I have no idea."

"Is she home?"

Quinn shrugs. "I have no idea."

An alarm goes off in Huck's head. "What do you mean? Where would she be if she isn't home?"

Quinn looks up from under his blue bangs. "Couldn't say. Because *I have no idea*."

"Well, when's the last time you saw her?"

Another shrug, this one more exasperated. "This morning?"

Huck's lungs contract. He's never considered the possibility that while he was looking for his wife, he could lose one of the kids.

"Has it occurred to you that Jordan's your sister?" he wheezes. "Your *little* sister. And you and Skyler need to look out for her, especially now that there's one less person around to do the job."

Quinn folds his arms. "Maybe you should give her a couple of hours to turn up before you start freaking out."

Huck thinks the word *oxygen*. "Vacation's delayed."

"Till when?"

"Next month."

"Good."

Huck eyes the memo, sucking in air. There's got to be a solution here. Something that'll make everyone happy.

"Skyler and I were wondering if we could have some money," Quinn says.

"What for?"

"Miniature golf," Skyler hollers from the kitchen, just as the second phone line rings.

"Don't answer that," Huck barks when Quinn turns his head to the sound. "Don't answer!" he calls out. He waits. Three rings. Four. Five. More rings than the phone would be allowed to ring if Jordan were in the house, he supposes. He leans backward to pick up the wall-mounted phone.

"Yello?"

No one. Or rather, just the subtle, live prickle of a human presence.

"Who's there?"

A breath.

It's the disgruntled worker. The one he hasn't heard from since the beginning of summer.

"Listen, you son of a bitch," he says. "You call here again and I'll—"

Another click in his ear. "Thanks for holding, sweetie," a voice says. "So anyway—"

"What the hell *is* this?" Huck continues on top of the other voice.

"Hello?" A woman's voice. It carries a note of offense.

"Who's this?"

"Suzie Gallegos. Is that you, Huck?"

"Dad," comes Jordan's remonstrative voice. "I've *got* it."

"Have you been on this line the whole time?"

"Mrs. Gallegos had to put me on hold," Jordan says. "So I was doing some homework."

"Were you listening in on my other call?"

"What other call?"

"Should I . . . call back later?"

Suzie. Whatever she's calling about, he's pretty sure it has something to do with birthday parties.

"Nope," he answers. "Lay it on me."

"Brittany broke her wrist yesterday. We're rescheduling the birthday party again."

"Well. That's a shame. You got that, Jordan?"

"Yes, Dad."

"Now hang up, little girl."

A "hmmph" and a click follow.

"I hope you didn't mean *me*," Suzie deadpans.

He tips back his chair. "She's not one of you."

"Excuse me? Are we talking about Brittany?"

"I mean Jordan. But you'll find that out soon enough."

"So, what do you say, Dad?" Quinn says the moment Huck hangs up.

"Can we take the truck?" Skyler adds from the kitchen.

An icicle of pain shoots through Huck's jaw as he crunches the remnants of his iced tea.

"Take that collar off," he tells Quinn as he slices the bills out of his wallet. "You're not a Doberman pinscher, goddammit."

Jordan appears in the doorway. "Take me with you."

Quinn snorts. "I don't think so, Jo-Jo."

"On the contrary," Huck says, rising as Skyler slides up. "That's a great idea. *And keep an eye on her.*"

The twins glare back at him. Then at Jordan. They give each other a look on their silent radio frequency.

On the dining room table, in the now empty room, the cordless phone rests upside down in the fruit bowl. Huck snatches it up. "You still there?"

A loud exhalation is the response. Then: "Yes, Huck."

"So where do we go from here?"

"That's what I've been trying to tell you," Larry Villalobos answers in a thin voice. "I've got one other lead. Because it seems that Rose Marie was—or possibly still is—in San Diego."

Huck lowers himself into his chair, a new spike of fear in his gut. Knowledge is power, sure. But what do you do with it? Create? Destroy?

Maybe nobody gets to choose which way it falls.

Across the top of the memo, he scribbles, "NO DEALS." Then he adds, "SORRY."

He leans back, feeling cleansed. "I'm listening," he says.

III

"I knew you weren't going miniature golfing," Jordan says when they pull into a parking lot downtown.

Skyler kills the engine. "Congratulations, baby Einstein." She exits the truck.

Quinn follows without answering. The bridge to Juárez is backlogged with idling cars. The parking lot is half-empty, the graffiti-smeared pay box listing to one side, the asphalt beneath their feet pocked and scabby. The air is heavy with exhaust fumes.

Jordan slams the door shut behind her. "Why do you guys want to come down *here*?"

Three men approach on the sidewalk, turning their heads to stare at Skyler as they pass. They look at the complicated, wheaty lumps of her hair and they look at her tits. Skyler pretends not to notice. She just makes herself smaller. Quinn they eye differently. They wrinkle their noses. They curl their lips. They say things to each other in Spanish.

Quinn coolly turns to the next person who stares, a chubby woman snugging a baby to her hip, and hisses at her like a cat.

The woman bristles and scurries away.

"We're here," he announces, "for the ice cream. Who wants ice cream?"

He sticks his finger into Jordan's ear before she can swat him away.

At the Alligator Plaza, where—according to her father, who Jordan does not believe, the city once kept a pen of live alligators—Quinn carefully places his head inside the glossy fiberglass jaws of an alligator statue, then brings his ice-cream bar to his lips. He shows them a game where they all stop in the middle of the sidewalk and look up and point and whisper furtively until some passerby is dumb enough to look up.

"Oh my God," Skyler murmurs as a woman weighted down with shopping bags has a look. "It's eating a pigeon."

At Wig World, Jordan selects a black beehive; Quinn, the sensible braid of a librarian. They stand side by side in front of the mirror, examining themselves with gravity.

"Look, look, you guys." Skyler bursts into the reflection behind them, pressing down on the wide, golden wings of her coif. "Who am I?"

The three of them grin evilly.

The light is draining out of the sky when they start to play Red Light, Green Light; the crush of people on the sidewalks thins. A gritty wind whips at their clothes. Jordan has never been out here on foot. Only in cars, passing through, in daytime. Now she stops and starts, stops and starts, Skyler calling into the shadows while Quinn races her using big clown steps. The pedestrians hurry away.

"Sa-bro-so me-nu-do," Jordan reads aloud from the window of a restaurant, and then "Ow!" when Quinn pelts her with a pebble. She volleys back a crumpled piece of tinfoil. "Quin-cea-ñera and wedding supplies, ow!"

"For Chrissakes, shut up," Skyler says, not throwing anything.

"Cambie aquí cheques de income tax."

People stare and stare and stare.

When they pass the doorway to a tenement over a grocery store, Quinn strides ahead and yanks open the dark doorway of a stairwell. "Be right back." His feet float up and disappear. Skyler settles silently on a bus stop bench, drawing her Birkenstocks up under her knees. Jordan lowers herself down beside her. *What's it like to be pretty?* she wonders. *To be tall?*

"Stop staring at me."

"I'm not staring. I'm just looking."

"What are you looking at?"

"You."

Laughter scrapes the air at their backs. Jordan turns her head slowly. There are five or six men this time, all speaking Spanish, their voices ragged and beery. Their eyes feel sticky against her own. She scoots closer to Skyler when she hears a kissing noise. Skyler examines her nails. Jordan leans, rooting her bottom to the bench. She thinks of the out-of-service phone in her purse. The twins had been outraged that she was the only one who got a cell. Their mother had offered them a lopsided smile. *I already know for a fact*, she'd said, *that you two don't know what an emergency is.*

When her father was still on the phone with the investigator, the woman on Jordan's line had coughed.

"Hello?" the woman said. "Are you still there, honey? How many times a year did you say you attend religious services?"

It was an old woman, or possibly someone pretending to be one. "Stop doing that with your voice," Jordan said crossly.

In the other room, she could hear her father saying his goodbyes. The woman warbled in Jordan's ear. Jordan clicked her off.

The other line was still live. She could hear breathing.

"Hey," she said to Larry Villalobos.

"Hello?"

"She's probably at the beach."

"Who . . . ?"

"Did you figure out yet where my name came from?"

After a pause came a humorless chuckle.

"On the day we met," Larry Villalobos said, "if I'd been given enough time to do my job, I would have been able to tell you that Jordan was your mother's maiden name."

"Good work, Poirot."

"What did you just say about the beach?"

She swiveled her stool. "Nothing. It was just a guess."

"You haven't heard from her?"

"Nope."

His fingers drummed the receiver. "Would *you* like to help me?"

She leaned forward. "How?"

"I've spoken with your grandparents, but . . . well. Do *you* think they've heard from her?"

Grandma Francine, Grandpa Jarvis. He didn't know how their voices sound like their faces, always pinched. "They said no."

"What about your mother's biological parents? Any reason to believe she's contacted them?"

"Her what?"

A silence hummed the line. A rustling of ill-fitting clothes. Larry Villalobos cleared his throat.

"Her biological parents. The parents she was born to, before your grandparents adopted her."

Jordan felt something rushing through her. The wind.

"You did know she was adopted, didn't you?"

"No."

"Oh boy."

She listened to him breathe.

"Look, m'ija, I'm sorry if I surprised you. I'd appreciate it, though, if you wouldn't tell your dad you heard it from me."

From where she sat, she could see Quinn, sidling up to their father in the dining room.

"You should definitely tell him if you think of anything, though. Anything that might help. All right?"

"Don't call me sweetheart," she said, but Larry Villalobos had already beaten her to the click.

Now, behind her on the bench, a man calls out: "Oye, güera. Güeritas."

Jordan's hand creeps up past Skyler's waist to close around the tip of a dreadlock. It's rough and dry, like something you'd scrub the dishes with. To her relief, Skyler doesn't know she's being touched.

They sit this way a long time, Jordan's neck prickling and her shoulders stiff and achy, until the men go away.

Quinn emerges looking sleepy and red eyed and happy. He aims a thumbs-up at Skyler.

"Hey, babee," he says in a fake accent, dropping his arms around both their shoulders. "Whatju girls do-eeng?"

"Quit," Skyler says.

"You smell." Jordan pushes against him with her palms.

"That's right." He takes a dreamy whiff of his armpit. "I smell beautiful." He hoists Jordan up and throws her over his shoulder. Buildings floating on air. Skyler kicking her legs upside down. Jordan's head thumps against Quinn's back as he marches in slow motion, humming, and she doesn't mean to giggle, but she does.

"Hey," Skyler calls out behind them. She lurches to her feet. "Hey, goddammit! Will you please *wait* for me?"

Even upside down, Jordan sees the little tremor of hurt moving across her sister's forehead. She tries to stop laughing but she can't.

III

Jerry goes for a drive, alone.

He drives politely, at an even speed, signaling generously and allowing other cars to pass. They roar past him with contempt. He keeps his hands on the wheel and cruises the wide boulevard that faces the mountain's crown of red-and-white radio antennae. He passes the vacant lot that, once upon a time, contained the drive-through hamburger joint where he entertained his young sons by tossing french fries to the prairie dogs that colonized the parking strip. He skims into downtown, past the sixties-era civic auditorium that has always made him think of a sombrero-shaped cake squashed in the box on the way home from the bakery. He slows and backs up the traffic in front of the glamorously dilapidated, single-screen movie theater where he took Chavela on their first date, the same theater where, in junior high, he and Inez rained spitballs and Jujubes from the balcony onto the unsuspecting patrons below, where, as a child, he'd watched animated Disney films with scheduled intermissions, *Bambi* and *Fantasia* and *Peter Pan*.

He idles at a stoplight before an ancient apartment building that, according to his maternal grandmother, was haunted by a hanged woman in a yellow nightgown who appeared in an upper-floor window, though who this ghost was or why she was haunting or on what authority his grandmother knew this to begin with, he cannot remember.

Rounding the blunt end of the mountain, avoiding the freeway, making his way along small curving streets that laze into and away from the boulevards, he slows to lowrider speed around Ascarate Lake—manmade pond, repository of weird suckerfish. The Ferris wheel still tumbles hypnotically behind the gates of Western Playland. El Bandido leers over his shoulder with his pistol, as though to acknowledge with Jerry a shared secret joke.

Beneath the blanketing stench of the oil refinery, he passes a Chico's Tacos and feels a pang that could be either hunger or its absolute opposite.

Onward, into neighborhoods of small flat-roofed houses with odd, added-on second stories, arched balconies, decorative fountains, potted plastic flowers, cars on the paved-over lawns. Wrought iron railing on every window. He might as well be driving the streets of Júarez.

He doesn't realize until, far on the other end of town, approaching the airport, having passed a shuttered Shakey's Pizza and the plaster snake–topped bar known since time immemorial as the Brass Asp, that he is actually going to Tavo's house.

He finds Tavo working on the engine of his car in the driveway.

His brother rears out from under the hood to squint at him. "What are *you* doing here?"

It's a good question. Jerry glides up under the carport. The corrugated plastic roof casts a greenish light. "I was in the neighborhood."

"What, you got lost? Don't tell me this is some kind of social call."

Jerry examines the house, a squat brick cube covered in wrought iron railing, its screen door partly detached. "Something like that."

"Pues entonces. Go ahead and start the conversation."

Jerry stuffs his hands into his pockets. "I got Chavela a new dog."

"What happened to the old one?"

"Eaten by coyote."

"Shit, man." Tavo turns away to spit on the lawn. "Maybe it was a mountain lion. I heard there's a mountain lion."

"There's no mountain lion. I saw the whole thing."

"You want to go inside?"

"No," Jerry demurs. "No, no."

"Then what's the matter with you?"

Jerry scuffs his heel against the concrete. The wind irritates his nostrils and dries out his eyes.

"Are you coming over to see Inez?" he asks finally.

Tavo jabs at something under the hood. "Is *that* what this is about?"

"This isn't *about* anything. I'm just wondering."

"Wasn't planning on it. She ever gonna leave?"

"Wish I knew."

"Isn't she driving you crazy?"

"What do you *think*?"

"Pues, por Dios, hombre, why haven't you kicked her to the curb?"

Jerry nudges aside a loose nail with his shoe. Did Tavo ever think of Marcus's ninth birthday party? Of other events, long ago?

"Well," he murmurs, "you know what she's like."

"Yup."

The wind tugs at their shirtsleeves. Wisps of cloud smear across the turquoise plate of the sky.

"Inez says it was actually the Chupacabra that ate the dog," Jerry adds, to keep himself from weeping. "In disguise."

Tavo laughs.

"She says it's evolution in action," Jerry continues. "We're encroaching on its habitat in the middle of a hundred-year drought. We've got less farmland, less livestock. But what we *do* have is an abundance of Pomeranians and miniature poodles."

"Of course, the Chupacabra is just the boogeyman. A bedtime story to keep the kids in line." Tavo chuckles and tightens something under the hood. "Or maybe to keep the Mexicans on the other side of the line."

Jerry snorts.

"Or maybe Inez was on the right track. Maybe your coyote really was something a little more . . . supernatural."

"Beg your pardon?"

"I mean, take a look around." Tavo gestures with his wrench. "Coyotes. Mountain lions. Gila monsters. Whatever. They're all totem animals. And we're part Indian, right? At least on the DNA level."

"Por Dios. What do—"

"That coyote was a sign, man. Life is full of signs."

"A coyote gets hungry and that's a *sign*?"

"Mira," Tavo continues mildly. "The coyote is resourceful and adaptable and playful. And it's a trickster, so it usually brings illusion with it. Chaos. The dark side. Because sometimes that's the only way you're going to get at the truth. So you tell *me*, Mr. *College*."

Jerry stops midstep, every hair on him bristling. "Don't *start*."

"Our ancestors were *Aztecs*. They talked to eagles and crocodiles and jaguars. But our people didn't exactly stay in that part of the world, now did they?"

"Por Dios. This too?"

"We didn't even stay the same people. We blended. Adapted. Like coyotes. Anyway, I guess you can study history or you can be a legacy."

"¡Basta!"

"It's like I told you all those years ago. You gotta hold on to your roots. Stand up for something. Claim what's your own. How else you gonna understand your place in the world?" Tavo looks down his nose. "Or your house?"

Jerry turns to him. Slowly. In the same way he did thirty years ago during televised football games when Tavo occupied his grad school efficiency apartment, decrying Jerry's outward lack of outrage toward a variety of commercials prevalent at the time: Juan Valdez illiterately admiring his coffee farm. The schemings of the Frito Bandito. The sombreroed Mexican on permanent siesta beneath the shade of the Taco Bell logo. And Jerry would rise from the TV tray where he was grading U.S. History 101 papers, and with a *Pues, I'll drink to that*, retrieve two bottles of Coors—boycotted by activists for busting the unions of its Mexican American workers, on sale that week at the Piggly Wiggly—smiling as he uncapped the bottles while his brother ground his teeth. Or he might offer Tavo something to eat. *Here, bro—I've got grapes*. All because of the "¡Uvas, No!" pin on Tavo's jacket, in solidarity with the migrant workers' boycott.

"I know who I am," Jerry tells his brother now. "I don't have to thump my chest about it in front of the world."

"Your first-grade teacher spanked you for speaking Spanish at school."

"Yeah, but I'm bigger than she is now."

"*History*—what good is it anyway? It already happened."

"So instead we should make it up?"

Tavo rolls his eyes in exactly the same way he did thirty years ago.

"We should probably erase some of it. Just ask my military record."

Jerry runs his tongue behind his teeth. He's not about to ask. It's not like Tavo's ever told anyway.

"Look, man," Jerry says. "It's time to let go of all this viva la raza stuff. It was just a fad."

"And yet the world still treats us like outsiders. This is our spiritual home. This 'fad' could've revolutionized your life."

"That's what they said about communism."

"Chíngate, traidor."

Jerry bursts out laughing. "I'm a lover, not a fighter. You should know that by now."

"You think you have all the answers, Mr. College," Tavo says. "And maybe you do. But one of these days, Momito, you're going to wake up and find out you don't belong anywhere. *Then* where will you be?"

"It's a *myth!*" Jerry spits. "Aztlán is a *myth!* You still think it's 1969!"

"Whatever. You're still lost."

"You're out of your depth! If you think you can handle the truth, I can provide you with scholarly research on the mystical beliefs of the first Mexican settlers in the region, which were mostly based in Catholicism and European folklore."

"Oye, pendejo. Why did you even come over here? Just to insult me?"

As though Jerry had never stepped between Tavo and Inez at Marcus's birthday party. As though he hadn't been willing to take the knife himself.

"Forget it," Jerry says. "Forget I ever came over."

"Know what I think?" Tavo calls out to his back. His words are tinged with a perceptible new delight. "Other than the fact that you have no sense of pride? I think you're scared shitless. Of *something*."

Jerry stops and turns hard on his heel. "¿De veras? ¿De qué?"

"No sé. But whenever something's freaking you out, you start pacing. You did that even when we were kids."

"Are you trying to tell me I don't know my own mind?"

"Well, that's the thing about history, ain't it? All you got is somebody's memory. No one can prove anything ever happened."

"That's exactly right," Jerry says, closing the gap between them and, in a dizzying moment in which he has no idea what he means to do next, pinches an inch of Tavo's shirt pocket and wrenches it hard to one side. "Ow! What the . . ." Tavo clenches and jerks back. "Did you just give me a *titty twister?*"

"Chíngate." Jerry spins on his heels, digging in his pocket for the car keys.

Tavo sputters with laughter. "*Now* where you going?"

Jerry yanks open the driver's side door. "For a drive!"

"Well, drive safely," Tavo calls back with cheer. "And drive fast. I think it's gaining on you."

III

Rose Marie is in San Diego.

Or, at least, she'd *been* there. Huck shifts his numb butt on the cool cement and sneezes, dislodging a cloud of dust. Larry Villalobos had traced a single email, the only one she'd made in the past four months—God knows she wasn't answering any, but Huck had guessed correctly that her password was still "rose_red"—which had been issued from a public computer in a library and directed that her dental records be forwarded to a certain address. This address proved to be some kind of weekly hotel. Did it have thin green carpet and a kitchenette? Were her neighbors hookers and small-time drug dealers? Where was the boyfriend in all this? Why did he feel so relieved? He had to stop himself when he realized he was mentally providing an account of the incredibleness of this situation to none other than Rose Marie herself.

Naturally, Larry Villalobos had suggested following up on location. This would entail travel expenses and lodging on top of the hourly rate. "Or," he'd intoned when Huck didn't respond right away, "you could always hire someone on the West Coast."

Obviously, they had found their vacation destination. Except that unless Rose Marie's presence there was confirmed, it would be a waste of time and, of course, money.

He emerges from his hole one leg at a time back into the dining room. The world outside smells of grilled cheese sandwiches and air freshener.

Outside, the sun. It bakes him as he stands at the edge of his lawn, facing Mexico and the city grid. The low greenery bunched around the Rio Grande has faded to autumnal brown. There's a solution here, he tells himself, or at least a lesser of several evils. If he can just stop over-looking something he's sure must be in plain sight.

An older-model, maroon-colored Volvo, square as a tank, whips around the corner onto his street and turns into the driveway three doors down with a jerk, as though the parking brake has been pulled before the car has fully stopped. Then Jerry Gonzales emerges to yank at his garage door.

It doesn't budge. Jerry does an about-face for the front door as he digs through his pants pockets. When he doesn't find what he wants, he pries open the screen door and rattles the doorknob. He leans into the door-bell with his thumb. He pounds with the side of his fist.

Huck rocks in his boots. He tells himself to stay right where he is unless he's called upon. But he doubts the likelihood of that. He knows when he's not wanted, even if he's got as much right as the next guy to check out obvious neighborhood home improvement projects, and any-way, Jerry's tugging at a small window at the side of his house, which he manages to pry open partway before it sticks. He stomps to the back gate.

The fence zaps him as he reaches for the gate latch. He swears, in Spanish, snatching his hand back and winding up for a kick, but man-ages to stop himself in time. Huck picks at a sliver of food stuck in his teeth. He wonders if Jerry can hear the hum of the fence from inside the house. Earlier in the week, when he himself sidled up close enough to get a better look, he swore he could actually *taste* it.

Jerry yanks, grunting. The window doesn't budge. Jerry backs up, searches the ground, and retrieves a landscaping rock the size of a plum.

Oh, the goddamned inefficiency of it all. Huck adjusts his hat and sets off in his neighbor's direction.

"Want me to call you a locksmith?" he calls out as Jerry leans back for the windup.

Jerry's arm stutters as his head whips around. He grips the rock in his hand.

"No," he says, "No. I'm fine."

"You could wait at my house. S'hot out here."

"No, no. I . . . really." His posture is stiff. "But thank you."

Huck eyes the window. "I could take a crack at that, if you want."

Jerry pulls himself up like someone about to protest. Then he throws down his rock in disgust. "Could we try it together?"

Huck cracks his knuckles. The windowpane's metal frame feels like the edge of a hot plate against his palms.

"Jesus Christ." He grunts as the window bucks in its frame. "When's the last time you opened this thing?"

Jerry grimaces as he braces against the lower part of the pane. "It's never opened more than two inches. Ever."

"Could you try another window?"

"This is the only one that slides. The rest are crank operated."

"These goddamned old houses."

"Yup."

They heave again and fall forward against the unyielding frame.

Huck lifts the bottom of a nearby juniper shrub with his boot. There. A largish branch, devoid of foliage.

"Mind if I bust that off?"

"Go for it."

The branch makes a dry crack as Huck tears it away. "So," he says into the silence that follows. "Looks like you've had a houseguest for a while."

Jerry huffs. "My sister. Though I'm beginning to consider her a tenant."

So *that's* who's been dogging him from the roof. Huck retrieves Jerry's rock and wedges the branch against the bottom of the sill.

"Both my brothers stayed with us for a week once." He taps the branch with the rock until he can feel it jamming beneath the sill. "I was ready to ship them off to the YMCA about halfway through." He pounds. "Course," he adds dryly, "sometimes I think the same thing about my kids."

Jerry chuckles. "I think Adam would opt out of his lease early if he could."

Huck leverages. "He's off to college, right?"

Jerry inhales as though to sigh, then catches himself. "Indeed."

"Whereabouts?"

"UC San Diego."

Huck's arm turns to lead. The stick splinters. The window frame jumps the sill.

"Sorry about that," he says after a beat.

Jerry pulls the window free. "No, no. It's . . . good."

He rubs his palms together and heaves himself up, bracing a foot against the side of the house, hanging in midair as he gains an inch or three of traction, and then falling, with a galumph, back to earth.

Huck resists the urge to pick him up by the collar and set him back on his feet. Anyway, the greater part of his brain is otherwise occupied. "Here." He lowers a knee, braces his shoulder against the house, and—though Jerry's expression is one of reluctance—offers him his upturned, interlaced fingers.

It's harder than he thought it would be. Jerry grunts as Huck gets his shoulder under his knee. Something twinges in Huck's back. Jerry's gut catches against the edge of the frame, and Huck stuffs him through with his hands on his ankles, as though he was feeding him into a wood chipper.

The feet disappear. A hollow thump follows.

"Be right out," Jerry calls out in a muffled voice, and then he climbs out of the bathtub.

Huck waits until he hears the front door unlocking. Jerry appears in the doorway, blinking in the sunlight.

"Would you like to come in?" he offers after a silent, fidgety moment.

"No, no," Huck demurs.

"I . . ." It seems possible that Jerry might be in actual physical pain. "I might have a beer or two in the fridge."

"No worries. Glad we got you in." He doesn't turn to go. He only looks out toward Juárez. "So I imagine y'all will be heading out to San Diego soon."

Jerry lets out his breath. "Next week."

Huck traces the shape of the horizon. He thinks of his wife in her apartment, with her green carpet and efficiency kitchen, indifferent, apparently with dental problems, the smell of the ocean in the air. He squares his shoulders to look Jerry in the eye.

"I wonder if I might ask you a favor," Huck begins.

His words, as they leave him, sound like a command.

10

GOLD

"BUENO," SAYS INEZ. "NOW SAY it again."

She fans herself with her cowboy hat in the shade of the covered stands.

Lourdes withdraws her teeth from her lip. "I am . . . raise . . ."

"Raising."

Lourdes grips the spiral notebook on her knees. "I . . . am raising . . . my rate."

Say it like you mean it!

"*Iamraisingmyrate!*"

A whistle blows in the field before them, a wall of helmeted young men grunting as they collide with a wall of foam blocks. Lourdes presses her thumb to her notebook's curly spine. She'd objected to this meeting place, but Inez told her to relax, on Saturdays they wouldn't be in anybody's way, wouldn't she rather be away from the house? Lourdes had to admit that she would. She couldn't concentrate during the lessons at the patio table when Inez waved and blew kisses to señora Gonzales, who watched through the window with pursed lips. The park was all right for a while, but there was nowhere to sit but the unshaded, bird shit–spattered bench by the empty playground. And where else were they going to go that didn't require spending money?

Money, money. Last week when she took her mother to the clinic, the doctor said *diabetes* and handed her a stack of pamphlets and instructions. Lourdes was skeptical. Did she really need the shots every single day? More than once?

"Lourdes," Inez says sharply.

Lourdes straightens on her bench.

Are you here?

Of course.

Do you want to learn, or don't you?

Lourdes looks out at the artificial grass. What she wants is to have the magical ability to speak English without having to utter a single word to Inez.

"Yes."

Inez folds her arms.

"All right then." She nods at the blank page on Lourdes's knee. "Write it for me. What you just said."

Shouldn't I be learning lists of words? Lourdes counters. Animals? Colors? I never understand how to make the verbs.

What you need is practice in everyday, practical conversation and in basic written communication. Or would you rather learn how to describe a zebra?

"Pero—"

"Write it."

Lourdes grips her pencil.

You do know how to write, Inez asks, looking down her nose, don't you?

"Claro que sí." Lourdes mashes the pencil to the page. "I," she scratches, "Em. Resin. Mairet."

Inez peers over her shoulder.

So you've been to school.

Lourdes stares hard at her own words. Almost to the end of eighth grade, she says.

The boys on the field crash and grunt.

You know that you will have to push yourself if you want to make progress, yes? You will sometimes have to be uncomfortable.

Inez shakes her head at the pages below.

Somehow, I'm going to have to teach you how to spell.

Lourdes closes the notebook. Her face burns.

"Por Dios, mujer," Inez says. Do you want people to keep thinking Mexicans are ignorant?

Lourdes runs her tongue behind her teeth.

"Fine," Inez continues. "Tell me instead—how are your girls?"

Lourdes folds her hands into her lap. "Bien, bien."

"In English!"

"Good!"

"I don't think I've asked you how old they are. ¿Cuantos años tienen?"

"Seven. Eight. Nine. Y seventeen."

Inez lifts an eyebrow. "Now, how did *that* happen?"

Lourdes turns her head to the field.

"¿Que pasó?" Inez presses. "Why is your oldest girl so much older?"

Lourdes makes herself shrug.

"Different father?"

Lourdes struggles to keep the flush out of her cheeks. No Mexican woman would ever ask another that question. Not that way. She fans herself with her notebook until, with the faintest of motions, she nods.

Inez allows for a very long pause.

"You must have been very young," she says.

"I is . . ." Lourdes keeps her voice even. "I was . . . young. A girl."

The whistle blows in the field. She feels Inez's eyes on her.

I had a boyfriend from Juárez when I was quite young, Inez says. She chuckles in her throat. These Mexican boys. They think they are a bunch of Romeos, no?

Lourdes looks at her own short nails and her double-knotted athletic shoes and the big white goalpost framing a frog-shaped cloud, as though one of these things might tell her where to go next.

"My daughter boyfriend, he of Germany," she says finally. "Un soldado."

"Híjole. One of those Germans at Fort Bliss? She'd better be careful."

"Yo sé." The yelling out on the field doesn't seem to fill enough of the silence. "You have childrens?"

Another chuckle bubbles in Inez's throat, farther down. "Do I *look* like anyone's mother?"

Lourdes shrugs, which means *no*.

"Tell me about the DuPre kids then."

Inez's eyes are suddenly bright on Lourdes's face.

I thought you knew them, Lourdes says.

Only their mother. And that was very long ago.

Señora DuPre? Have you seen her? Didn't you say you were visiting?

I haven't had the chance yet. Now, come on—you know everyone around here, don't you? Let's start with the kids. What are they like? Considering their father is such a hick.

It's a strange feeling, Lourdes thinks. Strange not to be surprised when you finally understand you have something someone else wants.

And also that it's what you must give in payment.

"Well?" Inez presses.

Lourdes takes a silent breath.

The older two are twins, she begins. The girl, la Skyler, she's nice enough, but maybe a little hysterical. Now el Quinn is another matter. He's trying to drive me insane. And have you noticed he paints his fingernails black?

Inez chuckles. What about the little one?

La Jordan. You will never meet a stranger child. But she is supposed to be very smart.

And señora DuPre? Is she an educated woman? My information is . . . out of date.

The loose wisps of Lourdes's hair lift in a cooling wind. She is burning to ask, How do you know each other? But this is a dance, the kind with a silence at its center.

"I don't know. But she very smart too."

Inez smiles at the clouds.

I see. And why do you suppose she left?

Why does anyone leave? Lourdes says. Either because they are running from the law or because they can't find work or because they're unhappy. They think they'll be happier somewhere else.

She thinks of Simón, of course. The money orders from Albuquerque, Pueblo, Bakersfield, Yakima. God knows where.

Maybe they never really loved the people they left behind, anyway, she adds bitterly.

Inez gives her a strange, cool look.

"You should say that in English," she says finally.

Lourdes looks down at her notebook, her heart suddenly pounding, uncertain of what she's been caught at.

I can't, she admits.

Inez gives her a slow half smile.

But you will. Eventually. If you want to badly enough. You understand more than you let on, Lourdes. You are a good observer. And you think before you speak. That puts you ahead of most people I know.

Lourdes examines her knees. Inez digs into the pack at her hip.

"Do you want to see a photo of another family?"

The photo she peels from an envelope is older than Lourdes expects. Black and white. Within its frame, a group of children of different ages— ten of them—stands in three crooked lines on the steps of a porch. There, near the center, is Inez, unmistakable, a dark little twig of about ten years old with bobbed hair and a devil's grin. Beside her, a serious-looking boy, barely school age, clasps his hands behind his back like an old man.

Gingerly, Lourdes touches the tip of the boy's chin. "¿Es señor Gonzales?"

"That's Geronimo, all right. Can you tell what a know-it-all he was already?"

In the back row, among the older kids, stands a stocky boy of fifteen or so who is unlike the others. His hair is not dark. Neither is his skin.

"Mira, qué güero," Lourdes remarks. "You brother?"

"Yes, yes. That's Lalo."

"Qué pasó?" When Inez doesn't answer immediately, she can't stop herself from adding, "Different father?"

Inez gives her a sudden, sharp look. Then she bursts out laughing.

Every once in a great while, she clarifies, a redhead pops up in my family. Or so my grandmother told me.

A redheaded Chicano, Lourdes says, shaking her head.

That's the Spaniards for you. Even five hundred years later, they're still messing with the Indian gene pool.

Lourdes doesn't answer. If she did, she would have to ask what a *gene pool* is. She looks at her watch.

Inez lifts an eyebrow. "You don't need to go already?"

Lourdes slips the notebook into her bag. Medicine or no medicine, the doctor said to start with the other things—what her mother should eat, free tests she could get. She digs for the doctor's papers and finds nothing, then realizes the last place she had them in her hands.

"I forget a thing." She rises, flushing. "En la casa de los DuPre. I go before coming the bus."

"Very well." Inez turns as though to allow passage, then stops. "But I have some homework for you. Bring me a photo. Una foto de la señora. ¿Me entiendes?"

Lourdes blinks. Where am I supposed to get a photo?

Inez laughs.

From their house, of course! Whatever they've got on display. You can put it back later. I only want to see it. To see *her*.

"Pero . . ."

If anyone notices it's gone, say you bumped into it accidentally and cracked the glass, so you took it to get it replaced. Tell them I told you to. Now give me your notebook.

She thrusts out her hand.

Lourdes studies Inez's thin, knobby fingers, snapping now with impatience, and reaches back into her bag. Inez writes the long phrase down on the page with "mairet."

"Repeat after me," she instructs.

Lourdes forces herself not to look again at her watch. The lumpy words fall out of her mouth.

"You'll bring it?" Inez says, grasping Lourdes's arm. "Traígamelo."

The wind gusts and rustles. *Free English lessons*, she tells herself. Even if there might be something a little too fervent in in Inez's touch, something under that devil's grin that looks like a grimace.

III

"Híjole," Miguel says, "this thing is heavy, man."

Jordan bends her knees and lifts her end of the biosphere onto her thigh, checking the safety glass for cracks. Miguel dinged the tank's square frame as he lifted it from the curb to the bed of his truck at the pickup area in front of her school, then again when together they dropped it onto the driveway in front of the house. Now the sedimentary layers are crooked, the rotting log askew, crushing the ferns and lichens, and the beetles look agitated, and some of the brine shrimp have washed out of the pond. She'll need to refill the humidifier. "It has to be heavy because the life-forms require a lot of organic matter."

Miguel readjusts his grip. "Right. So you want it where?"

"I think in my room."

"Upstairs? No way. Tell me another place."

"Okay, okay. The patio."

The biosphere lodges itself between them in the entryway to the kitchen.

From the front door comes a knock. She looks at Miguel from the kitchen. Miguel looks at her from the hallway.

She waves the knock away. "I'll get it in a minute."

Miguel squares off, pushing the tank with his shoulder. She tugs and wiggles it through the opening.

"I hope you're mowing the lawn today," she says, panting.

"Why wouldn't I?"

"The grass looked terrible when you went on vacation. My brother wouldn't mow it."

He huffs through his nose. "Yeah, I could tell."

"So where did you go anyway?"

Miguel, pushing, makes a low straining growl in his throat that ends in a bark. He steps back. For a moment, Jordan thinks he's not going to answer. "I told you. I got married. Then I had to move."

Her eyes dart to his hand. "But you're not wearing a wedding ring."

"That's expensive, man. Anyways, I don't have to. I'm the guy."

Jordan lifts an eyebrow. "Are you a male chauvinist?"

"I'm *what?*"

Another knock echoes, this one sounding more urgent.

"Push," Jordan says.

The doorframe creaks, dislodging chips of paint, until the biosphere skids out onto the tile.

"Chingado." Miguel rubs his shoulder. He spies the ribbon. "What, you won a prize?"

A sullen wave crests within her. "First prize. But not the *grand* prize."

The doorbell rings in a quick, skittish burst.

"Maybe you should get that," Miguel says.

A key jiggles in the lock at the front door.

"Ay!" Lourdes gasps as Jordan whips the door open. "I think nobody home!"

Jordan shrugs. "We were moving the biosphere."

"I leave papers," Lourdes says, looking flushed. "Doctor papers. You see papers?" She pantomimes a search, her hand shading her eyes.

"Oh," Jordan says. "We saved them for you on top of the toaster oven." She leads Lourdes into the kitchen, where Miguel leans over the tank, tapping on the glass.

"Hey!" Jordan huffs. "The organisms don't like that!"

"Pues, ¿qué tal?" Lourdes calls out in surprise.

Miguel straightens and smiles a little, sheepishly. "Bien, ¿y tú?"

Lourdes wrinkles her nose at the biosphere. "¿Qué es *eso?*"

Miguel shrugs and says something in Spanish and laughs, glancing in Jordan's direction.

"We have to move it," Jordan says crossly.

"Mira," Miguel says. He shoves the biosphere with his thigh in front of the obviously too-narrow back door. "It ain't gonna work."

Jordan crosses her arms. "Now what?"

Miguel adjusts his baseball cap. "I'll try to think of something this week."

Jordan scowls. "Your papers are on the *toaster oven*," she calls out to Lourdes, who opens the dishwasher to shake her head at its empty interior. The dirty dishes spill over the edge of the sink.

Miguel drags the biosphere back against the wall next to the pantry.

"Come on," Jordan tells him. "We can get it upstairs."

Miguel glances at the stairwell. "Maybe if you lift it on a rope outside or something, to the window."

"Do you have a rope?"

"I got no rope."

Lourdes scoops her papers into her bag. She hesitates, then shoves Quinn's skateboard out of her way, plucks a few items from the table—a hairbrush fuzzy with Cookie Monster–colored hair, a half-full margarine tub with no lid, a large plastic bow attached to a quiver of suction-cup arrows—and spirits them out of the room.

"I could give you my allowance money," Jordan continues, "and then you could go get some rope."

Miguel rubs his forehead with his sleeve. "Maybe you should ask your dad."

"He won't have time. And my brother and sister won't do it."

"Why you need it upstairs?"

Jordan tightens the knot of her arms. "Because I want to look at it. All the time."

"M'ija," he says, laughing a little. "I'm just supposed to drive you from school. I ain't strong enough to pull that thing up anyways."

Lourdes bustles back into the kitchen.

"The three of us," Jordan says. "All three of us together could do it. Come on."

Lourdes tilts her head.

Miguel laughs and explains in Spanish.

"What are you *saying*?" Jordan growls.

"Nothing, man." Miguel pats his pants pockets until he finds some keys. "I gotta go." He catches Lourdes's eye. "¿Ya te vas?"

"No!" Jordan says, stomping with both feet. "We can *do* this!"

"It'll be okay," Miguel says, turning.

"I need *help!*" Jordan bellows. She climbs onto her kitchen stool, balling her fists. "I can't do it by myself and I need you two to help me and we can do it, we can, we can, we can!"

Miguel and Lourdes pause. The look they pass each other seems to convey discomfort, or maybe just the fact that they are both suddenly very tired.

"Okay," Jordan says, hopping off the stool. "So, Miguel, you take this side, and you'll go forward on the lower step because you can take more weight. Lourdes, take the other side and go backward. I'll go underneath and push up."

Miguel glances skeptically at Lourdes. "I think it's too heavy for her."

Lourdes gives him an offended look and stoops to lift her end of the sphere.

They grunt. They puff. They get stuck at the bend in the stairwell near the top of the landing.

"Go left," Jordan barks. "Move your hand up to the top. Now go!"

They push side by side at the doorway of Jordan's room, the tank groaning against the frame as they shimmy it through. Then the whole thing pops through and thuds on the wooden floor.

They all stand panting, hands on hips, in the hallway.

"Thanks." Jordan beams.

Lourdes shakes her head. "Me voy."

"That means you're going now," Jordan crows.

Lourdes nods at the gray skid marks they have made on the floor. "Pon el Formula 409, eh? Before I come Wednesday." She makes a spraying motion with her finger.

She pauses, her eyes lighting on Jordan's head.

"What?" Jordan says.

"El 409," Lourdes reiterates, looking away.

"Later." Miguel offers a parade-queen wave to Jordan as he touches Lourdes's elbow and steers her to the stairs.

When the door closes, Jordan can hear the clock ticking all the way from the dining room.

Downstairs, she steps onto Quinn's skateboard and propels herself into the hallway. From the hallway to the den. From the den to the living room, her foot pressing hard against the slick floor.

In the old family photo propped on the liquor cabinet, her father is grinning over his tie. The twins' smiles are so wide you can see their missing eyeteeth. Jordan is a blob in her mother's arms. She studies her mother's face, the dark, fierce eyes fixed on the camera in a way that makes it seem like she's looking right at you.

She looks for as long as she can stand the gelatinous feeling in her chest and then turns away.

It's a moment before she registers that the photo she is looking for on the piano is gone. She leans over the top. A frame-shaped outline sits in the week's layer of dust. She peeks behind to see what fell.

Nothing. She turns in a circle, but nowhere is the photo in which her mother is snugged up against her father in his suit, her mouth partway opened in a laugh as her wedding veil floats up in the wind around the piled curls on her head, the freckles that makeup couldn't cover shining on her nose. The one in which they both look very young.

She traces a finger in the dust, then drags it down to the piano keys. She stabs out a note, then slams the lid shut. She doesn't know any songs. She had refused the lessons.

She skates to the window. Lourdes and Miguel haven't made it any farther than the curb. They stand close together. Lourdes clutches her bag. There's something big inside of it, something rectangular, with hard corners. The crucifix around Lourdes's neck catches the sun and gleams gold.

On the corner of Jordan's tongue, where what she feels sometimes solidifies into words, is a tangle that tastes like the endless rubber band she found inside of one of her father's golf balls, the time she smashed one open with a meat tenderizer.

But the words don't come. All she knows is that she knows *something*. She's not entirely sure what, but she's the first one to know it. She rolls the skateboard beneath her with one foot, back and forth, back and forth, its surface sandpapery against her heel.

11

IN LOVE AND WAR

"SEE YOU LATER, GABACHO," ADAM says, scuffing the toe of his shoe in the driveway.

Quinn slips his hands to his pockets. "All right, mojado. Have a good year."

"I'll be around. Fall break. Thanksgiving. Something like that."

"Cool."

At Adam's back, Dr. and Mrs. G lunge at the open doors and trunk of their Volvo like hummingbirds at a feeder. Luggage and taped cardboard boxes and stuffed garbage bags bulge from every opening.

"M'ijo," says Mrs. G, "did you remember the pants on top of the dryer?"

Dr. G digs through the glove compartment. "Someone moved the maps. Who's got them?"

"If you wear shorts in the car," Mrs. G says, "you're going to get cold. Don't you think you should change?"

"We're going to need to stop for coffee," says Dr. G.

Mrs. G peers toward the house. "Is that the kitchen light? Jerry, I thought you said you turned it off."

"It's off." Dr. G pats his shirt pocket and the back of his pants. "Where's the keys?"

"It's *on*." Mrs. G marches to the front door.

"Shotgun!" Adam calls out. He dumps his backpack into the front seat and dives in.

"Young man," Mrs. G calls back, "I am *not* sitting in the back for the next two days!"

The Chihuahua scales a garbage bag and howls like a little girl with a broken doll.

Adam rolls down his window and rests his arm on the hot sill. He wishes he'd gotten a Coke out of the fridge on the way out. He wonders how many miles it will be until someone lets him drive. His dad circles the car, shutting doors. His mom locks and rattles the front door of the house.

"I'm warning you," she calls out as she stomps back to the car.

"In," his dad tells her with a backward stab of his thumb. He inserts himself into the driver's seat.

Adam passes Quinn a look that means, *God help me.*

The dust that poofs up from under the tires as the car backs out of the driveway takes a long time to settle, even after the car has turned the corner and is gone.

Inside Quinn's house, the air tastes of Pine-Sol. A pile of his belongings has been pushed together in the entryway—a mateless slipper, half a dozen CD cases, a child-sized Mickey Mouse hat embroidered with his name.

He retrieves his slipper from the floor. "Hey, Lourdes!"

She pauses over her mop in the kitchen when he approaches, pushing back one side of her headphones.

"Have you seen my other slipper?"

Her face is inscrutable. "Slipper?"

He holds it up.

"Slipper," she repeats, like she's trying the word on for size. "One only I see. Allá en el pantry." She looks away, too soon.

He'd left both slippers in the pantry, where someone would have to step over them to enter.

She doesn't look at him. She's mopping.

In fact, she's cleared the kitchen. The countertops are crumbless, the floors free of newspapers and old mail. Even the paper clips that have been amassing in the broken coffee cup next to the phone are gone. He dips into his pants pockets. Out come his wallet, gum wrappers, two dollars and some change, a phone number written on the back of a matchbook, and the lint he scrapes up with his fingernails. He dumps it all onto the kitchen island. Then on to breakfast. He applies peanut butter to bread in two wide swaths and drops the sticky knife to the countertop, next to the open jar.

He hears a gratifying pause and hitch in Lourdes's mopping rhythm as he exits with his repast.

In the hallway, he encounters Jordan, descending the stairs in canary-yellow pants and a rainbow-colored knit poncho. There's a sprinkle of glitter in the part of her hair.

"What's the occasion?"

"Birthday party." She adjusts each of her Brillo-pad ponytails.

"Another one?"

"Do you have something I can use as a present?"

"Why didn't you ask Dad to get you something?"

"I *did.*"

He swallows a sticky mouthful. "Wait here."

He returns from his room bearing a small plastic alarm clock shaped like a chicken.

"That's *it?*"

He presses a button. "BOK-BOK-BOK . . . WAKE UP!" it shrieks, and then follows an electronic rendition of "Jimmy Crack Corn."

Her eyes flicker to life. "Do we have any wrapping paper?"

He snatches up a newspaper piled next to the jackets, rifles through, and extracts a color grocery ad insert featuring cuts of raw meat.

Jordan unfolds it with an approving look. "The party's at noon. I need a ride."

"Right. So where's breakfast? You've been slacking."

"I was about to make french toast!"

"No you weren't. There's no milk."

"Evaporated," she counters.

He stuffs the last of his bread into his mouth. "Evaporate *this.*" His elbow hooks around her neck, the better to scrub her scalp with his knuckles.

"Quit!" she says, squirming. "Quit it, quit it, QUIT!"

He grins and releases her. She storms away.

The kitchen, when he returns to it, is empty. The bills he left on the island have been folded neatly in half, the change stacked bottom to top in order of descending size. The rest is gone, except for his wallet, which has been smeared with a broad stripe of peanut butter.

He laughs, a stuttering hiccup that makes his shoulders jerk. He wipes off his wallet with a paper towel. He drinks the last of the orange juice from the carton, has a look into the dishwasher, almost full and redolent with the aroma of day-old spaghetti sauce, and unloads the contents back into the sink.

The dog skids in and jumps up to dip his snout into the dregs of Thursday's mashed potatoes. Quinn tilts the pot toward him for a more convenient angle.

The vacuum whines to life in the living room.

"Here," he says to the dog. He skips out into the hallway, squatting down to slap his thighs. "Come here, buddy. Here, here."

Ripley lopes out. He barks and feints back when Quinn plucks a rubber ball from the floor, then lunges after it as it bounces down the hall. Quinn saunters to the dining room wall.

"Dad," he calls, knocking beside the hole. "I'm going to need the truck this afternoon."

"Gas it up!" echoes a voice.

"I need some money!"

"Check the change jar!"

Jordan pushes against the armrests of a living room wingback, her legs crisscrossed in the air.

"Where's that photo of my mom and dad?" she calls out as the vacuum powers off. "The one on the piano."

A silent moment passes. Ripley drops the ball at his feet.

"Photo?" Lourdes's voice answers. "No understand, m'ija." The vacuum roars back on.

Quinn notes the empty spot on the piano's lid, dusted and gleaming with furniture polish, the flexing of Lourdes's broad shoulders as she mows the rug. Honestly, he's impressed—he didn't realize how far she'd be willing to take things.

He scoops up Ripley's ball and sends it sailing into the living room. Ripley scrambles after it.

Lourdes's shriek is audible even over the vacuum. When he looks, he finds his dog on hind legs, front paws on the other wingback, tail wagging, ball in mouth. Lourdes stands on the seat, brandishing her duster at her tormentor as though it were a fencing foil.

He laughs so hard he makes hardly any sound at all. Like one hand clapping. A tree falling silently in the forest. He leans against the wall to hold up his hollow body, the blood echoing in his ears.

III

"And this," the interpreter says, pressing a manicured fingernail to number twenty-six on the laminated menu. "Is ocean fish, or river fish?"

Skyler faces the Russians tenting their fingers around table four. There are five of them, sweating silently in dark suits, pale as scoops of Crisco. Has anyone ever ordered the fish tacos? Perhaps this bunch is under the impression that you can eat things that live in the Rio Grande. In any case, they're staring, and not entirely above her neck.

She slinks back to the kitchen, where, Ramón, the cook, hunches over a cluster of half-filled plates. He looks up at the sound of her voice, frowning, and casts a harried glance at the walk-in freezer.

What do you mean what *kind* of fish?

"River fish," she reports to the Russians.

They respond with an outburst of displeasure.

As she replaces their water pitcher with tepid glasses filled from the tap—"Why you give ice to drink?" the interpreter grumbled—management informs her that the phone is, once again, for her, and that this isn't her personal answering service.

Carlos coughs when she answers at the register. "So am I picking you up or what?"

"Well . . . that would be great." She turns toward the pink plaster wall in the silence that follows. A painted bluebird sails over an ear of corn. "What's wrong?"

Carlos sighs. "I thought you were quitting."

She sits on the floor beside her stowed tote bag and the rolls of used register tape. "I've gotta save up some money for next year, remember?"

Meaning that, insofar as there was no way she was going to keep living at home, and insofar as her dad hadn't yet thought to ask how the college application process was going, it was entirely possible that he would also eventually forget she was living a couple of miles away, with an empty dorm-sized refrigerator.

Silence on the other end of the line.

"We could still apply to state together," she says in a rush.

He exhales in the long, unhurried way that means he's smoking a cigarette. "Uh-huh."

"Don't be mad at me. We can hang out after I get off. As long as you want. Okay?" She snorts back the stupid tears swelling in her stupid sinuses. She smells like a corn chip. "I get off at nine."

"Yo! Güera!" comes a voice from the office. "Time's up!"

"*Okay!*" she hollers back.

"Look, sorry, babe," Carlos says. "Will you bring me some tacos?"

She picks up five orders of carnitas from the kitchen after she hangs up and deposits them without eye contact before the suits at table four.

The other waitresses hover at the far end of the dining room, casting furtive glances.

"¿Son la mafia, o qué?" Josefina whispers to Raquel as Skyler skims up beside them.

Skyler leans in. "I think you mean the KGB."

In tandem, they pass her a look that means, *Shut up, princesa.*

In the kitchen, Ramón immerses a pair of whole chickens in the deep fryer. The front of his white undershirt is speckled with grease, his hands shiny with kitchen-related scars.

She and Ramón are comrades in arms. Together they toil for minimum wage inside the machine of exploitation, their soundtrack an endless loop of piped-in Mexican radio. How had she not seen this before? What if she tried to fist-bump him?

Ramón looks up from garnishing his plates, wanting to know why this girl is always *staring* at him. And *smiling.* He smacks the pickup bell.

Skyler scoops up the plated chickens and delivers them to a pair of dime-store cowboys at table five, the younger of whom calls her güerita and asks if she's married.

I have a boyfriend, she answers primly.

The cowboy grins, revealing a gold tooth.

Well then, you're not married.

Something to drink? she says, flushing as she flips open her order pad. Or just water? And do you want ice or not?

She takes her break in the walk-in freezer, shivering with a kind of fever as her breath mists in the silent, frigid air. She rakes her fingernails across a row of frozen baggies on the shelf beside her, leaving frosty claw marks on a package that resembles a human brain.

"Pescado," it reads. It offers no expiration date.

"Yo! Güera!" bellows a voice near the stockroom. For the third time today, the loudspeakers blast a cumbia whose only words she can discern are "I love you, but I love your sister more."

With a sudden flush of rage, she stuffs the fish into her bra.

Her heart pounds as she bursts back out into the restaurant and stoops behind the empty register. She tugs her bra over her waiting tote bag. The prize drops with a thud beside her UTEP application.

III

At Clarissa Fontaine's house, Jordan stands on the crunchy grass, sweating in her poncho as she watches the relay race in progress, in which each player must transport an egg to the rear wall and back on a spoon clenched between their teeth. She twirls the warm utensil in her grip. Three girls wait ahead of her in line, each of them shrieking their encouragements as Taylor Apodaca—one arm stretched outward like a wing—makes the required lap around the gurgling stone fountain in the center of the yard and barrels back toward the relay line.

On the patio table, under twists of fluttering lavender streamers, the gifts lie nestled in pastel gift bags overflowing with crisp tissue paper. Jordan's meat-covered package, ribboned with the netting from a crate of grapefruit her father bought from a truck, has been pushed to the rear.

She wonders if Clarissa likes chicken clocks. If she doesn't, Jordan is totally going to ask for it back.

"Jordan!" the girl behind her shrieks. "It's your turn! Go!"

Jordan startles. She rips off her poncho and hurls it to the grass. The spoon handle tastes of salt as she bites down; the egg pushed into her hand is sticky and warm as a stone. The two girls on the other teams are ahead of her. She hits the ground at a furious shuffle, eyes glued to the path, hands cupping the air around her egg. She gains ground. Her feet almost meet the heels of the girl before her, and then, with a nudge of elbow against elbow, she darts to the inside lane around the fountain, and she passes her. Her eyes blaze. Her jaws cramp. Her lungs burn and ache, and the girls shout "Go! Go! Jordan! Go!" and she's closing in on it, she's rounding the final lap around the fountain, and then her feet slow.

The Roman-looking statue of a woman hoisting a water pitcher regards Jordan mildly from the fountain as she comes to a stop. She lurches back into motion again, but her feet move steadily now, without urgency. She is not moved by the cries she hears behind her: "Jordan! What are you doing? Jordan! *Go!*"

She will not be hurried. Even the girl who dropped her egg on the second lap passes her.

Clarissa and the other girls stand facing her in a knot at the finish line, glowering. Then they disappear into the house.

Jordan watches them through the sliding glass door. Mrs. Fontaine has been summoned. She bends her head to listen. She offers a few words in return and shoos them back out.

Clarissa approaches with a puckered expression. "Jordan," she says in a fake sweet voice. "Do you want to play musical chairs?"

Jordan glances at her watch and shrugs.

The CD player's volume surges in the den before the chairs can be dragged into place. "Ooh, I love this song!" someone squeals. Jordan watches as the girls succumb, one by one, to Britney Spears. They sing along on invisible microphones. They pop their bony hips and they drive the bus. Jordan takes a step back onto the plastic runner traversing the length of the white carpet. And another. And another one after that.

"Well, hello," a voice chimes behind her when she backs, at last, into the kitchen.

Mrs. Fontaine sits at the breakfast bar, her Sharpie marker poised over a large family calendar.

"Oh," Jordan says. "Hi."

Mrs. Fontaine regards her calmly, her glossy blond hair twisted into a knot at her neck. "Do you need something, honey?"

"No."

"Why aren't you hanging out with the other girls?"

Jordan traces an arc on the tile with one foot. "I . . . don't like to dance."

"Ah." Mrs. Fontaine flips to October with the tips of her Creamsicle-colored nails. "Well. Your mother always said you were climbing your own trail up the mountain."

Jordan's heart quickens. "She did?"

Mrs. Fontaine flips to November. "She also said that the mountain was made out of uranium and located on a remote Pacific island. And, for that matter, that probably you would build your own mountain someday, using a robot army."

Jordan folds her arms. "She did *not*."

"Oh yes. She meant it as a compliment. Your mother is nothing if not a good judge of character." Mrs. Fontaine flips the calendar all the way to January. "Except maybe of her own." She snaps the page flat.

Jordan studies Mrs. Fontaine with one eye.

"No one has heard from her, you know. I hope your father knows that. Tell him." The marker squeaks against the page. "I also don't believe for a moment that she's run off with some other guy. I would've heard about him. You can decide whether you want to tell your father that or not."

Jordan holds very still.

"It's just not right," Mrs. Fontaine says tightly, looking up. "Is it?"

On the kitchen table lies the sheet cake, frosted in lavender and white and bearing the legend "Happy Birthday, Clarissa!!"

Her heart thumps like a hind leg of a dreaming dog.

"Could I have some cake?" she croaks.

Mrs. Fontaine caps her marker. "What, you mean right now? Before the candles?"

Jordan doesn't answer. She only stares.

Mrs. Fontaine stares back. Then she rises. With a cake slicer, she carves off a neat corner topped with a lavender flower of frosting, slides it onto a paper plate, stabs it with a plastic fork, and presses it into Jordan's hands.

"Maybe you should have some pizza first," says Mrs. Fontaine.

But the fork is already in Jordan's mouth.

III

Why, Lourdes demands of herself as she trudges up the hill. Why didn't she just tell la Jordan, *I fix you photo, I bring soon*, and be done with it?

In her bag, she digs past her notebook, the heavy sandwich baggie filled with change, her mother's prescriptions rattling in their bottles. Her fingers close on a strange, soft shape. El hombrecito's slipper. She pauses to turn it in her hand, as though it were a brick of cheese, then tosses it into the weedy vacant lot beside her.

When she reaches the house, Pilar is out in the yard, tossing stones through a plastic hoop she rolls across the hard-packed dirt. Her round face is lit up, brown skin glowing, braids black as crow feathers. Her white school blouse, as well as the knees peeking from beneath her navy skirt, are both smeared the same shade of gray.

Lourdes clenches her bag and bursts through the gate.

What are you doing? she snaps. I told you there's not enough water to do laundry again this week! And *where* is your homework?

Pilar looks up and shrugs. Lourdes stabs a finger at the front door.

Inside, Chelita and Araceli drape themselves over opposite ends of the sofa in front of the TV, watching a young woman on-screen who sings and disco dances in leather underwear on the roof of a building.

The girls don't look up. Pilar plops in between them, pouting.

Lourdes kicks a pillow someone has left on the floor.

Who said you could watch this?

Chelita shrugs.

I see. And where is your grandmother?

Araceli frowns and leans to one side. Lourdes is blocking her view.

She's sleeping, Mamá. Rosario said she would lift her out of bed when she gets up.

An embarrassing pair of holes mar the collar of Araceli's blouse.

And where is Rosario?

She went to go borrow something from her friend Maritza.

The sofa creaks. The empty tuna can that has taken the place of the missing sofa leg has begun to cave in. The TV flickers. Too many people are using the electricity on the secret wire their neighbor spliced to the houses. Beside the ironing board, the unironed clothes and dirty laundry lie side by side in their plastic milk crates.

Her mother has always said, Your life is what God has decided for you. Better get used to it.

Mamá, Chelita says grouchily. Move out of the way.

She grabs her daughter's arm.

I do not work for you! she hisses. Do you understand?

Chelita looks back at her, wide eyed.

Lourdes releases her grip and snaps off the TV.

Get up! All of you! Where is your homework? I know you have homework, because you always have homework.

The girls squirm. They steal longing glances at the television. Pilar bites the pillow in her lap.

You think I don't know what I'm talking about? Even *I* have homework.

She plunges into her bag, removes a leftover half of a burrito, smacks it down on the ironing board, and extracts her notebook. A little shudder of hate runs through her, though whether it's for English or for Inez, she can't be sure.

See? she says. Here I am, doing my homework.

She clears her throat at the page she has opened.

"I would like a twenty-minute coffee break," she announces loudly.

A grunt comes from the bedroom. Girls! Who did you let into the house?

"I want a vacation!" Lourdes shouts, her finger following the words on the page. She steps on the heel of each shoe and frees her hot feet. "I want to go to California, visit the beach, and see the ocean!"

Mamá, Araceli scolds, Are you going crazy?

No, Lourdes snaps back. I'm learning. We're all learning.

Learning what?

Repeat after me: "Where is the grocery store?"

Who, her mother thunders from the bedroom, is in this house?

"The grocery stores in Texas," Lourdes shouts back, "do not sell alcohol on Sundays!"

She snatches up her burrito and stomps across the dented pink linoleum into the kitchen, where a güero in camo fatigues sits at the table
with a half-empty beer bottle on his thigh.

"Ay," she gasps. The blood rushes into her cheeks. She whirls to the
refrigerator.

Her daughter's boyfriend coughs, although it could be a laugh.
"Buenas tardes."

She yanks open the white door and stuffs the burrito inside. The
items on the top shelf are poorly arranged. She moves them around.
"Buenas tardes."

"Instead, should I say 'hello'?" Mateo says.

She shuts the door and turns back to him.

I didn't know you were here, she says stiffly. Otherwise, I wouldn't
have been practicing my English.

Mateo's blue eyes twinkle. For once, thankfully, his very white teeth
are out of sight.

I am not bothered. You can practice to me if you want.

Does her English sound like his Spanish? The sounds that come out
of his mouth are like rubber. She shakes her head.

In English, I speak more better, he continues. But maybe you know
some word I do not.

She snorts. So Rosario left you all alone?

Only for a few minutes. I am not bothered.

She eyes his bottle. What's the occasion?

He shrugs. I am German. We always drink beer. He takes a long swig
and adds, Unless we are in Texas on Sunday.

Shut up.

You would like one? He hovers the opener attached to his key ring
over an unopened bottle.

She looks hard at the bottle, then motions him to open it.

How is it? he asks after her first gulp.

She smacks her lips as she seats herself at the table. It's *weird*.

He smiles, turning the bottle to examine the label with all its busy *f*'s
and *w*'s. It's German, he says.

Ah. *That's* the problem.

Yes, yes. I do not drink this for very long time. Today I find. Very happy I am.

She takes a long, slow swallow. Mateo. It's the name she's given him. His real name is Mattias, but Matías was her father's name. She's never understood why the German army puts its soldiers with the American army at Fort Bliss. Maybe they practice their wars in the desert together. The young man who has been appearing at her table for months has a faraway look in his eye now.

You don't *look* happy today, she says. Not exactly.

I don't?

The smile crosses his lips again but falls away.

He says, I think I am sick for home.

She swirls her own bottle and takes another swallow. Does she want to know? Not really.

Tell me about your home, she says.

He shifts in his seat. She waits.

It rains, he says. A lot. Fall and the winter and spring, it rains, and the skies are gray.

She leans on her elbow.

This is near Frankfurt, he continues. Many, many ugly apartments. But outside of city is forest, very beautiful, very old. I do not see it now four years.

She leans. The silence blooms.

Are they going to send you? she says finally. To that war they're having with the Arabs?

He shrugs.

They might.

Something thuds beside them. Rosario shakes out her arms in the doorway, a plastic four-liter container of water at her feet.

I'm back, she announces. She eyes them both, her expression sweetening as she turns to Mateo. Ready, my love?

Lourdes tips her chin at the water. Who gave you *that*?

Rosario straightens, her ponytail swinging, her tea-with-milk complexion glowing with sweat. Always the lightest of her girls. The pretty one.

Nobody. I *bought* it.

Lourdes raises her eyebrows. This, when usually they fight over every last cent of Rosario's maquila earnings? I want clothes, Rosario complains, I want to go out, it's boring here, to which Lourdes provides the obvious answer: Then I guess you don't want us to eat.

I don't suppose the girls have had lunch, she says now.

I made frijoles, but nobody wanted any yet.

Are you working tomorrow?

Rosario tosses her head. When am I *not* working? She makes sarcastic, wire-sorting hand motions, kisses Mateo on the check, tugs him up from the table. Mamá, how do you say, "vámonos"?

Home by eleven, Lourdes says. She looks at Mateo when she says it. It's a disgrace, this gringo way of going out without a chaperone. She looks to Rosario. "Let's go."

"Let's go!" Rosario yanks Mateo toward the door.

He meets Lourdes's eye just before he ducks under the doorway.

She is safe with me, he says, with seriousness. He puts on his army hat and is tugged out.

Lourdes breathes in the silence that follows them. Then, from the back of the house, a shout: I don't care *who* you are—just get me out of bed!

Lourdes remains in her seat. The will of God. Quite frankly, it seems more likely to her that God, being busy, overlooks certain lives. The plans get stuck on his desk.

Let her eldest daughter believe. Let her believe that a man will solve all her problems. That he will change who she is. That he will never leave her, and that it wouldn't be for the best, no matter if he is kind. For where there is love there is pain, as the saying goes, and her daughter will learn this soon enough.

But how interesting, in the meantime, how strangely wonderful, to see what Rosario's faith makes of her.

Lourdes tips her beer to her lips. Where there is love, there is pain. This she learned long ago. Later there was Simón. No matter if she never truly loved him. There are many kinds of love. It is very hard to be the only parent. She closes her eyes to rest them for a moment. She finishes her beer and gathers her empty bottle and the one that lies opposite and sets them together by the sink. Then she rises to get her mother.

12

LONE STAR

MARCUS'S KNEES ACHE AS HE crouches in the dirt. The stand of creosote that shields him tickles his nose; his pulse throbs under his eyes. For a moment, he feels his weight almost give way, gravity tugging him backward on the slope toward the arroyo. Then a dark shape crosses his path, and he springs up and claps a hand to its warm chest.

"Siéntese," he whispers.

The shadow gasps and obeys, raising a poof of dust as it meets ground.

"Manos en la cabeza."

Another shape moves in the scrub. Marcus sinks back down under the weight of his belt, the baton thumping his thigh. Up. A heartbeat against the palm of his hand, a flinch. Down, to the ground. Somewhere out across from him, closer to the riverbank, Peña's voice barks out, "Alto! Migra!" Marcus holds himself taut until he sees him—a silhouette herding two others with the beam of his flashlight—then prompts his pair of shadows back onto their feet.

"¿Tienen armas?" Peña asks the bodies within the twin circles of light. He looks into each downturned face until a pair of eyes meets his own, every head shaking *no*. "¿Tienen identificación?" He pats his uniform pockets with his free hand for his notepad.

They seat the group on the ground in front of a knobby stand of cholla. Four guys this time, all of them young enough that Marcus could have gone to school with them, in jeans and sweatshirts, baseball caps, athletic shoes crusted in dirt. Knapsacks dangle from their shoulders.

"¿Nombre?" Peña asks the closest one. "¿De donde es usted?"

"Michoacán."

Are you sure? Peña prods. We'll find out if you're from Honduras or wherever.

"Michoacán," the guy repeats.

What about you? Peña asks the next guy. The same?

The scrub rattles in a cooling breeze. Marcus zips up his jacket. In the distance, the massive electric Lone Star on the flank of the Franklins makes a brilliant round blob. Apparently, Inez had left every light blazing on the bottom floor of the house all night long. So said his dad this afternoon when he called, just before they'd loaded up the car to cart Adam away.

And you? Peña asks the guy at the end of the line. What's your story?

My story? drawls a voice. Once upon a time, there was a guy who ran out of money.

Marcus cracks a smile. So does Peña. The guy returns a helpless grin, full of crooked teeth.

I hear . . . Marcus begins, then tries again. I heard that story before. How does it end?

It ends, Peña answers, after a short drive through the countryside, at the Zaragoza Bridge.

Well, I've always wanted to see your country.

Peña titters. The guy's nearest companion turns to him wearily. "Cállate."

The guy shrugs and keeps grinning.

Marcus glances over Peña's shoulder at the notepad. "¿Como se llama, hombre?"

"Cárdenas."

"Mucho gusto, Cárdenas. You're a real joker, you know that?"

The guy makes the slightest of bows. "Un placer, oficial."

Marcus digs in his pocket for the key to their vehicle. "I got it." He ascends the swell of the land at their backs where the Bronco lies hidden, the radio awaiting his call.

Afterward, he breathes for a moment in the dark cab, listening to the crackle of the receiver. On the phone, his father had asked him to check on Inez while they were gone. "Pop in on her," he instructed. "But for

God's sake, don't be predictable. Keep her on her toes. The safety of our home depends on it." He was not joking.

Something on the ground catches Marcus's eye. There. Poking from the scrub. He squints.

He takes care not to slam the truck door. The earth crunches under his feet as he crosses the distance. A pale, rounded shape comes into view in the beam of his flashlight. When, finally, he stands over the thing itself, all he can do is look down and down.

He returns to the Bronco and pulls it around.

"Took you long enough," Peña says when he kills the engine.

Marcus doesn't look at him. He only steps out and up to the guys who wait by the cactus.

Did you guys do that? he asks, tipping his head in the direction from which he came.

There's a shuffling, a passing of looks.

Do what? Cárdenas answers.

Did you kill a sheep?

We didn't kill any sheep, oficial.

Marcus says, There's a dead sheep over there. Blood everywhere. And its neck . . . on its neck . . . something that looks like . . . teeth.

Peña snorts a little.

"What, like from a coyote or something?"

"Maybe if it was a saber-toothed coyote."

"Mountain lion?"

"Jesus, I dunno, man. Wouldn't it eat what it killed? Plus, the head was like, fresh, but the rest of it was all shriveled up."

"Ooh," Peña says, wiggling his fingers. "Freaky."

Marcus whaps open the back door of the Bronco. "¡Vámonos!"

He can't resist driving past the scene of the crime.

"Whoa," Peña says, craning his neck out the window.

"You see?" says Marcus.

"Híjole, oficiales," comes the voice of Cárdenas from behind the plexiglass. If I had seen something like that, I would've eaten it.

"Cállate," mutters another voice. "Pendejo."

I hope you catch it, Cárdenas continues. There's some dangerous shit trying to get across the border out here.

Peña cracks up. Marcus can't stifle his smile. This whole thing is ridiculous, and so is everyone, and not just right here in this truck.

All right, all right, Marcus calls to the back seat. That's all.

"You mean 'es suficiente,'" Peña tells him dryly.

He passes Peña an equally dry look. The Lone Star on the mountain is like a distant porch light.

That's enough, he calls out. He faces front and hits the gas, barreling into the darkness.

13

THE SEASIDE MANO

"YOU KNOW, THERE'S THIS SAYING." Jerry draws a solemn breath. "Cuando de vista te pierdo, si te vi ya no me acuerdo." He looks to his son. "Did you catch that?"

"Um." Adam locates an itch on his elbow. "When you lose your view, I won't agree with you anymore?"

"Long absent, soon forgotten." Jerry pauses. Then he breaks into a devilish grin.

"Don't listen to him," Chavela says, blowing her nose into a tissue she pulls from her sleeve. She steps away from the footboard of an unmade twin bed to crush their son in her arms. Through the open window wafts the faintest whiff of the sea.

Jerry waits for Adam to extricate himself, then drops an arm around his wife.

"Mom." Adam reaches past Jerry's arm to Chavela's opposite side, sandwiching her between them. "I'll be back at Thanksgiving. Remember? That's, like, only two months from now." With a finger, he draws a smiley face in the air before her.

The door opens. In comes the roommate—a jocular young man from Pasadena, on a wrestling scholarship, whose acquaintance, along with that of his parents, was made this morning over the complimentary cheese danishes in the lobby. They'd described their passion for off-roading in all-terrain vehicles. Jerry now nods his greetings, claps a hand to his son's shoulder to murmur his wishes of luck, and with the lightest touch he can muster, herds his wife from the room.

He zigzags his way back to the hotel as Chavela turns away from him to gaze through her window.

Everywhere are sailors. Sailors in their white Popeye suits and Dixie-cup hats, sailors with the demeanor of Mardi Gras revelers waiting for the parade to begin.

He firms his grip on the steering wheel. California traffic, he has learned, is conducted at the speed of a silent movie, as though everyone is racing an ambulance. He turns off the air conditioner, because it's making him too cold, and cracks the window. Too muggy. He squints at the hazy sky. His Texas-strength sunglasses make his field of view too *dark*. He tosses them onto the dashboard and turns on the radio.

"Don't," Chavela says, as strains of The Doors fill the car.

"Oh, come on. It's only for a few minutes."

"I hate this music."

"Then find something else."

"There *is* nothing else." She snaps it back off.

He swerves and stomps the brake as a woman with three sports-uniformed kids in the back seat cuts him off. For the past two days, as the dog yapped and mewled every forty miles to be let out, his wet, rancid, miniature rawhide bones perfuming the car; as the desert gave way, finally, into farmland where they observed in objective silence the rows of late tomatoes and strawberries tended by brown people in big hats and long sleeves; as the faint blue smear of the Pacific finally appeared like a great mirage on the horizon, they have kept the conversation brisk. For how better to capture the last moments of their son's proximity than by racing alongside his quick thoughts? How else to fill the enormity of the space that might otherwise overtake them?

And now, here comes the space. He glances at his wife. They are officially unencumbered. Not even Inez is here to elbow between them.

Except that, with the radio off, it's too damned quiet.

He glares at the line at the turn signal ahead. "Should I sing instead?"

He feels the cool, silent look she gives him. "Actually, I was wondering what you want for dinner."

He shrugs. "Chinese maybe."

"That sounds terrible."

"Fine. Hamburgers."

"Ugh."

"Mexican!"

"They make it *wrong* out here."

True—when they first visited the school with Adam, they had stopped for takeout at Tacos Muy Macho, and despite the fact that he did understand they were visiting a coastal city steeped in Spanish and Indigenous history, he was unable to reconcile himself to the idea of fish in a *taco*. What's more, a taco served in a flour tortilla, which was, in fact, an abomination.

The turn arrow goes red just as he pulls to the front of the queue.

"Then what do you *want*?"

"I don't *know*. What do *you* want?"

She presses her hands between her knees. A plaintive note sounds at the bottom of her voice. An opening. He might press a key that backs things up a few spaces.

The problem is that he can smell the ocean. It rankles something in his blood. Something, in fact, has been building in his bloodstream for days, growing with every mile they have drawn closer to the Pacific. His wife looks out across the boulevard, lost in both past and future, feeling sorry for herself.

"Chinese," he mutters.

Silence. Then, a voice thick with chill: "I guess we could eat at the hotel."

He leans to one side, trying to see to the front of the line. "Perhaps we should just drive. We should drive until we see something that looks good."

"Not until we stop at the hotel. Kiko needs to go for a walk."

The bread delivery truck behind them delivers a brassy honk. He's sitting through the green arrow.

"How many potty breaks does that dog need in a day?" he snaps as he floors it.

"His bladder," Chavela answers hotly, "is very small."

He misses the turnoff to the hotel.

"You missed the turnoff to the hotel!"

Jerry grips the steering wheel. "No I didn't. I'm going back a different way."

"Como que 'No I didn't'? Give me a break."

"We don't always have to do things your way. ¿Me entiendes?" He turns on the next block and encounters a one-way street at the spot where he intended to double back.

"Or you could just admit that you don't know where you're going. Turn left." She tips her chin at the upcoming intersection. "Allá."

He passes three more streets in grim silence, pulls over, makes a six-point turn, and heads back in the original direction.

Chavela's fists clench on her thighs by the time he pulls into the driveway in front of the lobby.

"Go walk the dog," he tells her. "Have whatever dinner you want. Me voy."

She flares her nostrils at him. "¿Adónde vas?"

"¡Por un paseo!"

She's still standing in the driveway as he peels out.

He is sucked into the vortex of a mass high-speed chase of unknown motivation or destination as soon as he merges onto the freeway. He flips up his sun visor, the better to glare at the traffic that whips past him. How can anyone *think* at this speed? Where the hell is he anyway?

He is aware, of course, of the historical attractions that lie in every direction around him. He is nominally acquainted with the coastal missions, those lovely, severe, whitewashed monuments to frontier Christianity. He knows there's an Old Town at the center of this city that speaks of several centuries' worth of Spanish colonialism. He's fairly sure the local Indian tribes have been all but obliterated. For the record, he never had anything against politically aware Mexican Americans embracing their Indian heritage. If Tavo were beside him now, exercising his perpetual obsession, he would tell him that. You want to liken the migration of Mexicans to the American Southwest—before and after the U.S. occupation—to an instinctive return to a mythical Aztec homeland that legend conveniently locates to the northwest of Mexico? Fine by me. But *El Plan Espiritual de Aztlán*? It was the codification of metaphor into a political policy. Brainchild of old-school Chicano Power conferences. *This land is our land.* In having been denied a place in history, they would create a new history. They would blur the boundaries of history and mythology. They would design a creation myth.

Alongside him now, the rows of eucalyptus trees, the massive, looming gray towers of the naval ships parked in their ports. The Pacific, stretching to the other side of the earth, monstrous.

He exits and ends up in La Jolla.

Mansions on cliffs perch above him. Roads wind. The Volvo chugs toward a quaint business district lined with old-fashioned lampposts, pastel buildings housing Armani and Prada boutiques and restaurants where patrons sit on patios stirring drinks, their sports cars waiting at the curbs. Everywhere, the Spanish-style balconies explode with pink and purple bougainvillea.

He turns onto the grounds of a green and manicured park. He would like to turn back, but he has entered a parking lot with no outlet, and the air smells of salt; he is pulled by a terrible and magnetic force.

He steps out of the car.

Here he is, in front of the goddamned ocean. His sandals sink into a damp stretch of sand. The section of beach beside him has been cordoned off with a length of what looks like crime scene tape, behind which lies a disinterested phalanx of obese sea lions. He shuffles closer. A few lift their heads to belt out, "Ork ork ork." The water before him is vast. Vast like the skies over Texas. Infinite in the way of a mirror facing a mirror. In the distance, the water's brilliant surface is dotted with sailboats.

How very strange it would be, to grow up *sailing.*

He blinks back the dizziness unspooling at the center of his head and repositions his uneven feet. It is his understanding that illegals have been known to slog out into this water in the middle of the night, to the shallow spot just outside of Tijuana where the metal fence erected by the U.S. government peters out. Then they swim their way across the border into Imperial Beach. How they manage to resist the tidal pull on the liquids that move through their own bodies—how they function in the face of so much physical beauty—is beyond him.

Long absent, soon forgotten. He draws in a lungful of salty air and thinks of his son, lounging in his dorm room with the wrestler from Pasadena. His other son, who lies in wait near a smaller, sleepier body of water. His wife, clipping a leash to a collar with her small, sturdy hands, sitting down to dinner with a dog. He thinks of the task he was charged with before he even set out on this journey, which had nothing and everything to do with why he was standing here before the ocean—a task that, of course, he could just ignore. He could say he didn't have enough time, he lost the address, he couldn't find it.

The sea lions say, "Ork ork ork ork."

His nudges the rope with his thigh. "Is this to keep me safe from you, or you safe from me?" he asks the groaning heap of blubber beside him.

A gargling sound is the answer, a trembling snoutful of whiskers.

He blinks at the creature who meets his gaze. "What should I do?"

It shames him, the terror he hears in his own voice.

The sea lion regards him with velvet eyes, chewing the air, and offers a thunderous snort.

Jerry looks out to sea. He shakes the droplets of snot from his leg and returns to the car.

In his glove compartment is a map, and in his wallet, an address in Huck DuPre's blocky hand, scrawled on the back of a Costco receipt.

He turns back toward the city. Back onto the treacherous freeway, past the high trees and art deco buildings of Balboa Park, past Mission Beach and its slowly spinning Ferris wheel, past the captive whales of SeaWorld, back onto a wide thoroughfare he mentally christens Carne Asada Boulevard, and somehow, he doesn't lose his way—it's as though a path has been cleared for him.

He idles at a traffic light, where a group of pedestrians in front of a donut shop are speaking Portuguese. Two men wait hand in hand for the light to change. He tries to look, politely, elsewhere.

The lettering on the Seaside Manor Apartments is missing an "r," thus making it the "Seaside Mano."

He idles at the curb, studying the cracked white stucco of the façade, the worn wooden railings above the concrete stairs. *Why?* he asks himself. Why did he agree to this? It's not too late to return to his hotel room with a box of takeout and a conciliatory attitude. He owes his neighbor no favors. He can wave goodbye to the Seaside Mano.

But he's not here for his neighbor's sake. He can admit that much to himself. He kills the engine.

He ascends the stairs slowly. It's a two-level complex, six identical units sitting atop six more, like a prison cellblock. He passes a door where someone is having an angry Portuguese phone conversation.

All Huck had wanted him to do was check the mailbox. If he was up for it, Huck had added, he could hang out for an hour at some convenient time, watching to see if she emerged. If he was *really* up for it, maybe he could inquire discreetly among the neighbors. All he wanted was the slenderest thread of information.

But the name slot on the mailbox in question was blank. Of course, one would expect that from someone who's hiding, Jerry reminds himself as he glides across the landing, though there's always the chance the blank is concealing the presence of more than one person. Huck had alluded to that. He'd alluded, but the moment he had, Jerry somehow knew it to be untrue. Or just inaccurate, undercomplicated. He has no explanation for this hunch. Nor is he sure when he decided what to say: *Hi. Don't freak out. I'm just the messenger, I was already in town, I'm doing Huck a favor.* He will say, *Your family is worried about you.* He will say, *Would you like me to convey a message?*

He might even ask, *Perhaps we could get a cup of coffee?* Unless she offered one herself.

He could counter with dinner.

He holds his breath in front of the door to number eleven and knocks. And waits.

And waits some more. And knocks.

The door to number ten swings open.

He steps back to face an elderly Asian woman in a skirt, sneakers, and knee-high pantyhose who is aggressively wielding a large wooden spoon.

The woman regards him impassively. "She moved out."

"I see." He shuffles, unable to find the proper standing position. "Are we talking about Rose Marie?"

"Eh?"

"Attractive woman. Blond. Brown eyes. My age. Or . . ." He reflects for a moment, calculating, capitulating. "Actually, a bit younger. Ten years, perhaps."

The woman sniffs. "Rosie. She left a month ago."

Hope flickers within him. "Do you know where she went?"

"I don't know nothing about her. She was quiet. No visitors. She helped me move in my couch. I haven't lived here forever, you know."

He feels himself deflating.

"Of course," he says. He nods in a way meant to encompass the whole building. The world. "No one lives here forever."

"Drunk man crashed into my house and drove right through. Lucky I'm alive. My son has only a studio apartment. *And no couch.*"

Behind her, he glimpses yellow-and-brown plaid furniture, a thin green carpet. "I'm sorry about your couch."

"Why you want Rosie anyway? You police?"

"No."

"She owe money?"

"Not to me."

The spoon relaxes slightly in her grip. "You're her brother then."

He lifts an eyebrow. Maybe, he thinks, we all look alike to her. "No."

"Husband?"

"No, no, no. Not that."

"Lover." She refolds her arms, with firmness.

He blinks. Snorts a little, though it's really just a soft puff of air.

From some cistern within, the one that stores things absent or just put away, comes the distant sound of his voice.

"Yes. Something like that."

The smell of salt fills the air.

SHE IS WHAT SHE DOES and what she does is drive.

She drives, across days, through weeks. She drives even when the car, despite repair, begins to fall apart. How natural this seems to her now, how unsurprising. She watches calmly from inside a Blake's Lotaburger in Pojoaque, New Mexico, as a teenage girl with a milkshake in her hand backs into the Lexus in the parking lot with a pickup truck and dislodges the bumper before screeching away. Hailstorm outside of Salina, Colorado. Bogged in the mud outside a gas station in Ogden, Utah, until twelve pounds of kitty litter gives her the necessary traction. All things paid for, naturally, in cash. Sun scouring everything it touches all the way through Pocatello, Idaho, and into the Big Sky Country, deepening her freckles through the windshield. Against her leg, her finger presses a spot on the map, though it strikes her as more of a suggestion. She drives, riding the engine's new rattles and growls, and a part of her slips from the car itself to watch her own progress. She soars beside herself, casting shadow on the land below.

14

THE CAVERNS

HUCK SWINGS HIS HAMMER—A TEN-POUND Kobalt steel sledge with a thirty-four-inch fiberglass handle—and with a satisfying crack, sends the armrest of his rocking chair sailing into the living room wall. The remains of both end tables lie at his feet, along with a flattened metal umbrella stand, the silly antique pedestal meant to boost a single vase or plant but that had only ever showcased a doily.

He squats beside the fireplace and tugs at the flue. But the flue doesn't budge.

He hefts the kindling outside. The weather is as weird as it's been all week—the sky gray and lumpy with clouds, the air so still you could build a tower of playing cards on the hood of a car, not the slightest hint of moisture. He knocks off the trash can's lid with his knee. A San Diego vacation would have been nice about now.

"No clues?" he'd asked when Jerry arrived on his doorstep. "Nothing at all about where she might have headed next?"

"None whatsoever." Jerry's comb-over was askew, his hands rammed into his pockets as though he had just endured an unpleasant doctor's exam. "At least, not according to Mrs. Kim." He shuffled. "I'm sorry."

"No, no," Huck said. "You did me a huge favor, and I appreciate that."

He'd retreated to his dining room, where he widened the hole in the wall enough that he would no longer have to stoop and turn sideways to enter. Then he demolished Rose Marie's International Santa Claus figurine collection with a meat tenderizer.

Now he waves to Lourdes, who loiters at the end of the driveway as he smashes a lamp. From the corner comes the chugging of a low-riding pickup truck.

He reaches the curb just as Jordan slides out through the passenger door.

She frowns. "You're home again."

"Sure am." He lowers his head into the cab before she can slam the door shut behind her. "Hey, Miguel. I wonder if you might help me with something."

Miguel looks right, then left. "Well . . . I gotta go do a lawn."

"This'll only take a minute."

He leads the way to the house.

Jordan skips to keep up. "Are you home because we're finally going on vacation?"

"Sure. Eventually."

"Where? When are we leaving?"

Inside, Huck nudges aside the jackets and old newspapers beside the door. He has not yet reported the latest findings to the kids. The glimmer of hope struck him as too cruel to share.

"We'll figure it out."

"Dad," she says, but he's already turned down the hall.

The wooden armoire rests against the poorly placed wall that borders the kitchen.

"I could use some help moving this to the entryway," he tells Miguel.

Miguel eyes the cabinet with distrust.

"Dad," Jordan says. "You've been saying we're going somewhere for *months*."

"Well now." He squares off against the armoire's short end and feels around for a grip. "Not much I can do about that if nobody's figured out where your mother is yet, now can I?"

"But you're not even getting ready!"

"Honey." He waves Miguel around to the armoire's opposite side. "Do you think you could go do your homework for a while?"

"Dad. We need to make a *plan*."

He turns to face her and her jutting chin. The coffee-colored eyes. That orange-red *hair*.

"What?" Jordan huffs.

"Go watch TV or something!" He turns his back. "Let's do this." He repositions himself, feeling around the armoire's back for a better handhold, staggering against the resistance of Miguel's wiry braced shoulder on the other side. "And sorry. Things have been a little nuts around here."

"Dad!" Jordan hollers from the living room, "Where's all the *furniture?*" They heave the behemoth away from the wall.

"Since my wife left, I mean," Huck puffs. Miguel wobbles. Huck swings his end out, puts himself in the reverse position, waddles backward. "So. The rides home going okay?"

Miguel grunts. "Yeah!"

"How's life in general?"

"Good!"

They lower the armoire in the entry. It clunks against the wall, then topples forward like a drunk.

They shout as they rush to catch it.

"Goddamned old, uneven wooden floors," Huck adds as they leverage it back into place.

He waves his thanks as Miguel darts back out the door. At his back remains an armoire-shaped silhouette, ringed with a grayish crust.

He scrapes with a quarter from his pocket. If he wanted to take matters more firmly into his own hands, he could go to California himself. He could do his own grilling of the neighbors. He could contact the California Highway Patrol, insist they keep a lookout for a certain Lexus. He could call other state police. All of them. He could fire his private investigator, hire another one, leave tomorrow for a random destination on a vacation that had no purpose except to vacate the present circumstances, they could try Carlsbad Caverns again, maybe this time they'd actually make it inside, it'd be worth it.

Or he could install a garden. Granted, he'd have to learn about planting and fertilizing and pest control, so maybe he should just repaint. Or he could clean out the garage. Jesus Christ, he tells himself. Move. Get busy and stay busy. Get the electric bill paid, get the garden hose off the lawn, get the kids into college. It's time to set this house in order, because every person is responsible for his or her own happiness, he still believes that, and when Rose Marie came back, *if* she came back, she could decide whether or not she deserved to see him destroying what she loves, and it would be good for her, or maybe not, he actually doesn't know which, he knows only that he wouldn't mind a cold Dr Pepper, because his throat is closing up and his sweat has pasted his shirt to his chest and he has to hold himself up against his bare wall to keep from collapsing onto the floor because maybe he's going to die, right here, right now in his hallway on the Navajo-style area rug, which would be a goddamned shame, because he's kept it together this long, and so maybe he should reconsider this remodeling business before he gets in too deep, before it gets too weird, before anyone catches him here trembling against a wall with hot tears in his eyes.

The armoire topples over behind him with an ear-ringing crash.

He puts his foot through the wall. In the kitchen, Lourdes drops something that breaks.

His cell phone rings in his pants pocket.

"Yello?"

It's Mendoza.

He rests his head against the wall. "Does the term 'afternoon off' mean anything to you?"

"Huck." He hears the rattle in Mendoza's breath. "The peso just dropped."

No sound but the ticking of the dining room clock.

"How bad is it?" he hears himself say.

"It's not the flaming meltdown we had in '94. But it's bad enough."

"Do they know?"

Mendoza fumbles the handset. In the background, the usual electrical-mechanical ruckus has slowed. A rumbling of voices has taken its place. Many voices. Then comes the shouting.

"They know."

Somewhere within Huck, a light flares in a lantern. He lifts his head.

"Get out of there," he says. "Get the managers and admins out. Get back across the border. I'll be right there."

Outside, the sky is heavy with clouds. No rain.

III

Jordan turns up the TV as her dad roars out of the driveway. At the top of a fresh page in her social studies notebook, she writes, "Plans."

Who she should show these plans to, she cannot say. The twins are not home. The twins are a lost cause. The twins have better things to do and they do not care.

Her mother was the only one who would know what to do.

Like at Carlsbad Caverns. Which Jordan had been dreaming of, in the back seat—because it was *her* birthday trip, *her* idea, the vast underground chambers were waiting, slime-slick with stalagmites and mildew and bats—until thirty miles outside of town, when something popped from the brush and staggered across the blacktop, and her father swore at it and swerved as one of the tires popped, and the truck spun around and smacked into the guard rail.

The engine hissed. The dog howled.

It was hot. They opened their doors and slid out with liquid limbs into the encircling horizon. The highway was empty, the low scrub on either side broken only by a few tentative stalks of ocotillo and the brown, distant, indifferent mountains. The sky was a vast, throbbing dome.

A man stood immobile on the blacktop. He had on a baseball cap and a backpack and no sunglasses.

Her father folded his arms at him. "Thanks. A *lot*."

"Huck." Her mother stepped up. "You leave him alone."

"Oh, is he a personal friend of yours?"

Skyler lifted her dreads to fan the back of her neck and muttered, "I bet that guy is totally high."

Quinn sighed. "Did you bring the Game Boy?"

"What do you have to say for yourself?" her father called out. "¿Habla inglés?"

The guy had a weird smile on his face. Like he was about to sneeze, or was remembering a very strange dream. His knees went loose beneath him, and he sat down in the road.

"Agua," he said.

Her mother said, "Oh shit," and leapt for the cooler at the back of the truck.

Jordan retreated to the truck's shadow. If *she* stumbled onto the road and made someone crash, she would apologize for messing up their birthday. In her tote bag, she had a biography of Marie Curie, a small folding chessboard, two peanut butter sandwiches, three pencils, a pad of graph paper, and her cell phone. *For emergencies only*, her mother had said when she'd presented it to her, though no one asked her to make a call now. Not that she could find a signal. Her heart beat in her throat. She extracted a pencil and wrote at the top of the pad: "Plan A."

Her mother inched up to the man in the road, extending an opened can of RC Cola.

"We don't have any agua," she said. "Except for some that's already been in the dog bowl."

The man reached for the can very slowly. As though it were a dream can.

Her mother backed away.

"See if the truck starts," she said. "We should offer him a ride."

Her father straightened. "You want to put a stranger in the truck with us?"

"But what'll he do out here?"

The man in the road emptied the whole can into his mouth. The soles of his feet were visible through the holes in his shoes.

"Have you stopped to think about what it would mean to get tangled up in that guy's mess? What about when we hit the checkpoint?"

"Oh, of course," her mother said. "This is all about *you*."

Jordan sketched out a schedule for cola consumption, a sandwich ration, and a scheme for extracting gasoline from the truck's tank for use as a flare after dark, while her parents argued about whether to walk or flag down a passing vehicle.

"That gas station was two miles back!" her father said. "But if you want to go, fine. Go. Just take a damned cola with you. Skyler, ask this guy what his plans are."

Skyler looked at the guy and turned red, as though the words were stuck in her mouth.

Her mother offered the man another cola, then opened it for him when he couldn't make his fingers close around the pop tab.

Jordan bit off the rest of the eraser. It was satisfyingly chewy and tasted a little like those rubber balls dispensed from gum machines.

"What the hell?" Skyler whispered. "Are you eating a *pencil?*"

"Jordan, come on."

Jordan looked up with surprise to find her mother standing before her. "What?"

Her mother's hair was coming down from its french twist in limp chunks. Beads of sweat had formed on her upper lip; her freckles stood out on her cheeks like drops of blood. "You're coming with me."

Jordan's heart did a strange tap dance. "Just me?"

"Are you out of your skull?" her father said. "You're not taking her anywhere!"

The twins jiggled their eyeballs at each other. Then they jiggled them at Jordan.

Jordan swallowed. The heat shimmered the air. Her father stood facing her, willing her still with the fists he pressed into his hips. Her mother gazed at her steadily as though into her very center. Her mother held out her hand.

The whoosh from the approaching 18-wheeler turned their heads. It let out a throaty honk and swerved around the man in the road, then again around her father as it pulled to the shoulder.

"Jesus Christ!" the driver said as he swung down with bright, crazy eyes. "The hell's that guy doing out there?"

Ripley whined and panted. Jordan's heart beat in her head as she inched away from the truck.

"Mom." She extended "Plan A."

Her mother read it in silence.

"My God," her mother said, peering over the top of her sunglasses. "This is . . . impressive."

"I know."

Her mother's eyes made a fierce flash, but a smile lifted a corner of her lips.

"Good."

Her father stooped to rub Ripley's ears before he hoisted himself into the cab of the semi. "If I'm not back in half an hour, send out the Saint Bernard."

"If you're not back in an hour," her mother said, dropping sideways into the passenger seat, "we'll drink the Saint Bernard's blood."

The driver said, "Screw it, I'm giving that guy a ride. He stays out here any longer, he'll be dead."

Jordan looked to her mother, to see if this was true.

Her mother popped back onto her feet and said, "Oh *shit*." The man was face-planted on the blacktop.

Her mother took his pulse on his neck and whapped him on the cheek and snapped at Quinn when he wouldn't help her roll him over. She pushed on the man's chest a long time. Then there were radio communications, and more waiting, and trucks, and uniforms, and the snap of a blanket unfolded, and a whole lot of silence and swallowing.

Now Jordan wonders what her mother would do if she were here to see their dad kicking down the walls. If her mother were here, would he be kicking down the walls to begin with? Would she say, *Huck, for God's sake, stop studying that child! Do you think she's going to sprout wings and fly?* Her mother, who was still lost, who apparently had a whole other secret mother and father if you believed Larry Villalobos, but whatever.

She bites off her pencil eraser. The "Plans" page is still blank.

III

As far as Huck can tell, from his vantage at the high point on the road leading into the industrial park, the crowd that has massed around the maquila is only growing.

Which means that it's not just his maquila that's in on this. It's a bunch of them.

He stands with one foot outside the truck. People are out of their smocks, sitting on the asphalt, milling around the entrance. Already, they're hanging their hand-painted banners and handing out signs. He can taste the dust in the air. Time to go home, make a report, and await further instruction. Or castigation. Company policy in the event of a walkout is for administration to stay put at their desks until closing time.

He rolls onto the lot and parks at the edge of a boiling sea of young women.

They surround him before he can even meet them halfway. Sure, he can feel the pounding in his chest as they chant their slogans at him, but it's somebody else's chest, someone farther away.

"Y'all," he begins, raising his voice and making himself tall even though he's already the tallest one on the lot. A few pockets of men push forward. He looks for someone who might be in charge, someone he can reason with.

His eye catches a woman who huddles against the building's beige wall, bug eyed, her purse clutched close.

It's Carmen. When she tries to move forward, a dozen hands press her back.

Sweet Christ. He shoulders his way hard through the crowd, shaking off anything that touches him.

"You okay?" he shouts when he reaches her.

Her face turns up to his. "They won't let me go home."

"Did everyone else get out?"

"As far as I know."

"Is anything smashed up inside? Where the hell was security when this happened?"

"They were the first to leave."

He tugs down his hat. "I'm getting you out of here. You can come back for your car later."

They've taken three steps when they're intercepted by a baby-faced young woman carrying a cardboard sign that reads, "HUELGA." A blockade of other sign-wielding women whooshes to her side.

He turns to Carmen. "Help me talk to them."

She gives him one of her looks.

"Listen," he calls out, "this isn't the way to solve the problem."

Carmen talks.

"If you don't get back to work, you're not getting paid. Plus, you'll probably be fired. I don't want to fire you but I might have no choice. And other people are just going to come in and take your place."

He's pretty sure that each of Carmen's lines begins with the clarifier "He says."

He says, "Look, I'm on your side. It's not my fault the peso was devalued. It's not even this company's fault. If you want to be mad at somebody, be mad at your government. That's who's gonna raise the price of
food and gas now."

The baby-faced young woman looks back at him, quivering, as
though the sternness of his tone has had its intended effect.

Then she erupts.

"Are you stupid?" Carmen translates, deadpan. "Are you joking? The
maquila makes millions of dollars. We get paid sixteen dollars a week.
I've got five kids and no husband and two jobs. My twelve-year-old
doesn't go to school so she can take care of the little ones."

The surrounding women cheer with rage.

"And you cancel all our vacations, so we're exhausted but we *still* can't
feed our families. And we tell you again and again, but nobody listens,
nobody cares, nobody does anything. So now we're doing something.
Until somebody gives us a raise. And a union of our own. That piece-of-
shit union we're supposed to belong to is in bed with the maquila. And
the government."

A man pops up from the rear of the line to shout his own two cents.

"We also want food that doesn't have worms in it," Carmen translates
helpfully, "when we even have enough time to get to the front of the cafeteria line. You want to have lunch with us, güey?"

A numbness descends upon Huck. Even his lips are frozen.

He leans in to Carmen. "What does 'güey' mean?"

"Let's go, Huck."

Ice. Freezing him over, adding weight like snow on a roof.

He turns, slowly, to the cafeteria guy. "Y'all planned this way in
advance, didn't you?"

"I'm not saying that," Carmen interjects.

The cafeteria guy puffs his chest. A sudden hot rage floods Huck's
veins.

"Did you call my house?" He lurches forward. "*Did* you?"

Someone lunges to hold back the cafeteria guy. The crowd foams
over. Huck grabs Carmen by the wrist, half-dragging her behind him as
he rams with his elbow and knee through the wall of bodies, then pushes
her into the truck. He slams the door behind himself.

They breathe hard, Carmen gripping the hole in the knee of her pantyhose.

"Well, Huck," she says finally, "you certainly showed *them*."

Maybe he'd have a comeback if the crowd wasn't trying to tip over the truck.

III

In the night comes a whirring sound in Jordan's dreams, like a toy helicopter. No. A giant hummingbird, beating its wings just outside her window and looking down its dagger beak with an unfathomable liquid eye.

She opens her eyes in the dark. The sound is still there. She stumbles out of bed, stepping on the cuffs of her pajamas, and falls and lands on her hands. She creeps to the window. There, on the ground. She lifts up the window, eyes blurry with sleep, cold air smacking her face.

It's Miguel, in a thin jacket and gardening gloves, his slight, slumped form pacing up and down the yellow grass. He's mowing the lawn with a mower that doesn't have a motor, just blades that whirl around and around as he pushes.

"Why are you mowing in the middle of the night?" Jordan calls out to the top of his head.

The whirring stops with a violent jerk. "Who's there?"

Jordan blinks down at him.

His breath makes a smoky puff in the air as he spots her. "Sorry. Did I wake you up?"

Jordan nods.

"I wake anybody else up?"

She peers over her shoulder. Turns back. Shakes her head.

"I couldn't sleep." He smiles a little. "You ever have that problem?"

"Sometimes."

He shuffles a flat spot into the grass. "So, what do you think? Should I keep going?"

Jordan sways. Her father's truck still isn't back in the driveway.

"If you want."

"You know, your mom . . . ," he says, his words turning into little ghosts in the air. "Your mom is . . ." He looks away. Down. Back up again. "Go back to sleep, m'ija," he says softly. "I'll be done in a minute."

She stands there swaying, looking down at him, the top of her head feeling light.

It's not until she shuts the window and burrows back into her bed that she feels the huge, echoing ache in her gut. She falls down, down into a dream where everyone rises at night, goes to school at night, bustles through streets and stores at night until the light rises up from the bottom of the sky and the people of the world fold themselves up in their bat wings to sleep.

15

OUT WALKING

HOW DO YOU SAY "IT looks like it might rain"? How do you say "Shut the door," how do you say "I need to leave by four thirty," how do you say "Where is the nearest post office," never mind if you'd never mail anything from this side anyway, nobody's going to take you seriously if you can't lighten up your accent, for God's sake, stop putting an *e* in front of all your *s*'s.

Inez tips her chin at Lourdes.

"Say 'how,'" she commands.

Lourdes picks at her notebook's metal spine. "Jau."

Inez gives her a dubious look. "Say 'where.' Use your lips, not the back of your throat. Like you're blowing out a candle. *Wh*."

"Juerr."

Inez looks briefly to the heavens. "Say 'spaghetti.'"

"La foto," Lourdes says. She wraps her notebook in her arms. "When do you giving it back?"

Inez leans against the guardrail. The city below smokes like burnt soup in a bowl.

"You're still thinking about that silly photo? It's somewhere in my room."

Can you find it?

I'm not sure. I'll have to look for it.

I'll look for you. Your room needs to be cleaned anyway. Badly. You can't keep me out of there forever.

Keep your hands off my things! That's a standing order.

Lourdes feels the start of a headache behind her eyes. Her clothes lift with cold puffs of air as the afternoon traffic whizzes past.

I'm the one who's going to get blamed for this, you know.

Inez steps up onto the concrete bench before the railing and stretches.

Well then. If you can't do the time, don't commit the crime.

Lourdes straightens. I'm not a criminal!

Oh, come on. I know you were doing me a favor.

Yes, too much of a favor.

Inez cackles. Ooh, you're getting feisty these days.

Lourdes squints furiously into one of the viewfinders. Because she has not plugged it with change, all is dark.

Couldn't we have found someplace warmer to go? she grouses.

Where? The library? Do you want to whisper through your lessons?

If that means you'll talk less, sure.

Inez nods at the notebook in the crook of Lourdes's arm. How do you say "library"?

"Library."

Tell me you want to go to there.

"Next time we go library. We read. No talking."

Inez laughs and leaps down from her perch. Lourdes trots after her.

You know that, eventually, señor DuPre will notice the photo is gone, right? It's his *wedding* photo.

What makes you so sure he's going to notice?

I can't be sure of anything, Lourdes snaps. He's smashing the walls of his house! He's destroying his furniture! He yells and throws things and he gets so upset he almost passes out, and last weekend I had to check him to make sure he wasn't having a heart attack! Someone probably should be concerned for the children.

Indeed. Inez lifts her head into the breeze. Maybe it's something in the water. My brother has been acting like a mad monk ever since he came back from San Diego.

Lourdes tugs her sweater closer. When she arrived at la casa Gonzales this morning, el profe was holed up in his office, shades drawn and clock radio blaring, with what looked like a week's worth of dirty dishes at his desk. He regarded her with beady eyes when she greeted him with a smile and a polite tap of her mop handle against the floor. You may leave this room uncleaned, he instructed her. Something clattered at the end of the hallway. No you may not! la señora called out.

I've noticed, she tells Inez now.

Well, if there is anyone who's crazy in my family, it's him.

Are you kidding? You're all crazy.

Am I? Tell me in English.

"You are crazy woman."

Inez cackles. "Muy bien." And then, before Lourdes can finish gnawing on the gristle of her mood, Inez adds, Your first child, she was born out of wedlock, no?

Lourdes lurches a little in her step.

"Por Dios," she mutters.

Oh, come on. Nobody cares about these things anymore. It's not like this is 1950.

You think so? Lourdes retorts. Then you don't know anything about Mexico.

Inez jerks her head back this time when she laughs.

Well, I like to think I know a few things about being *Mexican*.

Chicana, Lourdes corrects. She allows a long, cool moment to pass before she adds, I already told you how young I was.

Inez studies her with the look of a scientist.

Your family must have helped you, no? she says. There's no other way.

They march. Lourdes's athletic shoes make a squeaky crunch on the asphalt. What should she say? That when she could no longer hide her belly, her father slapped her so hard she fell?

That's one way to describe it, she says.

I see, Inez says as a truck bearing frozen foods whips past them. And the father? Did he ever give you the time of day again?

Are you interviewing me for a job? Or is this supposed to be my confessional?

Oh, *relax*. They usually don't.

Lourdes opens her mouth. And shuts it.

And so I would guess you don't have any baby photos of your eldest, Inez continues.

Lourdes blinks against the sun. *What?*

You know what she looks like *now*. But do you have any photos to remind you of who she was?

Lourdes kicks a stone in her path. It skitters into the street.

No.

Inez picks up her pace.

A shame. But then again, maybe you wouldn't want any.

"What you talking?" Lourdes blurts. "Why you say this thing?"

Inez smiles. And shrugs.

Sometimes we want to remember the past and sometimes we don't. Or sometimes we have to go looking for it.

Lourdes looks at her sideways. Then out at the city.

The past doesn't always stay where it belongs, she finally says.

I had a baby too, Inez responds crisply. I was also very young. Probably younger than you were.

The traffic flits past, first one car, then a space, then another, like bees returning to their hive.

"Por Dios," Lourdes says. You have a child?

A girl. Or so they told me. I never saw her before they took her away.

Lourdes kicks another rock.

You'll get the photo back, Inez says. I just want a little more time with it. With *her*.

Lourdes draws a sudden breath. She darts another glance.

Señora DuPre must be about the same age as your girl, no? she begins carefully. What a coincidence.

Inez keeps her eyes on the horizon.

I suppose that when you're looking at photos, Lourdes says, it's easy to imagine your daughter's life.

Inez pauses. Then she chuckles.

Very easy, Lourdes. Very easy indeed.

Perhaps you returned because you've been looking for her.

Again, Inez chuckles, though there's sharpness beneath it.

Perhaps you should start working as a private investigator, Lourdes. Or a psychologist.

How, Lourdes wonders. *How is this possible about Inez and señora DuPre?*

You haven't found her, she says.

Are you offering your services as a bloodhound?

You probably don't know what to do next, Lourdes says, for this, at last, is something about which she is an expert. She says, You probably don't know how much longer you can stand it.

Inez's lips tug into that maddening half smile.

Well, as long as my brother can stand it, I suppose.

Lourdes lets the silence rest on their shoulders. Inez is using her. Of course. Even if, for an instant, something in Inez's face—beneath her face—looks paper thin.

What if you don't find her? Lourdes asks.

What *is* this—the Spanish Inquisition?

You started it.

Yes—and apparently, I've created a monster.

Lourdes almost smiles. She looks at her watch.

What, Inez says, already? Let's write down a few phrases before you go.

No, no. Another time.

"In English, mujer!"

Lourdes huffs. "Again, a time."

"No, no, no! Get out your notebook. Where's your pencil?"

Lourdes snatches out a pen as she digs into her bag, launching into midair the key ring that is hooked around the pen's cap.

What's that? Inez asks as Lourdes retrieves the ring from the sidewalk. The key to your kingdom?

No, the key to la casa DuPre.

Inez stops abruptly.

You have a key to that house?

Lourdes stops a pace ahead of her.

Yes, she answers uncertainly.

How long have you had a key?

Lourdes shrugs, her heart thumping.

Inez leans in, so close Lourdes can feel her body's heat. And you never told me?

Lourdes crosses her arms.

You have a key, Inez says, a wondering look spreading across her face. And then with a sudden blaze in her eyes, You have a key.

Don't, Lourdes says, and she shoves the key back to the bottom of her bag. But she can't turn away, her own eyes ablaze now, and she doesn't know who is looking at whom.

III

"So," says Chavela. "You've stayed in here all day again."

Jerry repositions one of the unread midterm essays fanned out before him.

"Are you depressed?" The doorframe creaks as she leans against it. "Is this your way of empty-nesting?"

He turns an unread page. "I'm not depressed."

"Then what's the matter with you lately?"

He clicks his red pen. It is true that he has had little appetite for anything more than slices of American cheese and RITZ crackers. Has he slept? Not since they came back from San Diego. He would like his wife to move away from the door.

"I don't know what you mean."

Through the window, he spies a small dark form at the corner, wrapped against the wind. It approaches with a contemplative gait.

"Inez seems to have lost her partner in crime," Chavela notes tartly over his head. The floor creaks.

Jerry clicks. "She'll find another." The form pauses in the middle of the sidewalk to look back over its shoulder, as though to gaze upon something it had just left behind. A gritty gust rattles the leafless mulberry trees below. He feels a draft near his feet. It had been warm in San Diego, with a softness to the air, an underlying moisture that eased the parched edges of the soul.

Of course, he did not reveal to Chavela the errand he undertook at the Seaside Mano.

"After Christmas," Chavela says, her voice dropping to the low end of her register. "New Year's at the latest. That's her deadline."

The form on the sidewalk throws a long, late-afternoon shadow as it ponders the DuPre house.

"I'll put it to you this way," she continues. "You'll have to choose one of us."

He rises.

Chavela moves to the center of the doorway. "Are you listening to me?"

"Yes."

She tosses her head as he brushes past her. "Then where are you going?"

He is unable to provide a satisfactory answer to this question.

"Oh, wait," she hisses as he heads for the stairs. "Let me guess. *For a walk.*"

The screen door whaps shut behind him as he steps outside, jacket-less, into the chill.

Inez regards him with mild surprise as he intercepts her on the sidewalk.

"What are *you* doing out here?"

He shrugs. "What are *you?*"

They appraise each other across their crossed arms. Then, as though they had heard the same starting gun, they begin walking.

They make their way past kids on bikes, dogs leaping behind gates to snarl at their passage, a neighbor Jerry doesn't know who, drought be damned, is washing his car. He is grateful for the silence Inez allows him. Will they make their way around the block and down the hill, toward the boulevards below? No. The destination is inevitable. They turn back. Back toward the opening in the wall between houses. Together they step onto the foot-trampled path that leads to the foothills, into the desert.

"Have you been tormenting my maid again?" he says as they pick their way through the creosote.

She offers a sidelong glance. "Not much."

The sky opens over their heads like a vast gray parachute marred with blue claw marks. His chapped lower lip has begun to split open.

"What the devil is wrong with the weather?" he grouses.

"Is it so different than usual?"

"Only marginally."

"Grouchy today, aren't we?" she notes pleasantly.

He points the top of his head into the breeze. "Do you believe in letting sleeping dogs lie?"

"I don't know, Momo. It depends on what kind of dog it is."

"Fine. Then tell me this—have you ever forgotten something so completely, ever pushed something so far from your mind that it essentially ceased to exist?"

"Isn't that like the tree falling in the empty forest? How would you know it exists if you can't remember it?"

"It's like groundwater," he says. "It's like, one day, in a corner of your backyard, you find a puddle. You ignore it for a while—you think it's a fluke, a plumbing leak, maybe your neighbors dumped a bucket over the fence. But eventually it starts trickling. Then one day you wake up and you have a stream. A pond. And you look down and see your own reflection."

Inez plants her next step and stops.

"Hermanito, what's this metaphorical crap? What's your prob lately?"

His feet skid in the dust as he stops just ahead of her. The snake of freeway traffic pulses below. Beyond, the river, placid as chocolate milk.

"What if I told you something?" he says.

Inez shrugs. "Go for it."

"Can I count on your confidence?"

"¿Como que 'Can I count on your confidence?' Por Dios."

"I think I was unfaithful to Chavela once," he blurts. "Long ago."

And with the utterance of these words, something at the center of his being simultaneously clenches and releases, radiating to the horizon.

He lurches back into motion. He doesn't look at Inez as she trots up beside him. He only feels the low hum of her surprise.

"You *think* you were?" She adjusts her hat, examining the freeway. "Well, were you or weren't you? Unless you're about to launch a political career, you shouldn't be massaging the semantics here."

He squints. Somehow, even in cloudiness, it's too bright.

"I mean I don't remember. Not entirely."

"What? Why the hell not?"

He tucks his hands into his pockets. "I may have had a few at the time."

She snorts. "Sounds like more than a few."

"Oh, give me a break. You showed up at my house after a fifteen-year absence and demanded to be served tequila at breakfast. This occasion was an *exception*."

"Okay, Mr. Teetotaler. So why now? Why remember this woman at all?"

"Let's just say I've had occasion to be reminded of her, of late."

She studies him.

"I see," she says. "So, all right already. What is this flotsam? Guilt? Nostalgia? Old feelings returning? What?"

He nearly shudders with gratitude. "All of the above, I suppose. Though, in some respects, it's all mostly irrelevant."

"You're not actually considering telling Chavela?" she asks sharply.

"God, no."

"Smart man." Their feet crunch in the dirt. "So, what's the problem then?"

He looks to the river for an answer, but of course, it's in no hurry. It just waits. Ditto the white-and-green Border Patrol vehicle parked at the near bank, casual as a shrub. Behind his eyelids is the imprint of a certain face. A fierce, dark-eyed gaze, a sweep of wheat-colored hair. Damn it all.

"The problem," he says, "is that the more I don't know, the more I don't know. And lately I've had the feeling that something is about to bite me in the ass."

Inez skips over a toppled nopal cactus.

"This is news? Life is always biting us on the ass."

"I'm beginning to wonder how much of my life has been predicated on an unknown history."

Silence. The breeze rattles the creosote.

"So, what are you going to do?"

"Shut the door, I suppose." He rubs his chilled arms. "Wait it out. Let it go. Chase it off. Send it back to where it came from. As many times as necessary. Whatever happened, I'm certain it was a terrible mistake."

Inez seems to absorb this speech with such tranquility that, for a moment, he wonders if she's heard him. Then she lifts her chin.

"Agua que no debe beber, déjala correr," she says.

Water that you shouldn't drink, let it run.

A rueful laugh escapes him. "In other words, 'Let sleeping dogs lie.' I haven't heard that one since our grandmother scolded us with it."

"I have a question for you."

"Mm?"

"Are you actually trying to protect Chavela? Or are you just trying to cover your ass?"

He side-eyes her. "Well, both. Obviously."

"Hmm."

A prickle of warning warms the back of his head. "What do you mean 'Hmm'?"

She shrugs.

"I just think it's interesting, how worried you suddenly are about the feelings of someone you're having such a hard time getting along with lately."

He turns to her. "The last time I checked, that situation was independent of any part of this discussion."

"And yet," she continues, a note of mirth lifting her voice, "one would think you'd be putting some extra effort into your marriage, considering your desire to bury the past."

"I *beg* your pardon?"

"All I'm saying is you might want to consider the possibility that you are engaged in an act of self-sabotage. Or just an unadmitted desire for"—she searches the air for the words—"some kind of *escape*."

"You know," he says tightly, "there just might be a few other stressors at work in our household. Because the last time I checked, the only escapist around here was you."

"You asked," she growls. "You asked me a question about sleeping dogs. But you don't even know which dogs are yours."

He meets her incandescent look with his own. There is a door before him. Inez has cracked it open. He could still follow his sister inside, follow her onto the path that has led her here.

"Chavela wants me to lay down some kind of deadline for you," he says instead.

Inez's look narrows. "I see. And are you going to lay it down?"

"I haven't decided."

She throws her hands into the air.

"Ooh, the great benefactor hasn't decided. Well, maybe there are a few things I haven't decided either."

"And what's *that* supposed to mean?"

"Well, we've all got our cards to play, now don't we?"

He almost laughs. Hadn't she said the same thing a million years ago? To the frat boy? The one who'd called them spics and said *Speak English* as they'd emerged from the campus library? The steak knife out of her pocketbook before he could blink, the boy's throat mottling as she pressed the blade and said, *Sure thing, white bread.*

Her Second Notorious Incident.

He glares into the embers of her eyes now, imagining he could push her off-balance with his mental powers. "Is that some kind of threat?"

She steps up to meet him with a dark flicker of a smile.

"Ask your dogs," she calls out as she strides away. She disappears behind the rise of the land, lofting a trail of fine dust behind her.

III

Marcus runs into his aunt as he crests a foothill on his way into the desert. Her dark head pops from nowhere on the opposite slope, the dust billowing up from their feet as they both stop short.

"Hey, tía," he manages. "What's . . . up?"

Inez casts a sardonic glance at the massive, puffy, flat-bottomed clouds blowing past overhead.

"Out for a stroll?"

She eyes his uniform. "What are *you* doing?"

He has come after work, looking for his father. Instead, at the house, he found his mother, alone and in a very bad mood. She scolded him for leaving footprints on the floor her maid had just mopped. He excused himself to unearth some books he'd left in his former closet and told her he was heading home to crash. But first he wanted a few minutes to himself.

"Guess what I saw last night?" he begins. "Not just one goat, but two. Both of them totally desiccated and—I shit you not—with three-pronged fang marks on their necks."

Her foul expression blossoms with delight. "No!"

"Oh yes."

"And what did you do?"

"Left 'em there."

"What do you think did it?"

He chuckles. In truth, he wonders about the logistics of offing two animals at once, how more than one person would have to be involved, what tools they might have used to puncture the necks, how the hell they managed to drain the blood from the bodies, no trace on the ground.

"I was going to ask my dad that."

Inez draws a sudden breath, as though she were about to sneeze.

"By all means. Ask him. Ask him what he knows. He saw a lot of things out in the field, back in the day." She pins him with a gaze full of flint. "He was a party to them."

Marcus chuckles, but in his chest he feels a rattling of unease. "Any idea where he is?"

"Oh, he's out walking. Somewhere. Just like the rest of us." She tosses her head. "But who knows, m'ijo? Maybe a coyote did it." The sharp thing in her eye catches the light and twinkles. "Though I've never actually seen one out here. Have *you*?"

He shakes his head, his laughter a murmur in his throat. She links her arm to his. It's time for him to go home now. To sleep. But Inez's step is quick, her eyes bright and burning, and so he allows her to tug him back down the hill, along the worn path. Back to the house of his mother and father.

SHE WAKES BEFORE DAWN, RISING from her narrow bed in her narrow room, greeting the day with silence. Silence as she readies the breakfast dishes with Brother Thaddeus. Silence as she washes the dishes with Brother Constantine, silence again at lunch and dinner, silence as she mops the floors. After sundown, when the vow lifts, she still clings to silence. Because here, inside these echoing days where she lives almost entirely through the actions of the body alone, untouched among untouchable men as she feigns Catholic prayer, her pulse slows. Her blood cools. And when the blood cools, the thoughts cool.

Yes. This. Get me to a nunnery.

She does some writing. Snippets. Filaments.

Except that Brother Bartholomew, public relations liaison, takes her aside and suggests to her—not unkindly—that, because her retreat has been "unusually long," that perhaps the time has come to pay some form of rent.

Which, in truth, hurts her feelings.

She leaves in the middle of the night, again. No note. No dignity except that found in silence.

And then—still silent—she is on the highway again, under the wide-open Montana sky, as though she had never retreated from anything at all. There is only the sense of needing to arrive somewhere else, now at a terrible volume, of reaching for something she can barely grasp.

She drives and she watches herself drive. She drives north and west.

16

ALL THAT FALLS

SOMEWHERE IN THE UNIVERSE IS a neutron star with a mass (m) equal to the mass of the sun, 1.98 x 1030 kg, and a radius (r) of 12 km.

"Hey there, sweetheart."

Jordan looks up from her physics book. Sunlight stripes the foot of her bed.

"Hi, Dad."

She points her nose back into the book.

The floor creaks. "How's your day going?"

"Fine."

Her father shuffles in from the doorway and leans. "Whoa. Remind me what a neutron star is?"

The cold chicken leg she has arranged on a paper towel rolls toward her elbow. "A collapsed star of extremely high density."

"Sounds heavy."

Her father waits. Last week, he came home at breakfast time with the truck looking like someone had taken a baseball bat to it. "Strike," he'd announced, then slunk off to bed. He hasn't been to work since.

"Are you going to Costco today?" she asks now.

"Wasn't planning on it."

"I need some frozen vegetables for dinner. And we're out of toilet bowl cleaner."

"I'll see what I can do."

"I have a permission slip."

"What for?"

"For my class to visit the Tony Lama factory."

"Put it in my hat. I'll see to it in the morning."

She returns to her book. The neutron star is the only object in its quadrant of space. Her father drifts backward and parks at the foot of her bed.

"So." He sighs. "How *is* school?"

She reaches for her graph paper. "It's fine, Dad."

"Do you like school?"

She clenches her toes. "Mm-hmm."

"Do you have any friends at school?"

The equation demands the calculation of the free-fall acceleration at the neutron star's surface. "What?"

"I mean, are you happy?"

Jordan exhales and looks up. Her father's hands are fists in his pockets, and he leans forward as though into the wind, his face a desperate crumple.

She looks past him through the doorway, hoping for a glimpse of someone. Why can't he lean into Skyler's room? Why not Quinn's?

"Dad, I've got a lot of work to do."

She doesn't know why her voice is suddenly so quivery, or why her heart knocks so loudly she's sure he can hear it right through her chest.

His face tightens. He's a tall, blocky, semi-handsome, stubbly-looking dad in the doorway, and Jordan can feel him—both of them—hanging in space, like Galileo's feather and the ball of lead. If her mother walked through the door right now, would he turn? Would he ask whether she'd gone to see her real parents, would he wonder whether her mother resembled these strangers since she wasn't like anyone else, would he wake up to talk to Miguel from the window as he mowed the lawn in the night? The next thing climbs up her throat from her stomach. She could let the words drop: *Am I adopted?*

"Dad," she says instead, because the blades of the lawn mower had sounded like something hovering outside her window, watching her sleep. "You know what weird thing happened the other night?"

"Sorry," her father says stiffly. "Sorry to have bothered you." He ducks back out.

Jordan's throat feels thick. She bites her arm just above the crook of her elbow.

Footsteps on the stairs. Quinn pokes his head inside the door.

"Hey, are you ready to go?"

Brittany Gallegos's birthday party. She'd forgotten all about it.

III

"Look," Jerry says, holding out a palm. "Just stay away from each other. Okay?"

Chavela clenches her fists. "My silver serving tray," she hisses. "You hocked my *silver serving tray*, ladrona!"

Inez rolls her eyes. "I didn't *steal* anything. You'll have it back next week, after I'm repaid a loan I'm owed. Anyway, when's the last time you used that thing—the Reagan administration?"

"Tranquilo," Jerry suggests to them both.

"If you needed money," Chavela hisses, "why didn't you ask for it?"

Inez shrugs. "You would've said no."

Chavela grimaces. "When's the last time you washed your clothes?"

"Ask Lourdes. You'll feel better if you make her do everyone's laundry. Where is she anyway?"

"She's late," Chavela snaps. "And I don't like *that*, either."

"Tranquilo!" Jerry turns away with the phone. "Sorry, Son. You were saying?"

Adam makes an exasperated sound in his ear. "What about fall break? Or maybe a weekend? What if I came home a couple of weekends from now?"

A moment ago, they were negotiating the travel arrangements for his return trip for Thanksgiving. Wasn't it only six weeks ago that this boy disappeared from their lives?

"Son," he says, "I'll call you back." And then into Chavela's ear, "I'll deal with her regarding the tray. In the meantime, can't you just ignore her? You're supposed to be the *reasonable* one."

She steps back to give him that look of cold reason. "And *you're* supposed to be on my side."

She strides from the room. The front door slams.

"Great," Jerry hisses.

Inez leans against the refrigerator, not looking at him, gnawing hard at her thumbnail. "It will pass."

The ignition of Chavela's car turns over in the driveway.

"Is that so?"

"I guess it depends."

"On what?"

"On whether she and I can come to a certain understanding."

Outside, a vast bank of blue-gray clouds has moved in to plaster over the sun.

"Here's what I understand," he says now. "I think you should go somewhere else for a while. At least for a few days."

"I'd prefer not to."

"I beg your pardon?"

"You heard me."

"This is *my house*."

"And *I* have some business to take care of."

"Business?" He stands away from the counter. "Would you like to explain what business this is, exactly? You've had 'business' for six months now and I see no evidence of any transaction."

"It doesn't concern you," she says, her knee bouncing.

"On the contrary," he says. "It concerns me greatly."

"Then perhaps you should take up a hobby, to take your mind off things."

At his center, something flames white, then blue.

"Perhaps you should go upstairs and get your coat and go for a walk," he says through his teeth. "Right now. Before something happens that we both regret."

The knee bounces harder. "I don't think so."

"Am I supposed to apply my foot to your ass?"

Inez folds her arms and looks up. "Are you going to?"

The mirth has drained from her face. In its place is a look that seems to perch at the edge of a cliff, on the lip of an aircraft's bomb hatch, the same look she had given him all her life every time he stole back his paper route money from her, or pointed out her incorrect literary quotations, or threatened to tell on her for sneaking out at night (but never did).

He meets her dark gaze.

"I am not afraid of you," he says.

III

It takes Jordan ten minutes to change into a purple jumper with tights and to wrap her collector's edition of *Ripley's Believe It or Not!* in the comics-and-horoscope section of Thursday's paper.

Mrs. Gallegos had called again last weekend, of course. Brittany had no broken bones. Her lungs were strong, her tonsils free of infection, her allergies under control. She had cleared her social calendar. The party was on. At last.

And yet Jordan had neglected somehow to pencil it into her appointment book. Her legs are restless against the seat as they skim the freeway, over murals painted on the T-shaped support posts—American flags and eagles, a brown-skinned Jesus Christ on a cross in the perfect shape for the *T.*

By the time Quinn noses the truck against the juniper-hedged curb in front of Brittany Gallegos's house, something is knocking around in her chest. She turns to him and says, "I'm not going."

"What?"

"Take me with you."

"Jo-Jo, come on. I've got things to do."

"Don't call me Jo-Jo."

He pops the automatic locks. "Jo-Jo, get out."

"Make me."

"You're not seriously doing this, are you?"

She turns back to face him. Her chest lifts. Her body becomes an octopus body, a million suction cups sticking her to her seat.

He thumbs off her seat belt and lurches for her door handle. She wraps her legs around the gearshift. He claps his hand down on her ankle, but she wedges her palm against his chin and he only succeeds in removing her shoe.

"I don't have time," he pants, prying, "to take you home."

She loops her arm back into the seat belt. "I don't want to go home. I want to go with *you.*"

He clamps onto the back of her neck and twists. She seizes the black, gelled points of his vampire bangs.

"I can't deal with this," he says as he hooks his arm around her waist, then squeezes her claws until her fingers splay. He stomps against her door with both feet, and together, they tumble from the truck to the curb. She scrambles back up, but he snatches her by the back of her coat, and suddenly she's upside down over his shoulder, pounding her fist against the pointy bone at the top of his butt. "I cannot *deal* with this," he reiterates, staggering up the walkway. Her legs scissor the air.

He drops her halfway up the walk. She ducks as the gift whizzes overhead and feels the thump of her shoe against her thigh as he sprints off.

By the time she's picked herself up, he's already pulling away.

III

The smell! howls Lourdes's mother. The smell is giving me chest pains!

I won't permit it, Lourdes says, pushing the towel along the bathroom floor with her foot.

Rosario follows with the mop.

Why? Chencha says they're looking for someone right away. The lady that was taking care of the kids had a family emergency and had to come back here.

And how do you expect to get over there?

I just will, Rosario says, pouring more Clorox into the bucket.

I'm dying! her mother calls out from the kitchen table.

You don't have a card, Lourdes continues. Have you saved the money to pay for one? All of that takes time. You have to think ahead. Everything's different than it used to be.

Well, if I can't get *this* job, Chencha says I can find another one like it, easy. And it would pay more than I make at the maquila anyway. So, what's the problem?

You've killed me! yells Lourdes's mother, as though she wasn't the one who poured last week's stew down the toilet. You've killed me, I'm dead, and now who is going to take me to the doctor?

How are you going to take care of somebody's kids if you can't even talk to them?

Nobody cares about that! Rosario dumps the bucket into the kitchen sink. They all want you to teach the kids Spanish. Anyway, Mateo will help me learn whatever words I need. He knows what words to use.

Mateo will teach you. Has *Mateo* ever taken care of a bunch of kids? Lourdes plunges a wooden spoon into the beans on the stove and stirs, too fast, the way she always warns her girls not to. Today would have been a good day for *Mateo* to pick you up.

No dogs allowed in the house! her mother interjects.

Rosario bangs the coffee cups together.

Now tell me your plan, Lourdes says, if Mateo happens not to be around every single second you need him. How you would say in English "What time do the kids go to bed?" Or "How do I reach you if the house burns down?" Have you thought that far ahead?

There's more than one way to plan, Rosario says.

Who's planning on feeding me? grumbles the voice at the table.

Does anyone here understand that I need to get to work? Lourdes barks. Does anyone understand what would happen to us if I got fired?

My point exactly, says Rosario. What if this stupid strike never ends?

A voice in the front room shrieks, No, it's mine, give it back!

You could take in laundry, Lourdes says as Rosario shakes her head. Ironing.

Pilar wails, Mami, Chelita took my—

What makes you think, Lourdes says, that you can just walk up to some gabacho's door and get a job?

Because I'll offer to work for less than the next girl who applies.

"Jesus y María."

"Mami," Pilar howls in the doorway, and Lourdes looks up to find her youngest cradling one hand in the other as it drips a bright stream of blood.

Lourdes snatches up the dish towel and descends on her.

She tugs her to the sink. Finds the gash at the knuckle where the red wells up and out. She dips a mug into the pot of boiled and cooled water on the stove and dabs on the dishwashing soap while Pilar screams.

Press this with me, she commands when she's wrapped up the hand.

I cut my finger, Pilar sobs, and she stamps each foot, back and forth.

You crushed the beans, her mother says, peeking into the pot. Lourdes lifts the towel. There. It's slowing down now. Chayo, bring me a piece of clean rag.

Rosario presses her lips but does as she's told.

"Ya." Lourdes knots the bandage. "Sana, sana, colita de rana."

Pilar sniffles, little dewdrop tears clinging to her lashes. Lourdes sighs and runs her hand once over the smooth black hair. In the front room, Chelita and Araceli are conspicuously silent.

Well, Lourdes says to no one, or everyone. Simón always thought the grass would be greener on the other side too. To the living room she calls out, "¡A comer!"

It's about time, her mother says to the bowl Lourdes sets before her.

Lourdes looks at her watch and gasps.

III

"Well, well, well." Inez leans against the refrigerator, gnawing at her pinky nail. "Look who's growing a pair."

Jerry pulls a grim smile.

"Times have changed. And you can't stay here forever."

She lifts an eyebrow. "Is that so? It seems to me that the more things change around here, the more they stay the same."

"You have a choice. You can make a good faith effort and come up with a timeline or a plan, or—"

She spits a sliver of nail in his direction. "Or what? I just don't know what to do with all this macho energy."

She drops into a chair at the kitchen table and snaps open the crime section of the newspaper.

The light explodes behind Jerry's eyes, but still, he turns. He ascends the stairs.

The door to Inez's room bangs against the wall when he flings it open, motes of dust spinning in the sunlight. In the air, the ripening scent of untended laundry and bedsheets. He steps through a maze of sealed cardboard boxes to the window, its adjacent wall plastered to the ceiling with books. The taxidermy wombat regards him from the corner with its glassy-eyed, frozen hiss.

How much? he asks himself as Speedy Gonzales, nails clacking the floor, comes to stand trembling and bug eyed between his feet. How much responsibility does he bear for those who enter his house?

He kicks over the wombat. Its skull makes a satisfying thunk against the hardwood. Speedy Gonzales dodges away as Jerry yanks a pillowcase from atop the unmade futon and chucks in the contents of the nightstand—toiletries, grooming implements, an open package of granola bars, a transistor radio from the Jurassic era, a half roll of toilet paper nestled beside a pile of wadded, spent squares. Also a half-full fifth of Wild Turkey, which he empties into the potting soil of the dying ficus tree by the window before adding it to the collection. This he tamps down with a few select items of clothing from the floor and the second volume of *The Complete Works of Plato*.

He jogs downstairs and drops the collection at her feet.

She lifts a languid eyebrow at him. "And what's this?"

"Your luggage. You're leaving. Right now. There's enough here to keep you going for a few days. Then you can call me and we can discuss what to do next."

Her smile is arch. "I don't suppose you reserved a hotel room for me."

"Last time I checked, you had a great number of siblings."

"As if. Would *you* stay with any of those people?"

"You know," he continues, "you could explain yourself. You could ask for whatever it is you need. Nicely. For *once* in your life."

"So you want me to beg."

"¿Como que 'beg'?" he says. "I took you into my confidence. Are you afraid that if you do the same, you won't have anything to hold over my head?"

The laugh that bursts from her is strangely flat.

"Mira qué self-righteous. Am I supposed be afraid of *you*? Of being sent away?" Her eyes combust. "You're the one who doesn't *do* anything."

He freezes. Just as he had frozen at the window a thousand years ago, as their father and the next-door neighbor dragged Inez from the house. Creased her, flattened her like a box that wouldn't stop popping open. And yes, he stood mute as his mother wept, as his siblings pinned their eyes to the floor, their hands anywhere but at each other, he obeyed when their father returned with a face of cast iron and orders never to speak of the day again.

Leave it to Tavo to be the one who asked. Who crouched with his arms over his head as their father brought the belt down on his back and still asked *why* and then *why* again.

And when Inez returned after the months of her exile—so thin her clothes hung off her, abject, lethargic, but with a look in her eyes that came straight from the pit of hell—still, he did not speak. And if he had overlooked any opportunity over the years to inquire, to clarify, to get the real story, to connect the dots that, of course, became obvious the older he got—for what other reason were Catholic Mexican American teenage girls forced to disappear in small-city Texas circa 1959?—if in his gut, in the place where there is understanding but no articulated thought, he has known the truth for decades, then perhaps he is to blame. But at some point, the past morphs into a person's private business. And then you have to ask yourself how late is too late.

"Por Dios, I was ten years old," he croaks now. "What could I have done?"

"You never asked," she hisses.

He lifts his palms. "You never told."

"So why don't we take a page from the past? Let's pretend there's no problem. Then it won't exist."

His blood aches in his veins.

"I told you to leave Tavo alone at Marcus's birthday party," he says quietly.

Inez sniffs. "His fifth girlfriend in the course of two years had just left him. A person with that kind of track record should be prepared for some ribbing."

"And you couldn't take the same?"

"It *wasn't* the same."

"You turned Marcus's birthday switchblade on Tavo. And when I stepped between you, *you turned it on me*."

"Then why did you let me back into your house? You already knew what I was."

His blood gathers above his neck.

"You," he tells the woman before him, "have made your choice."

He yanks open the back door, props the metal screen door on its sliding hinge, and extends a hand toward the great outdoors.

A gritty breeze gusts between them. Inez turns her gaze to some point in the distance, settles in the chair, and lifts the newspaper to eye level once again.

And then he's behind her, his hands under the backrest of the chair, heaving it with his full strength.

Inez thumps onto the ground like a scarecrow weighted with a brick.

She sits there on her knees, eyes wide, braid askew, until she rises to brush the imaginary dust from her sleeves. "Cabrón," she calls him, chuckling. Then she whirls and shoves his breastbone so hard he barks like a seal.

He reaches for the crockware jar of kitchen implements on the countertop and yanks free a metal soup ladle.

She snorts at his implement and reaches for the overturned chair.

The chair makes a *crack* against his shielding forearm—or is that his arm cracking?—as she brings the chair down over his head. He has no time to study this pain as he swings the ladle and connects it with her hip. She howls and raises the chair again, but he grabs the rungs between the chair legs with one hand, pushing unsteadily against the force of her exertion. She lunges again, and he ladle-whacks her bony little ass.

She stumbles and drops the chair and clamps her claws on his weapon, pulling.

"So," she pants, "it's you and Chavela against me at last."

"I don't see anyone here but me," he grunts.

She yanks the ladle hard enough to tug him down almost face-to-face with her. "And your fat fucking ego."

He bares his teeth. "I need it to protect me from your breath."

"Come mierda."

"Primero *tú*."

She stomps on his foot.

He yells, hopping, and snatches the collar of her shirt. Together they fall sprawling across the entryway to the living room.

She scrambles away from him before he can firm up the grip on her ankles.

"You know," she laughs while he coughs on the floor, "even after all this time, you still fight like a little girl."

One of the end table lamps comes crashing down beside him.

He rolls onto one hip, snatching a cushion off the love seat to use as a shield against the other end table lamp as it comes sailing his way, then crab walks up to hurl the cushion at her head.

"¿Sabes qué?" he spits as she stumbles sideways. He snatches up the other love seat cushion and whumps it against her rib cage. "*That* is for every wedgie you ever gave me"—whump—"every time you pantsed me"—whump—"every time you forced me to sing embarrassing songs in front of your friends."

Inez seizes the floor lamp, its polished chrome stem as tall as she is, and charges him like a soldier with a battering ram.

He blocks with his cushion, grunting with the force of it before he swings again.

"That's for every goddamned empty potato chip bag you've left around this house"—whump—"and for every favor you've freeloaded without gratitude." He shudders as lamp and cushion collide. "And *this*"—whump—"is for all your wasted talent"—whump—"for your grand exits and burned bridges and all the people you've left behind"—whump—"for your entire sorry, misspent *life*." His last swing misses. "Just ask Tavo."

Who, in the moment before the knife met his collarbone, had said, "What are you, my mother? You're *nobody's* mother."

Inez pants, her eyes wild, the lamp raised now above her head like an axe. Her hair makes a sweat-dampened rat's nest around her head. She lowers the lamp slowly to the floor.

It's impossible to ignore the trembling of her hands.

Jerry turns his head, a sluice of nausea washing through his stomach. He leans and braces his hands against his knees.

"Madre de Dios, hermana," he wheezes. "Have you had enough?"

An energetic grunt is his answer.

He looks up just in time to see Inez lifting—impossibly, wobbling at the limits of her reach—Chavela's heavy, wooden Mexican trunk-style coffee table. With an inhuman roar, she rushes him.

He makes no sound as he lurches to meet her. He only feels the ping in his back as he wrests the table away from her and allows it to crash to the floor; his knees pop as he shifts his weight and closes his hand on her thin arm. She leaps sideways, then cries out as he twists her arm behind her back. It's an immobilizing twist, the twist of a trained law enforcement agent, the surprisingly firm maneuver of a man who has not used his hands this way in a very long time.

She struggles, and he torques her wrist.

"You," she snarls, "are going to regret this."

He torques again. She cries out. A weird thrill rises up in his blood.

"Actually, I won't. Tell Chavela whatever you want. We'll find out which one of us she believes."

"Chavela?" She chuckles low in her throat. "Who's talking about Chavela? We both know there's more on your conscience than your pathetic indiscretion. Maybe it's time people learned what you're *really* capable of, *Agent* Gonzales."

For a moment, the world tilts.

"Get out of my house," he rasps finally. "Stay away from my family."

He releases her with a shove. She whirls, crouching, as though preparing to pounce again. But she only pulls herself upright, crowning him with the bitterest of smiles.

"You were the one," she tells him. "You were the one I thought I could count on. But you're just like the rest of them."

She hooks her arm around the potted aloe on the entryway table on her way out, sweeping it to the floor. The pot cracks and spills its dark dirt.

He stands at the center of the thunder in his ears. He wants to climb onto the roof of his patio with a broken lamp held aloft in a gesture of victory. He wants to fall into his recliner with a bag of microwave popcorn in his lap and a cigar, the television turned up to a volume no one else can stand.

But his legs won't hold still, so he plucks his jacket from a peg beside the door and goes out.

III

Jordan stoops to retrieve the gift and mashes it to her chest. She scrubs her scuff-marked tights with a licked thumb.

What she needs is a plan. A plan, a plan, a plan. A nippy gust of wind blows up under her coat, and she pulls it tighter around herself. She paws through her purse. She doesn't have her notepad. She has a wrapped collector's edition of *Ripley's Believe It or Not!* she's read eleven times and twenty-two cents and the pink, lifeless shell of her cell phone.

She scoops it out, just for the feel of it in her hand, and strokes it with her thumb. Her mother would get it reconnected, if she came back. Some kind of pop music leaks from the house, high pitched and bouncy. Jordan bites the inside of her cheek. It's cold. Inside, there's cake. If it were her birthday and her mother were here, she would give Jordan a party with a thousand balloons and magicians and rented ponies.

She screams and hurls the phone to the sidewalk.

It cracks on the concrete. Beneath the sweet, mouthless cat-face decal, its legend—Hello Kitty—seems to her now like a sigh, a message meant for her alone.

What if she's been looking at it backward? If the phone had been working to begin with, *then* would her mother call? Was that what she was supposed to make happen all along?

A curtain whisks aside in the house's front window. Brittany Gallegos, looming, her hair hanging in two dark, shiny sheaves to her shoulders. Jordan stares back for a long and unblinking moment. She picks up her phone. She's not going in. She's not going anywhere. The curtain swishes back down. Brittany doesn't want her, she already knew that, but not how to change it, and this makes her tighten her arms around the gift until the corners of it feel like they're bruising her through her sleeves and her eyes get hot and blobbed up. She's just going to wait. Right here, in the middle of the sidewalk, until she turns to stone or somebody comes and gets her and takes her wherever it is she really belongs. Up goes the curtain. Brittany. Jordan shivers and sticks out her tongue.

The doors of the house fly open. Here come the throngs in their cone-shaped hats, their plastic Hawaiian leis whipping away from their necks. They swirl around, closing in, bringing the adults with their cheerful voices and brisk limbs, who touch her and exclaim her name.

She covers her head with her arms. She's been tricked! *She's* the guest of honor, the girl at the heart of it all.

Except that everyone rushes past. "My God," someone's mom says. "My God, look at this!" "It's *October!*" gasps another. Jordan peeks between her elbows. The air is whirling and fuzzy. Tiny clumped flakes land on her arms, her bangs, her nose, melting as soon as they touch. The crowd jostles and laughs and sticks out their tongues. She tilts her head back. The clumps sting her face. It's like being hypnotized. It's like being more awake than awake. If she were a balloon, she'd float up and the sky would hold still. But the sky comes down, dizzying and deep, so she sways on her feet and keeps looking.

III

"Vámonos," Lourdes mutters at the bodies blocking the way as she exits the bus. "Vámonos, vámonos." Every face around her turns up toward the white fluff that swirls down from the sky, and she turns up her face too—only once in her life has she seen anything like this, and her heart makes a strange, startled leap in her chest—but there's no time for it now; she hustles along the long street to the bridge, through the slow crowds, past the open-air shops blaring music in two languages over racks of clothes and jewelry and kitchenware, shivering in two sweatshirts as she drops her coins into the slot and nudges along the covered walkway over the irrigation canal, the river in its concrete bed, the barbwire-topped chain link crowned with the wind-whipped remains of a thousand plastic bags—"¡Mira, mira, mira!" everyone says, pointing into the sky—into the line, where she waits, scoots and waits, scoots and waits, until she faces the green uniform at the desk.

She slides her card forward. Ahead, at the front of the line, people slip from the building into the white flurry, disappearing as they descend. Her toes tap in her shoes.

An unfamiliar series of beeps emanates from the card reader. The guard looks away from the window and back at his computer screen.

"Señora," he says, a sharp note in his voice.

She looks at him more quickly than she means to. With his freckles, he looks like a boy who has suddenly grown old. "Díaz" says his name tag.

He leans forward on his elbow and says, This has expired.

A strange, tingling numbness spreads through her hands.

Expired?

You'll need to get it renewed before you can cross again.

She reaches for her billfold.

No, no. You have to fill out the paperwork on a computer and pay the fees. And, he adds, glancing at her card, this kind of card is obsolete now. You need the new one.

A computer?

You also need a passport to get it this time. Have you started the process?

A passport, she says.

He says, The regulations have changed.

He points to the flyer taped to the front of his desk, his boyish face showing neither impatience nor sympathy.

The grace period is over, he says. There have been commercials all over the TV and radio. The notices have been posted for months.

When she doesn't respond, he slips the card again under the little beam of light. A beeping of refusal follows. She barely feels the card's weight when he returns it to her hand.

In fact, all her limbs now feel as though they have been rubbed with an ointment that tingles and cools and burns. Her feet almost float over the ground as she backs her way out the building, back over the brown river in its concrete bed, past the barbwire and its plastic-bag crown, past the newspaper hawkers and taxis that cluster like flies and the Indian girls, barefoot and begging, wrapped in their blue-striped rebozos. The white flakes come down and down.

Her feet meet the sidewalk. When she pauses to look back, she feels like she has frozen in place. But the world keeps moving anyway, so she turns back around. She points herself toward home.

SHE SPEEDS THROUGH THE CITY along the double-decked highway. She looks up and up at the shining buildings, at the massive white volcanic cone in the distance seemingly suspended in midair. She drives winding tree-lined streets hemmed with beautifully restored little dollhouses, past a fishing terminal filled with ugly, picturesque fishing craft. She finds her way to a dense wooded tract in the city's heart. In the parking lot, she sets the car alarm for the first time in many months.

Here she hikes through a primordial swath of fern-laden forest and emerges onto a path between thickets of blackberry bramble. She shuffles downhill, past a huge golf ball–shaped radio tower and a cluster of uninhabited homes and outbuildings—former army fort, her map says—to a wide sweep of grassy fields. In a pattering of rain, the damp grass punctuated with small, placid black rabbits, she squishes her way to the overlook. Here she stands, in Donna Karan pants stained with ketchup, hair whipping, head reeling. The gray waters stretch below, vast. The fog wreathes the green spit on the horizon, beyond which rise the icy, nippled tips of the Olympics. Apparently—or so says her map—the water is not the ocean, but a *sound*, whatever that is. It looks like the ocean to her. A barge plows out to sea. Sailboats dot the water like rose petals. The sun is wrapped in a gray bag somewhere on the other side of the clouds.

She falls. Right into a cross-legged heap. For a moment, she thinks she's been overcome by the height, or exhaustion, or maybe just beauty. But she knows, then, that it's the water. There's a depth to the water here, a claustrophobic chill—you can't see what lies underneath. It's another substance altogether than what she has left behind in the Baja, and it exerts a force to which she has no natural resistance.

She turns up her damp collar and surveys the green land behind her. It seems possible to her that in this place she might eventually break out in a riot of leaves and tendrils, like one of those invasive species that swallows telephone poles and porch posts and cars parked too long. She imagines enveloping the Lexus and digesting it slowly, consuming all means of return. She looks out over the water that is but isn't the ocean, and she sways.

17

ALL THAT RISES

"IT'S HIS BIRTHDAY," ADAM ANNOUNCES.

Dr. G looks up from a TV tray stacked with stapled papers.

"Is that right, kid? What's the damage?"

Quinn slips his hands into his pockets. "The damage is mostly to my brain."

"Congratulations. Aren't you doing anything with your family tonight?"

"Nope."

"You must have plans with them this weekend."

"Nah."

Dr. G raises an eyebrow. Quinn shrugs. Adam's back for fall break.

Dr. G rises. "Then I guess it's going to be boys' night in." On-screen, a clutch of Gila monsters hatch from their eggs.

"You still watching this, Dad?" Adam snatches up the remote and surfs into a sixties-era *Aquaman* cartoon.

Dr. G disappears into the kitchen. Quinn relaxes the clenched hands in his pockets and lowers himself to the sofa. This morning he crunched his first bowl of cereal alone in the lamplight of the family room. Jordan stomped downstairs at first light and fixed him another bowl, so he ate that one too. Before school, Skyler gave him an unwrapped, pirated CD—The Cure, live in concert, no less—instead of her usual hippie shit. The kit he'd wrapped for her in Snoopy-patterned paper contained a squat glazed pot; a shriveled, sprouting potato; and an instruction booklet. Potato bonsai. "What a stupid present," she said, grinning. And that was all. Just a clean exchange, no expectations, not even for the words "happy birthday," because that would be like saying it to yourself, and beyond that, what more was left to say?

Now Dr. G glides past the screen with a bottle tucked under his armpit and a trio of shot glasses bulging from one hand.

"Gentlemen." He pauses halfway up the stairs as they gawk. "Is there some reason you're not following me?"

Adam pulls back his head. "Are you serious?"

"I'm serious."

"Where's Mom?"

"At your grandmother's, until late. Now get up here."

Quinn laughs. Adam's mouth is shaped like an *o*.

III

"If *Moby-Dick* was written today," Carlos asks the ceiling, "do you think Melville could get away with two-hundred-page descriptions of whale biology and all that harpooning and skinning and oil harvesting?"

Skyler, on the bed, lifts a white, ruffle-encased pillow with her feet and chucks it to the floor. A poof of dust rises. She sighs, thinking of Lourdes. Should they be worried? Probably she had just gotten tired of their slovenly ways and found some better, less disgusting family to work for.

"Because it's freaking amazing, the way he handled language, but if it was published today, people would be like, 'This book drags! Let's get to the action! Where's my dictionary? I can't fit this book in my carry-on!' Anyway, literary qualities aside, think about it—he had a Polynesian character, and some Africans, and an Indian and an Arab, and they all lived together happily, and who wrote anything like *that* back then?" Carlos reaches for the eyelash curler in her hand, which is crimped around a smoldering stub. "It was, like, utopian. You should totally read him."

She kicks another ruffled pillow from the bed. "This has turned out to be kind of a weird day."

He exhales toward the open window. "Oh," he says. "Here." He rolls over to paw through his jacket, then pushes a plastic rectangle into her hand.

It's a cassette. A mixtape, no less. Hendrix's "Foxy Lady," Zeppelin's "Since I've Been Loving You," G. Love's "Baby's Got Sauce," and more, more songs, more words in Carlos's tiny, cramped handwriting, so many words.

"Happy birthday," he adds, grinning.

She studies the little window between the spools, the way the tape itself wraps around and around in ever-tightening circles. Hadn't her brother once pulled the guts out of one of these things just to see how long it was?

"Awesome," she says.

He bows his head a little. "Sorry it's a tape."

"No, no. I love it."

"If I ever get a computer, I'll burn you a CD."

"It's great. It really is. It's totally meaningful." She sighs. "It definitely beats potato bonsai."

He kicks the opened box beside the bed. "It *better*. Hey, are you hungry?"

An hour ago, he took her to dinner at Texaco using his sister's gas card. They ate ham sandwiches out of plastic cartons and shared a Coke under the gas station awning as the sun set. This was totally romantic.

She shrugs. Her lip quivers. Her eyes brim over.

"Whoa." He drops the eyelash curler in a coffee cup on the dresser. "What? What's wrong?"

She covers her face with her arm. Last week, when it snowed, the world had seemed magical and portentous, at least for the fifteen minutes it lasted. This week she has been visiting the mailbox. She has separated the junk mail from the bills and the magazines each day, and this morning when she and Quinn had exchanged their gifts, she almost said it: *Mom didn't send a card.* But she knew he would only say, *So what?* with his eyes. And so there was tomorrow. Even the day after that, something still might arrive. Basically, you could wait forever.

Or you could decide to stop waiting.

"I'm just tired," she says now, flushing.

"Did something happen?"

Had it? Did *anything* ever change around here, in the fundamental ways? Like her own self, for starters? She examines the freckles on the backs of her pale, pale hands.

"Forget it," she mutters.

He sits up. "No, no. I want to know. Truly."

"Well, I don't really want to talk about it."

"Oh, come *on*. Just tell me."

"I just hate this house," she blurts. "Okay?"

He sighs and lifts a fistful of dreadlocks to rub the hot crown of her head. "Why?"

"Because it's stupid," she spits. "Everything about it is twisted and fake and materialistic and just totally"—she searches the ceiling, the bedspread, her own palms—"white. White *bread*."

His hand stops. He makes a weird little chuckle at the back of his throat.

"But your house is so *cool*."

The air conditioner ruffles the bedspread. There's something in her mouth. She can't figure out what it is, why it's there, why it tastes so much like shame, whether—if she doesn't say anything at all—it will just disappear.

She swallows. "Let's put on your tape."

"Let's get out of the house."

Her limbs absorb all the gravity in the room. "I dunno."

"I mean," he says, and when she turns to him, something shifts under his face. "I mean . . . seriously, let's go. Let's just get out."

"What are you talking about?"

"We could go," he says. "Really go. You could pack a little bag right now, and I can get by on nothing, and . . ." His mouth stalls. "I mean . . ." He yanks on his ponytail, as though to straighten his thoughts. "Let's just *blow* this town."

She sits up and meets his gaze. Her blood hums in her veins.

III

The departure of his sister has not brought the peace of mind Jerry imagined.

He turns the corner onto the shadowed landing at the top of the stairs, juggling the glasses and bottle in the crook of his arm, wrestling the latch of the french doors. Of course, he made phone calls. Even if, in talking to Ofelia, and Beto, and Lalo, and Delfina, and the rest of them, including the auxiliary relatives, the trajectory of his conversation ran along the lines of "Have you heard anything? Anything she might be saying about me to someone else? Because, of course, you know better than to believe anything she says." He instructed Tavo to call him immediately if he heard from Inez, then told him to shove it when Tavo said he would probably have more luck finding his own backbone.

He tossed Inez's forsaken possessions from the guest room into yet another cardboard box and stuffed this—with the others—back into his garage.

Chavela should have been happy. Granted, there was the wreckage of the living room, but otherwise, wasn't the turn of events cause for celebration? "You should have seen it!" he insisted at first. "You should have seen *me!*" Instead, she'd been circling him, like a raptor that has not yet spotted the morsel for which it is willing to descend. She swoops in when she wants to know when he's going to take out the recycling, where is Kiko's collar, why does he keep staring out at the desert like that? Then she consults her to-do list, and does things. He retreats, in turn, to his study with a lumbar-support pillow and a bottle of ibuprofen.

In fairness, there had been little time for them to achieve equilibrium before Adam poured himself out of the battered Volkswagen van in which a dorm acquaintance had given him a lift home. "I just need to chill for a while," he'd said, though from the look in his eyes, Jerry knew his affliction to be homesickness, or rather, something more complicated—homesickness for a home one is sick of. And if, in fact, a return home so early did in fact verge on ridiculous, if Jerry was at all secretly worried that Adam might be the next son of his to throw away an opportunity for higher education that he took entirely for granted, the kid had at least managed to finagle a week's worth of assignments in advance from his teachers, which, mostly, he seemed to be completing. And so, Jerry decided, he would give him some space. Which is exactly what a man should offer another man. Even if his return trip required a plane ticket.

Chavela said, "M'ijo, you could enroll here at UTEP next semester. It's not too late."

He and Adam had rolled eyes as one.

Then this morning, as he ripped the ripe sheets from Inez's bed to spare Chavela the chore—because what the devil had happened to Lourdes anyway?—he found the photograph, wedged facedown between the mattress and box spring.

He turned it over. His heart fibrillated. For what he held in his hands was the wedding photo of Huck and Rose Marie DuPre.

He looked over his shoulder, flooded with panic: *whowhywhenhow.* Had Huck, in an end-of-marriage pique, tossed it out? Did Inez trespass on private property to scavenge it, having guessed at the object of his ancient indiscretion? He pictures her pawing through the neighbors' garbage, clapping her hands in delight at her fantastic luck at having extracted, at last, an instrument of blackmail. Or just torment.

Far, far worse was the possibility that she, nosing around la casa Gonzales in some sealed and forgotten storage area, had found it among his own personal effects. For it wasn't out of the question that, in his long-ago madness and stupor, he'd taken a souvenir.

Chavela was in the kitchen, blocking his path to the garbage cans outside. He stuffed the offending object back under the mattress. Then he went for a drive.

And now, at this hour, he is left only with his thoughts—his oozing, itching, maddening thoughts. He will allow them no quarter. For he has already decided that this evening marks the beginning of the reoccupation of his house. Together, on this evening he and the boys who sidle behind him, tittering, will build a den, a bastion of maleness, a fenced fortress impossible to penetrate. Here he will repose, unmolested. Safe in his own nest of demons.

He flips open the wall-mounted keypad control and turns up the fence's voltage. Then he shoves open the door.

III

Quinn's shot glass meets the tabletop with a thump.

"You two took that like a couple of pros." Dr. G's gaze is cool and arch.

Quinn sucks on his lime wedge, concealing a gag. "Dr. G, let me assure you that your son is strictly an amateur."

Adam snorts. "Oh *yes.*"

Dr. G narrows one eye and salts his hand. "Personally, I only drink this stuff on special occasions. I hardly even bother to crack open a beer these days." He tips the bottle to the glasses. "Should you choose to disclose the events of this evening to your father, please inform him of that. Then tell him I left town. Until then, here's to attaining the age of reason." He raises his shot glass. "Salúd!"

Adam turns to Quinn. "Salúd!"

"Salúd!" Quinn retorts. A fat blossom flames in his gut.

"Wait a minute," Dr. G says, dealing for five-card stud. He probes his remaining cards. "We are not playing with a full deck here."

Adam offers a wide smile. "I wouldn't know anything about that."

"This from the kid who plays solitaire in the bathroom."

"How else am I supposed to pass the time?"

"Go. Return with some other form of entertainment."

Laughing, Adam disappears into the house.

A heavy calm descends in his absence. The palm and the mulberry trees in the yard creak and rattle their leaves. Dr. G folds his hands on his gut, serene as a Buddha. *Don't squirm*, Quinn tells himself.

"You know," he blurts, "it's very cool of you to do this."

Dr. G gazes out over his head. Little pinprick stars have begun to poke into the sky. "My own father did something like this for me when I turned eighteen." A breath of silence. "How *do* you get your hair to stand up like that?"

Quinn probes one of the cones of his hair. "Knox gelatin. And hair spray."

Adam barges back onto the deck with a cardboard box.

Dr. G leans on an elbow. "This one has been known to use pancake syrup and model airplane glue on his head."

Adam drops the box. "Hey, viejo, at least I'm not using spray-on hair."

Dr. G pats his head. "I'll have you know that every bit of this is mine."

"What's left of it."

"There's not going to be much left of yours when they shave your head at military school."

Quinn slaps the tabletop. "That's right, mojado!" Adam's on scholarship at UCSD. Personally, he's headed for community college next year. He laughs, the corners of his eyes moistening, until he sees that both father and son are peering at him silently over the elegant hooks of their noses.

A flush of heat, prickly and nauseating, travels from the top of Quinn's head to his navel. *You know what I meant*, he thinks at Adam, who gives him a look that says, *You dumb shit.*

"So anyway," Adam says, "here's a game." He drops into his seat.

Dr. G offers Quinn a sharp glance before turning his attention to the box before him.

"What's *this* nonsense?"

Adam shrugs. "It's kind of all we had."

"Oh, come now. We have to have something more dignified than this. Risk. Monopoly. Scrabble even."

"I happen to know the Monopoly set is missing several mortgage cards. And also the race car and the shoe."

"You can't drink and play Life!"

But Adam, to Quinn's immense relief, is already unfolding the board. In fact, the familiar rainbow-hued dial, the white plastic buildings—church, mansion, hospital, the bridges encased in plastic green shrubbery standing out in miniature relief—are all a comfort to Quinn. He pinches a game token shaped like a white plastic car between his thumb and forefinger. On the topside of the car, the little round holes where you plug in the tiny pink people and blue people. How old was he the last time he played this game? Ten maybe? Nine?

Three spins and he's rocketing up the career path. Adam screams up behind him, moves ahead, lags, and pulls into his square. Dr. G, having been forced to attend college first, straggles behind.

"I'm fired and have to start a new career," Dr. G informs them gravely during his next turn. He pours a splash of tequila into his glass, downs most of it, and chooses his career card. It seems to fill him with optimism. "I'm going to be a salesperson!" When Adam comes home from the hospital with a baby girl, Dr. G mutters, "Madre de Dios," and reaches for the rest of his drink. Quinn wins a dance contest, which pays for an African safari.

Taxes. Car accidents. Payday. Payday. Payday. Quinn discovers the sheaves of paper money at his elbow—pink, yellow, minty green, and blue. He ruffles them with his thumb in their sectioned tray.

"Who's the banker here?" he asks dreamily.

"*You* are! *You* are the banker!"

"Are these glued on?" Adam reaches for Countryside Acres retirement home and pops it free of its slot.

"Spin!"

Suddenly, Quinn's laughing again. He doesn't know what's so funny, but here it comes. Then he's past the point of stopping, of caring, and maybe that's why this time they join him. They hoot together. They slap the tabletop. They throttle their armrests and guffaw until they cough and go limp in their chairs.

"So, kid," Dr. G begins. "How's your father these days?"

A few linty clouds smear the sky. The metal chair cools the back of Quinn's neck. If he doesn't move, maybe the question will go away. The only question worse than this is how he himself is, as asked by adults who look strained and earnest and like their sympathy isn't offensive. They do it because they can't ask about his mother. How she is. Whether he's heard from her.

Dr. G's question hangs in the air, as palpable as dust.

"He's okay, I guess."

"I'm sure the labor strikes aren't exactly helping."

Nobody has to know how his father mopes. How he looks too much like a kicked dog.

"They say time heals all wounds." Dr. G straightens in his seat, lifting his shot glass to the window's light. "But in my estimation, whoever said that didn't get it quite right."

Quinn slumps and scrapes at the tiled tabletop with his thumbnail.

"There's a saying I learned when I was young." Dr. G lowers his glass, tips the bottle.

"Uh-oh," Adam says.

Dr. G gives him a sharp look. "Listen. I'm trying to tell you two something important. Someday you're going to change."

Quinn puts his mind somewhere else, somewhere far out of reach.

"When you were a boy," Adam says, "you had holes in your shoes the size of corn tortillas and had to walk ten miles uphill to school. In hundred-degree weather. Through swarms of cicadas. Right?"

"I'm not done."

"Dad, please."

"Listen." Dr. G leans forward onto one arm. "This is what I wish I'd known when I was your age. Someday you won't want that war paint in your hair anymore, and you'll find that all those rings and bolts in your face are more of a nuisance than anything, and you'll discover that different things are important to you than once were. And you'll figure out that the answers to all the questions you've been seeking are irrelevant because you were asking the wrong questions. There's this saying . . ."

He recites something in Spanish. A poem maybe. Adam's eyeballs jerk to catch Quinn's before he points them directly at the sky.

"From time, I ask time," Dr. G translates. He leans back in his chair. "'To time, I give time. Time is a good friend. Time will undeceive us.' That's the key, boys. Time doesn't heal us. It only enlightens."

"*Okay*, Dad."

"We have been here," Dr. G continues, and there's something deliberate in his tone, a way he is looking but not looking at Quinn, "for ten generations. Ten. Our family has been in Texas that long. We didn't even cross the border—it crossed *us*. And we've learned a few things in that time. Therefore, you should remember—"

"You know what?" It's a moment before Quinn realizes he's blurted this, another before he registers the angry set of his jaw, the way his eyeballs throb with his pulse. Dr. G's eyes glint sharply in the low light, and Quinn senses the tensing of Adam's shoulders. One or two thrilling words. That's all it would take to collapse this summit.

He jerks up his shot glass instead. "Let's drink to that."

Dr. G leans on his elbow, jowl tucked. The considerations roll across his eyeballs.

"¡Salúd!" Dr. G stabs his glass into the air.

"¡Salúd!" The rims of the three glasses chime.

Quinn excuses himself before anyone can spin again. He teeters toward the deck railing, heat spreading through his stomach.

"Whoa there, easy does it." Dr. G reaches out to steady him. "I think this is where the experiment ends. You need to build up your endurance with this stuff."

"Quinn, pal." Adam grins enormously. "You're totally wasted."

"Shut up. It's my birthday." Quinn's ears pop, and this gives him the sensation of having burst from a huge, slick bubble. The evening's first cricket grinds. He startles and looks for it between his feet.

Dr. G, looking much like the Mona Lisa, shakes his head.

In the can, Quinn holds himself up with a hand pressed to the wall. Mrs. Gonzales's little translucent soaps and lotions line the base of the mirror. He wonders what everyone at home is doing. Are they worried? Pissed off? Are they watching TV? How long until his father calls over here? Will he call at all? I mean, what are you going to do? Call your eighteen-year-old son and say, *Get home and have your birthday party! Right now?*

His mother would. If she knew.

He flushes. He double-checks his zipper, leaning over the sink toward the mirror. A longish face meets him there, the left ear ringed with hoops, a pointy chin fuzzed with blond stubble, black cones of hair drooping. A zit rises in a red dome beside his nose. Is there anything distinguished about this face? Anything interesting or even remotely good looking? He splashes water on his eyes, makes a puddle on the countertop that he doesn't wipe up. Most people he knows, their parents are divorced already. It's not like he's a kid anymore. He'll be moving out next year. He puts his nose up close to the mirror, shutting one eye. Except for one giant gray-blue eyeball, he's a blur. He stumbles sideways against the towels. Time will enlighten us. Thanks, Doctor, for that priceless advice.

Out. Back out to the deck, to the air.

"My turn," Dr. G says, heaving up out of his chair and none too steady himself. "If you'll excuse me, gentlemen."

Quinn falls into the seat beside Adam's, tracking the bright white of Dr. G's shirt as it disappears into the house.

"Check out the moon." Adam tips his chin toward the sliver poking like a cat's claw from behind the mountain.

Quinn reaches idly for the rainbow dial. He spins and lands on *Buy a house!* "Yeah. Cool."

"We should go hiking up there. Before I go back."

Quinn lifts a card from the house deeds deck. "So you're going back for sure?"

"What else am I gonna do? Hang out here in Chuco Town and watch cable?"

According to his card, Quinn's new home is the farmhouse. Located on fifty rolling acres, with garbanzo bean crops, prizewinning pigs and dairy cows, and a spacious barn with silo.

Adam shifts in his seat. "Anyway. Want to go tomorrow?"

Quinn snorts at the card in his hand, sets it down. He wonders if Skyler is eating cake.

"Hey. Gabacho. Are you trashed or what?"

Quinn blinks and unlaces his hands from the back of his neck. "No."

"Having a good birthday?"

"Sure."

"What do you want to do now?"

Quinn leans back in his chair. The hills make a purplish, almost invisible silhouette against the navy horizon. He reaches for his empty shot glass and suctions it to his eye socket like a monocle. With his free eye shut, all he sees is a round haze of city light. On the Mexican side, it's darker. The river is so far below, so slow and smooth it might not even exist.

"I bet you and your dad had a serious party on your birthday."

Adam chuckles dryly. "Well, it was observed. We went out to eat and saw a movie. But we sure as hell didn't do *this*."

A ripple passes through Quinn, something that opens and opens. He removes the glass. Adam's black sideburn, the peacock bangs, the familiar ringed brow—each of these parts seem suddenly strange to Quinn. It's as though he's looking at someone he's never met who looks exactly like someone else he can't remember.

"Why don't you say it?" he says.

Adam raises an eyebrow.

"Come on." Something builds in his tight chest. "Say it."

"Say what?"

Quinn plants his knees wide. "Do you think I'm stupid?"

"The hell are you talking about?"

Quinn grips his armrests. He can see everything. He can see all the way through Adam now, into his center, to the chamber where he keeps both pity and contempt because they are actually the same thing, and he sees how this trove has been reserved just for him.

"Spit it out, *mojado*," he barks. "You know you want to."

Adam's face hardens. "Don't tell me what I want. *Gabacho.*"

They sit unmoving in the silence that follows. The fat palm tree at the side of the house rustles incessantly. A haze blooms in Quinn's brain. His hands look heavy and strange in his lap, like gloves filled with sand.

A heave rends the air.

Adam twists, raking his eyes through the dark. "No way."

Then again, from inside the house—a retching. Heave-ho.

Adam shuts his eyes. "Oh, *no*."

Quinn hiccups one note of a laugh. He means this as apology. But it trips into a giggle. It grows. It pitches upward into a high, crazy cackle, he can't help it, and when Adam's eyes fly back open he gives Quinn a look of outrage, a look that means, *You crazy fucking white boy*, and he shakes his head, he laughs through his nose. Everything's fine. The face before him is lit by two brilliant crescents. Somewhere below them, an engine rattles and falls still.

"Crap!" Adam coils. "Is that my mom?"

III

"What exactly do you mean," Skyler says with her heart beating up into her throat, "when you say, 'blow this town'?"

Carlos's warm knees press her leg. "I mean . . . we could just blow *away*. Away from everything that makes you unhappy and makes me crazy. To somewhere that's just *better*. I mean . . . you're eighteen! It's not like it's against the law."

"Do you mean for a while?" She levels her gaze at him. "Or for good?"

A look of wonder passes over his face. "I don't know."

"Where?" she breathes.

"How about Mexico?"

"You want to go to *Juárez*?"

"No, no. Farther. Baja maybe."

"And do *what*, once we get there?"

"I dunno," he says. "Set up camp on the beach. People stay out there on the beach all the time." He slides an arm around her shoulder. "I mean, imagine it—the ocean, stretching out all the way to forever. We're in our swimsuits. We have this tent set up under some palm trees, and a campfire, and fishing poles, and a cooler of beer—nobody cards in Mexico, right?—and books, a massive pile of books inside our tent. Best of all, the beach is empty. There's nobody there to tell us what to do. Nobody to tell us who we are. Just the ocean, pounding beside us." A sheepish look passes over his face. "Or something like that. I've never actually been to an ocean."

She sees her own reflection in his eyes. The ocean tumbles and smashes. She turns in his arms and kisses him.

"Mexico!" she says, laughing, when they come up for air.

He shrugs and laughs back. "You speak Spanish. Better than I do anyway."

"I could start packing tonight," she says, though of course they'll have to write a note telling everyone not to freak out, they're okay, they'll get jobs, and would they be taking his mom's car? They'll pay for the car.

"Oh no!" he says, twisting to look over his shoulder. "What time is it?"

She blinks and shows him her watch.

"I was supposed to pick up my sister twenty minutes ago!"

"Come back after you take her home."

"Monica's going to kill me." He gets up from the bed. "My *mom* is going to kill me."

"Okay, but wait. When can we talk about this?"

He squeezes her hand. "We'll figure it out."

"I've saved up some money," she continues. "If you got a job before we left, we could—"

"Sounds good," he says, shrugging into his jacket.

The slap of his feet follows him down the stairs, then the careful creak of the front door. He pauses with one foot inside his mother's station wagon to look up to the open window where she stands.

"We'll figure it *out*," he whisper-calls. "Eventually. All right?"

She stares down at him in the dark, her blood strange and hot, galloping in her veins.

III

On the Gonzaleses' deck, Quinn cackles. "Beats me."

"You asshole, shut up. Was that in my driveway?" Adam's chair screeches against the cement and then clatters backward. Somewhere below, the metallic, heavy creak of a door. "Crap! It *is* my mom!"

A door slams. When Quinn looks to Adam again, he understands what is necessary. Their feet leave the ground at the same moment; together they are leaping, flying, crashing against each other outside the bathroom, where Quinn finds himself pounding the door.

"Dad! Dad, get out of there!" Adam throttles the doorknob. He presses the door with his shoulder until it pops open. "Mom's home!"

Dr. G smiles up at them from the floor, pale and peaceful, his back against the wall beside the toilet.

"Save yourselves, boys," he says. He flushes pink. Then pomegranate. His face crumples and he clutches at the air with one hand. "Abandon ship! It's too late for me. Now go. Go!"

They go. Toppling down the back steps, out the gate, into the street, they run. The street is empty and still, and they understand that this silence should be filled with their voices, without sense, without words. Adam plucks up a rock from the curb and hurls it at a streetlight and misses. Quinn stumbles into a parked car. The alarm shrieks to life, and he jerks away, imagining his father rising in solitary outrage from his recliner to whip aside the living room curtains. They go, scrabbling around the corner at the end of the block, and somewhere behind them is Dr. G, left to his fate by the toilet. His face had made such a joke of it all. Had Quinn only imagined something desperate in his eyes? Like the guy outside Carlsbad. He should have helped him. Should have hefted him up with an arm around his back, but the look in Dr. G's eyes was a version of what he saw in the other guy's eyes, and Quinn couldn't touch either of them. He turned away.

There's no one in Adam's driveway. That's the stupid thing. The stupid thing is that Quinn dreams of his own mother, has dreamt of her since the first broken days after she left. He would tell Skyler this if he could. Their mother comes into his room while he drifts in the zone between sleep and wakefulness, looking furious but also like she's about to shatter into thousands of tiny pieces that he knows he will never be able to fit back together. And he wants to wake up completely, but he can't; he can't move until morning, when he wakes in the dark, choking on something. A question. What if? What if she's dead? How would any of them ever know?

Adam raises a fist to the sky. "She'll never take us alive!"

Quinn's sneakers skid and then stop. A porch light pops on nearby. Then another.

"Come on!" Adam calls. "Come on, hurry up! Jesus, what's the matter with you?"

Quinn sways in the street. The darkness pools around him in ripples that spread for years in all directions. Here's what he really needs to know: what he will see in his sisters' faces when he comes back to say, *Yes, I left you behind.* What if he said, *I'm sorry,* what if he cried like a stupid baby, would that change anything, would that make him any better than what he is? He wobbles, bends, sinks to the ground. The asphalt's loose pebbles cut into his hands. Someone once told him he had the hands of a pianist, someone who didn't know how many years it had been since he quit playing. How long ago had that been? Who had he hoped he would be?

The sharp smack of a rock stings his arm.

"Come *on,* gabacho!"

Quinn shuts his eyes. Adam is waiting, and his knees ache on the pavement, and it's not even midnight. He closes his hand on the pebbles beneath him and flings them as hard as he can. Then he rises, staggering onward.

III

In the dark of the front room, the stars through the window look so small and cold, they don't even twinkle. Only Rosario is awake.

She kneels before her borrowed backpack, brushing dust from its latches. This she has hidden under her bed for weeks now, has cradled the weight of it in her arms as she tiptoed in socks from the room where her mother and grandmother converse in cooing snores. Everything is packed. Clothes and toothbrush, soap, water bottle. All in its place. As though there were any other way it could be. She pulls the zipper tooth by tooth.

Now, before she steps into her shoes, she looks back at the kitchen table, to the note she has placed there. Maybe she's said too much. Maybe not enough. Maybe her last paycheck, cashed and stacked neatly beside the note, speaks its own language. Better that than to be useless inside these weeks of worry and waiting, to learn to want less your whole life instead of more.

Behind the sheet to the girls' room, she hears someone turning in bed. She can hear them all breathe, their mouths on their pillows. She could probably guess who is who, just from the sound of their breath.

She places a fork on either end of the note to keep it in place. Quietly, quietly, she opens the door.

Mateo is waiting. He leans at the edge of the yard against the glass shard–topped wall, barely visible in the glow of the streetlights blocks away. He wears his regular clothes, jeans and a sweatshirt, and as he gazes out toward the parked truck, he looks serious and tired. Still, he smiles when he catches sight of her. He steps up to take the pack from her shoulder. The army blanket he drapes over it, as he nestles it onto the floor where she too will curl herself, turns it into something invisible.

She looks north, to the other city—toward many other cities—and then back. Ten thousand miles away, someone else's war rages on.

Are you sure? she asks with her eyes.

His sky-blue eyes in the dark could be any color at all. But his teeth are the color of the first light of day. They almost glow. He holds out his hand.

And together they go. They go.

EL TIEMPO ES UN BUEN AMIGO

TIME IS A GOOD FRIEND

2006

18

EL OTRO LADO

THEY'RE DEFINITELY GOING TO NEED to stock up on appetizers before the party. Not to mention ingredients for the main course—something people could eat with their hands would be a good idea. Of course, there will be cake. And two kinds of ice cream. And hot fudge sauce. Jordan digs with one paw through the chest freezer. Up come the frozen pizzas. Assorted Salisbury steak dinners and potpies. An open box of Otter Pops. Chicken thighs with a sell-by date of two years ago. A huge ziplock bag containing a mass of gray lumps is labeled, in magic marker, "pescado." She wraps it in a towel used for drying the dog and steps out onto the driveway, into the echoing roar that is Miguel crisscrossing the lawn with the power mower.

"What does this say?" she asks when he cuts the engine.

He dips into his shirt pocket for his glasses.

"'Fish.'" He gives the bundle a dubious look. "You gonna eat that?"

"Maybe," she says, getting ideas.

"Remind me I'm not gonna eat at your house. You have a good New Year's?"

She shrugs. She and Quinn watched Dick Clark and drank 7UP mixed with orange juice. The Christmas lights are still on the house.

"School starts on Tuesday. Are you still driving me?"

He removes the grass clippings bag. "If your dad wants."

"He wants."

In the kitchen, she shoves the fish into the other freezer. The blender sits beside the sink with half a smoothie in it. The garland of Christmas cards she hung from a string over the kitchen island offers embossed wishes from the so-and-sos, who were mostly wearing Christmas sweaters in their photos and smiling with their teeth under the studio lighting.

On Christmas, there had been take-out chicken enchiladas and cable TV and presents her dad had ordered, prewrapped, from Amazon. And phone calls. Granny DuPre had huffed in her ear, "Well, if I'da known y'all weren't coming, I'da jumped in the truck and drove out there myself." Grandma Francine had been more restrained. "Sugar," she said, sounding, as always, like she was sitting upright on a glass chair with a small purse clutched in her lap, "I just think it would be better if we all waited until your mother comes home."

Her father had spoken to neither grandmother. He looked like a bear roused too early from hibernation as he lay in the recliner listening to Willie Nelson CDs.

But now it's a new year. And in a new year, you have to start doing new things. Especially when the old things were gone for good. Because, even though Grandma Francine seemed to think otherwise, that's how it was going to be from now on, wasn't it? Even the Christmas cards had been addressed to "Everyone" or "The DuPres" or "Huck and Family," without mention of a certain name. And anyway, her father had given her a pogo stick and a biography of Stephen Hawking for Christmas, both of which she'd liked very much. She dumps the rest of the smoothie down the sink. She's going to need to start making a guest list. But who would it include? The kids in her class, who didn't invite her to *their* birthday parties? The girls whose parties she'd been to this year? Brittany Gallegos even?

Maybe.

In the dining room, Quinn stares down the sheet-covered hole.

"Dad." He braces his hands against his knees. "Let's try this again. So there's no progress with the labor negotiations or whatever?"

Skyler straddles a backward chair beside him. In the living room behind her, the browning Christmas tree lists to one side.

"When is Lourdes coming back?" Jordan grouses.

Skyler grips her chair. "Wish I knew."

"Dad," Quinn says. "Seriously. You can't go to work at *all*?"

Jordan points at the floor with her toe. "Whose socks are these?"

"Dad?" Quinn presses. "Hello?"

A mirthless chuckle issues from the hole. "Work is closed until further notice."

Quinn looks to Skyler. She bites her lip and nods.

"But I thought you wanted—" Quinn begins. "I thought we were going to—" He looks again to Skyler, who pushes her fists into her eyes. He faces the sheet. "I mean—what happened to our *vacation?*"

He braces at the same time Skyler does, teeth clenched.

Silence in the hole. Then a release of breath.

"I'd certainly *like* to go on vacation at some point."

Quinn drops his shoulders. "You haven't set anything up yet."

"Nope."

Skyler rises. "Okay. So Quinn and I, or better yet, Jordan"—she glances encouragingly in Jordan's direction—"will set something up, and you'll come. Out. Right?"

"Let me know when you've got some ideas."

"California!" Jordan blurts, standing on her toes. "Didn't Larry Villalobos say that Mom was in—" She stops with her mouth open. The air feels suddenly poisonous.

Quinn makes an impatient hand gesture that means, *Go on.*

Jordan shuts her mouth. She irons all expression from her face and lowers herself to the ground. Her old life is gone now. "Never mind. I don't want to go on vacation."

Skyler gives her a murderous look, then turns to Quinn, imploringly.

Quinn straightens and bumps the table behind him, triggering a small avalanche of empty Pop-Tart boxes and toilet paper tubes.

"Jesus Christ!" He kicks the phone book at his feet out of his way. "Where the hell *is* Lourdes?"

Jordan clamps her hands to her hips. "I don't KNOW. And guess what? Before dinner, I want everyone to take their dirty laundry to the hamper. After dinner, your dishes need to go in the dishwasher."

Skyler turns in her chair. "Excuse me?"

"Everyone—and I mean everyone—is going to need to clean up their messes before my party." She turns toward the hole. "That means you too, Dad."

Quinn rolls his eyes. "Jo-Jo. It's *four months* until your birthday."

"Exactly," she says, liking how fierce she sounds. "Now are you going to pick up those socks or what?"

III

As Chavela sips her coffee on the bright, chilly deck, listening to the hum of her electric fence, she represses a sigh. The shopping is over. Also the cooking, the visiting, the wrapping and unwrapping, the in and out of the boys—she only dabbed her eyes a little as she sent Adam through the turnstile at airport security for the second time in two months.

Below: her husband, on foot, making slow but purposeful tracks away from the house.

Jerry. Who had emerged from the holidays not with dissatisfaction and lethargy, but with a strange energy. He jiggles his legs under tables. Scowls, mutters, paces. Of course, he walks. And when he's not walking, he's driving. And when he's not driving, he's working. And when he's working, he avoids his home office—filthy, disorganized space that it is, she can't say she blames him—retreating to his campus office instead, no matter the hour or day of the week. And then she is alone. In a house that no longer contains Inez. Which ought to make everything right.

Now her husband pauses on the sidewalk before the DuPres' house, where Miguel edges the lawn. The edger sputters to a stop. They speak, heads inclining toward each other, like two men at a table playing checkers.

Chavela whacks down her mug. ¡Oye! she could shout. ¡Espérate allá! Then she could walk over and ask Miguel if he knows anything about Lourdes.

She and Jerry had fought over whether to fire her. Could he really invent an adequate reason for not doing so? "We should give her a chance to explain herself," he said. "Pues, y how long are we supposed to wait?" she countered. "Until Easter?"

He said, "A lo menos, debes considerar that she was a stabilizing force for Inez."

"Maybe so," she retorted, "but Inez shouldn't have been using her as a force for anything, y ya no está aquí, now is she?"

"No," he answered coolly. His nostrils twitched with what she recognized as the silent language of blame.

"You never even wanted a maid!" she hissed as he left the room.

Below, with a nod, Jerry takes his leave of Miguel. He rounds the street corner like a man with an appointment.

She downs the rest of her coffee. Snatches up her BlackBerry and drills down to her list of housekeeping leads—Claudia, Jimena, María, Amaralis.

No. She taps a phone number on the speed dial instead.

"Oye, cuñado," she says when Tavo picks up.

He grunts. "Chavela? Or is it one of the other ones?"

"Listen, I need to ask you something."

"Bueno, let's get right to the point. Don't ask me how I am or anything like that."

"I'm not asking because I thought you hated being asked. Pero, ¿como estás?"

"Lousy."

"That's what I thought."

"So, what's the occasion?"

Good question. She lets out her breath. "I want to know what's the matter with your brother."

He snorts. "Who, Momo?"

"Have you talked to him lately? Do you know if anything weird happened to him?"

"You mean, like, other than being born a pompous ass?"

She tilts her head to the sky. Cloudless. "Other than that."

"It's been a couple of months since I've seen him." He clears his lungs noisily. "What seems to be the problem?"

"It's like . . ." She bunches up in her chair, unable to shut her mouth. "It's like something is bothering him but he's not saying what, he's not saying anything, we're not saying anything to each other anymore, and I just want to know, is it just some male midlife-crisis thing, or is there something else, is there anything you know about?"

The squeak and snap of a recliner chair opening. "What makes you think I would know, of all people? He's usually pissed off at me."

"Well, he doesn't get along with Inez either, but she was the only one he talked to. And you're sort of the next best thing."

A silent moment follows. Then an eruption of laughter.

"¡Que la chingada! Finally, somebody comes right out and tells me I'm second best!" The laughter crests, then subsides. "Mira, other than when he called me after Inez took off, the last time I actually talked to him he came over to my house unannounced and picked a fight. Then he gave me a titty twister."

"¿Cómo que 'titty twister'?"

"I mean, I don't know what he's got to complain about. He's got a job, even if it's a pointless job. He's got his health, his family, and he's got a damn nice house. Nice neighborhood, that's for sure." He falls silent again, then chuckles. "Nice *neighbors*."

Chavela rubs her temples. "Eh?"

"Does that good-looking güera still live down the street from you?"

"Who?"

"That little belle of the ball from Dallas. What's her name—Rosie?"

A strange sensation descends upon her, as though she's standing below a cliff over which a fine curtain of sand is pouring. And yet she cannot move out of its way. "You mean Rose Marie DuPre?"

"That's the one!"

The french doors at her back creak open. With a leap, Kiko's in her lap.

"You've met her?"

The chuckling turns lecherous.

"Yeah, and maybe I should meet her again."

Kiko wobbles. "She's gone. Left her husband."

"¿Verdad?" The recliner creaks. "Well, *that* is a shame."

"You know you're a pig, right?"

He laughs. "Haven't you heard that pigs are one of the smartest animals?"

Kiko turns a circle in her lap and settles, gazing up at her with googly eyes. "Well," she says, "at the very least, when you meet a pig, you get a pig. You know they're going to roll in the mud." She rubs Kiko's ears.

He's still laughing. "Anything else?"

"Only if you want to tell me what it's like to eat garbage."

The laughter roars in her ear.

She clicks off the phone and looks out over the foothills at the dust-colored, creosote-tufted land, the brown stripe of the river, the toxic gases rising over the city. Everything hazy but also washed out with light, indistinct. She shades her eyes. There—over the houses of her neighborhood, the commercial buildings beyond, the smokeless smokestacks of Asarco, past the freeway—the mountains lead the way into the desert. What is it her husband sees when he stands out here taking in every slope and crevice? What does he want to see? It's like he's studying the body of a woman.

A little fissure opens somewhere within her. She has no words to describe its exact nature. But she knows it's a feeling she hasn't had for a very long time.

Kiko leans from her lap to the tabletop to lick the inside of her coffee mug.

"I guess that's the difference between dogs and coyotes," she murmurs as she pulls both dog and mug back into her lap. "Dogs don't slink around."

She drags her nails through Kiko's coat. The fence below makes an electric pop. Her gaze returns to the desert. Space that begs to be filled with something. Questions maybe. *Where are you going?* would be a good start. And then, of course, *Where have you been?*

III

At first, the voice Marcus hears is so distant, so indistinct, he thinks he's hearing it on a radio. It's lost in the idling of a hundred car engines. The guy behind the wheel of the battered Lincoln Town Car—jowly, soul-patched—isn't talking. The car's plates are from Texas. The tabs are expired.

"Your citizenship, sir?" Marcus repeats.

The guy looks out over the dash. "Mexicano."

And so it goes. With a tilt of his head, Marcus signals to Ortiz and Mueller. Mueller brings the dog, a German shepherd that trots up alertly, hoping for a whiff of controlled substance.

The dog sits down at the front of the car and looks back for his biscuit.

Pull over to the inside lane, Marcus instructs the driver.

The guy looks around, too quickly, seemingly for any route but the one before him. As if. Marcus bites down on the edge of his bad mood. "Temporary rotations will be in effect," the department memo said, "in order to best utilize our resources during the current agent shortage."

Pull over, he reiterates, with more force.

"Ayúdame!" says the radio voice, growing in volume. "Ay, por favor!" A woman's voice. Marcus's eyes dart from dashboard to back seat.

Turn off the car, he barks.

The driver clutches the wheel.

"Ayúdame!"

"Jesus Christ," Marcus says. He bangs on the hood. "Open it up! Ábrelo!"

The woman is spread-eagled over the engine, facedown, on a singed blanket. He peels her off as she sobs.

"Jesus Christ," he repeats once he's lowered her to the ground. She's tiny and round, Indian-looking and strangely familiar in a way he can't place, with bobbed black hair. Her face and hands and the fronts of her thighs are raw and pink with burns. How long have you been in there?

I don't know, she says between sobs. A few hours.

Ortiz and Mueller make a swift dance of removing first the guy from the car, then the wrapped brick of meth from under the engine block.

Where are you from? he asks the woman.

"Chiapas."

Are those your drugs?

Her face clouds. What drugs?

He sighs. Did you give that guy money to bring you?

She looks away, lip trembling.

He settles her in the office with apple juice, saltines, and a tube of first aid ointment while she awaits her ride to the detention center.

"Maybe she can get a job jumping out of a cake," Peña calls out from his lane when Marcus trudges back outside.

Ortiz waves a car through. "You hear about those people who got dumped outside Samayaluca yesterday? She should consider herself lucky."

"She should ride in the fridge next time," Mueller says. The nine guys who were pried out of the freezer compartment of a semi in Laredo last week were curled under stacked sides of beef.

Marcus snorts. Last week, on the last night he'd been out on field duty, they'd run into none other than Cárdenas the Joker.

Twice, man? Marcus asked as Peña's flashlight beam joined his. Seriously?

Cárdenas offered his toothy smile. "¿Qué tal, oficiales?"

Peña, chuckling, shook his head. You know what's going to happen if you get caught again, right? Three strikes and all that.

Cárdenas looked chastened. "Sí, sí, claro." He let out his breath. "Seré mas listo en el futuro."

I will be—Marcus picked apart the words in his head, cinching the plastic cuffs around Cárdenas' wrists—more smart. Smarter. In the future.

"¿Oficial?"

Something in his tone made Marcus hesitate. "¿Sí?"

Cárdenas lowered his voice. "¿No hay otra manera de . . . manejarlo?"

Down at his thigh, Cárdenas rubbed his thumb against his fingers.

Marcus blinked in the moment it took him to understand. Then he choked back a laugh.

"No, no, no, no!"

"¿Veinte?"

Marcus shook his head. "Dude, keep your twenty. It's hopeless. Busca trabajo *allá*." He tipped his chin in the direction of Mexico.

Cárdenas shrugged. "No hay trabajo."

Then apply for citizenship, Peña told him.

With what money? I don't have a job.

They escorted him to the Zaragoza Bridge and put him in the line going south, where Cárdenas grinned and said, See you next week.

Watch out for you-know-who, Peña called out as he disappeared behind the chain link. Remember that sheep?

Of course. When those agents in San Elizario discovered the exit to a hand-dug tunnel underneath a Honey Bucket on a dairy farm, Peña crowed, "Now we know how the Chupacabra has been getting over here!" The time that wet shot the agent in the leg out near Van Horn,

Peña said, "They never caught the guy, right? That's because it was actually the Chupacabra!" Then came the standoff. Agents versus Mexican soldiers, each claiming the other had trespassed into each other's country in some hazy, unfenced area miles from the river—"an encounter that almost became an international incident," the news had reported. This, at last, gave Peña some pause. "Forget the war on drugs, man," he told Marcus, shaking his head. "We're at war with Mexico." He'd waited two breaths before he'd added, "Although I think it's time somebody admitted that the Chupacabra is head of the main drug cartel around here."

"Órale!" Peña calls out now. "Why drive when you can fly? How do you top that airplane dude? Can that even be topped?"

Last week some guy had sneaked onto the runway at the airport in Tijuana and hitched a ride to Sacramento by chaining himself to the fin of a 747. And survived, albeit deeply in shock and with none of his clothes.

Marcus looks to the office. The woman wipes her nose on her shoulder, slumping over her cuffed hands, head bowed. And suddenly he thinks, *Inez*. The woman in the office might be heavier, her hair shorter, but the resemblance is obvious, even if his aunt has never sat that way in a chair in her life.

Inez. Who is gone.

He looks away. The light burns his eyes. His line is backed up to eternity. The dog pants and whines on his tether in the shade, as though sensing something. Something that rings inside all of their heads, almost inaudible, like a voice on somebody else's radio. As though the world has been turned up to a higher frequency.

"Just wait," he answers, though he's not sure if anyone hears him.

III

"Where's Lourdes?" bellows the voice at Miguel's back. "Why hasn't she come back? Is she on vacation?"

La Jordan. Again. He looks up from his crouch at the rear of his truck. She presses her fists to her hips, hair sticking out like an orange feather duster.

"I dunno."

He feels her waiting behind him as he fiddles with the toolbox, opening things, shutting them. He doesn't turn.

She huffs and storms away as quickly as she appeared.

He tosses in the rake. He hasn't slept well in a week, and now he's supposed to be Lourdes's keeper. Even his jefe Gonzales, cornering him on the sidewalk an hour ago with pleasantries about the weather and the lawn care business, finally asked, Would you happen to know if Lourdes is planning to return to us?

Miguel raked grass. "I don't know nothing about it."

Gonzales had raised an eyebrow, as though appraising him on a different matter entirely. "I don't suppose you . . . live near her?"

Miguel raked. He shook his head.

"I guess that means you live . . . ?" Gonzales circled a finger, as though searching for something nearby on a map. Miguel raked. Gonzales clasped his hands behind his back and turned his gaze toward the clouds. "Is there anything worse than vacation? It puts people in a bad mood because there's nothing to do. Then it puts them in a worse mood because they know they have to go back to work."

Someone—Mrs. Gonzales, probably—was watching them from the Gonzaleses' deck. He could tell by the way she was leaning over the railing.

Of course he knew Lourdes was gone. Did they think he was blind? If his mother wasn't still mad about him and Luz moving out, he'd ask her to look into it. But it was also Lourdes's private business if she wanted to ghost these people, and anyway, didn't he sometimes fantasize about doing the same thing? Maybe Lourdes was the only one who actually had the cojones to do it.

He brushes away the dry grass from the underside of the mower. *Well, what do you wanna do?* he imagines his father asking him now. Personally, he'd like to ask his wife the same question. But Luz had looked so sick and gray this morning—too much like Papá had looked at the end—that even now his tongue feels thick in his throat. He wouldn't trouble her. There was more than one kind of trouble, and of course, he would never be able to discuss any of it with her.

The funny thing was that it would be Lourdes's ear he would bend now, if he could. He would wait for a glimpse of her and then cross the street, looking over his shoulder, to say, *You're not going to believe this.* And then he would tell her how, this morning as he was pulling dandelions from the front planter, before anyone else in the neighborhood was awake, their jefe DuPre had come out of his house, unshowered, uncombed, to ask him if he knew anything about cleaning a house.

"We could use some extra help," he said.

Miguel set down his spade. "Well, I got a lot of jobs already."

DuPre chuckled bitterly, his eyes bright on Miguel's face, as he ran a hand through his hair. "Well, but my wife is gone."

Lourdes would laugh about that. No further words would be necessary.

Which was perfect, because, of course, he wouldn't be able to tell her what he really saw in DuPre's eyes. That behind his vacant expression, there was also something hard. Something that wasn't saying as much as it could. It had been there all along. Hadn't it?

There was no one he could tell that to. No one.

III

Your passport, señora, says the man across the counter from Lourdes, and he slides it across the countertop.

She flips it open to her own unsmiling photo, her breath caught in her throat.

And the border crossing card? she asks, trying to sound all business. *I need another application, no? Another fee? How long will it take?*

The man stamps a paper without looking at her, scratching a fleshy mole on his nose.

Everything requires an application and a fee. *The card isn't a requirement. It's just a convenience, so you don't have to carry your passport around everywhere. You should keep your documents somewhere safe.*

She nods in the dismissive way that means, *Of course.* Her nephew had filled out the form for her on the computer down the hall, pushing the right buttons with one finger. She can see the line of people waiting for a computer from here. She peeks in her book again. She *exists.* Even if, as with the birth certificate she paid for at the back of an auto repair shop with Simón's last money order, her birth date is the wrong month and has made her a year older. What, you want a *Mexican* one? the man who took her order asked. There were twelve of us, she told him, and none of us was born in a hospital. Anyway, do I look like I speak English? He shrugged. Does it matter?

Next in line! the passport man calls out with impatience, his voice echoing in the cavernous gray room.

She opens her English notebook at an empty bus stop bench at the end of the block.

The creased pages flutter in her lap. On a blank page, with a blue-lead pencil, she prints a single word.

"Inez."

Maybe she should write, "Dear Inez." Except that it sounds so cozy, it makes her slightly nauseous. And in which language to proceed? She presses her pencil to the page again, willing it to move. This would be so much easier if she had her employers' phone numbers. Or a phone, though it raises her pulse to think about figuring out how to punch in all the numbers on a phone card—she might as well call Russia.

On the little TV at the newsstand behind her, an announcer's voice says, Early this morning, the mutilated bodies of three more young women were found in the desert outside Ciudad Juárez, bringing the total this year to one hundred and thirty-seven. In other news, the U.S. war in Iraq—

A hot lump rises in Lourdes's throat. Last week, she opened her door to two huge uniformed güeros and an American in camouflage whose name tag read, "Cpl. Ramírez." The güeros said, "Guten Morgen." The corporal said, You're not in trouble, as she tried to slam shut the door. He asked if she knew where Mateo was and tried not to smile when she said, I don't even know where my own daughter is, much less that son of a whore. They persisted anyway, the güeros asking Ramírez questions in their throat-scraping, impossible-to-understand English, Ramírez turning to her to ask if she thought they were still in Mexico, or if they had gone to the other side.

Lourdes folded her arms. Don't worry about us, Mamá, Rosario had said in her note. Mateo has friends who will help us. We'll send money when we can. At least you'll have one less mouth to feed.

I have no idea, she told them, which—strictly speaking—was true. How did you even find me?

Someone on base knew which maquila your daughter worked at. Before the strikes. Did he mention any reason he might—

Maybe he didn't want to go where you're sending him.

Ramírez lifted an eyebrow. There's no official word on that yet. Technically, Germany is opposed to the war. But yes, there are rumors. Things could change.

What if you don't catch him?

They'll catch him, Ramírez clarified. Wherever he is, there's only so long he can get by. He's not a citizen of either country.

No, she thought. He's not. His eyes had traveled far, far away as he sat at her table. He'd said, I think I am sick for home.

She looked from Ramírez to the two big güeros compacting the dirt before her front door, trying not to show the tremor in her own hands.

Who is going to tell me? she insisted. Who is going to tell me if you find them?

Ramírez spoke to the Germans. The Germans spoke to each other. They eyed her and made German sounds until the taller of the two reached into a pocket and, with an encouraging smile, produced a business card.

You can call them to follow up, Ramírez explained. They can usually find a translator.

She stared at the card in her hand.

Now a bus belches to a gasoline-scented stop before her; the people elbow their way out. She should have asked those gabachos how to spell the funny-sounding word that means Mateo had left them without permission. She could have written it down in this very notebook. And wouldn't Inez love *that*?

"Deer Inez." She erases the greeting with force, as though señora Gonzales herself were looking over her shoulder. In English, no. And not to Inez. It will never work. Nothing will work. Her handwriting looks like a child's.

Farther down the street, a cumbia plays on a tinny radio, and someone calls out, selling chicharrones. A whole family of Indians begs on the corner. She turns away from them, the women in their threadbare rebozos, their dirty feet in their sandals.

Five days. That's how long until her grocery money runs out.

"Estimado señor!" she begins.

19

TRESPASS

"FROM LOURDES?" JERRY TURNS OVER the folded, pencil-smudged paper in his hands. "¿En serio? How did you get this?"

Miguel shrugs. "From my mom."

"Lourdes gave this to your *mother*?"

"No. She gave it to my tía."

"Wait. So you . . . know each other after all?"

Miguel shrugs. "We're cousins."

And Jerry can only look on in wonder as Miguel bids him an "Anyway, see you later" and retreats toward the idling heap of his truck.

He reads as he drifts into the kitchen.

"What's that?" Chavela wants to know.

He hesitates, then passes her the note. "A message smuggled from prison."

She sets down her bottle of spray cleaner and frowns into the page. "Well, it's her own fault if she didn't get her papers in order. And there are plenty more where she came from."

He watches from the corner of his eye as she resumes her countertop scrubbing. She has yet to find a satisfactory replacement for Lourdes, but she's still conducting interviews. He allows a long moment to elapse before he answers, "Indeed."

She slows, not quite looking at him. "But *what*?"

"Nothing." He settles in at the kitchen table and lifts the newspaper. "Not. A. Thing."

She spritzes the food processor. "You know, these people choose to work here."

"Oh yes. Of course. Absolutely true."

"And they know what's going to happen if they aren't reliable."

"I'm certain they do."

He can feel her eyes warming the side of his head. Outside, Miguel's truck has moved, as though teleported, to the opposite side of the street. "Why are you agreeing with me?" she asks.

"Is there some reason I shouldn't?"

"Because you don't."

He turns a page. "I don't believe I said anything of the sort."

"But I know what you're thinking."

"What I think," he says, "what I *have* been thinking, is that maybe we still need a vacation."

"Involving what? Some isolated cabin in the woods?"

"I was thinking somewhere bigger. More worthwhile. Like . . . Europe."

"You're kidding me, right? Have you forgotten that we're putting a kid through college?"

He casts a languid eye in the direction of the lawn mower that roars to life farther down the block. "No. But neither am I unaware of the illegal expenses in our budget."

She whacks down the spray bottle. He folds the newspaper and rises.

"Going somewhere?" she asks with ice in her voice.

"To the neighbors'!" he announces. His voice sounds bold in his ears, full of conviction and cheer.

And yet as the celestial gonging of a particular neighboring doorbell dies away between the Grecian-style porch columns at his back, he finds he's gritting his teeth. He zips his jacket against the late-winter chill. Downwind, the breeze has lightened the brown haze of the city to the color of pantyhose. A voice rises sharply within the house and is answered by another. And another.

Cacophony. The junior DuPres, it would seem, in the midst of some kind of squabble. Perhaps, he tells himself with a sudden rush of hope, this is a bad time. He could still scuttle back down the driveway. Except that, damn it all: Lourdes. Lourdes and her smuggled note, addressing him as though he were some sort of divine intercessor—"I am sorry I have not been to work señor I did not mean to go Awall, if you permit me to come back to clean for you maybe everybody else will not be so mad." She had put her trust in him; she had asked for his aid, *his* specifically, and that had touched him. And it made him angry, that he was touched. It made him angrier still that he felt compelled—independent of any suggestion!—to help her further. This called, on some level, for self-punishment.

He presses the doorbell again.

From within, a crashing. The sudden roar of a television. The voices rise again. "Don't answer that!" yells a female voice, and then the door jerks open.

It's the youngest DuPre, a girl, and she greets him impassively.

He had hoped for Quinn. "Good afternoon, young lady."

"Hi."

"Who is it?" yells the same female voice from within.

"Adam's dad," she yells back, without turning around.

"Shit," he thinks he hears the voice say.

And then there is a longish pause, after which a disheveled and surprised-looking Quinn elbows his way into the doorway.

"Dr. G," he says, blinking through smudged eyeliner. "What's up?"

An unexpected swelling of gladness fills Jerry's chest.

"M'ijo!" he booms, and he claps Quinn on the arm before he can stop himself. "I don't believe I've seen you since your birthday."

Quinn swallows and smiles feebly at his socked feet. "Yeah."

"Right. Well." Jerry's hands find his pockets. "I was actually hoping to speak with your father, if he's around. I have some information for him about Lourdes."

"Where is she?" the girl demands, still lodged in the doorway beneath Quinn's elbow.

"She's in Juárez. Now if I could just tell your father—"

"Um," Quinn begins.

"He's not really available," the girl finishes.

But here, the elder DuPre girl, her rat's nest of hair looped in a Gordian knot atop her head, appears behind them both.

"Oh, yes he is," she says, forcefully. "Come on in."

The look Quinn gives her as Jerry steps into the foyer does not escape him.

Something crunches beneath his loafers. He lifts a foot from a crushed dog biscuit, then steps off a trail of soiled paper towels and the fallen fronds of a brown holiday garland dangling overhead. The air is redolent of sandalwood incense and sour milk.

"Can I get you some coffee?"

The younger girl is all business now. The other two have fled.

"Please remind me of your name."

"Jordan."

"I appreciate the offer, Jordan, but I'm already sufficiently caffeinated."

"We also have tea. And Tang."

Atop the lamp on the entryway table, a topless Barbie doll rides a white rubber rat.

"I'll keep that in mind."

"Dad." The elder DuPre girl's voice, in the next room. "You have to come out."

The response is muffled.

"He's waiting. He knows something about Lourdes."

Muffle, muffle.

"No, he wants to talk to *you*."

Muffle, muffle, muffle.

"Fine then. We're coming in to get you."

Next follows an irritated grunt, an exchange of sharp words, and the slow shuffle of slippers on hardwood. Jerry clasps his hands behind his back, fastening a pleasant expression to his face.

Huck DuPre could stand to run a comb through his hair. He could use a shave. A change of clothes might not be a bad idea either, unless the stained sweats he's wearing are meant to be pajamas. But who is he, Jerry tells himself as Huck teeters slightly before him in the entryway, to judge someone's appearance on a Saturday morning? Even if the needed shave clearly should have happened several days ago.

"Huck," Jerry begins. "Hello."

"Afternoon." Huck's gaze, focused at the top of Jerry's head, is strangely vacant, like a Civil War soldier in an old photograph.

"I wanted to let you know about Lourdes," Jerry begins quickly. "She's had a mishap with her paperwork, but she extends her apologies and hopes you'll take her back when she—"

"Fine. Send her over. Whenever."

"Okay, great," Jerry says, already turning. "I'll let her know."

He cannot explain why, once he is free of that vacant gaze, he turns back.

"Incidentally," he says, and he glances around the room in what he hopes is a circumspect manner, "I think we'll *all* be glad to see Lourdes again. I know how challenging it can be to keep up with things, especially when you've got a houseful of kids."

Huck grunts noncommittally.

"Right." He should go now. "Well." He should flee. "So, Huck. Just wondering—is everything okay?"

Through Huck's nose comes a faint puff of air. "Everything's terrific."

And with that, Huck shuffles back out. A rattling clatter in the adjacent room follows, as though someone were climbing into an enormous package of cheese.

"I'll let myself out," Jerry says to no one.

But here appears Jordan, this time with a cup of coffee in each hand and a can of 7UP in her hoodie pocket. She regards him stoically, disappears into the next room, and reappears almost instantly, less one mug.

"It's better when he has some coffee," she tells him. "Or a Dr Pepper." She extends the steaming mug to him, as though the offering were both a question and a command.

He retracts his hand from the doorknob and accepts the mug. "I see."

"I have an IQ of 154," she says, once he's taken a scalding mouthful. She pops opens her soda can.

"Not bad." He sips. "Jordan, is everyone getting enough to eat around here these days?"

"Of course," she says, with offense. "*I'm* cooking."

"Ah, forgive me. Is everyone managing to get to school?"

"As far as I know. Miguel takes me."

He raises an eyebrow. "Really?"

"Is Lourdes okay?"

"As far as I know."

"Is she coming back?"

He takes another sip, a long one. The coffee is of middling quality but well prepared. He asks himself what he is still doing in this house. How he could have possibly arrived at this moment in his life. Whether kindness is actually the cruelest act of all.

"Honestly," he says, "I'd give it about a fifty-fifty chance. I hope it works out. But perhaps your father can find someone else to help around the house if—"

"*No.* I want Lourdes."

He studies the girl before him, her freckled face turned up toward his like that of an intense and determined sunflower. She bears a remarkable resemblance to her mother. Her elusive, unobtainable, irrelevant yet still unbearably attractive mother. Who had, incidentally, abandoned her own children. He takes another sip. "Of course you do."

They drink their beverages together in the foyer, with space between them, in silence.

III

Marcus comes for dinner, straight from work, still in uniform.

"Welcome," Jerry says in the tone one would use to greet a visiting dignitary.

"Howdy." Marcus tosses his keys and sunglasses into the change bowl and unbuttons himself at the throat.

Chavela is all aglow upon Marcus's arrival. Her hands alight on his shoulders, his elbows, his wrists as she guides him to the dining room. Adam finds this amusing. "She's in *love* with him," he whispers to Jerry. For Adam, too, is home once again—a so-called midwinter break. Marcus bears his turn patiently. He smiles, answering his mother's questions about his day as she scrapes a fat chicken breast onto his plate. She even glances up at Jerry, a private glance, her expression knowing and nostalgic.

It takes him aback, this moment of softness. Then she looks away and it's gone.

He stirs his mashed potatoes. He cannot begrudge his wife this pleasure with their sons—to actually have both boys in the house at once, at the dinner table, filling up the space between their parents. Perhaps it's evidence of nature's sense of humor that despite their trappings—police versus punk—the boys' resemblance to each other, and to Jerry himself, is unmistakable. Chavela gives him another look across the table, reading his mind, brimming with the same thoughts.

It strikes him as possible that things are returning to a state he vaguely recalls as normal.

Either way, Chavela relinquishes Marcus to him after dinner, and for that he is grateful. He brings his son up to the deck at sunset.

"Jesus. So that's what it's like back here with that thing on."

Jerry doesn't even bother to follow his gaze. The buzz from the wall isn't so much audible as tactile—it makes the hairs inside his nose vibrate.

"I guess it *has* been a while since we've seen you."

Marcus leans for a better look. "How can you stand it?"

"I'm told it's for the protection of Speedy Gonzales."

"Why doesn't Mom just keep him inside at night?"

"I guess she thinks there's no such thing as being too safe."

Down in the yard, the minidog is zipping from end to end, chasing imaginary birds in the waning light. Jerry reaches into the plate of snacks he has spirited to the patio table and tosses down a few chunks of smoked cheddar cheese.

"I guess it might keep out the illegals," Marcus continues.

Jerry assumes a dry expression. "Ha ha."

"Or maybe it'll just keep you out of Mexico."

"Very funny." He drinks deeply from his Diet Coke and imagines Lourdes, under cover of night, trying to scale the rear wall into his yard, only to meet with five thousand volts of disincentive. "Speaking of which, how's work?"

Marcus shrugs. "Fine."

Jerry allows for a moment's pause.

"Of course," he says, "the job's different than it used to be. The border is different. The *world* is different."

Again Marcus shrugs. But something shifts in his face. Under his face. Wherever he is as he looks behind his own eyes.

Jerry leans over the table. "Look, Son, if you ever take it in your head to finish school, I just want you to know that you have my full support."

"Dad."

"I'm trying to tell you something here."

"Dad."

"There will come a day," Jerry says quickly, "later in your life, when you look back at the sum of what your experiences have been thus far, at the things done and not done, and you'll have to reckon with your legacy, with the life you have created for yourself, and then—"

"Dad, are we really talking about me?"

"What else would we be talking about?"

"You tell me," Marcus says, and he turns to him.

A strange cooling sensation descends upon Jerry, as though a wind were blowing through some aperture in his jacket. "Whatever do you mean?" he asks lightly.

Marcus looks at him but also does not look at him. His knee has begun to bounce under the table. "Yeah, well, things might be different, but . . ." He shrugs. "I mean, the more things change, the more they stay the same. Right?"

Jerry leans back in his seat. "I don't understand."

"Oh, come on. You were La Llorona. You can't tell me that was the only thing you ever did."

His son's gaze refocuses, and within it is a sharpness that is in jest but also not in jest.

Jerry sets down his drink. "Did something happen at work?"

Marcus offers the faintest shake of his head.

The chill moving through Jerry turns to flame. "Who have you been talking to?"

Marcus stiffens. "No one." He looks away. "Forget it."

"Forget about what?" calls a voice as the back door scuds open, and then appears Adam, plopping himself down into a deck chair beside them.

"Work," Marcus mutters.

Adam cracks open the full-sugar Coke in his hand. "Ooh, exciting."

"I actually happen to be pretty good at it," Marcus clarifies without looking at Jerry.

Adam lifts his soda can, swirling it before him like it's a good glass of wine. "I'm pleased you find your career so rewarding," he responds with a fake British accent. "I, however, require a greater center of civilization."

Marcus spears a cheese cube with the corner of a cracker. "Last I heard, San Diego isn't exactly paradise either."

"Well, there's more to life than *this* place, that's for sure."

Jerry swallows. "This city isn't so bad. It's your home. It's what made you."

A silence precedes his sons' nearly simultaneous answer: "Right."

The sunset is like the world ending in orange and pink.

Marcus drains his soda can. "I've gotta split, Dad."

He and his brother shake hands, facetiously. To Jerry, Marcus submits to the clapped hug, the quick "See you later, Son." Not that he meets his father's eye, exactly, but in his unhurried retreat is the silent acknowledgment that all is water under the bridge. Jerry suddenly is too tired to accompany him downstairs, to lean against the door and watch him drive away, as parents do, to impart their invisible seal of safety in travel. Marcus is a big boy now. He can take care of himself. His footsteps thud down the stairs.

From the den emanates the chatter of the evening news—the latest incursions, Jerry gathers, the explosions that might be American or might be sectarian. He looks to his younger son and finds himself welling up with gratitude that he has lived to see a time when his country's military draft seemingly won't be put to use again. Adam leans in repose over the deck railing, his striped hair ruffling in the breeze. Jerry doesn't know what his son sees. He doesn't know what he's thinking. His heart squeezes plaintively in his chest.

"Did you know," Jerry tells him as the dog zips below, "that they love the original Speedy Gonzales in Mexico? By the time Warner Brothers admitted to America that the character was racist and pulled him from the cartoon lineup, he was already a symbol of Mexican national pride."

Adam gives him the *You are insane* look.

Jerry laughs. "Good night, Son." He gives Adam an arm clap as he passes, as casually as he can manage. Adam responds, not skipping a beat, with a soft, quick whack to Jerry's forehead. Jerry reaches after him and misses, and they're both laughing as Adam disappears into the house.

Jerry sits.

He doesn't know how long he's been there before he starts hearing the night around him. Chirp of crickets and rustle of mice. In the absence of human sound, the fence assumes the faintest audible pitch, a low monotone. And there, just at the edge of his hearing—something else. On the other side of the wall, down in the blind spot. Something paces, four legs back and forth, figure-eighting as though in hunger.

He steps quickly and quietly down into the yard, plucks up a rock from the landscaping, and lobs it over the wall. It whizzes silently and he doesn't hear anything scrambling away and he doesn't hear the rock fall.

He knows, then. It's not four legs he hears, but two. And with a pull in his body as deep and tangled as the roots of a tree, he knows to whom they belong.

III

In the bolt and screw aisle of Home Depot, as he scouts for something that could reattach the temperature dial of his washing machine, Jerry steps back from the shelves and bumps shoulder to shoulder with the body behind his, which turns out to be Tavo's.

His brother lifts an eyebrow at him as they right themselves. "Since when do *you* know how to operate a screwdriver?"

Jerry straightens. How many months has it been since they've seen each other? Since they've even spoken?

"I wouldn't worry about *me*, hermano," he says with a once-over of Tavo's physique. "But I'll bet you haven't operated *your* screwdriver in a while."

"Pinche cabrón," Tavo fires back, and then he laughs.

They walk to the checkout together.

"So. Heard anything from Inez?" Tavo asks as the two of them make their way to the parking lot. The Mexican day laborers at the periphery gaze hopefully in their direction.

The sky has begun to darken under a raft of fast-moving clouds. "Not since she tried to murder me," Jerry begins.

"You are shitting me," Tavo says when he's heard enough. He shields his eyes from the thickening grit in the breeze. "So who won?"

Jerry dons sunglasses. "Both of us. Neither of us. Actually, I have no idea."

"Figures. She was always pretty strong. Remember that time she pushed Papá's Chevy off the curb?" He shakes his head. "What do you want to bet we'll never see her again?"

Jerry zips up his windbreaker. He could tell him. About what he heard on the other side of the fence.

Instead he says, "Hold tight for another ten years and I guess we'll see."

"We'll see." Tavo digs through the purchases in his plastic bag. "So. Still pissing off your wife?"

The wind gusts. Jerry winces against the grit but doesn't turn.

"I beg your pardon?"

Tavo retrieves a packet of washers and shakes them, as though he finds their size annoying. "Well, she was pretty fed up with you, wasn't she?"

A strange chill has begun to permeate the air. A nosebleeding dryness. "How would you know?"

"She called me."

Jerry pulls back his chin. "She *called* you?"

"What, you didn't know?" Tavo laughs and tosses the washers back to the bottom of the bag. "That was weeks ago. She wanted to know what was the matter with you, hombre."

Jerry takes hold of the spindly tree rattling its leaves in the parking median. "What's the *matter* with me? What makes anyone think there's something the matter with *me*? Why was she asking *you*?"

"Tranquilo," Tavo says. "She didn't know who else to ask. Plus, anyways, what's the matter with asking *me*?"

"And what did you tell her?" Jerry's voice rises. The laborers, collars up and cap brims down, look up and turn back to their huddle. The air is like sandpaper in a wind tunnel.

"I said I never had any idea what the hell is wrong with you. But whatever, man. I guess I shouldn't have mentioned it."

"Right. Right. Let's keep things secret from Jerry, shall we?"

Tavo rolls his eyes. "You're right, Momito. There's nothing the matter with you *at all*."

"Talking to my wife behind my back—" Jerry sputters.

"When you finally piss off all the people you know," Tavo calls out as Jerry stomps toward his car, "where you gonna go *then*?"

Jerry's foot is heavy on the gas as he wheels out of the parking lot.

Home. It looms before him, looking real but not real, like an artist's rendition of his house, as he pulls into the driveway. The door of the Volvo echoes when he slams it.

"So," he says, bristling in the kitchen doorway. "I suppose you've heard that saying about loose lips."

Chavela is at her laptop. The expression on her face is one of someone who has heard little but is still annoyed at being interrupted.

"Loose what?"

"If we were in the navy, we'd be halfway underwater by now."

She looks up. "Como que 'navy'? Are you speaking English?"

"¿Qué importa? Apparently, you had plenty to say to Tavo about our private affairs."

There's no mistaking the ripple of guilt that moves across her eyes. He could stop here, he tells himself. He's made his point.

"Or maybe these days," he hears himself hissing, "you just find my brother more . . . *interesting* than I am."

Chavela's expression cools. "Is there some reason you think you're any better than him?"

He regards her with a bitter smile. "I could provide a list, but I tend to think the reasons are self-evident."

"You think you're better than everybody, don't you?"

Deep within him, at the feet of the discontent that has slithered and pressed inside him these past months, rears a dark and powerful urge.

"At the very least," he retorts, "I don't think I'm any better than the hired help."

"Por Dios. Is this about Lourdes again?"

He shrugs. "Sure. Lourdes. Definitely. But maybe we're talking about *all* Mexicans."

She gives him a look that—he sees now for the first time—his sons had inherited from her.

"What I think," she says, her chest rising, "is that I am an American citizen."

He leans against the archway, his leg bouncing. "Your father came in on the Bracero Program. Your mother married into her citizenship. You're only one step removed from Lourdes."

The sting of his words flashes across her face and then disappears. "I see. And did *your* ancestors come over on the *Mayflower*?"

"That question is irrelevant. As you know, my family has been here for ten generations. *Ten.*"

"Are you trying to out-American me?" she rasps.

"So, what do you think Marcus thinks of your employees? You've never explained your economic policy to him, have you?"

She slams shut the binder. "I know what I'm about. And I'm not obligated to explain my decisions to my children."

"Ah, I see." He smiles bleakly at the ceiling. "Don't ask, don't tell."

"Bueno," she says. "Maybe you're right. Maybe that's been our policy for too long around here."

"She chose me," he barks. "She chose *me*, over anyone else."

"What? What? Who? ¿De quién estamos hablando?"

"Lourdes, of course. Who else would we be talking about?"

"You tell *me*."

The look she offers him is so black, it seems to suck the light from the room. Once upon a time, he'd whisked this woman away in an orange Ford Pinto and together, hand in hand, they'd fled—she from her father, he from . . . what?

He turns heel.

Chavela rises. "¿Y *ahora* a dónde vas?"

"¡Por un paseo!" he roars.

"A drive," she calls to him as he stomps back out to the Volvo, "is *not* a destination!"

He scrapes the car's undercarriage as he guns it out of the driveway.

Anyway, Chavela's got it wrong. He knows where he's going. He plows down the freeway, exiting at the opposite end of the city, turning south and east, into the Lower Valley. Grit blows in gusts against the windshield. A greening panorama of cotton and alfalfa crops, still only shin high, lean at a hard, windblown angle in the distance. He turns down a dirt road, pebbles whacking around in the wheel wells, until—there, just ahead, in a weed-choked swath of land lying prone against the river and the belly of Mexico—there is the bare patch of ground where once stood the squat adobe house of his paternal grandparents. He idles beside the irrigation ditch where he'd spent countless hours pitching rocks. A short distance away he can discern the remains of a pen that had once been the home of an enormous, foul-tempered sow, who could be poked with sticks to provocative effect. Beyond the fields, in the now annexed village of Ysleta, he and his siblings had traipsed in the afternoons to consume pan dulces by the dozen, or after dusk to descend upon the drive-in movie theater, orange-crate benches in hand. Here. Where the wind blows the wild yellow grass. Where his grandparents and great-grandparents were born Americans but never spoke English.

He drives.

He cruises into the old village, passing the whitewashed walls and silver dome of the Misión de Corpus Christi de Ysleta del Sur, place of his baptism. Across the street, kitty-corner, lie a Carl's Jr. and the Tigua-owned Speaking Rock Indian casino, now offering bingo on Wednesday nights.

He is seized with a desire to change direction. To the north and west, say.

He wheels north onto a familiar boulevard, moving into the heart of the city, as his parents once did, so that they might sweep the floors of office complexes and sew Levi's jeans and cowboy boots in factories and send their children to public schools where they would be spanked if they spoke Spanish. And here, where once was a horse pasture, now lies a pizza parlor. In the middle of a cotton field, with both the Ysleta-Zaragoza Port of Entry into Mexico and a waterslide park in sight, a Kmart sits. On the street where a rainbow-bright mural of the Virgen de Guadalupe peers all-knowingly through the pumping bay of a gas station, one now encounters the Templo Palabras de Vida Eterna and the Centro Cristiano Restauración and the Iglesia Cristiana Pentecostes—evangelical imports from points farther south. He motors past the cemeteries with their plastic flowers ever at attention; past La Llanta Tires and Wheels and its accompanying ecosystem of auto paint, parts, and body shops; past First Cash Pawn and the giant white horsehead of the Bronco Swap Meet; past the neighborhoods of low houses, squat and brick, some of them painted—in the tradition of another country—in shades of lavender and aqua and bubblegum pink. Wrought iron bars encase every window and door.

He emerges in the east, into a universe of sixties-era split-levels with two-car garages, video superstores, Walmarts. He aims west. Downtown. Past lawyers' offices and a day spa and a carnicería and a tortillería and a Kentucky Fried Chicken and a palm reader; past the cedar-lined park where in his youth his extended family would gather for barbecues, a preposterous number of guitars in tow so that adults might all sing "Solamente Una Vez" and a pre–Ritchie Valens "La Bamba" and "Cielito Lindo" while the kids rolled their eyes and begged for Elvis; past La Botánica Divina Luz, advertising a special on charms that will both ward off the evil eye and promote luck after DUI arrests; past a billboard promising pristine new real estate somewhere at the edges of the incorporated city.

"Welcome to my world," he mutters aloud to himself. As though he were his own passenger. "Welcome to El Chuco, Sun City, the Pass to the North."

At his flank now, the port of entry known as the Bridge of the Americas.

He squints down the street before the light changes. Is he only imagining that the grid of idling traffic is less dense than it was a few months ago? Is the human tide thinner?

There, he scolds Chavela inside his own head. *Just what you wanted, right? You're like the United States after the annexation of Texas. Invite them all over to work, then send them home when you decide there's too many of them.*

He passes the movie theater of his youth, its ornate stone façade now lit with a blinking modern marquee—and, thinking of a certain afternoon in the company of his sister, long ago—swallows the fierce knot in his throat.

I'll bet if you could, he continues at his wife, passing the old downtown plaza where he was once spanked for successfully aiming a slingshot loaded with used chewing gum at a live alligator, *you'd pull a Herbert Hoover. Is the economy in the toilet? Are you losing popularity among your constituents? You know who's to blame for that. Time to deport!* "Repatriate!" *By the hundreds of thousands!*

He turns to avoid the downtown Sunday flea market, then slips onto the freeway, evading the speed trap under the Sunbeam Texas Best Bread factory sign. The golden-haired-girl logo munches her slice at him. *Speaking of having it both ways,* he continues, blood rising, *I guess you'll have to come up with a new guest worker policy at home. But watch out—the ghost of Cesar Chavez might organize against you.*

He exits the freeway, into a residential area where he cannot help but slow, as though he were a passenger in one of the raucous, slow-cruising vehicles of the Saturday nights of his youth, turning his head in front of an asphalt parking lot at the juncture of two streets, toward an edifice modified beyond all recognition.

He might linger. But the house he grew up in was transformed into a bail and bond service long ago.

The more things change. He turns the corner, and to imaginary Chavela again. Satisfyingly, she can barely meet his eyes. *And so. Shall we have another Operation Wetback? Or perhaps a new Operation "Rescue." Let's round 'em up and get 'em out! With violence, please. And forget due process. Separate the families, while you're at it. Or just send back the children. Even the acculturated ones. And the non-Spanish-speaking ones. And the ones who are actually U.S.-born. God knows it's been far too long since it occurred to anyone to do* that.

He cruises yet another street of sagging bungalows. *Look.* He lets out his breath. *We all know the rules. The limits. We know.*

He slows in front of a stone-porch bungalow, former home of one Marilyn Lawson, brief high school girlfriend. Briefer than either of them would have liked. Another knot rises within him. What if, during this era of his youth, he'd instead met Rose Marie DuPre? Somehow. Somewhere. Whatever her name once was. Would she have looked twice in his direction? With what expression etched on her face?

He guns the engine, hard.

He goes west, slipping exactly between the red-roofed university above and the imposing baroque stone below of his old alma mater, El Paso High, rising among those slumped bungalows, rising with Mexico at its back. He continues around the brown shoulder of Mount Franklin, toward the school where he sent his kids instead, and although the fading, silent smokestacks of Asarco lie ahead, here at the side of the wide boulevards sit new-construction apartments overlooking willow-shaded golf courses. Virgin hillsides sprouting billboards for car dealer-ships. Au Gold Jewelry, Persian Rug Gallery, Ethan Allen—all nestle in graffitiless strip malls stuccoed a tasteful adobe brown.

What do you think? he asks his wife now. *Are the upgrades worth it? Do they make you feel safe?*

Unbidden, another voice—male—pushes into his mind.

Like you're not enjoying it yourself.

He almost turns in his seat.

You're jealous! he rails at Tavo. *I escaped. You didn't. And now all you want to do is to drag me back down into the muck.*

Tavo smirks. Jerry's knuckles whiten on the steering wheel.

Por Dios, he huffs. *We've each earned our lives. We know who we are. I mean, come on*—he drops a hand, palm up, on the empty seat beside him—*isn't it pointless to chew endlessly on history? To allow it to haunt you?*

He wonders if that woman ever saw her child again.

If Jerry weren't operating a moving vehicle, he might close his eyes. Then maybe he wouldn't see himself laughing as he rose from the water that night outside Fabens. Shaking off his wig. Unwinding his sheet, unrolling the damp pant legs of his uniform when his bare feet touched ground. McAlister, Soto, his partner Whitman—all of them chortling as he called out, "Just kidding!" Their captives, startled, struggled not to roll their eyes. "Sorry!" He laughed. It was time to load up. Time to go.

If only, he says under his breath now. If only that woman had followed the script.

The others, men and women both, kept their eyes on the ground as they answered the questions. But this one looked up at McAlister from under her thick bangs and refused to give her name.

"Oh really?" said McAlister. "The silent treatment?"

When he reached for the cuffs, she twisted in his grip, eyes spiraling with panic, and kicked him in the shin.

"Now you've done it." McAlister captured her arms behind her back, cuffed her, wrestled her toward his vehicle. He shoved her inside. "As for you," he said, grabbing the shadow that had been standing behind her, "you're going with them."

The shadow was a skinny kid of about ten, with a solemn, macho demeanor and velvet doe eyes. He did not protest when McAlister loaded him into Jerry's vehicle.

The woman screamed. Every word was a variation of "no." When she kicked the back of the seat with both feet, McAlister shackled her ankles.

Through the window the boy's doe eyes met Jerry's and didn't blink.

"Um," Jerry said. Whitman—six years his elder, five years on the patrol to his six months—offered a warning glance. Jerry turned away. "You're not going to drop those two off in two different places. Are you?"

McAlister, breathing hard, slammed the vehicle door and spat on the ground. "Why not?"

Jerry glanced back at the truck. "Well, for starters, he's a kid."

"What do you want me to do? Let 'em go?"

Whitman and Soto, loading the rest of the group into the vehicles, paused to look back at the two of them. McAlister wiped the sweat from his forehead with the back of his hand.

"Well?"

Jerry shrugged. "Well. They're not smuggling dope and they don't have any firearms. No reason we couldn't just drive them back to the bridge together and let them out. Right?"

The woman screamed. "Por favor. ¡No se lleve a mi hijo!"

McAlister stepped up into Jerry's face.

"How long do you think you and your bleeding heart are gonna last out here, Gonzales?" His breath smelled of coffee. "You've got a job to do. And if you don't do it, I will personally make sure you are not only out of a job but that your ass gets handed to the inspector general."

Jerry stared back at him. "My heart does not bleed."

McAlister snorted. "Glad to hear it, Shakespeare. Now look at this."

He turned toward the stunted mesquite that stood a few feet away. In the beam of his flashlight gleamed a cache of plastic gallon water jugs, in front of two small whitewashed wooden crosses.

They were far out into the desert on this night, two dozen miles from civilization in any direction. It was June.

McAlister lifted a jug.

"Fucking human rights groups." He unscrewed the cap. "They think they're helping the situation? Jesus. Let me tell you what's the nicest thing you can do for these people—teach them not to come back. And not to bring their damned kids with them, idiot parents. Jesus Christ." He glanced up at Whitman. "Take the kid to the checkpoint. We'll see you tomorrow."

He poured out the water from the jug. He poured every jug.

What Jerry wanted, as the damp pooled on the hard-packed ground, was to lurch forward. Close the distance. Shove McAlister down and snatch the jugs and set them back under the tree. But he couldn't move. All he could do was look over his shoulder once more at the boy, and then at the mother who screamed. Whitman, backlit by the open truck cab, wagged a finger at him. And then Soto called out from the darkness. "What's the problem, man?" He laughed. "She your cousin or something?"

Now, behind the wheel of his car, the heat on full blast, Jerry's dry eyes burn. The mountain disappears behind him, brown and furrowed and backlit with haze.

I did what I had to do, he tells himself. *What I was supposed to do. At the very least, it wasn't my child. The people who abandon their own children are the worst of all. Right? Any other indiscretion pales beside it.*

He passes the exit for the interstate running north. Memory is a vault. He barrels toward the city limits. Memory is a door that can be permanently shut.

"Right," he blurts.

Then he coughs, sputters, choking—it's as though he is at the confluence of many streams joining, rising past any height where he can breathe, and all he can do is nod. Yes. Yes, he watched as McAlister drove off with that woman in the night, yes, he took her son to the thoroughfare on the Juárez side of the checkpoint and, handing him a twenty-dollar American bill out of his own wallet, bid him good luck and good night. Yes, he held Rose Marie DuPre in his arms, yes, this too, he felt her warm body pressed against his and tasted her waxy lip balm and pressed his sticky lips to her bare shoulder, he doesn't know what he was looking for as he felt the clasp of her bra snapping open, improbably, in his hand, but he was drunk, she was probably drunk, everyone was drunk at that party, each of them lost to one another, and beyond that he truly cannot remember, he cannot, he cannot, not even if every action or inaction in history has a consequence, a ripple, a legacy. Even if we never know what they are.

His tour is not over.

Because, of course, if a person were to drive the route he is driving—having made a sudden, hard U-turn back toward town—he might insist to his wife that whatever she understands herself to be means both everything and nothing. He might remind himself that time is the great leveler, and all the places we have known or loved will one day change, and who can say for certain what is right or good. He might ridicule the long-ago certainty of his brother, Mr. Viva Aztlán, who once warned him that a man who no longer belongs to the world from which he came would one day belong nowhere. Or perhaps the tour guide might grasp, at last, that the history of the city he is touring alone is actually one of perpetual longing. And what else is longing but a desire to be somewhere else? Which is actually the urge to return home, which always seems to be just ahead of where the tour guide is, or possibly behind, and so he pulls over and exits his car to turn in circles to read the brochures, which inform him, in any case, that the place he seeks doesn't really exist.

He could swear he hears Inez's voice in his ear: *I could have told you that.*

Enough, he tells himself as he struggles to push the Volvo's door shut against the wind. The more practical concern is how to proceed into the desert in the midst of a full-blown sandstorm. He grits his teeth, pushes his sunglasses as far up his nose as they'll go, tucks his nose behind the zipper. He staggers as a fresh gust blasts him sideways. The ground beneath his feet slips as he proceeds, head down, over the foothills, past the charred and melted patches of scrub, where it seems like ages ago he doused a series of flaming art sculptures—for he is not so far from home now—and although he feels a momentary start at the sight of a newly arranged heap of rubbish (milk crate, skateboards, potted plant wearing an assortment of mittens), he cannot lift his head, does not pause. And when he reaches the base of the mountain's slope, he climbs. And when he can no longer stand upright to climb, he crab walks. His palms sing with the pain of every unseen prickle he grasps; his forehead and cheeks feel as though they've been scraped with steel wool. His throat is dry, his eyes burn, his nose runs with what feels like mud. He sinks to his knees. It would be best at this point, he understands in the reptilian portion of his brain, to ball up and cover.

He turns, struggling upright, glimpsing only a washed-out streak of sky, the smudge that was once the horizon, the merest suggestion of city streets visible through the howling curtain of sand.

"¡Chíngate!" he screams, and he raises both fists toward the great beyond to deliver a double bird.

And then he simply roars, reaching down to scoop rocks, sticks, garbage, handfuls of dry earth, which he hurls again and again into the wind. Everything flies back into his face. He hurls anyway. He knows what he is. In some climes, the rain is what would wash a man clean.

"Sir," calls a voice from the depths of the tempest.

Jerry startles. He lifts a forearm to his brow, blocking just enough grit to be able to see the pair of wraparound sunglasses that emerges from the haze. An olive-green uniform. A badge.

The uniform bends under the force of the wind. "¿Habla usted inglés?"

Jerry mutters. "Are you shitting me?"

The uniform takes a step closer. "¿Tiene identificación?"

Jerry narrows his eyes. The uniform straightens. The wind howls.

20

REGRESANDO

HUCK LEANS OVER THE TABLE.

"So, what you're saying is that your salary demands are still for a thirty percent raise, minimum, outside of the transportation subsidies."

Yesenia Fernandez Aragón leans forward to meet him. Without her sign, she looks even tinier than she did in the parking lot; her dimpled hands and elbows make him think of a gingerbread cookie. She turns her round face to whisper something in the lawyer's ear.

"Yes," says the lawyer, after some nodding. "My client, all the employees, they do not change their mind. Also, they want you give to them back the company team of fútbol."

The two men in the group of supporting instigators sitting behind Yesenia Fernandez in the conference room nod and fold their arms.

Huck leans back from the table. Is he authorized to put the defunct company soccer team back on the table? What would the company do if he upsold the morale component and put it on the hook for team uniforms and league dues? He has no idea. He has no idea *what he is doing*. He'd said as much when HQ tapped him to conduct the negotiations, and then he reminded them that these people had recently mobbed him.

"That was just a symbolic gesture." So said the disembodied voice of a board member during the conference call. "These workers know you. You understand the day-to-day realities. Even if they're angry, they're going to want to deal with a familiar face, not high-level management parachuting in to—"

"So let me get this straight. Nobody else is coming?"

"We're sending legal counsel."

And here they are—two high-end suits who arrived on the red-eye to El Paso International, their faces glossy with sunscreen. In the opposite corner, the two Juárez labor attorneys in shirtsleeves who are working pro bono.

He's sweating as he turns to his human resources manager. "Melinda, let me see the terms again."

She slides them over with a manicured hand before he's even got the words out.

"Let's go back to salaries," he says, scanning. "The thing is, I'm not authorized to offer you more than six percent at this point."

Pro Bono Number 1 reads his lips and says something to Yesenia Fernandez. She regards Huck in the manner of a doll on a shelf who follows you with its eyes, then turns to the others and speaks in a low voice. A hot burst of whispering follows.

"My client say thirty percent," says Pro Bono Number 1. "Or maybe to begin hungry strike."

Jesus Christ. "How about we talk about the vacation situation for a minute? I know you're not happy with the consolidation of all the various saints' days into one holy week, but it's always been pretty disruptive to have to stop production in the middle of the week so you can—"

"Es cultura mexicana," says Pro Bono Number 1, pleasantly. "Will you like to celebrate Christmas on the twenty-seven of December?"

Huck pastes on his own smile. "We're willing to explore outside cafeteria vendors instead of keeping it in-house. What are some of the options you'd like to bring to the table?"

"My clients will like to introduce you their representatives for the new union."

"We'd like to see proof that your current representatives aren't doing their jobs."

"Please, you show the accounting for the union monies my clients pay."

"The accounting department's pretty busy. We're losing eighty to a hundred grand a day right now. Don't you think that the most important thing—for everyone concerned—is to get this maquila up and running ASAP?"

"Bueno, we talk overtime," says Pro Bono Number 1, while his partner furiously scribbles.

"Look," Huck says, and he can feel the heat rising in his face. "What I'm trying to do—"

Melinda clears her throat. On her legal pad, at her polished fingertip, she's written, "Rehiring incentives??"

"Huck." Roberts, one of the company lawyers, drops his hand on Huck's shoulder. "Let's take it down a notch, yes? Remember that you're here because they know you. They know, on some level, that they can trust you. We're here to back you up on the limits of the negotiation. Let's just choose one of the paths before us and follow it. Or better yet, lead the way. Yes?"

Huck grips his ballpoint pen. Can he suck it up? Even if he can smell himself now? He takes care not to raise his arms as he sets down the pen.

"Let's start over, everyone."

He catches Yesenia Fernandez watching him with the expression of someone who already knows what he is.

A gust of fresh rage whooshes up in him. But he puts a lid on it.

"Ms. Fernandez," he says carefully. "What is it you want from *me*?" He turns up his palms on the table.

Pro Bono Number 1 gives him a funny look. Then he turns to the group.

"My clients will like to demand termination of certain managers," he says when he turns back around.

"All right," Huck says. "Let's start there. Who are we talking about?"

Yesenia Fernandez folds her arms.

Pro Bono Number 1 smiles a very polite smile. "We start with *you*, Mr. DuPre."

III

The neighborhood dogs are going berserk. They light up, one by one like a string of musical Christmas lights, at whoever has the audacity to use the sidewalk on a Thursday afternoon. Ripley bellows from behind the back gate too. Huck oozes up to the small, high window beside his front door and glimpses Lourdes as she barrels up his front walk and lands hard on his doorbell.

He scuttles away from the window, his back to the wall, heart pounding in his ears. She didn't see him. He's not here. Nobody's home. When the second chime dies away, he figures he's in the clear.

And suddenly her face is in the window, her eyes and the top of her dark head bobbing above the frame as she hoists herself up onto the porch railing and braces her hands on the windowsill. She catches him hunched under the entryway chandelier and waves, with enthusiasm.

"Good morning, señor," she announces as he eases the door open. "He regresado."

"Lourdes." He reaches to scratch beneath his new beard, then thinks better of it. "Morning."

"You want I clean today?"

"Got things straightened out, I see."

"I start right now," she says. "No hay problema."

"I don't know about that."

Her gaze drifts, discreetly, past his shoulder. He can't help but look with her. It's like an avalanche behind him, a garbage dump, like the scenes you see on TV after an earthquake somewhere in the world.

She turns her face up to his, beaming. "I do it. All of it. Every days you want."

He would like to close the door.

"You key," she adds, as though it was the last thing she could think of to offer him. "I have."

She extends it in her cupped palms.

For Chrissakes. He waves it back at her, waves her into the house. She releases what might be a breath of relief.

He sighs in return. "You want coffee?"

"Por favor." She marches to the kitchen, harvesting the dirty laundry as she goes.

He trails after her and installs himself at the coffee maker. This much he can do. He scoops and flips the switches as Lourdes, her back turned, unloads the dishwasher. The negotiation table had been just as silent— only more echoing—in the moment after the bomb dropped. And then his lawyers erupted and started talking about bad faith and moving the finish line and everyone in the other camp rose, agitated, and he too rose, inflating, as the words he tried to hold back rocketed toward his mouth: "*Everyone!* Look, there's a lot to understand here, and I'm not understanding all of it, but I'm trying, I really am, and I guess I didn't understand what you needed before, I didn't understand you"—he heard his voice break here—"but I wasn't listening, the entire company wasn't listening, and I'm sorry about that. Do you understand? I'm *sorry.*"

In the fresh pin-drop moment that followed, the two men in the group of workers looked at him with a kind of horror that was at least nine-tenths disgust. As for Yesenia Fernandez, the look of pity she gave him was the kind meant for someone you don't feel pity for at all.

And now? When he asked Roberts in the emptied room whether he, Huck, was going to continue to be a part of the negotiations and what, exactly, the overall value of his job was to the company, Roberts had laid another hand on his shoulder.

"That remains to be seen."

Now, at the sink, he sets down a mug of coffee beside his housekeeper. She nods her thanks. He picks up the lampshade that has been sitting on the floor beside the breakfast bar for a week and shuffles away.

In the living room, he cranks open a window, craving fresh air. A truck pulls up to the curb.

"Here's your invitation to my birthday party," he hears Jordan say as she pours herself out.

In the cab, Miguel dons his glasses to examine the card she thrusts at him. "Who else is gonna be there? A bunch of little girls?"

"Everybody. Whoever I feel like inviting."

He taps the gas before the engine dies. "You feel like inviting *me?*"

"Well, are you coming?"

He laughs. "We'll see, m'ija."

"You've got one month to think about it."

He pulls away in a cloud of exhaust as Jordan watches, hands on hips, a Little Bo-Peep ready to whack her wandering sheep on their butts with a big hook.

Huck heads for his hole.

Lourdes overtakes him in the entryway. "You shirt, señor," she says, bustling up to toss him a rumpled button-down. It's been a while since he's seen this one. He opens his mouth to ask where she found it, but she's already back in the kitchen, crashing around.

He wads the shirt into the lampshade. It belongs with the lamp in the den, he realizes now, but that room seems impossibly far away. He lowers himself into the decorative antique lion's-head chair until his elbows meet his knees. Ripley approaches and thunks down at his feet, releasing a groan. A new ruff of fat rises from the back of the dog's neck.

Of course, he would be talking to Rose Marie about this whole stinking mess, if she were here. If everything was different instead of what it was. An ache wells up in his chest. Maybe she wouldn't understand anyway. Oh sure, she understood basic economics and the interruption of supply in the face of demand, but could she *understand*? He'd made sure she'd never actually *had* to work.

He rummages in his pocket for his cell phone and dials Mendoza. Just to say hi.

But Mendoza doesn't answer.

He looks to the kitchen, biting his lip. "Lourdes?" he calls out.

The front door whacks open.

"Dad. What are you *doing*?" Jordan steps out of the eye-searing light and drops her backpack. "Have you picked up the party decorations yet?"

He shakes his head.

She rubs Ripley's ears. "Do we need more dog food?"

He nods. The dog's tail thumps the floor.

From the kitchen comes the sound of water filling the sink.

She frowns. "Who's home?"

Lourdes appears in the entryway in pink rubber gloves, holding a damp pair of cowboy boots.

Jordan blinks with her mouth open. Then she rushes her.

"Did you know that solar flares can disrupt the electromagnetic field of the earth so much that cell phones stop working?" she asks Lourdes breathlessly from a toe length away. "I'm doing an experiment at school that shows how the aurora borealis works, except nobody understands what it is because we don't have one here. Skyler got a speeding ticket. Are you going to be here all the time again?"

Lourdes looks half-amused, half in need of a Tylenol. She reaches her free arm around Jordan's shoulder, and gives it a good shake. "¿Qué tal, m'ija?"

"It's my birthday in a month," Jordan continues.

Huck's chair creaks. Jordan blabs. Lourdes nods and smiles. He folds and refolds the shirt on top of the lampshade, trying to remember why he opened the door. Possibly, quite possibly, he only wanted to hear another adult voice in the house. It wasn't so much to ask. Was it?

Except that now, she flings out her arm and exclaims, "¡Y mira qué sucia! ¿Qué pasó? In here es un disastro."

"I *know*," Jordan says with a roll of her eyes, and then she glares in Huck's direction.

He slumps. "What?"

Jordan and Lourdes give each other a look. Without a word, Jordan exits.

Lourdes wipes down the boots with a rag she extracts from her waistband and deposits them under the shoe bench.

Huck pivots minimally in her direction. "I guess you ate your Wheaties this morning."

She doesn't glance up. "Eh?"

Jordan returns, bearing whisk broom and dustpan. She marks him with another look and squats to slide the broom beneath his chair. Lourdes wipes down the dust-encrusted picture frames on either side of him.

"For God's sake." He widens the space between his knees. "Isn't there some other place you could clean first?"

"Dad." Jordan rams him with the dustpan. "Can you move your foot?"

He responds by rising, moving his chair to a corner three feet to the left, and plunking back down again.

Thus he can see into the kitchen without being seen as Quinn trudges up the back steps and whacks open the screen door.

"Whoa," Quinn says, stopping short.

Lourdes offers Quinn a very tight smile and turns back to the stove top.

Quinn pauses, then digs into his jeans pocket. He eases open the silverware drawer.

Lourdes spins. Quinn smiles and palms his spoon—armed with a taut rubber band—but her eyes follow the clap of his hands.

The back door smacks open.

"What are *you* doing here?" Skyler drops her bag. "Are you ditching?"

Quinn snickers. "I know I am, but what are you?"

Skyler gives him a look. He tips his chin toward the stove.

When she turns, her feet seem stuck to the floor. Then she lurches.

"Lourdes!" She throws out her arms. "We thought you were never coming back!"

From Huck's vantage point, it's like watching an octopus strangle a butternut squash. Lourdes's hands rise into the air, her face registering—finally!—a moment's alarm. But she gets it under control. She pats Skyler's back, tut-tutting a bit, and disentangles herself.

"Ay, m'ija. Está bien. I miss you too."

Skyler turns back to Quinn. "You better be helping her."

"Of course," he says.

Lourdes meets his gaze with menace.

"Here," Jordan says, suddenly in Huck's face with the scent of M&M's on her breath, and then she plunks down eight copies of *House Beautiful* on the shirt atop the lampshade.

Huck claps his palm on them before they slide off. The magazine covers look familiar to him, though he has no idea whether he's seen them before. The damned subscription just keeps coming and coming, like a never-ending calling card from Rose Marie.

"This is for my birthday party," Jordan says back in the kitchen, extending a blue envelope.

Lourdes takes it gingerly from her hand, as though accepting the kind of secret message that blows up ten seconds after reading it.

Quinn shakes his head. "Jo-Jo."

Jordan straightens. "Don't call me Jo-Jo."

"Jo-Jo," he continues, "I wouldn't get your hopes up too high about this party thing."

Lourdes extracts the card with a thumb and forefinger.

"I'm inviting you," Jordan says.

Skyler darts an embarrassed glance at Lourdes. Out of the side of her mouth she singsongs, "You're gonna be ma-aad when nobody co-oomes."

Jordan inches forward, leaning. "Are you coming?"

Lourdes looks as though she's digging for words inside her own head with a shovel.

"Pues, m'ija," she begins.

Jordan her lifts up on her toes.

"M'ija, I think . . ." Her nose trembles, as though she might sneeze. "Maybe I clean you party. You daddy—he want I help with you party?"

Jordan skips out to Huck's chair, tossing him his two heavy key chains—they jingle as he wriggles to keep them from sliding off his lap— then stuffs a fistful of dark socks into his shirt pocket.

"Can Lourdes help at my party?"

"Crap!" he hears Quinn say. "Dad's home?"

"Well?" Jordan drags over a metal contraption that screeches against the hardwood.

"What the hell is that?" Huck says.

"The shoe tree from your closet."

"How did *my* stuff get into the kitchen?"

"You left it there?" Jordan says. "Duh."

The shoe tree falls on the dog, who groans and turns his head away.

"Watch what you're doing!"

"I wouldn't have to if you put something away."

"In case you hadn't noticed, my hands are kind of full here."

"So get rid of something."

"Fine." He hugs the magazines back into a stack and thrusts them at her. "Here."

Jordan's expression flattens. She folds her arms.

It's a moment before he realizes he is locked into a stare down. Dammit.

And then he is elsewhere. Ages ago. The hospital room where, once, a short, brown-skinned nurse had lifted newborn Jordan from Rose Marie's arms into his with a skeptical look that somehow left him feeling unworthy.

What's he worth now? he wonders as he locks eyes with the prize. He traces the magazine edges with his thumb.

"I don't need these," he hears himself say.

"Fine," Jordan says, lifting her chin. "Put them down."

"I don't *want* them."

"Throw 'em out!"

The keys fall from his lap. "That's enough bossy talk out of you, missy."

"Are you doing it?"

"Goddammit," he roars, rising. The dog jumps to his feet in alarm. The heads of his other two children prairie-dog from the sides of the kitchen archway, Quinn with smeared eyeliner, Skyler's dreadlocks swinging in the empty air. Lourdes's sneakered foot freezes.

"Will everybody just stop looking at me?" he shouts.

The twins roll their eyes simultaneously, as though they had set a timer, and pop back out of view. Jordan makes a *w* with her thumbs and forefingers. *Whatever*, she mouths, following.

He breathes heavily, clutching *House Beautiful*, the socks flopping out of his pocket like a boutonniere. He doesn't have to do *anything*. No one can make him.

Except that, for a single sharp instant, he sees the house around him for what it is: a collection of what Rose Marie has saved and what she has discarded.

He looks down at his hands. The part of him that had touched her face, her body, a thousand times over and still had never reached the most essential part of her.

"Everyone," he calls out to the quiet house. He slumps. "I'm sorry."

Then he kicks the shoe tree. Crosses the room and dumps his cache into the wastebasket. He snatches up the lampshade—lying now on its side—and wrestles it back onto the base in the den. The rest he leaves on the floor.

It's enough for now, he tells himself as he slouches back to his hole. Quite enough.

SHE LIVES, IN HER RENT-REDUCED room, with a partial view of the community garden, atop three stories of patinaed brick and wide wooden stairways, above converted live-in art studios and small offices, beyond the statuette of a lamb-wreathed Jesus greeting all who enter from a niche above the main entrance. Insofar as the Good Shepherd Center was formerly a home for the kind of teenage girl that once would have been described as "wayward," she regards this scenario as hilarious.

No one is in on the joke. Not the artists, the natural health practitioners, the employees of wilderness conservation organizations, not the custodial staff, an Ethiopian man and a Cambodian woman who are the only brown people apparent in a five-mile radius but with whom she still had assumed a certain kinship. Polite but distant, all.

The grounds, in any case, are hers to tame. She rakes and weeds, plants and trims, waters and can't quite cover expenses. Gets a second job wrangling a small herd of lawn-mowing goats. Drives them in a trailer hitched to the Lexus to the overgrown vacant lots, the obscure public parks, the highway embankments choked with blackberry bramble. Is this weird? Plenty weird. Who cares? She sits at the edges of fields and thinks. And doesn't think. And can't think. Because the northwestern spring is cold and insanely green and profuse with fecund, blooming things, the sky so heavy and low with gunmetal-gray clouds that it makes her head hurt. The sun, when it shows itself, never passes directly overhead but only makes a high arc over the horizon. She never has any idea what time it is.

She has unfolded the note from its envelope, more than once. Folded it back. She would like to write her own notes, retroactively. To Huck, for starters, last June. To the twins in September. But every birthday card she begins ends up shoved back into whatever bedside table she's sleeping next to. Like life, it's a spiral. The more she stays silent, the more she can't speak. The farther away she is from the beginning, from any point of reentry.

Now she sits in her folding chair as the goats graze ivy and ragweed on the back lot of a furniture warehouse. The note is in her pack, at her feet.

She closes her eyes. There's no escape from the beginning of her beginning. Even now. It's a point so far behind her, it seems to disappear with the cloud-covered sun over the curve of the earth, but still it rises on the horizon before her in the gray morning. The beginning that is the ending that is the beginning. Snake eating its tail. As though you couldn't move toward anything resembling the truth without facing the truths that lie somewhere in the wake of your life.

A goat says, "maaaah." She opens her eyes and meets the gaze of the creature who stares back with rectangular pupils, chewing, looking bored.

She packs up again in the night. No notice (why start now?). Just the key on her doormat, the hard, flaring growl of the Lexus. Her hands are cool and light on the steering wheel as the darkness blooms around her, frogs calling out from hidden puddles, the magnolia trees unfolding like ten thousand pink butterflies opening their wings, and the heavy, nodding lilacs wafting their dizzying perfume.

She holds it all under her breath, just for a moment. Then she turns out of the parking lot. Toward the freeway. South.

21

SPOOKS

IF JERRY WERE TO FLY—LIKE an owl, or a hawk, or a mosquito—in the dark early hours over the city, skimming past its brown mountain, dipping over the house-speckled foothills to light on a fence post near a particular window, he might find himself alone at his desk.

His focus at the desk is resolute. He rolls his sleeves to the elbow, slips his bifocals to the tip of his nose. The stacks of his students' midterm essays are blinding in the lamplight. He hears his own breath beneath the scratch of red pen. His steaming coffee and the silence of his house are one part loneliness, one part balm.

The sun rises. Small birds begin their twittering on the telephone lines.

And then he is halfway up the mountain again, head bowed to the pressure of the wind, the grit stinging his face, screaming.

He swivels in his chair toward the scrape of a broom against hardwood.

"Lourdes," he says. Outside, the mulberry trees swell with neon-bright buds. "Rápido. ¿Como se dice 'primavera' en inglés?"

Her plump hands still themselves on her broom.

"E-spring." She returns to her work.

He, home alone, had been the one to greet her at the door on the day she finally returned, her hands clasped before her heart. Was it surprise? Supplication? Unmistakable was the relief that welled up in her eyes. He was only glad, with a degree of force that startled him, that she had not disappeared forever. He let her in.

He turns back to his desk. He will work until noon, breaking only for sustenance and, of course, a walk. His walks are short, of late. They have purpose. He maps out a trajectory in his mind beforehand—home to mall parking lot to small, disused park space at the edge of the neighborhood—so that he might only stretch his legs, cool his mind without temptation to wander. He does not wish to wander.

The mountainside takes on a pinkish hue. Something in the scrub recoils and raises a sudden dust cloud.

He reaches for the blinds. The sun swells. The sky stretches to the limits of his vision. Then comes the voice that called out to him over the shriek of wind, the uniform materializing, olive green beneath the dark glasses in which he could see his own reflection as they drew near, a vision from some other quadrant of time and space, a hallucination. "¿Tiene identificación?" the specter wanted to know. His accent was passable; his face was as brown as Jerry's own. The low muttering in his throat ignited. "I am a goddamned native-born citizen of the United States," he roared. "I am ex–Border Patrol, and when I report you, Agent, you are going to learn that I am your superior in every way." The uniform halted. "What's your pay grade, sir?" Jerry worked his jaw. Five years he'd spent in the trenches as a young man; he'd made it to journeyman. Didn't the passage of time convey seniority? He took a step forward. "What's *yours*?" The agent's posture went hard. "Stop right there. And show me some ID."

"And so," he says now, the blinds fully opened. "How are you today, Lourdes?"

She breaks no stride, stooping to retrieve a wad of paper from the office floor. "Muy bien, señor."

"Try it in English," he suggests.

She blushes at the floor, then firms her shoulders.

"I am . . . good today."

"Bueno. And are things finally returning to normal for you?"

She glances up at him with alarm.

Had he looked the same way when he showed his ID?

Because Jerry was gone then. Flown away. To the living room where he met the parents of Marilyn Lawson, that brief high school girlfriend, her parents' faces registering him with cold disbelief. To the office of a junior high school counselor who shook his head, laughing, as he removed him from honors English before the first day of class. The movie theater where he and his sister once slipped their coins over the counter for the matinee of *Bambi* and heard, "You're not allowed here," the teenage ticket boy pointing to a sign Jerry couldn't read. Inez pushed their money forward. "We're Arabian," she said haughtily.

On the hillside, he glowered before his detainer. Whippersnapper. Bearer of his gene pool. Inheritor of a world that did not come in translation.

Inez's effort to teach Lourdes English had been motivated by more than just a desire to irritate him, of course. He'd known it all along.

"Kind of a weird time to be hiking, don't you think?" the agent said, as he thrust Jerry's driver's license back at him.

They both swayed under a new blast of grit.

"Do forgive me," Jerry responded in a low, acid voice. "After all, *I'm* supposed to be the one to apologize."

"La vida," he clarifies now, in his study. "¿Es más normal, hoy en día?"

Lourdes emits a little bark of a laugh. She shakes her head. "Is never normal."

He offers a smile in return.

A throat clears itself in the hallway. "Have you seen my red jacket?"

Chavela, at the door with an expectant expression, wearing authoritative business attire.

Lourdes snaps up the broom and busies herself with the floor before the bookshelves.

"I haven't," Jerry responds quickly, hoping to peel Chavela's eyes from Lourdes's back.

Chavela takes a halting step into the room, as though she wished to say something else. He waits with his hands tented over his papers. She looks once more to Lourdes, the line of her mouth hardening. She turns to go.

"Perhaps you should try the bottom of the hall closet," he hears himself say. "I found my blazer there not long ago."

She disappears behind the doorjamb. "Thanks. I'll check."

"Would you like to have lunch before you go?" he blurts.

Her step pauses midcreak. She leans back into the room.

He cannot entirely articulate to himself what he hopes to gain by his offer. He only knows in the inscrutable moment that passes between them that, even more than his impulse to seclude himself, he wants to see the light of recognition in his wife's face. And he could say, *Sorry about Lourdes*, who escapes now through the doorway as discreetly as possible, having been extended a reinstatement of employment, with a pay raise, without Chavela's consultation—even though he isn't actually sorry about that, not at all. He might say, with more sincerity, *Forgive me my moods and my excuses and my walks.* He might look down at his hands and say, *Forgive me for something more. It was a very long time ago.*

"It's nine o'clock in the morning," Chavela says.

He twiddles his pen. "Right."

She waits for more. But he cannot speak.

Nor did he tell her of his encounter on the mountainside. For he had only the smallest sliver of pride left in him at that moment, a gleaming, broken blade, and were he to lay bare this thing he held so close to his heart, perhaps there would be nothing left of him at all.

And so now his wife, with a roll of her eyes, walks away. Outside the door, Lourdes sweeps.

III

"What are you up to after work?" Peña clinks open his Zippo.

Marcus dips into the bag of Red Hots wedged beside the parking brake. "Sleep."

"Me and Cabrera are going for beers. Wanna come?"

Marcus grunts and slumps against the headrest. Two weeks ago, they were put back on nights. On his way into work today, at the bank, he'd run into Ashley Gutierrez, who was on her way home. How long had it been since they'd seen each other? Six months? "You look great," he enthused as she tucked that thick, caramel-colored hair behind her ears. "Oh," she responded. "I guess that's why you stopped calling me." He blinked at her, groggy and stupid, like someone who'd been sleeping on a plane. "I've been . . . busy," he said, though what he really meant was "I'm sorry." What he didn't say was that he gave up because she seemed undecided about him, because he couldn't quite muster the cojones to face the result of a potentially wasted effort. Which, apparently, he should have made. She extracted her keys and, with a withering look, turned heel. Marcus stood light headed before the teller, who had to ask him more than once, "May I help you?"

"I kind of want to get up before noon," he says now.

"Screw that," says Peña. "Come with us."

"Not this time."

The Zippo clinks open. Shut. "When is there ever a time? Dude, live a little."

Marcus eyes the lighter with malevolence. "I'm really stinking tired."

"Amateur."

Marcus raises his middle finger.

Peña laughs. Marcus checks his watch. People have their new papers by now or they don't. Border Patrol has just released an insane number of new recruits into the field. This afternoon, well before his encounter with Ashley, as he still lay behind the thick curtains of his sleep, his father called.

He dragged the phone across his face. "Dad."

A pause followed, as though his father were preparing to make an announcement.

"You haven't seen Inez, have you?" he said finally.

Marcus pulled back the window shade above his head and, wincing against the light, slapped it back to the sill. "Inez? God, no. Have *you*?"

"I haven't seen her." Another pause. "Just be good out there, Son. All right? Be one of the good guys."

Marcus frowned into the receiver. "Excuse me?"

"And be careful."

"When am I *not*?"

His father bid him a good afternoon and hung up.

Now, in the truck, all is silent, save for the crickets. And the clink of Peña's lighter. And the sticky, cinnamon crunch between Marcus's teeth.

The radio crackles, and they both lean up quick from their seats.

They wait. For a voice, the trip of a sensor. Anything.

Silence. They fall back.

Marcus throws open the door of the truck.

Peña clinks. "What?"

No moon tonight. The dark seems fuzzy, irresolute. "Remind me to tell you later about this prank my dad used to play."

He scuffs away on the hard-packed dirt, the city a dull glow on the western horizon, the irrigated fields by the river furrowed and dark, until he spots a nopal that looks like it could use a watering. *I've been busy.* He snorts to himself and imagines unfurling a hidden cape. *Busy fighting for the forces of good, I'll have you know!*

He catches sight of the tent-sized lump on the path before him.

He zips up and clicks on his flashlight. Beams it brighter, centers it. It's a cow. Shriveled, stiff, its head thrown back seemingly in midbay. Three quarter-sized wounds puncture its still-oozing neck.

He stares. He turns the beam of his flashlight into the dark.

III

"I'm glad you came," Jerry says across the Formica tabletop.

Tavo reaches for one of the greasy taquitos nestled into the cardboard holder before him and douses it in a thin, orange-hued salsa.

Jerry reaches for his own dripping roll. "And so." He taps a blunted end against his paper napkin and tries not to sigh. "How's things?"

Tavo crunches. "Same as they ever are."

Jerry's roll shatters under his teeth but is still chewy enough that it's difficult to bite a piece free. He gnaws. Pop music assaults them from the sound system.

Tavo slaps down his taquito. "Órale. What's up?"

Jerry shrugs.

"Since when do you have nothing to say? Am I supposed to ask how things are with *you*?"

Jerry chews. It was an impulse that led him to call Tavo, to blurt into the stiff silence that followed the hello: "About that conversation in the parking lot—sorry." Just as, by making the phone call in the first place, he had been subverting a deeper impulse to go for a very long and unstructured walk. Just as now, he could—perhaps, just possibly, here inside of a Chico's Tacos—relate to his brother a certain anecdote.

"Things are uneventful," he begins, because this is also, in a sense, true. "Quiet." He brushes the shards of tortilla from his lap.

A group of teenagers erupts with laughter at the next booth. Outside, beyond the yellow expanse of grass and the bright lake in its man-made bed, behind the gates of Western Playland, a crew of workers scales the roller coaster, applying loud hydraulic tools. El Bandido grins through his dismantlement, devilishly.

Tavo wipes his fingertips on a napkin. "With Chavela too?"

Jerry looks back to catch the smirk on Tavo's face. Testing him, of course. Or just salting the wound. He refocuses on his taquito. "She's tolerating me, I suppose."

Tavo regards him with a ruminative silence.

"Yeah, well," he says. "Good luck with that." His tone is not sarcastic. "How's the kids?"

Jerry upends a minitub of salsa into the remaining tube of his taquito. "Good question. They're living their own lives. As they should."

Meaning that Adam is away at school, as ever, except for when he returns to the crash pad for the purpose of out-of-house socializing, and that Marcus is working. Always working. Marcus being, of course, the most logical person with whom he might share his story.

And he had tried. Tried to form the words. Tried.

The roller coaster crew pries loose a huge metal beam. El Bandido grins. In another era of his life, that grin had struck Jerry as one of solidarity, a shared amused outrage. Now he sees no recognition at all in the furtive cartoon eyes.

"Marcus is overworked," he clarifies. "But it's also possible he likes it that way. I honestly can't tell whether he's happy or unhappy anymore." He exhales. "Incidentally," he continues in a low voice, "you won't believe this, but on the day we last met, in the middle of that storm, I hiked out into the foothills and—"

"It's your own fault, man."

"What? *What* is?"

"You passed on your genes." Tavo dabs the orange ring from his lips. "Your smart-ass, extra-smart, smarty-pants genes. Haven't you ever heard that smart people are usually the least happy?"

He grins and shoves another taquito into his mouth.

Jerry takes a very deep breath. "Al contrario, hombre. I think a legacy has less to do with genetics and more to do with choice. The decisions made and not made. They get passed down the line."

"I guess that's what they mean by 'karma.' Personal karma. Ancestral karma."

"You read too much Carlos Castaneda in the seventies. What I mean is that surely, one day you'll realize you have changed. And then you'll see that different things are important to you than once were. And that the answers to all the questions you sought are irrelevant because you were asking the wrong questions. And you'll grasp that you've built a life around everything you believed to be true about yourself, only to find that—"

"Mira, Mr. *College*, maybe you should also pass on your superior knowledge of *life* to your son. I figured this shit out in Vietnam while all you pendejos stayed behind."

Jerry whacks his palms down on the tabletop and rises, abruptly. If the table wasn't bolted down, he might flip it.

But when he meets his brother's gaze—suddenly piercing and hollow all at once—he lowers himself back to his seat.

"Some legacies shouldn't be passed on," Jerry says quietly. "I say let the sins of the fathers end with the fathers."

Tavo's expression dissolves into something that is at first baffled, then perhaps bemused. His eyes grow distant. He makes a sound that is half snort, half sigh.

"What do you suppose Papá would have made of that idea?"

Their father. Construction worker, night watchman. He of the drink and the temper and the propensity for tears when listening to certain Lola Beltrán albums.

Jerry offers a faint and wry smile. He reaches for his Diet Coke. "I think the answer would've been in the belt on our asses."

Tavo lifts his orange Fanta in response. "We're getting old, hermano."

Jerry nudges forward his cardboard container. It's still half full. "Have a taquito."

Tavo stares down the offerings. "Man, these are just as bad as they were in high school."

Jerry opens another tub of salsa. "Without question."

They finish their meal, slowly but meticulously, as though they were eating the evidence.

III

"Okay, fine," Peña says with an opening clink of his Zippo, "If a human rigged up that cow, how'd they do it?"

Marcus's leg jiggles under the steering wheel. "I dunno, man. Ice pick? Chain saw?"

"That neck wound was pretty fresh. I didn't hear anything. Not even a moo. Did you?"

"You're missing the obvious," Marcus says, "which is that the perpetrator snuck up behind the cow with a rag soaked in chloroform."

The lighter clinks shut. "Of course, it's only a matter of time before it gets a taste for human flesh. One of these nights, they're going to find some guy in a lawn chair in his backyard, clutching his neck with one hand and a crushed can of Budweiser in the other, and—"

"Jesus Christ," Marcus mutters.

"*Now* what?"

Marcus casts a malevolent glance at the silent radio. "I'm *bored*."

Peña nods, an unlit cigarette dangling from his lip. Then he reaches into the glove compartment and tosses over what looks like a bottle of vitamins.

Fake blood capsules. The brand name is Spurt.

"What the hell is *this*?"

"I got it just in case."

"In case of *what*?"

Peña smiles. "I've got an idea."

Marcus tosses the bottle back. "No you don't."

"You got any neck under that collar?" Peña leans in for a look. "Okay, not much, but you're still vulnerable. If you got attacked, man, you'd be covered in blood. After you went to investigate weird sounds in the dark. Hypothetically speaking, of course."

"Forget it."

"You mean after I yell, 'Oh my God, it's the Chupacabra'?"

Marcus rubs the bridge of his nose. "Is this because I told you about my dad? You should use his thing as your prank. That one works, at least."

"La Llorona is totally passé. Not even my abuelita believes in her anymore."

"Your grandma doesn't believe anybody landed on the moon."

Peña chortles. "Pendejo. You're not bored. You're boring. Even your old man knows how to have more fun than you do."

The lighter flares and releases a foul cloud of smoke before Marcus can snatch it away.

Marcus cracks open the door. "The second part of that," he responds with more bitterness than he intends, "is probably true."

They sit. And wait.

III

"*Finally*," says the girl at the door, and then she thrusts forward a blue envelope. "You've been extremely difficult to find."

Jerry squints against the bright early light. The girl in question—the young Miss Jordan DuPre—has temporarily subdued the marigold-colored puff of her hair with a terry cloth sweatband. "Have I?"

"Here." She jiggles the envelope.

He accepts it with mild cheer. "Good morning, by the way."

"This is an invitation to my birthday party next week. Lots of the neighbors are coming."

He raises an eyebrow. God help them all if he is meant to observe the birthday of every DuPre who enters his house.

"I see," he says, unfolding the prize. "Congratulations to you, young lady. And thank you for thinking of us. But I don't think we're available on this date."

From behind him comes a firm footfall. "Are you sure?"

He turns. Chavela meets his gaze with an impersonal pleasantness, as though he were a prospective client.

"Quite sure," he says.

She snatches the envelope from his hand. "Let's double-check. Good morning, m'ija!" she adds brightly. "How are you?"

The girl softens her ramrod posture. "Fine. And you?"

"Wonderful!" She examines the document. "And there's no problem with this date at all. We'll be there."

The girl, beaming, skips down the sidewalk.

"Excuse me," Jerry says once the door has been shut, "but ¿qué te pasa?"

Chavela folds her arms. "I thought you *liked* spending time with those kids." Her voice suddenly undulates, riding currents that are somehow both darker and brighter. Her face retains its pleasant expression.

He pulls himself taller. "I wouldn't describe it as simply as that."

"Is there some *reason* why we shouldn't go?"

"To a fourth grader's birthday party? Surely, you jest."

"It doesn't sound too different from a block party to me. Or is there some reason you'd rather not go?"

"No."

"Any reason you wouldn't want *me* in that house?"

"No."

"Any reason you wouldn't want me to have any conversations with the people who live in that house? To see how they're doing? Considering what a rough year they've had over there?"

The look in her eyes makes him think, *Whirlpool.* "No."

"Then I guess it's settled."

His fists, in his pockets, are clenched. "Why don't you go by yourself, si tienes tantas ganas? You're the one who loves parties."

"Oh, no, no. Vámonos *juntos.* Haven't you always wanted to see the inside of that house? I know I have." Her smile is small and hard. "Sometimes you just have to enter the belly of the beast. No?"

And then he is alone, the dust motes riding the shafts of spring light around him, his tongue much too dry in his mouth. Somebody's else mouth. He watches himself from a perch at the top of the shelves, like a crow.

III

"No way," Marcus says to the shadow before him. "¿Otra vez?"

Cárdenas looks up from beneath his baseball cap, offering a toothy, helpless smile. "Oficial. ¿Qué tal?"

Marcus shakes his head. "Dude."

I thought you said you'd be smarter next time, Peña says.

Well, I felt pretty smart until five minutes ago.

At Cárdenas's elbow, a young woman with a fat, sleeping baby in a sling rolls her eyes. Her jeans are wet below the knees—pulled across on an inner tube, no doubt. The legend stretched across her T-shirt reads, in English: "Don't Touch the Knobs, I'm Perfectly Adjusted."

Marcus chuckles and seats a squat, middle-aged couple. They clutch plastic bags of damp clothes.

"Oye, guapo."

Marcus turns his flashlight to an old woman the size of a child. *Hey, handsome?*

When he approaches, she asks, "¿Habla usted español?"

First, a pause that he immediately regrets. Then, quickly, "Sí."

I speak a little English. You want me to tell you in English?

"No."

She smiles, her face as creased as a walnut, her sparse hair combed straight back.

She says, You remind me very much of an officer who caught me once when I was young. He was very good looking.

He laughs.

You forgot to ask us how many are in our group, she scolds. Another group is meeting us. My granddaughter is with them. I don't want to get separated.

He turns back to Cárdenas. Is this true?

Cárdenas looks to the old woman.

Six more, he says, when Marcus steps between them. A half hour behind us. Just regular people.

Including her granddaughter, Marcus prods.

Cárdenas nods. My niece.

Wait, Marcus says. He looks to the old woman. Then, is she . . . ?

Cárdenas summons the grin.

My mother, oficial.

I know you're going to wait for them, she tells Marcus crisply. She folds her arms. You'll do the right thing. I can tell you're a good boy.

Marcus shakes his head all the way to the truck.

The radio crackles after he hangs up. He laughs out loud in the dark cab, feeling strangely—for the first in a long time—like himself.

The glove compartment is barely visible in the moonlight. He hesitates. Pulls it open. The bottle of Spurt is still inside. He taps out five capsules, a shade of red so deep they look almost black, and slips them into his shirt pocket.

Back at the trees, Peña greets him with the clink of the Zippo.

"So, what's up?"

"The van'll be here in an hour." He offers two bottles of water from the crook of his arm to the middle-aged couple. The man has a lazy eye that floats loose over the bridge of his nose.

"By the way," Marcus adds, "I brought something else with me."

"Yeah?" Peña fills his cupped hands with a flare of light.

Marcus hands a bottle of water to Cárdenas, who cracks it open. "*Yeah.*"

Peña looks back at him blankly. Then his eyes widen.

Water for the young woman. She gives him a simmering look and turns her head away, patting the baby's bottom. He sets down the bottle beside her. The old woman takes the last one from him with both hands.

"Gracias, guapo." She nods toward the scrub. Could we talk?

He leads her to a creosote bush a short distance away.

Well?

She smiles. Do you have any children? She lowers an upturned hand toward her knees, in the Mexican way, to indicate their height.

He shakes his head.

You're married?

"No."

Well, then soon. A big, good-looking boy like you—you hardly even look Indian. You're more like an Arab.

He laughs. The baby squalls. He glances in its direction.

My son is going to jail this time, she says, examining the thin clouds.

Marcus shifts his weight. I know.

It's a shame, she continues mildly. He's such a good boy. Like you.

He rakes through his words.

There are rules, he settles on finally.

Yes. Rules. Though I've heard sometimes people bend them.

"Ándale pues," he says in his breeziest tone, leading her back by the elbow.

Cárdenas looks up glumly from his knees as they approach. The baby squawks again.

The woman tut-tuts and adds in a low voice, The baby's mama is going to jail this time too.

His eyes slip toward the young woman. Of course, she catches him. Her chest heaves as she jiggles the baby.

What a shame, he says.

Yes, the old woman agrees. A shame.

When she raises her eyes to his, a coy smile flickers over her lips. She tips her head at the young woman, as though in encouragement.

For crying out loud.

"Hey." He turns toward the river, hardly recognizing his own voice. "What was that?"

Peña looks up from his charges. A smile slips on and off his face, quick as a blip of radar. "What? You hear something, Gonzales?"

There's nothing to hear, of course. Just the crickets and the shuffle of feet, a brief crackle of walkie-talkie static. The river is too slow and thick to make any sound at all.

He sets off toward the river with a tug of his collar and the slightest upturn at the corner of his lips.

Something scrapes in the brush before he can take his third step.

He whips his head. Silence. Then again—scrape. A thump and drag. Marcus mutters, "Crap," and snaps his fingers to quiet the people under the tree. Peña crushes his cigarette beneath his heel. A soft, quick splash echoes from the riverbank.

They wait until there's nothing to do but give the all clear.

The old woman stretches. Maybe it was La Llorona.

"Ay, señora." The third woman makes the sign of the cross. Don't talk about that.

No, no, the old woman continues, teasing now. Maybe it was her, making that noise. She turns her face up to Marcus. You think?

Marcus scans the dark.

Do you even know who La Llorona is?

The witch, he mutters.

She grins. "A compass"? What are you talking about? La Llorona is the one who looks for her children in the river. She drowned them and now she wants them back.

I *know*.

Of course, she doesn't always cry, she continues, picking her teeth with a thumbnail. If she thinks you're one of her babies, she sneaks up on you. She gets closer and closer, and then . . . *Rah!*

She reaches so abruptly, claws out, that Marcus's hand jerks toward his holster.

I thought you knew all about her, she says, cackling as he lowers his hand with clenched teeth. She's for real, you know.

"¡Mamá!" Cárdenas whines. "¡Por favor!"

The others titter. Even Peña turns away in silent laughter.

Do you believe in the Chupacabra? The force in Marcus's voice makes the old woman straighten. Behind her, Peña bugs eyes at him with disbelief. Then he clutches the air as though witnessing a losing play in a football game.

The Chupacabra? The old woman snorts. That's not real.

Her companions giggle. Cárdenas too.

Marcus barks, That's enough. He motions the group to its feet. "Vámonos."

The woman's laughter dies away.

What about the others?

We'll send someone else.

It was only a joke, guapo.

Do you think I'm an idiot?

The only answer is another splash from the direction of the riverbank. There is nothing more to be said. He waves Peña toward the group, scuttles to a rise in the embankment, crouches in the dark. Nothing else exists. There is only this moment—his mouth dry, his pulse thrilling, the muscles of his legs coiled, trembling, at the edge of every possibility.

"Siéntese," he whispers, springing upright. Hand to a chest with its own thumping heart. The thud on the ground. "Siéntese," he repeats, again and again. "Siéntese."

The new group of people at the center of Peña's beam flinch and turn their heads as they crest the rise. One silhouette staggers sideways—a girl, sixteen or seventeen, though it's hard to tell in the light.

"M'ija," the old woman says as their hands meet.

"Ay, abuelita."

Everything will be okay, the old woman murmurs.

Peña opens his notepad. Marcus seats the new arrivals beside the others. The young woman's eyes burn at him in the dark.

But now, from behind him, comes a cry. Or more of a gasp. He whirls. The group still huddles, shoulder to shoulder, bound by a low, agitated murmur.

"¿Qué pasa?" Marcus calls. Peña's beam joins his to make a bright oval. The group goes quiet as the old woman rises into the light.

"Señora," Marcus says, with sternness. "Siéntese."

Her eyes only dart to something in the dark. Then she lets loose an earsplitting screech.

Another female scream follows, then another, and Marcus is on his belly, the gun somehow already in his hand. The others shout, scattering. The old woman stands rooted, an accusing finger pointed toward the river, and only now can he make out their words.

La Llorona.

They plunge for the scrub, for the fields of alfalfa and cotton, toward the river, Peña bellowing behind them, "¡Alto! ¡Alto!" before he throws himself onto the man with the wandering eye. Marcus springs to his feet and is nearly knocked down again, someone whacking a shoulder to his. Cárdenas—his arms clasping a fat bundle to his chest. For an instant, Cárdenas marks him, his eyes spiraling, his eyes on the gun. Marcus leaps, shoving his weapon back to its holster, closing a hand on a backpack, tearing it open as Cárdenas breaks free, a dozen small parcels spilling from the bag to the ground. *You motherfucker,* he thinks, even as he snatches at the next thing that streaks past him. A smooth arm. He already knows whose it is. She struggles against him, and when she kicks him, she connects hard with his shin. He catches her hand and rolls it over until it locks.

Her arms are empty. His heart pounds with fists in his ears.

Where is your baby?

The young woman tries to yank loose. He twists her wrist, and she cries out. The baby howls up ahead as someone stronger and faster than she—Cárdenas, of course—hurtles with it toward the river. Maybe he's the baby's father. Maybe he's betting no one will separate a mother from her child. She leaps away from him again, surely knowing it will hurt, and this time she chokes out, Let me go. He looks from her to the ruckus of splashing to the baby's cry.

Something oozes down the length of his chest. Something sticky and warm.

In the dim light, he can just make out the blotch blooming through his shirt pocket. He stares at it dumbly, a dizziness spinning apart his brain. He clenches the hand in his tighter.

The hand's owner yelps. Her lips tremble and her eyes are liquid and wide.

And he realizes: Fake. Fake blood. He's an idiot. He sags in relief, his free hand grasping her shoulder.

She recoils.

He reaches for her again, as though in apology.

She twists in his grip.

He clutches her by both shoulders, not meaning to pull her back to him. But he does.

She spits at him with the force of a viper.

For a moment, he's numb, slow as he wipes his cheek with his sleeve. Then he clamps his hands on her anew and turns her. Together, they struggle—like furious dancers who both want the lead—toward Peña, who curses and wrestles the man in the dirt. The woman jerks and bucks as he urges her forward, gasps as he turns her arm behind her back and something pops. When the cuffs meet her wrists, she goes limp.

"Por favor," she says, weeping now.

He pushes her, facedown, to the ground, beside the scattering of little packages Cárdenas has left behind. They're diapers. He can see that now.

"Por *favor*." The flashlight in the dirt makes a bright, jagged slice of her face.

Yards away, the man beneath Peña stops flailing under the clamp of the cuffs, but his one good eye still rolls, wild with fear, toward the river. To the hag that surely awaits them all.

The old woman waits beneath the mesquite. Marcus goes to her on his unsteady legs, feeling for the cuffs on his belt, the baton. At his back comes the hard clink of the Zippo, the sudden flare and breath. The old woman smiles without mirth and offers him the tender undersides of her wrists. Then she lifts them as if to say, *Hurry up.*

THE ORGANIZATION WAS STILL BASED in El Paso, with a correlating arm in Dallas. She'd known about it for years. Yes, the woman on the phone had admitted when pressed, they did still run the home for girls in Juárez, it was a cost-effective arrangement, some families preferred the privacy of the location, especially the Catholic ones, but it wasn't really open to the public. She requested a tour. Offered a donation. Explained that she just wanted to see the place where she was born.

Which both was and wasn't true.

Now she crosses at the point of entry. The guard looks quizzically at her documents, then at her. She tells him she's just planning to stay for the day. She follows the byzantine directions along potholed, no-speed-limit freeways, then onto quiet streets. The building is nondescript—a dormitory, or an old motel.

Nobody has any idea why she's here. Girls—American girls; her parents would have of course taken comfort in knowing the mother would be an American, would have insisted upon it—chatter and waddle behind their bellies through the lobby.

"What can I help you, señora?"

She turns to face the matronly woman in a suit who waits behind her.

She has practiced the words in her head.

"I was born here," she stammers. "Could someone tell me who my birth mother is?"

The woman accepts, with dignity, the two folded twenties Rose Marie tucks into her palm, beckons her into a file-cabinet-lined storage room, and asks for her fecha de nacimiento.

The minutes pass. The woman looks. Looks again.

"Lo siento," she says finally. "No here, this one. Is a long time ago."

A door, shut. Just like that.

Just like it always should have been.

She spends a numb, leaden afternoon wandering and enduring stares at a crowded outdoor market in front of a cathedral, wishing for an earthquake or for some other chasm to swallow her. Then she wipes her tears and bucks up.

It's time to go home. Face the shitstorm. Ready her apologies. Jordan's birthday is coming up and that's exactly the time she should be back in El Paso. The past is gone. Definitively. The questions have no answers, and honestly, it's a relief. She can only look forward now. Nothing at home is likely to be any different, but all of it is perfectly imperfect. Herself included. Her mind feels strangely clear, her heart calm.

At the border, the guard looks at her documents and wants to know where her passport is.

She doesn't have one, she explains tartly, hasn't needed one the entire time she's been in and out of Mexico this year.

Whereupon he informs her that she can't return to the United States without one. The regulations have changed.

She insists that she's an American citizen. Her *parents* are American citizens. *All* of them. He points out that she was born in Juárez, then tells her she'll have to wait in a secondary inspection area while they verify her identity. Then she'll have to pay a fine. She's down to her last eleven dollars. Doesn't she have a credit card? It appears, she informs him icily, that she's been frozen out of it. Well then. She could have quite a wait.

And in the days that follow, when she's moved from inspection room to holding cell, as she repeats her story again and again, reminding whatever uniform that appears that no, she doesn't have her phone with her, she left it at home, yes of course there's someone who could pay her fine but she would *prefer* not to involve them, couldn't they just let her go first and then bill her, they have her permanent address for God's sake, until a weary-looking guard her own age who also looks like he's been sitting behind a desk for the last twenty years says, "Por Dios, mujer, we'll make the call for you." And when she tells him she'd prefer that he didn't, he says, "Fine. Then Mexico can have you."

She calls his bluff all the way through the phone call she watches him make through a glass panel, even as she's marched down a concrete slope past the barbwire. Then, the seating in a similar room, only more shabby. A similarly weary-looking official. "I think I need a lawyer," she tells him stiffly.

The guard looks up from his paperwork. "¿No habla usted español?" More days. In a different building, a room with a cot. A visit by some kind of social worker who also speaks no English but offers her a toothbrush and a rosary. She paces and writes letters on the mini-notebook she keeps in her purse for grocery lists. "Post office!" she demands. "Teléfono!" The guards tut-tut and say something about international long-distance charges. You can send a telegram, they suggest. She turns her imaginary pockets inside out. They shrug and offer her a fax machine.

The next time she sits down in a room with her paperwork, she demands books or at least crossword puzzles from her interviewer. And a shower. Also, better food. Goddammit, she's an *American citizen*!

He slams down his coffee cup. "¡Cállate, güera! Aquí no das las órdenes, ¿me entiendes?"

She sucks in her breath, fear—at last—an icy puddle in her stomach.

The guard leans toward her over the desk, his eyes bulging. Then he flings the papers toward her in disgust and goes out.

Her return transfer is astonishingly swift. The same agent who detained her on the U.S. side is there to meet her. He exchanges a look with the Mexican guard, who rolls his eyes. Somebody shoves her car keys at her. The inside of the Lexus smells strongly of a barnyard; the seats are covered in goat hair.

The ignition sputters as she turns it over. She guns the gas, and the entire car bucks. She guns harder. It floods out. Panic rises in her throat. The car is worthless. It knows no place but nowhere. It no longer knows how to move forward.

She puts her foot on the brake, wondering how far she can walk. But with the next turn of the key the engine seems to remember itself, or at least what it once was, and it roars itself back to life.

22

FIESTA

"OKAY," HUCK SAYS IN HIS bathrobe. "Let's put out those tables and chairs."

Jordan huffs after him onto the patio in an apron that reaches her knees. "We need to get the food ready."

He whacks open a pair of metal folding chairs. "They'll need to sit before they can eat." He extends the legs of a folding table. "Grab the end of this, will you?"

They open all the tables. They array the chairs. They drop a floating mass of yellow balloons, weighted with a chunk of cinder block, into a faded plastic swimming pool.

"Now help me with the tacos," Jordan grouches.

"What I'm gonna do," Huck says as he surveys the unopened bags of tortilla chips, unpeeled avocados, intact cabbages and tomatoes, unreconstituted dips and the frozen plank labeled "pescado" in the sink, "is send your brother or sister out to Chico's to pick up a few dozen taquitos. If they ever wake up."

"No!"

"Honey." He lowers himself into a chair to meet her at eye level. "I'm trying to make this whole shindig easier for you. For everybody."

"I don't want an easy party! I want *my* party!"

"I believe that I said at one point I'd do my best to make sure you had a better birthday than your brother and sister did this year. This is how I'm doing it."

He leans back in the chair, folding his arms, offering an immovable smile.

She thrusts a cutting board at him. "Make the salad!"

He skirts the enormous cake on the countertop behind her. Two layers of chocolate, sandwiched together with some sort of beige goo, beneath concentric rings of miniature marshmallows and maraschino cherries speared on Pixy Stix. He heard her crashing around in the kitchen even after he went to bed, didn't try to stop her.

He centers a cabbage on the cutting board. "We can do this." He whacks the cabbage in half, then in quarters, then shreds.

The doorbell rings. He whirls with the knife in his hand.

"Good God, are they here already?"

Skyler answers the door in Spanish.

"Morning," he says with relief when Lourdes appears with her bag and big sneakers.

Jordan saws the frozen fish blob with a meat cleaver. "Hi, Lourdes."

Lourdes eyes the room. "First cooking or clean?"

Huck's heart lifts. "You can cook?"

Skyler pours herself into the kitchen.

"Dad, why didn't you just spring for a party at Chuck E. Cheese?"

Jordan hacks with both hands. "Chuck E. Cheese is imbecilic."

"Agreed," says Quinn. He slumps against the doorway in his pajamas.

Skyler glares at the empty coffee maker. "How long has everyone been up *without making coffee?*"

"M'ija," Lourdes says, snatching the cleaver from Jordan. She casts an unconcealed, exasperated glance in Huck's direction. "¿Qué es esto?"

"Careful with that," he tells Jordan. He turns to the rest of his offspring. "Time for you two to get dressed. I need you to look for some stuff in the garage."

"Coffee," Skyler mutters, pawing through the cabinet.

Quinn smiles at the huddle that is Jordan and Lourdes and picks his eye corners with a black-painted fingernail. "Will you guys make me some hash browns?"

III

Marcus drops onto on a green metal park bench splattered with pigeon shit and faces the alligators. He rolls his dirty sleeves to the elbows. He's walked all night, and his eyes burn. He wears his uniform still, unbuttoned now under his thin jacket; his shoes chafe his ankles. On the brightening horizon, a vapory scud of spring clouds. At the checkpoint there was coffee, enough to fill a whole thermos. The usual forms to fill out. The silent eye contact he and Peña made over the tabletop. No one asked them anything.

Now he wants to go home. Not to his apartment, with its discount furniture and wide-screen TV and the heavy-footed neighbors above him. Somewhere farther. Somewhere back in the known world.

Except that the back of his head tingles. Someone is standing behind him. Too close.

He turns, his hand on the backrest, feeling slow, slower than he needs to be, than he should be, ever.

"Tía," he says. Her face is deeply tanned, creased with sun, with wind. With time.

"Wondered if that was you," Inez answers.

III

"El baño, m'ija," Lourdes barks as Jordan whaps open the back door. "Clean or no?"

Jordan wrestles the garbage can back inside and outfits it with a new bag. "I'm on it."

She skips from the room as Skyler enters hugging a pair of full wastebaskets.

"We're out of toilet bowl cleaner," Skyler reports. "No hay Ajax."

Lourdes opens the refrigerator and extracts a box of baking soda, scrubbing the air with one hand. "Esta. Con vinagre."

Skyler dumps the trash and hurries after her sister.

Lourdes wipes her forehead on her sleeve and turns down the burner. The fish sizzles in the pan. She prods with a spatula. Today is a birthday inside of a birthday. If the coincidence surprised her at first, however, she doesn't have time for it now. Rosario is eighteen years old today. Last week, someone wired her 135 American dollars from a place called North Carolina without a note; Simón at minimum always signs his name. And now? She would like to wish her daughter a happy birthday—in English, as a joke; she wouldn't even yell at her. But she can't, and so Rosario should have sent word. Called. Written a letter. Anything. The fish spatters as she squeezes a lime. As though any child could understand the importance of her own birthday to the person who gave birth to her.

And now here comes el hombrecito with his tiny earplug headphones, his radio thing tucked into his waistband.

She gestures toward the fish in its pan, to the mountains of pico de gallo and cabbage in the serving bowls at her back. "You have plate? Un grande?"

Quinn removes an earplug and smiles. "Did you say something?"

She presses her lips, steps onto a stool to open the cabinet over the stove, wrestles out a tray, and thrusts it at him.

He accepts it languidly.

She retrieves her own headphones. The music station from El Paso is playing something with a hard beat, a sneering male voice with a woman's howl behind it.

Quinn grins. "Holy crap! Are you listening to the Stones?"

She says, You should help your sisters, little prince.

"Say what?"

She takes the tray back from him, gestures to the broom beside the doorway, points to a folded stack of black shirts on the countertop, points in the direction of his room.

His elbow knocks the broom to the floor as he reaches for the shirts, disappearing with the easy gait of the innocent.

She props the broom back against the wall. The CD case she finds behind the blender clunks when she drops it into the garbage can.

She turns back to the fish. She wraps the tortillas in a kitchen towel. She will ask Jordan to push the right buttons on the microwave. There is work to be done here. Work, work, work. Her friend, work.

The music howls. She turns it up.

|||

"It's me," Marcus says, and the sound that escapes him is part bark, part laugh. He pushes up his already rolled sleeves. "But I'm not sure I believe it's really you."

Inez spits on the ground behind her. "You're right. I'm actually Marilyn Monroe."

"Have a seat."

She hefts her backpack higher on her narrow shoulder, teetering sideways under its weight, and lurches. And then she's on the bench beside him, a little brown bird with wings that twitch and flap as her pack slips to the ground.

"So," he says, feeling light headed. "What's . . . new?"

"Not much." She smells of cheap whiskey and a week without a shower. "How about you?"

He shrugs.

"Then why are you looking at me like that?"

He smiles weakly. "We missed you. Worried about you. We wondered where you were."

"I was where I always am. Here and there. Everywhere."

The passersby turn heads in their direction.

"But now you're back," he says. He's not sure if it's a question.

She levels her gaze at the alligators. "So it would seem."

The palm trees rustle in the rising breeze. A cloud of pigeons hurtles to the ground before them to strut and peck in circles.

"Got any plans?" he says.

"I was thinking." Inez sways in her seat. "I think I'll pay a few visits today." She coughs and spits over the back of the bench. "Your father among them."

"Do you come with an olive branch? Or a just a big stick?"

The chuckle that escapes her is an acid one. "I just can't seem to stay away."

If only. If only he could blow the fog from his mind. Weigh the options, step back. Breathe.

"I know what you mean," he says lightly. "I was headed over there myself. Want a ride?"

"A ride," she repeats, as though trying it on for size.

"Except we'd have to take the bus back to my apartment first. I . . ." He glances down at his uniform, looking—what? Rueful? Embarrassed? "I walked."

"Me too," she says, sounding very far away. Her head lists to one side, as though pulled down by her braid, by years of gravity. "The difference, sobrino, is that *you* look like shit."

He laughs, hiccupping. "I'll buy you lunch."

"You sure you've got the time?"

"Anything for my favorite aunt. I'll call my folks and let them know we're coming afterward."

Her gaze drifts past the alligators. "Feel free."

No one answers the landline. He leaves a message, his tone casual, they should give him a call, sooner than later would be great, like, *really* soon, he'll try them again in a while. Three buses have nudged up against each other across the street, nose to tail, like elephants. He dials his mother's cell phone.

First, the truncated ring of a device that, uncharacteristically, has been turned off, then the voice mail. His dad's phone does the same, per the usual. *Just call your mother*, his dad would insist, in the face of complaint. *She always knows where I am.*

"Well, tía," he says once he's left the next chipper message. "Let's just head out to my place, and then we'll call them again."

But when he looks back, she's already gone.

III

"Good afternoon, young lady," Chavela tells the girl in the doorway. She extends her wrapped gift with a realtor's smile.

The birthday girl, dressed in a ruffled orange skirt that matches her hair and a hot-pink blouse that does not, accepts the gift with cheer and throws open the door.

Chavela's elbow jabs Jerry's arm. "Happy birthday," he says neutrally.

"You don't have to take off your shoes," Jordan responds. "Part one of the party is outside."

She beckons them into the high-ceilinged foyer. They follow, past a wide sitting room, empty save for an uncomfortable-looking antique sofa and a lonely piano. They follow past the dining room, where a bed-sheet has been tacked to the wall, into a kitchen that, he is surprised to see—that he sees Chavela sees—is smaller and somewhat less well-appointed than their own. The back door has been propped open with a pasta colander.

Outside, the young Miss DuPre deposits the two of them at the edge of the pillared patio and disappears.

Jerry shifts between feet. Exactly seven people are gathered at the patio's center—all adults. They do not appear to know each other well. They flash awkward smiles, crowding the hors d'oeuvres table. Invisible speakers pipe in the sort of music that he supposes his sons would call "techno."

He tugs his jacket closer. "Well." The sun has begun to disappear beneath a paste of darkening clouds. "This looks fun."

Chavela reapplies her smile, though it is not aimed in his direction. "It's all about the attitude, malhumorado."

She steps away from him to corner a towheaded scarecrow of a young man who has just raised a chip loaded with guacamole to his lips.

"And how do you know the DuPre family?" she asks cordially after a self-introduction and handshake that necessitates the young man wiping his hand on his pants first.

Jerry counts to ten and steps up beside his wife. Every time he's caught her, lately, studying him from behind newspapers, from around corners, beside him in the Volvo, her expression narrow and all-knowing, he is provoked to blurt, "*What?*"

But she hasn't told.

He offers the young man his own hand. Chavela is bluffing. How can it be otherwise? For, from what source other than her own imagination could she have possibly derived any sort of suspicion? She hadn't been here. She'd taken the boys to her sister's in L.A.

There could have been a witness.

His pulse quickens. In all the years since that summer night, had he truly never considered this possibility? It had been a party, after all, a block party, people in the streets and on their lawns.

There is a difference, Jerry tells himself, between refusing to acknowledge history and losing it somewhere in the black hole of memory.

Also, Rose Marie left her family for reasons that had nothing to do with him.

"Well, I'm glad this family finally has something to celebrate," Chavela tells the young man as he inserts a chip into his mouth. She breezes away from them both.

Jerry looks at the young man. The young man looks back.

"I'm sorry," Jerry says, trying hard not to follow Chavela with his eyes. "How did you say you know the DuPres?"

"My parents own the Pic Quik." He bounces on his toes. "My mom is supposed to meet me here, but she's still stuck at the store, so she sort of sent me ahead. Like, an ambassador."

Or a scout, Jerry thinks. "So you hardly know them at all?"

"Well, I know their favorite slushy flavors."

A glance across the patio reveals Chavela chatting up a pair of heavy-set women—the younger in pink sweatpants, the elder in crepe-soled shoes. "Nice to meet you, ambassador. Now if you'll excuse me."

He slips up beside his wife as she and her cohorts burst into laughter. She offers not the slightest glance in his direction when she introduces him in Spanish.

"Sheri and Lupita work in the school cafeteria where Jordan goes to school," she adds.

He inclines his head politely. "¿Verdad?"

"I was just telling them how you once worked in food services."

"Where at?" asks the younger one.

He describes the dishwashing job he held as a fifteen-year-old at Luby's cafeteria as Chavela glides away once again.

"Pues, my friend that works at the mess hall at Fort Bliss," the older one says, "she told me once on accident somebody slopped a bucket of mop water into the soup, but they gave it to those guys anyways."

Chavela has inserted herself in the midst of two men his own age and a preteen girl who are nodding, all nodding like bobblehead figurines that can't stop.

"De todos modos, la Jordan is like the only kid who talks to us," says the voice beside him. "Except she's got this thing about . . . ¿cómo se dice? 'Space debris'?"

The back door, having lost its colander, now slams open. A short, round figure emerges, rump first, rotating slowly with outstretched arms on which rest a pair of food-laden platters.

A tremor of elation moves through him.

"Lourdes," he calls out despite himself.

She halts, the trays swaying in her arms.

He begs the pardon of the women before him and hurries up to Lourdes's side.

"Buenas tardes," he tells her with what he realizes is much too wide a grin, and then he moves to relieve her of a tray. "Permítame."

She eyes him with what he could swear is annoyance, her hand gripping the tray before she releases it. "Buenas tardes, señor."

The tray contains tacos of an indeterminate filling. He follows Lourdes to the table and shimmies it into a spot between the plastic cups and napkins.

"¿Y como está?"

Lourdes sets down her remaining tray.

Busy, she tells him with firm cheer and relocates the first tray to another spot on the table.

And do they have you working as a waitress today?

She shrugs.

Work is work. You know?

He inclines his head.

It certainly is.

He watches as she rearranges the plastic flatware, the heavy bass of the music punching the air between them.

Please excuse me, señor. I still have a lot to do.

Of course.

He watches as the screen door slaps shut behind her.

Behind him comes a stir of voices. His neighbors, the Andersons—Jared and Tammy—have come shuffling with a ribboned gift bag through the gate. He thinks to wave, but already, Chavela is upon them.

"*Now* it's a party!" he hears her say.

He turns back to the hors d'oeuvres. He scans the precisely hedged yard and the house's façade with a posture of absolute nonchalance. But his eyes are peeled for Huck DuPre. Of course.

III

From his bedroom window, from between two slats of venetian blinds tweezed apart with thumb and forefinger, Huck looks out over the gathering crowd on his patio and thinks, *Shit.*

He clacks the ice tongs in his free hand. All he needs to do is take them downstairs and shove them into the ice bucket, freeing the waterlogged wooden spoon he stuck there this morning. Hadn't he been happy enough to find these tongs in his nightstand? Even if it recalled the period of time, after Rose Marie's evacuation, when bedtime required a prophylactic nightcap.

There's Eugene Radosevich, waving to someone in the crowd. And the Andersons, unloading a case of beer onto the beverage table, and here comes Edwin Espinoza and he would bet Mimi wasn't far behind, and—Christ, was that his mailman? Whooping it up with Chavela Gonzales?

Which means Jerry is here. Huck locates him lurking by the guacamole, no doubt waiting for the opportunity to make someone feel like a mental midget. Or just judged, somehow. Judged, judged, judged.

He's sweating so much that he can't keep a grip on his tongs.

A chorus of voices float up the staircase, muffled and jovial, as Jordan greets someone at the door. His eyes fly to the glass doorknob. Goddamned wobbly, rattling, nonfunctioning, old-fashioned keylock. He's vulnerable here.

Outside, the music changes to something involving a sitar.

If he waited for a moment for the activity in the entryway to die down, he could dash downstairs and—if he ducked, crab walking into the dining room—enter the hole undetected.

But no. He wipes his palms on his jeans, manning up.

He keeps his pace measured on his way down the stairs, taking no pains to muffle the clack of his boot heels. The chatter of the party fills the air.

At the bottom of the landing, he stands with his hands on his hips, as though daring someone to talk to him.

They're all outside.

He looks at his watch. Takes a step toward the rear of the house. Then another. He two-steps with the sitar through the entryway to the empty dining room.

He snaps the tongs, staring down the painting of farmers threshing wheat. There are many things in this world, he tells himself, that hurt no one if you do them for only a few minutes.

He dives past the sheet, feeling no pain as his knees hit the pavement.

III

The back door slams open.

"I do *not* believe you," says the woman who comes tripping in. She sets down an empty beer bottle on the breakfast bar, smiling vaguely at Lourdes before looking away.

Her companion adds her own empty to the bar. It tips over. "Get over here and I'll show it to you."

Off they go, tittering, toward the bathroom.

Lourdes sweeps the bottles from the countertop into the recycling bin. Outside, the trash bags tied to the patio posts are already overflowing.

The breeze is turning into a wind. It rattles the metal trash can lids at the side of the house as she stuffs in a trio of loaded bags. Fat, gray clouds crowd in over the mountains, and is that a drop of rain on her arm? When was the last time they even had any? She might have to move the damned food.

And yet she imagines what it would feel like—that release, the coolness on the skin, everything damp and cleansed. After so long. Maybe it's raining where Rosario is. Maybe somebody has given her a party. She wrestles down the can's lid. The street is empty. Everyone is at the house behind her. Shuffling in their good sandals. Laughing with beers in their hands. Filling their plates again and again.

Except for one lone figure, making a dark shape at the side of la casa Gonzales. At first, she thinks her eyes are playing tricks on her—it's a shadow, a roll of old blankets, a sack of leaves. But now it moves, stumbling, to the front of the lawn, to the next house's lawn, to the carport of the house beside the one where she stands.

"Madre de Dios," Lourdes whispers.

Inez, with a half curl of a smile, raises a hand to wave. Then she touches a finger to her lips.

III

From her perch atop the desk in the upstairs office, where she is afforded an unfettered forty-five-degree-angle view of the backyard, Jordan observes Ripley in action. He wags with vigor as he butts his head against the backs of knees—each of them buckling, their corresponding elbows flaring outward in surprise—then snarfs in midair the food that is spilled from plates above.

Also, her neighbors, the Espinozas, clinking beer bottles in a "cheers" with Doug from the Pic Quik. The Andersons, chatting up the Taylor-Gutierrezes, who show little reaction when Mr. Anderson touches his head with his thumbs to make reindeer antlers. Her teacher, Mrs. Woodward, who has wandered in through the back gate looking concerned about keeping her hair in place. A cluster of adults she's never seen before sing a song unintelligibly, with French accents. Sheri from the cafeteria plays an air guitar behind their backs; Lupita swats her. Mr. Gonzales stands alone beside a trash bag, an almost visible storm cloud over his head, then joins Mrs. Gonzales, who glides away from him once more. A couple of country-club moms have arrived—Mrs. Conklin, Mrs. Crowder—around whom revolve a small solar system of girls. Behind the beverage table, out of sight of their mothers, three of these girls have clumped together to stick out their tongues at the fourth. Girl number four bursts into tears, then punches one of her tormentors in the collarbone.

Jordan radiates with joy. This is where she likes it best—watching, from afar. Even better would be if she had a control panel of some sort, buttons to push and big screens from which to command the operations, in which case she would have jettisoned the Chico's tacos that have appeared on the buffet table.

Also, she would have pressed the cancel button on the weather forecast. The sky has turned a deeper shade of gray, swallowing the sunlight, and there's grit in the air. But it's not going to rain. No. Not possible.

With the weary but cheerful sense of duty borne by those who must come down at times from the mountain, she descends.

She runs into Brittany Gallegos in the kitchen, reading *Teen Beat* magazine at the breakfast bar. Jordan gives her a good, long stare.

"My mom told me I had to come," Brittany tells her, flinging her shiny hair over her shoulder.

Jordan stares.

"This music is weird," Brittany says.

Jordan stares. "My cake is going to be way better than your cake."
When she finds Quinn crunching away beside the Chico's tray, she
scowls. He shrugs back. She ascends a folding chair at the patio's edge, a
wooden spoon and a metal pie plate tucked under her arm.

"All right, everybody," she calls through her cupped hands. A few heads
turn her way. She bangs the spoon against the plate until she's got a quo-
rum. "For part two of the party, we're playing games. Everybody form two
lines in alphabetical order of your last name, line one ends at 'L.' We're
playing, Human Periodic Table Hopscotch, with Special Handshake."

A number of sounds emerge from the crowd—groans, warbles of
confusion, barking laughter.

"Can I have another beer first?" someone quips.

"I'm only doing it if roller skates are involved," calls someone else.
"Can we do that?"

So many eyes upon her. So much held breath.

"Sure!" she announces. Her heart is a bright flag whipping in her chest.

III

Lourdes steps away from the house. She looks back over her shoulder.
She cuts across the yellowing grass out of the front door's line of sight,
and when she reaches Inez, she looks her over, the pack at her feet, her
face, her heavy-lidded eyes.

You're drunk, she says.

Inez snorts.

I found my way here, didn't I? And hello to you too, by the way.

Lourdes hugs her elbows.

Los señores aren't home. They're at the party.

A cheer erupts in the DuPres' backyard. Inez lifts an eyebrow in its
direction.

I see, she says, and a new smile spreads across her face. She bends to
lift her pack.

No, Lourdes says, lurching, and she closes her hand on Inez's thin
arm. You can't.

Can't what?

It's a birthday party. Why do you want to ruin it?

Inez tenses under her grip.

Who says I'm going to ruin it? I'm just going to go check it out. Whose birthday?

La Jordan. The youngest.

And how old is this girl today?

Ten. Inez. What are you trying to do?

Inez makes a low, growling chuckle in her throat.

After I say hello to my brother and sister-in-law? What I always do. Talk to people. Just talk. I've been away a long time. Surely you understand the solitude of being a stranger wherever you go?

Lourdes says nothing.

Besides, Inez continues with growing cheer. I've always liked a good party. What's one more person in a crowd like that?

She's not here, Lourdes blurts. You should leave them alone.

Inez snatches back her arm.

Who do you think *you* are? The gatekeeper?

She says nothing as Inez stumbles back under her pack, toward the house. It's out of her hands. It's none of her business, it isn't her family, it isn't her party, she can just walk away.

Except that before her she sees a lost woman who doesn't know the way home.

Damn you, she mutters, and she marches up to grab the loop on Inez's pack.

Inez yips as she's jerked sideways.

Damn *you*, woman. What do you think you're doing?

Lourdes lowers her head as she pulls Inez up the front walk, into the wind. She plants Inez against one of the pillars surrounding the front door and looks to each side of the house. Seeing no one, she turns and rattles the doorknob. It doesn't budge.

She extracts the DuPres' house key from her pants pocket.

Inez's face transforms.

Son of a whore! You're smuggling me in?

The door creaks open. Lourdes sticks in her head. No one.

I'm doing no such thing, she says. You need to sober up before you go outside. I'll bring you a Coke.

Now that's more like it! Inez grins.

Lourdes gives her a black look. Don't get used to it.

Inside, the metal chandelier sways over their heads. The jackets hang in orderly rows on their pegs.

Well, Inez says, turning unsteadily to survey the room, with pleasure. Well, well, well.

Don't touch anything, Lourdes says as she pulls her by the elbow into the formal living room. The music floating in from the patio, dampened under the chatter of the crowd, has taken a bouncy new turn, like dance music for robots. And put that down! she adds. She yanks a family photo from Inez's hand and returns it to its shelf. You never even returned the last one.

Inez sniggers. She turns in another slow circle, her eyes lighting on the staircase.

Lourdes stifles a gasp and blocks the doorway with her body. You can't go up there!

Inez drops her pack beside the piano. Come now. Who would it hurt?

Stay here, Lourdes says through her teeth, and read a magazine. Act like you're waiting to use the bathroom. I'll be back in a minute. Don't you understand how much trouble I could get into?

Relax, says Inez, and she flops down onto the fancy sofa with its turned wooden legs. She rummages under the coffee table beside her and finds a Victoria's Secret catalog, which she regards with amusement.

If anything happens, she adds, donning a serious face but suppressing a giggle, I will accept full responsibility.

Oh, of course, Lourdes snaps as she moves for the doorway. You're such an expert on that.

III

In the echoing space between dining room and living room, from deep in his hole, Huck lifts his head from his slump at the sound of his maid's voice, arguing with a woman he cannot identify, in a language he cannot parse, and wonders, *What the hell?*

III

Marcus tries the doorbell for the third time. He rattles the doorknob as the chimes die away, then sorts through his key collection once again, eyes sticky with exhaustion. Where is his spare key? Is it possible he never even had one? He can't say for certain that, in the years since he moved out, he's ever been to his parents' house when they weren't home.

There's some kind of ruckus going on down the street—music, a party. Okay. If they're not home, she hasn't surprised them. Unless they've already murdered each other. He can leave a note on the door. Under the door. That is, if he had anything to write on. He feels around on his belt again, in his uniform pockets. If he had a goddamned key he could wait, in a horizontal position, on the sofa.

He's zapped the moment he touches the latch on the back gate.

A car pulls into the driveway behind him as he peers furiously through the front window. It's an unfamiliar sedan, windows tinted but in need of a paint job. Down comes the driver's-side window.

"Yo," a voice calls out over the still-running engine. "Sobrino."

"Tío," Marcus blurts. "What's . . . up?"

Tavo gives him the once-over and turns off the engine. "I might ask you the same, kid. Anyway, I just saw Inez."

"Me too!" Marcus hustles down the walk to meet his uncle, who is now hefting himself out of the car. "She told me she was headed over here, but I can't get ahold of my mom and dad."

"Well, I'm glad it's not just *me* your viejos are ignoring."

"So she didn't want to come with you either?"

Tavo shrugs. "I offered her a ride, but she told me to shove it up my ass."

"And now she's not here."

"Nope."

They stand in silence, the light going from gray to almost blue around them. A cheer thunders up from the party down the street and then a raucous chant, as though from the spectators of a race. A raspy wail from the sound system rises above it. A few members of the crowd join in.

Tavo says, "Are they listening to Janis Joplin over there, or are they sacrificing a goat?"

Marcus peers toward the noise. His eyes meet his uncle's.

"Crap," they say simultaneously.

They hit the sidewalk together, elbowing their way forward like speed walkers, just ahead of the storm.

III

"It's starting to rain," Jerry remarks.

Edwin Espinoza, his abundantly cologned neighbor, swipes a few drops from his forearm. "Don't worry—it'll go away in a minute."

Beneath the contorted branches of a Mexican elder, Chavela has engaged an older couple whose expressions suggest they have settled in for a pleasant religious sermon.

"I'm not so sure about that," Jerry says.

"Are you kidding me? Since when does it rain here in April?" Edwin swigs from his beer. "Has it even rained at all in the past year?"

A fat drop splashes Jerry's eyebrow. Another collides with his taco. Its texture had surprised him upon his first bite, the mysterious filling revealing itself in the salty tang that coated his tongue. It wasn't bad, not bad at all, though perhaps there was a whiff of the freezer beneath it. He doused it with a good pico de gallo from a nearby bowl. The only other alternative was the tray from Chico's that had appeared during the game of Blindfolded Lawn Bowling with Famous Movie Lines.

On the other side of the lawn, next to the barbecue grill, Pete Davis is flailing and hollering in a dance likely to elicit offense among certain ethnic groups.

"Bring it, man!" someone shouts out from the crowd that has gathered around him. "But first, go stand on my lawn!"

Edwin shakes his head. "Pointless."

Jerry takes another bite. "Have you tried the fish tacos?"

"Fish *tacos*? You mean tacos with *fish* in them?"

Chavela, now beside the juniper hedge, has cornered Quinn DuPre.

Jerry squints. The kid has the slip of a smile on his face, but he looks antsy, shifting from black sneaker to black sneaker with hands in his pockets. Chavela laughs and throttles his shoulder. As though he was hers for the questioning. Jerry turns his whole body in their direction. Let her catch him. He dares her to.

He lifts a hand to the bullseye of pain that suddenly sings in his sinuses. The air pressure has dropped, it would seem. Like an anvil. And above them all, the gray, cloud-heavy sky seems to still itself, holding its breath.

First, an explosion of thunder. Then the sky splits open.

A cheer detonates in the yard.

There are those whose first impulse is to rush out to twirl and tip their heads back into the great, wet gush. There are those who crowd onto the patio, jostling the tables and prying open the back door, hooting and opening fresh beers. Chavela he loses sight of altogether.

Beside him, Edwin leans on the patio post, looking to the sky with something like outrage.

Jerry's sinuses reinflate. He reaches for another taco. And a beer.

"You're right," he tells Edwin as the crowd in the yard, riding a wave of exclamations and curses and squeals, comes stumbling in to join the rest of them. "It's not raining."

For from the sky now pour huge lumps of ice, a million golf balls thumping down to crack the heads of those below, crusting the world over in white.

III

Huck takes a tentative step from his hole.

Three reasons he's got for this: One, his unbearable curiosity at the sound of Lourdes—Lourdes!—scolding someone. Two, an insane racket of precipitation has begun to pound the roof and windows of his house, and that, too, he's got to see for himself. Three: For God's sake, it's his kid's birthday.

He clears the sheet just as the entire party comes crashing into his house. They arrive bearing bowls of food and the buckets of ice, the folding tables and chairs, the plastic swimming pool heaped now with gifts, laughing and hollering as they wrestle the goods past the dining room to set them down God knows where, and he knows he should recognize the faces he sees but all that comes to him now are motions that blur and make strange kaleidoscopic shapes.

A shadow goes motionless in the doorway.

He grips a chair until a body—slender, female, woolly headed—comes into focus.

Skyler. Regarding him as though she had just come upon a buffalo behind the dining room table.

He takes a step back. Her eyes narrow.

He takes another step, groping behind for his sheet with one hand. Her eyes go wide.

"Oh no you *don't*," she snarls, and she dives into the room faster than he can think about moving, and throws herself in front of the hole.

"Lemme in," he says, glancing over his shoulder toward the crowd. He sidesteps from one side of her body to the other.

She starfishes her arms and legs across the opening. The face she turns up to him is a freckled mask of cold fury.

III

Jordan glowers at the sky.

"No!" She stamps her foot. She jumps up and down with clenched fists, rattling the lamp on her bedside table. "No, no, *no!*"

Down comes the hail, piling onto roofs and lawns and parked cars like frozen jumbo marshmallows.

She stomps out to the landing at the top of the stairs, watching through its small window as the party disappears indoors. The music blasts on in the den. It's not fair. She planned and planned. She flinches as a ball of ice hits her windowpane with a "crack." Downstairs, people are whooping it up again.

Outside, there's a guy pressed flat to the side of the Andersons' house. A battered white pickup truck hunkers farther down the street at the curb, a lawn mower abandoned at the end of a mowed stripe in the lawn.

Miguel, looking shivery and wet and very surprised, huddles against the house as she approaches with a pair of three-ring binders tented over her head.

She gives him a good long stare. "Why aren't you at my party?"

He wipes off his glasses. They steam back up immediately.

"'Cause I'm stuck under this house."

"You weren't coming," she tells him. "You weren't coming at all."

"I've been busy."

"With what?"

"*Things*," he says. "Come on. It's not like you could even invite me for reals."

"Why not?"

"That," he says, "is something you're gonna understand real good someday."

"Lourdes is there."

"So?"

"I get to invite whoever I want."

"Like who? Who? Who all's there?"

There's something in his exasperation that strikes her as a weakness, a crack in a wall she could widen. It makes no sense why she's the one who suddenly has tears in her eyes.

"Nobody!" she yells. "Everybody. So do you want to stay out here and be all wet and stupid, or do you want to come inside and eat food?"

She shoves one of her binders at him.

The hail roars down. She winces as it clobbers her arm.

"Híjole," he says finally, snatching a binder. "Just for a couple of minutes. That's all. Got it?"

She snorts back the tears and leads him to the house, underneath the falling sky.

III

A new clap of thunder booms overhead. Marcus and Tavo duck under the DuPres' front porch. "Is this for real?"

Tavo wipes his face with the back of his sleeve. "Maybe it's the end of the world."

Marcus knocks.

Inside, a woman's shrieking laughter rises above the noise of the crowd. The music changes abruptly from a hippie song to something goth.

Marcus presses the bell. He looks to Tavo when no answer is forthcoming. Tavo looks to him. The doorknob rattles in Marcus's hand but doesn't budge.

Tavo rolls his eyes. "Vámonos."

They hoof it around the house with their arms braced over their heads, through the back gate, to the abandoned and trash-strewn patio, the back door rocking open slightly on its hinges, just as the DuPre girl and his parents' gardener appear from around the opposite corner of the house, both of them with school binders on their heads.

Like four cars arriving simultaneously at a four-way stop, they all stall. The girl—is her name Jordan?—regards him solemnly with wet, flattened hair. Miguel squints behind his foggy glasses.

Marcus clears his throat. "Hey. How's it going?"

Jordan straightens. "It's my birthday."

"Cool. Happy birthday. I was . . ." The words feel like they're sticking to the sides of his brain. He glances at Tavo, who stirs the air impatiently with a hand. "My uncle and I were wondering if my dad was here."

"I think he's still here. Want to come in?"

And then he's suddenly at the periphery of a crowded kitchen, next to a bowl of vegetable dip, wedged several inches closer than he would like into the personal space of his companions, minus their hostess, who has disappeared.

He looks to Tavo. Tavo looks to Miguel. Miguel looks to Marcus, his hands diving into his pockets. He eyes Marcus's uniform.

"Wow, man. I didn't know you're a—"

"La migra's here!" A hand, Marcus can't see whose, claps him on the shoulder as it travels past. "Cuidado, hombres. This party's gonna get busted!"

"Look at that mess outside!" comes another voice, loud and too close to his ear. "My whole life here and I've seen five, maybe ten minutes of this stuff. But I've never seen anything like *this*."

"*Who's* dead?" Tavo squints in the direction of the droning voice emanating from the sound system.

A teenage girl in heavy eyeliner oozes past. "Bela Lugosi," she clarifies.

Marcus finds himself clutching a celery stick dipped in ranch dressing. Miguel has disappeared. The music changes to that Queen song his dad always liked, the one where they tell you to keep yourself alive.

"This is weird," Marcus says, to no one.

Tavo plucks a Bud Light from a nearby ice bucket and shrugs. "It's not so bad." He tips his chin in a way that means, *Keep moving.*

III

"Move over," her father tells her, lurching to one side of the hole.

Skyler lurches with him. "Forget it."

"I'm not negotiating," he says as beads of sweat form around his hairline. "You wanna get grounded?"

Her heart pounds in her ears. "You can't do this. Not this time."

"Goddammit." He reaches to pry her shoulder from the wall.

"Oh hey, baby," calls a voice from the doorway. "There you . . . are."

"Hi, babe," she calls back in a bright, brittle voice.

Her father freezes, reddening, and drops his hand.

She can see the starburst colors of Carlos's tie-dye in her peripheral vision as he takes a stutter step into the room, then pauses, then sidles up the rest of the way.

"Everything cool?" he chirps.

"My dad wants to hide in his hole," she says. "We thought he was over it, like maybe he was ready to start acting like a normal person who's in charge of his own life, but apparently, he'd still rather hide instead of showing up at the party in his own house—which, in case he's forgotten, is *Jordan's birthday party*—and we're *not* going to let him do that."

Carlos glances at her father. "Baby," he says, his voice low with alarm.

"Young man. Go wait in the other room."

Skyler whips her head. "Don't. You. *Dare.*"

Carlos blinks back at her.

She doesn't have time for it. Not for a lot of things. Like, for starters, the way he crosses his arms whenever she asks him about his plans after graduation, since she has, in fact, registered for her first classes at UTEP, and she's just been wondering what it is he's going to *do* next, other than smoke weed, and watch TV at his parents' house, and not quite manage to get a job. Which is to say nothing of the way he continues to avoid any further discussion about the possibility of getting out of town.

"What do you want me to do?" he asks out of the side of his mouth.

"I don't *know*," she bawls.

"Jesus Christ." Her father wipes his temples with the back of a hand.

Carlos swallows. Although his experience with girls on the verge of hyperventilation runs deep, where grown men in this state are concerned, he has entered new territory.

He averts his gaze from Mr. DuPre. Skyler clutches the sides of the hole her dad has punched in the dining room wall, as if it were a breach in the hull of her ship and she were about to be sucked out into space, or maybe just into the storm wrecking the world outside the window. Skyler, who has been with him all summer and yet somehow only half with him, her eyes always far away, looking in the direction where she was slipping, sideways, out of his grasp.

Except when she surfaced from herself to nag him, like she was his *mom*. And also when she actually seemed to prefer his mom's company to his, which was kind of weird, because if she wanted to be part of his family, wouldn't that make her sort of like his sister? Which was to say nothing about how she'd started to complain, practically every time she passed in front of a mirror, about how *blond* she was, how *pale*, she's so *boring*, she wished she had his skin, his eyes. His genes. "You're so lucky to have a *culture*," she told him bitterly. "I have no context whatsoever."

Now Skyler's eyes are the blue pilot lights of a gas flame.

There's really only one choice here. He looks up at the old man—two heads taller, a good forty pounds heavier than he is—and asks himself if he's got the cojones.

"So, Mr. DuPre," he begins, heart thumping. "Do you want to . . . I mean . . . you should check the party out. It's a total rager."

Mr. DuPre grunts and works his jaw.

"I mean," he continues as Skyler nods at him energetically, "it's pretty killer, considering it's supposed to be a birthday party for a ten-year-old girl. Did you plan it that way?"

Mr. DuPre glares at the table.

"Jordan planned it. The forces of nature took over from there."

"Totally!" Carlos jerks his head toward the window. "Can you believe the way nature is kicking our butts?"

"I am fairly certain," Mr. DuPre says, as though trying to climb out of a hole at the center of his brain, "that my oleander bushes are destroyed."

"Yeah, and your windshield might even be cracked! Have you checked out your truck?"

Skyler releases one of her hands from the hole's edge to grip Carlos's shoulder, which she squeezes. Her face is firming back up.

Mr. DuPre exhales. "Might be a good idea."

Carlos straightens out of his slouch, feeling giddy now, weirdly competent. He gives Mr. DuPre a friendly tap on the arm with the back of his hand. "Maybe you should even take it for a drive, after things slack off out there."

Skyler gives him a *what the hell?* look.

"Or," he adds quickly, "maybe you could help us figure out where to move the living room furniture? Because there isn't enough room in there right now, and I think people are trying to dance."

He senses Skyler's exhalation beside him as she steps up and takes her father's arm. "Let's go check it out, Dad."

"I dunno," her father says, shaking his head at his feet. "I dunno."

Skyler gives Carlos a look he can't entirely parse, but it seems to say something like "yes" and "let's go" and "now," and he can feel the old current running between them, tightening its slack, and he steps up to her dad's other side, and will he dare take his other elbow? He will. He does.

The three of them take a step, as one, toward the doorway.

"Oh!" says the short, dark-haired woman who suddenly appears there before them. Her coiffure doesn't move, even when she jerks to a stop. "Huck! Hello!"

She enters without awaiting a response.

"Hi, hon," she says with a kindly nod in Skyler's direction. "Huck! I was wondering when we were going to see you! Listen, I wonder if you'd mind doing me a favor! I'm listing a Southern revival house— it's a lot like this one!—and I'd love to compare some of the features, moldings and light fixtures and whatnot! Would you mind showing me around?"

Mr. DuPre doesn't resist as she touches the elbow Carlos has dropped and escorts him from the room.

From the living room comes the thumping opening chords of that Santana song.

"Who was *that*?" Carlos says.

"Our neighbor, Mrs. Gonzales."

They look at each other.

"OYE COMO VA," everybody yells in the living room, singing.

III

"This crown molding is beautiful," Chavela tells Huck as together they face the ceiling in the den. "Is it original?"

Huck tries not to meet any of the eyes he can feel on him. Everyone is smiling.

"I think it's original," he says. "At least, I don't remember doing anything to it. Unless Rose Marie took charge of it at some point."

"I see." He can sense the solicitous tilt of Chavela's head, the way her body leans toward his, in a posture of concern. "Speaking of which, Huck—how are *you* doing lately?"

It takes all his effort not to bury his face in his hands.

III

There's his wife, cozying up now to his least favorite neighbor.

Jerry slides closer to the entryway to the den, wedging himself behind a fully laden coatrack, where he is out of the sight of his prey. He nudges aside a red windbreaker, peering past clots of partygoers. He supposes "cozying" isn't the right word. Because it's not as though he's jealous. Oh, no. But as Chavela's body makes a subtle three-quarter turn, her hand coming to rest lightly on Huck's bicep, the hair on Jerry's arms bristles. She's after something, of that he can be sure.

Huck emits a manic laugh. "I'm terrific!"

Chavela lowers her chin, her expression kind and brimming with patient disbelief.

"This still must have been a very difficult year for you. I mean, dealing with the kids alone? That's no picnic."

Huck's puffs out his breath and chuckles, feebly.

"I'm sure you've missed Rose Marie."

Jerry leans abruptly up on his toes, straining to hear over the music. Huck coughs a little. "I guess that depends on which way you look at it." He turns just enough that Jerry catches the wry look on his face.

"Oh my!" Chavela says, with a tinkling laugh. "Are we talking irreconcilable differences? If you don't mind me asking."

Huck straightens and puts a little swagger in his shoulders. "Well, I can't say I thought of it that way. But apparently, *she* did. And so did her boyfriend."

"No!" Chavela's face conveys sympathy and horror and the enjoyment of scandal all at once.

"Oh yes."

"You're joking!"

"I *wish*."

"Aren't they cute," Jerry mutters to himself.

Chavela leans closer. "And did you suspect?"

"Can't say that I did."

"Ay, ay, ay." Chavela shakes her head. She looks right to left, then tilts her head conspiratorially. "Was it anyone you know?"

Jerry rises onto his toes.

"Ha! To this day, I still couldn't tell you who it is."

Jerry lowers himself back to earth onto a cushion of disappointment, onto which is tacked the thinnest sole of relief. Perhaps he is, in the end, nothing more than a fool.

"Do you think," Chavela continues, almost whispering now, "I mean, is it possible—do you think there were others?"

Jerry's heart stops. It's a cold brick in his chest.

"That never occurred to me," Huck says wonderingly, and then a shadow of distress crosses his face.

She waves her own words away. "I suppose she's still in town," she continues without skipping a beat.

Jerry grits his teeth. Does she give up? Ever?

"That," Huck says with a rueful smile, "I couldn't tell you either."

"You mean you haven't heard from her?"

"Not a word. I was able to follow her credit card trail for a while. And the PI I hired tracked her to Mexico. Then San Diego. But you already know about that one."

"About . . . what?"

"You know. The favor I asked Jerry, when y'all went to San Diego, to take Adam to school."

Chavela tilts her head. Jerry white-knuckles the sleeve of the red windbreaker. Maybe he should just tie it like a blindfold around his head now.

Huck looks down at Chavela, on the verge of alarm. "I . . . asked him to check and see if she was at the address the PI found for her. She wasn't there. But I guess Jerry took it seriously when I asked him to keep it all under wraps."

"I see," she says uncertainly.

"Of course, that was nearly a year ago."

In the agonizing moment that passes, Jerry can hear the wheels turning—grinding, smoking—in Chavela's head.

"And you're sure she's . . . okay?" she says finally.

"If you're asking if she's alive, my guess would be yes. I'd like to think so anyway."

Jerry can see his wife draw in her breath.

"You know," she says, lowering her voice, "if you ever do hear from her, if you see her, please feel free to send her my way. Because, you know, maybe she'd like to talk."

AHA! Jerry thinks, *aHA, aHA!* The coatrack sways around him. Here, finally, is the heart of the heart of his wife's objective—not to question him, not even to question Huck, but to question Rose Marie herself, to root out for once and for all whatever version of the truth about him she imagines Rose Marie alone possesses. And maybe Rose Marie does in fact have the answers. But guess what? *Chavela wasn't going to get the chance to find out.* Nor was he. Nor was anyone. Fate had spoken. That chapter was over. Good for them all.

"All right," Huck says.

"I just mean woman to woman. Sometimes people are more willing to share with people they don't know well, you know what I mean?"

"Thank you," Huck says with moist eyes.

Chavela returns a similar gaze. "You're welcome."

Jerry steps out from behind the coatrack.

"Huck!" he calls out with aggressive cheer. "¿Qué tál?"

Huck startles. "Jerry."

Chavela eyes him coolly. "Oh. There you are."

Jerry steps between his neighbor and his wife. "Well, well, neighbor. This is quite the party. Quite the collection of guests."

Huck shuffles in place. "Sure is."

Jerry holds Huck's gaze until he looks away. Then he slides toward Chavela, ever so subtly, until his arm presses against hers. She stiffens.

"If we don't stick with our own around here," he adds breezily, "we're liable to get lost. Don't you think?"

He scrapes at the polished floor with one hoof.

III

You, Lourdes says in the doorway, her voice tinged with horror, should not be in here.

Inez stretches and sprawls at the edge of the bed, which has been made, though with no great care.

Shouldn't I?

Lourdes presses her lips together. It has been the better part of a year since the door to this room was left unlocked.

You don't belong here, she says.

Well, neither do you. Come on—it's only for a few minutes. There's no place for me to wait downstairs, and I've still got to sober up. Remember?

Inez giggles.

Lourdes glares. She closes the door behind her, then moves to straighten the photos of the children on the dresser. She swipes the dust from the bedside table with her bare hand and tucks a loose cord into the box of dismantled electronic equipment on the floor.

For God's sake, woman, Inez interjects. Take a break. They're working you like a dog.

Lourdes shoves a lump protruding from the bed skirt with her foot.

I can sit in the kitchen if I want to.

Oh yes, that's a good place for the help. Do they have a separate entrance for you?

Shut up.

Inez cackles and pats the mattress beside her.

Come. Sit.

It's el señor's *bed*!

I don't see anywhere else to sit, do you?

Outside, the world has gone strangely silent. The force of the blood pumping through Lourdes's body recedes too. It's what happens when you stop moving, lose focus, and if you make this mistake, damn it all, the weight of your whole day, of the months behind you, will collapse on you like the ceiling of a cave.

Her shoulders sag as she lowers herself.

You're tired, Inez says matter-of-factly.

Lourdes gazes out the window, toward some point in the distance she cannot see.

I would vouch for you, Inez rasps. If they found you here, I would take the blame.

Lourdes turns to her. The gaze that meets her is a deep one, the lined, weathered face as dark and straightforward and utterly without makeup as her own. Is that why she feels like she's looking at herself? Her future self. Her mirror self—the one that isn't her but shows her what she is.

She turns away.

What do you want from me? she says, and maybe she's talking to Inez and maybe she's not. Why are you here?

Inez remains silent for a moment.

The second one is an existential question, she says as she rolls onto her back.

Lourdes frowns.

What kind of question?

Inez laughs fully now. Just like that. Just like the sky clearing outside, the sun beaming through the clouds, as though it never had been dark.

Oh, why are any of us here? Inez continues. Living the lives we're each living? There's no answer. Only choices. The choices we make and the choices made for us. Then back to our own choices. An endless loop.

She stretches, as though she'd just awakened, in this room, this bed.

I want the secrets, she continues. All the secrets you've got. What's the gossip around here?

Lourdes's head swims. It's like someone has spun her in circles.

I don't know any gossip.

Oh, there has to be gossip, Inez says, rolling to face her again. There always is. And you know who I want to hear about.

She smiles, but her eyes burn bright with need.

Lourdes rubs her palms on her knees. What does she owe Inez? Six months ago seems like a decade ago now. She could turn away from her. Refuse her altogether. It would be her right.

Except that, inside this moment in which she feels like the thinnest hollow eggshell, she chooses kindness.

No one has heard from la señora, she begins quietly.

So I gather. But have they heard *about* her?

Only a little. She was in Mexico. Then California. Now . . . nobody's sure.

How do you know?

Because they talk to each other. They think I can't understand them.

Inez snorts softly. What's going on here in the house?

Business as usual. I mean, as usual as it can be, ever since la señora left. Lourdes lifts her face. But you know what? The kids actually seem to be doing well without her. Even el señor is starting to act more normal.

The light goes back out of Inez's eyes.

Of course, Lourdes adds quickly, it's not just the family who has missed her.

Mm?

I think, Lourdes says, trying to sound conspiratorial, not quite believing she's daring to say it, I think also señor Gonzales was sorry to see her go.

Inez raises back up on her elbow. My brother?

Well, Lourdes says, facing her now. On the day señora DuPre disappeared, when he asked me what was going on over here—I didn't want to know, mind you, if she left el señor for some other boyfriend, it was none of my business—but when I told him, it surprised him so much, he dropped his water glass.

The look in Inez's eye grows uncertain.

What do you mean?

Everything outside is dripping. The world glitters.

Obviously, he had a crush on her. Maybe more.

Inez pushes herself up, slowly, back into a sitting position.

My brother? she croaks.

The air in the room feels suddenly strange. Too thick.

My *brother*? Inez repeats. Do you have any idea what you're saying?

Lourdes blinks. Then she gasps. *Oh!*

Inez's face flames over.

And you never thought to mention this before?

Lourdes sits up, scooting away. Inez rises and leans into her face.

It must have been extremely enjoyable, keeping this secret for your own, Inez says, the whiskey thick on her breath. Have you been on their side all this time? I've spent the last year of my life circling my brother's world, feeding off his scraps, when all along I've been played for a fool. And worse.

I didn't mean—

I was wrong, Inez hisses. Wrong about you. I thought you were the one person in my brother's house above reproach. The only one with any moral character at all. But, she says, her eyes raking Lourdes's face, a horrible smile lifting her lips, you're a hypocrite. Just like the rest of them. The rest of *us*. You had a baby, a baby out of wedlock, you were little more than a child, and what kind of a girl did that make you? Did your father call you a *whore*?

I'm not, Lourdes hears herself say in a tiny voice.

Oh really? What makes you think *that*? Did you *love* him?

Lourdes doesn't answer. She only closes her eyes.

Pathetic, Inez says. That pointless desire to reach across the chasm that separates us all.

Lourdes breathes. There once was a boy, his skin was the color of milky tea, his eyes yellow-green, like a cat's. But now her blood lights up in her veins.

It's time to go, she tells Inez now.

Inez snorts.

And where are we going, little maid?

Lourdes moves to the door and pulls it open.

Take a look, she says into the hallway.

She can feel Inez's narrowing eyes. But she pours herself off the bed. As Lourdes knew she would.

What? Inez demands as her eyes sweep the hallway.

Gingerly, almost apologetically, Lourdes grasps her shoulders—she's so light, it's like lifting a stool—and shoves her to the other side of the doorjamb.

Inez spins to face her. Lourdes meets her wild eyes.

It doesn't matter if I ever loved anyone, Lourdes blurts. Only that I kept living anyway.

She slams shut the door.

First, an eternity of silence, her body trembling as her back presses hard. Then from the other side, the scrape of a voice: Do you think I need *you*? For *anything*?

A short, sharp exhalation follows, and then Inez's unsteady footfalls recede down the stairs.

Lourdes cracks open the door. A clear blob of spit oozes down its center.

She allows herself to rest against the doorframe for only a moment. Then she pulls a tissue from her bra and wipes off the door. She tidies the stack of magazines under the bedside table. She snaps smooth the blankets on the bed, until the shapes their bodies made are gone.

III

"Dad!" calls a voice from across the room.

Jerry lifts his head. For he is the one who is being paged. He is hard-wired to respond to this name, to this voice and any urgency it conveys, even after all these years. He knows what belongs to him.

And sure enough, there, at the entrance is Number One Son, in uniform, waving urgently. Behind him is his brother Tavo.

"What the devil?" he asks aloud, and both Chavela's and Huck's heads whip toward the object of his gaze.

"Dad." Marcus wades toward him through the crowd.

His son stops. His eyes dart past Jerry's shoulder. He tips his chin. The smile on his face is mannequin stiff.

There, at the end of his son's gaze, at the room's other entrance: a small, scruffy, dark figure, leaning, breathing heavily, watching.

Inez.

In the eternity of seconds that follow, Jerry needs to know only this: how he's going to get his sister out of a room in which there is no other possible escape route, how to conceal her, contain her, he can already see the mushroom cloud in her eyes, and now there is only this moment, which is in so very many ways like the moments so long ago in the dark, when he crouched in his own uniform, waiting, on the verge, with no time, no time, no time.

"Hermana!" he calls out with cheer, and he swoops across the room to drape an arm around her shoulders.

The bewildered look she gives him is perhaps the most priceless gift he has ever received. He scoops her back across the room.

"Hermano." She stiffens in his grip. "Get your hands off me."

"I'm very glad to see you too!" he responds, more loudly than necessary. "Allow me to introduce you to my neighbor and the host of this party, Huck DuPre."

He deposits her before the neighbor in question.

"Huck, this is my sister, Inez. And over here"—he signals for Marcus and Tavo to join him—"we have my elder son, Marcus, and Tavo, my brother."

No one moves. Inez glowers. Jerry widens his eyes as he grins, with a certain aggression, at Marcus and Tavo. The two of them, with a glance at each other, edge forward.

Huck studies each of them, his face a rippling sheet of bafflement. "Nice to . . . meet y'all."

"Well, yes," Jerry begins, "you see, it was really very nice of Jordan to extend her invitation to everyone in my household, and—"

Tavo makes a loud exhalation, as though clearing his nasal passages, and thrusts a hand at Huck. "How's it going?"

His demeanor, as Huck accepts the hand and tugs it firmly, is one of great and sudden amusement.

Jerry digs into his shoe heels. "And since I had forgotten we had all been planning to get together today—"

"Sorry for just showing up," Marcus interjects. "My folks weren't answering their phones." He bumps into the fringed lamp on the end table beside him, which he fumbles to catch.

"I'm with *him*," Tavo adds helpfully. He takes the lamp from Marcus's hands and restores it to its original spot.

"Pues, Inez," Chavela says with excruciating politeness. "How nice to see you again." Her eyes are liquid nitrogen.

Inez kisses the air between them.

Jerry, vibrating in the wordless moment that follows, no longer has any idea what the hell he thought he was doing.

But here a strange sound escapes Huck. Laughter.

"So," he says as he looks down at Inez. "How'd *you* manage to crash my party?"

She lifts her chin. Her eyes dart toward the stairs, the second floor. But she straightens and turns back to her host.

"Well, cowboy," she says with an insouciant roll of her shoulders, "I just followed the music to the hoedown."

Huck cracks up again.

"And I suppose you're here to ride the bulls?" He wipes the corners of his eyes. "You'll have to take up the music problem with my kids."

"I think a musical blockade might be in order. Are these the birthday girl's choices?"

"I doubt it. Maybe we can put the other two in some kind of reeducation program."

Inez responds with a throaty guffaw, though she shoots a final dagger look at Jerry before she turns her back to him.

"So, what's a girl have to do to get a drink around here?"

Again, Huck laughs. "Not much." He steps into the hallway, where someone has pushed an ice chest up against the wall, and retrieves two beers from its interior.

At waist level, Jerry's hands make a sudden flurry of warning. He tries to catch Huck's eye. It goes unnoticed. Huck and Inez face each other directly now, clinking bottles. The two of them have edged away from the rest of the group.

Jerry turns back to the rest of his family.

"What the hell is going on here?"

Tavo returns from the hallway, opening a beer with a car key. "We were trying to save your ass, but as I suspected, it's unsavable."

Jerry faces his son.

"What happened to *you*? You look like the rodeo clown who got dragged by the bronco."

Marcus opens his mouth but manages only to shake his head. And anyway, Chavela is already upon him, frowning and dabbing with a tissue at his neck at the claw marks throbbing just above his collar.

"Life." Tavo belches wistfully into his fist. "Everything always ends the way it began, only weirder."

Jerry looks to his wife. "Have we had enough yet?"

Chavela clucks her tongue at Marcus's neck and tucks the tissue back up her sleeve. Across the room, Inez and Huck are slapping their thighs at each other, tipping their beers.

"We should have set these two up months ago," she says.

III

"Attention!" Jordan bellows into the kitchen. "Attention, all partygoers!"

A few eyes light in her direction, then—bright with distraction—turn away. She backs into the hallway.

"Attention!"

She captures a few smiles, a nod.

"Hey, sweetheart," says someone who touches her head as she passes.

She ducks and lowers her megaphone, which she has constructed from duct tape, the plastic-cone collar Ripley once wore home from the vet, and a metal kitchen funnel, and heads into the den. The remote for the stereo breaches from a bowl of popcorn.

"May I have your attention, please?" she bellows, once she's cut the music.

She is met with several lusty cries of protest, which lift her spirits further. She steps, shoeless, onto an ottoman.

"The music will resume in approximately ten minutes," she announces. "We are now entering part three of the party: the surprise."

A few chortles rise from the crowd.

"What surprise is that, hon?" calls a woman's voice.

Jordan feels herself expanding. She has arrived at her pièce de résistance, the heart of the heart of the party, the moment into which she will arrive, as though plunging into a body of water from a great height, fully ten years old at last.

"The surprise that makes it a surprise party. Like if *you* had planned this party, instead of me. In a moment, I'm going to go outside and you're all going to hide and get very, very quiet, and when I come back in, guess what you're going to yell?"

"She wants to do *what?*" says a voice that sounds like Brittany Gallegos's before it's shushed.

"Jo-Jo." Skyler suddenly appears beside her, looking flushed and embarrassed. "Please. Don't even."

"Oh, I wouldn't worry about it too much," says their father, lumbering up out of nowhere. "It's her birthday. Make her happy." He dips into the ice chest and shuffles away.

Jordan rises onto her elated toes.

"Underneath the living room furniture, you'll find small ziplock bags of confetti," she continues through the megaphone. "Please share with your neighbors. The surprise will be followed by cake and ice cream."

"And more beer?" a male voice calls out.

"Sure!"

The cheers erupt from all corners.

She dismounts. She waves goodbye from the door like a starlet boarding a plane. Outside, everything is dripping, gleaming. The windshield of the car next to the driveway has been cracked in two places. She treads across the crushed grass to the side of the house, to the thickest of the juniper hedges, and crouches behind them in the dirt. The house is all muffled shuffling and shifting. Then, quieting.

She waits a full minute in silence, leaning forward to nibble a juniper frond, savoring its sharp, ginny flavor. Then she steps out.

"SURPRISE!"

The cheer reverberates in the belly of the house. She spits out the frond nub in outrage. That was too soon! Too *soon.*

She stomps up the walk, even though the whole world has grown abruptly silent again. Stops short in the doorway before the damp, confetti-dappled figure who waits on the other side, still as salt; who turns as the eyes in the room all turn to fall on Jordan; whose eyes meet, with remoteness and wildness all at once, Jordan's own.

They are two deer, meeting in the forest. Jackrabbits scampering across the dark desert floor.

"Did you come for my birthday?" Jordan asks.

And her mother, as though she possesses no human language at all, inclines her head in a way that surely means *yes.*

23

HEART OF HEARTS

"WELL, LOOK WHAT THE STINKIN' cat dragged in."

The voice cracks open the room. Then comes a slender girl's form, her head a halo of ratty blond coils. The narrow, barely hooked nose, the eyes of blue flame. They rake over her now, head to foot.

Behind this girl, a boy. Hair raven black, blond at the part. Eyes secret as the bottom of a well.

"Shh," he says to his sister, sharply. They lock eyes, speaking to each other inside their silence. As they always have done.

The shuffle of feet, the coughing, murmuring, the skittish laughter that comes in anticipation of a punch line. A sudden blast of music fills the room, midsong, and is restored to a polite volume. Only her youngest child faces her openly.

With the smoothest pivot she can manage in her rubber gardening boots, Rose Marie turns to the crowd.

"Afternoon, y'all!"

But Skyler is already pulling her away by the arm.

Up, up the stairs they go. To the landing. Skyler whirls.

"I should tell you to get the hell out."

Quinn pours himself into the space behind his sister and hunkers.

"Where," Skyler says, "have you *been*?"

Rose Marie counts the beats of her pulse. "Mexico."

"Mexico!" Skyler folds her arms. "Vacationing with your boyfriend?"

"No."

"Oh, let me guess—you're over him now and think you can just waltz right back home."

The house is warm and smells of the kitchen. Fried food. Something sweet.

Here comes Jordan, shambling up the stairs, rounding the banister, beelining. She stops just short and stares.

Rose Marie breathes. "I was supposed to be gone for two weeks."

"It's been a *year*," Skyler spits. "And you never so much as sent us an email."

Rose Marie smiles a weird smile. "The car broke down."

"Mrs. Du Pre!" A body wafts onto the landing. "Hey, you're back! It's totally great to see you. You wanna come downstairs and hang out?"

Skyler clenches. Quinn rolls his eyes.

"Baby," says Carlos. "I just thought—"

"We'll talk later," Rose Marie tells her two elder children. "I need to find your father."

To Jordan she says nothing. Jordan has a frizzy cowlick behind her left ear. Jordan ducks predictably when Rose Marie reaches out to smooth it down.

But Jordan's footfalls make a firm squeak on the stairs behind Rose Marie as she descends.

III

The queasiness unfolding in Jerry's gut conjures the image of a fat, oily snake awakening from a long nap. He belches convulsively.

Tavo, studying the scene across the room on his toes for the better view it affords him, pauses to give him a once-over. "What's *your* problem?"

"Tacos," Jerry grunts. He's sweating. His ears feel like they've been stuck with hot needles.

"The ones from Chico's? What are you now, a lightweight?"

Jerry's hands meet his knees. "The fish tacos. I think there was something wrong with them."

Tavo marvels at him a moment. Jerry looks up, with hostility. But Tavo only returns a very odd smile. He bumps Marcus's elbow. "Was there something the matter with the tacos?" he asks innocently.

Marcus twitches against the wall with his eyes half-closed. "What?"

Tavo looks to Chavela, as though he didn't mean to, but couldn't help it.

Chavela seems not to register him. Through the haze of his nausea, Jerry notes her erect posture, her seeming impulse to cover the distance to the woman who has squeaked in her boots back down the stairs. The expression on Chavela's face contains so many emotions, none of them can be named.

And then she turns to him.

"I need air," he says, and he staggers toward the back door.

Marcus watches as his father lurches from the room and wonders whether there is anyone in his family who isn't starring in some kind of private drama. He considers Adam, far from harm in his college dorm, a little refrigerator at his bedside, posters tacked to the wall. He was insulated. It was worth resenting.

He has reached the point of exhaustion where the floor ripples and swells.

His mother, as if hearing his thoughts, startles and turns to him.

"¿Qué te pasa?" She applies a warm hand to his forehead.

He knows where he is. He's at the eye of the most focused vortex of concern he is ever likely to know in his life, the one that he long ago learned to sidestep or laugh past or shrug through. He meets his mother's insistent gaze. He's staring down the alpha and omega. Deny it if you will, he tells himself. In the end, your mother is always waiting for you. The last day and night of his life have merged into a unit of time that has no name. He could tell her everything.

"Don't," he says before he can stop himself. He shakes the hand off. "I'm fine."

Whereupon Chavela, watching her son slouch off in the direction of the bathroom, swallows the lump rising in her throat and turns away from her brother-in-law, so that he won't see the things that might show on her face.

And *that*, Tavo tells himself as he pretends not to notice Chavela's expression, is something he's not gonna touch with a ten-foot pole. Though it's a shame she feels so bad. His brother is the one who should feel like an asshole, though honestly, he feels bad for him too. He rises onto his toes again and secures a fresh view of the new guest of honor.

Personally, he'd like to stroll right up there and slap her on the back and say, *Welcome home, Rosie!* No hard feelings toward anyone concerned. Personally, he feels just fine.

III

Skyler looks down over the second-floor railing, feeling light headed and shaky. Her mother, having clomped down the stairs in her huge rubber boots, takes two purposeful steps into the living room and then stops.

Skyler lets out her breath. She could go to her room and lock the door, but who would be held accountable then? The fresh blood rushing into her skull feels almost restorative as she pounds down the stairs.

Jordan intercepts her on the last step.

"It's time for cake and ice cream," she announces.

Skyler grits her teeth. Although it goes against her general principle of feeling sorry for her sister in any way, she can't help noticing that Jordan looks uncharacteristically pale and hunched and wide eyed, like a cat in a carrier who is not going to come out at the vet.

Meanwhile, here's this vacant woman turning to them now with her faraway eyes, who has traded in her linen pantsuits for overalls and a bandanna over her head and no makeup, and it occurs to Skyler that there might be something truly *wrong* with her mother, something that's gone past its expiration date.

This only increases the volume of her rage.

"You're right." She pins her gaze on Jordan. "You spent weeks planning this party. People were having a good time. You made this ridiculous cake, and now it's time to eat it."

She faces the room. "Excuse me, everyone."

Her voice is louder than she realized. The heads turn. She tries not to blush.

"We're going to have cake and ice cream now in the dining room. After we sing 'Happy Birthday.'"

People swallow the last of their beverages. They edge away from each other with polite expressions and conclusive pats on the arm.

"Come on, everybody," she continues. "It's Jordan's birthday. She worked hard for this. Let's not worry about anything else right now, okay?"

A lonesome voice rises from the back of the crowd. "Is there any beer left?"

"In the bathtub," she reports.

A weak but sincere group cheer comes from the contingent at the back.

"Turn up the music!" she hollers. Someone obliges. The crowd slides toward the dining room. She clasps her sister's shoulder. "Come on, Jo-Jo. Let's go."

But Jordan only looks up at their mother. Not blinking.

Their mother, apparently back in her body, looks down at Jordan as though they are the only two in the room. "Go on, sugar," she says. "I'll watch."

Not Quinn, though. Skyler looks away from this lovefest just in time to catch him with his hand curled around the front door. The look he gives her needs no translation as he backs out into the bright light behind him.

Fuck this, he thinks as he shades his eyes. He's already heading into the hills.

III

Using the key to his garage, Huck cracks open a pair of fresh beers and hands one to Inez.

"What the doctor ordered," she says, and clinks her bottle against his. "Unless you've got whiskey."

"It's in the den."

In the outer world, following a few moments of speechifying by Skyler, a new cheer erupts. Inez waves a dismissive hand. He exhales his relief. Of course, they'd missed the big moment, the surprise, he felt bad about that, but there's still plenty of party ahead. For now, he's likely been forgotten in the shuffle. Which is fine by him.

"I like this," Inez says now, as she glides from one wall of his hole to another. She appraises the round jute rug he added last month, the beanbag chair, the camping mattress and battery-powered lantern, the wicker basket containing reading materials, the thrift store bedspreads and tapestries nailed to the upper beams in order to define and brighten his walls. A vagrant's idea of luxury. Which, from the look of his guest— seriously, what cat had been dragging this woman in and out of his neighborhood?—might be the reason she's taken a shine to it.

He chuckles. "My home away from home."

"Oh, it's a man cave, to be sure," she continues. "But I what I like . . ." She reaches for one of the tapestries, pushing against the orange-and-yellow hippie mandala thing at its center to the wooden beam behind, which she grasps with both clawlike hands. "I like the idea of being at the heart of the heart of the house. I like that I can touch its bones."

"So do I," he says, wonderingly.

Of course, it was still unclear to him how he had led this woman here to begin with, though it might have to do with the beer sloshing around in his system. Add to that the satisfaction of getting his way in the end, despite Skyler's tyranny. Either way, he has to admit now, it feels strangely natural. He's got a guest. He isn't hiding—he's inviting. He's created a space on his own terms into which, just possibly, some small, willing, sympathetic sliver of the world might join him.

Inez releases the beam. "So have you attained enlightenment in this den, or have you just been smoking opium?"

He laughs. "Mostly listening to baseball games on AM radio and watching the dust float by."

"You should take up mad science. You could build a bomb in here. Or bring the dead back to life."

"Maybe I can get Jordan to work on that with me."

Inez joins his laughter with a cackle of her own. What's so funny? He has no idea. But they're both hiccupping, dabbing the corners of their eyes, erupting again, and then comes a shifting of sound in the outer world.

Voices move closer. Footfalls. Huck cocks his ear toward the wall. The crowd is packing into the dining room. Shuffling, clinking. He hears someone say "cake."

"Uh-oh," he says.

The strains of "Happy Birthday" fill the air.

"Goddammit," he says, and he lurches for the sheet-covered entrance. "I have to get out there."

But does he stride right out of his hole and into the crowd as though it was nobody's business, nothing strange about it? No. First, he peeks. And what he sees, as he cranes to see around the people standing four-deep near his wall, past the dining room table, over the bent marigold head of his daughter, who looms over a monstrous cake, glowing in the light of ten flames, is a stranger. A strange woman. Lingering near the doorway at the very fringe of the crowd, like a bird both hoping for and insisting on crumbs.

It surprises him, how slowly he straightens. How everything slows.

"What's the matter, cowboy?"

"I believe," he hears himself say in a very faraway voice, "that my wife has returned."

The response is one of long silence. Then a stumbling.

"Where?" Inez growls.

III

Where? Rose Marie asks herself as Jordan blows out the flames. The crowd cheers. Where is Huck, where should she stand for the cake cutting, where has she put her keys, where do you go when you finally reach the end of the line?

She might ask someone that. It would be an icebreaker, a joke. But first someone in the room would have to look at her instead of smiling pleasantly and pretending they can't see her.

She steps back and looks over her shoulder. Her housekeeper is watching her with a single eye from behind the archway to the kitchen.

Rose Marie lifts a slow hand and waves.

Lourdes waves in return.

Rose Marie crosses the distance. "Hey there, Lourdes."

"Señora. ¿Como está?"

A strange chuckle escapes Rose Marie's throat. "Can you believe it?" She looks to Jordan, settling in now before her cake. "Ten years old."

Lourdes seems to hold her breath. "You want . . ." She looks at her feet. Exhales. "Venga conmigo, señora. Come in."

When Rose Marie can't move, Lourdes takes her lightly by the arm.

"Siéntese," Lourdes says, indicating the kitchen table. She rummages through the refrigerator and emerges with two Dr Peppers.

Rose Marie eases into the chair. "You're a good host."

Lourdes seats herself. "No es mi casa."

"But you're here." Rose Marie cracks open her can. "You're *still* here."

Lourdes sips. "Este weather. Muy ugly."

"It's insane. Never seen anything like it."

"You travel?"

"I was in Mexico."

Lourdes lifts her brow. "México."

Rose Marie takes a long swig, then studies her chapped hands with their broken nails. It's how she's going to keep the tremor out of them. "I was looking for someone."

Lourdes snaps off her soda tab. "You find?"

Rose Marie summons her most pleasant smile. "No."

"Por eso you come back."

"That's part of it."

"Maybe," Lourdes says quietly, "esta persona find *you*."

"I don't think so."

"You family miss you. *All* you family."

"Did they?" Rose Marie sips from her soda.

"Señora," Lourdes says, and her voice planes a sharper edge. "Mira. Why you leave? Hay más, ¿no?"

Rose Marie sets down her soda. Good God. Should she provide the summary of causes? Everything that it all boiled down to in the end? Other than medium-grade marital discontent; parental emotional exhaustion; the curse of effortless affluence; the increasing sense of uselessness in the face of the slow leak of everything that might have once been her potential; rage as a form of depression; stupid and impulsive acts as a cure for depression; the sum total of her life and whether or not she had ever been, in any meaningful way, happy?

There was a note. It had come for her in the mail—that much is true. But it was more than just a note. It was a whole stinking lifetime.

"There's always more," Rose Marie tells Lourdes now, and she's surprised by the softness of her tone. "Isn't there?"

Lourdes folds her hands, one over the other. She doesn't look at Rose Marie directly—it's a bit maddening—but in her eyes is something fierce. She nods, once.

They sit in silence, sipping, while the crowd natters in the next room and the music pipes back into to the sound system.

"El pastel," Lourdes says finally. "You go. Eat cake."

Rose Marie lets out her breath. "Right." She tilts back the last of her soda and collects Lourdes's empty and drops everything in the recycling. "Lourdes?" She turns back. "Gracias."

Lourdes meets her gaze urgently. "Mira, señora—"

A fist raps at the window over her head.

A pair of dark, quick eyes widens next through the pane, though whether this is due to surprise, or horror, or the old-school, Coke-bottle glasses that magnify them now to an unnatural size is hard to say.

"Oh, Jesus Christ," Rose Marie says now.

Miguel, in seeming agreement, ducks his head and disappears.

III

"Now she's gone," Huck says, and he stoops, quickly, to exit.

He finds himself crushed against the broken drywall. Inez has wedged herself through at the same time.

He offers an incredulous look to the top of her head. "You mind if I get out there first?"

"I wouldn't if it was over my dead body."

He shoves forward, his knee pressing into her hard, pointy elbow. "What's *your* hurry?"

"It seems we've all been waiting for this a long time."

"Look," he says, the heat rising in his voice, "no offense, but maybe this isn't your business."

She twists just enough to retract. He steps into the gap.

She lurches again. This time when they stick, she manages to wedge both elbows and knees through before his. She tears the sheet down.

III

There's always more, Rose Marie tells herself as she slips from her own house.

Such as the morning before she left, when she spilled coffee down the front of her blouse. Cursed in the empty house as the lawn mower roared in the yard. Removed her entire outfit, lying on the bed in her slip even though the United Way luncheon was in half an hour. Not moving until the knock.

It's funny, it occurs to her now, how stepping backward makes your disappearance less conspicuous. She backs across the patio, wondering whether she might be mistaken in thinking she could meaningfully address her mistakes. Whether she could have made herself feel any differently the night before the spilled coffee, when she'd donned the champagne-colored negligee that Huck ignored and asked how he would feel if she were to take a vacation alone, as if she were going to get the kind of answer she needed instead of a suggestion that she take up a hobby instead of a vacation, *but whatever go ahead honey, zzzz.*

She'd whisked open the door without putting on so much as a bathrobe.

"Whoa!" Miguel turned away, a garden-gloved hand raised before his face. "Sorry! I'll come back later!"

"No," she said. It sounded cheerful but also enough like a command that she actually stopped him in his tracks. "Come in, Miguel. We owe you for the month, don't we?"

She wrote the check at the kitchen table as he shuffled near the breakfast bar. She concentrated on her handwriting, on making perfect ones and zeroes. Maybe she could take up penmanship as her new hobby. She lifted her eyes and held out the check to him without getting up. He kept his gaze averted. The only way to get him to look at her was to grasp his now ungloved hand.

It was callused and warm and rigid in her own. She peered up at him calmly, taking in his stunned expression, the way his black hair fell over one eyebrow. His frame was small, wiry, his skin a warm shade of caramel. He was older than her children, thank God, but still very young.

"I never realized," she murmured. "You have antelope eyes."

The eyes grew wider, traveling to her neck. Below. She knew what she was—a well-preserved woman cresting the far side of her forties, still chesty, gloriously blond. He didn't move away. She rose from her chair. This particular scenario, she noted with amusement and despair, was a cliché. Like the letter that came in the mail, it echoed of something long ago.

She could feel Miguel's breath on her ear. His hand trembled and brushed her collarbone. *What a cliché.* Her hand was steady as she reached for the brim of his cap.

Now, as she backs around the corner of what was once her house, in the break in the hedges where the garbage cans sit, through the back gate, she turns and nearly collides with a man slumped against the wall.

Her heart. It slams against her chest.

"My goodness," she chirps. "*Everyone's* here."

Jerry, for his part, with his hands on his knees, turns his face up to the woman before him with what he recognizes within himself as pure terror.

"From what I gather," he says, after a long moment, "the guest list is Jordan's doing."

Rose Marie nods.

"And how are you?" she adds with excruciating politeness.

He attempts to straighten but the nausea rises up in him again. "That is a difficult question to answer."

Silence. An eon of it. And inside of this eon, he tries not to look at her but fails at this also. Outwardly, Rose Marie's face is as cool as a receptionist's, but he can see the heaving of her breath beneath her overalls. Her bandanna has slipped sideways, giving her a pirate-ish look. He is uncertain whether he has ever seen her without makeup before, ever glimpsed her near a window of her house on a morning in which some sort of bedhead similar to the unraveling straw-like plait before him would have been evident.

And she is still indisputably beautiful. Perhaps more so now that she carries so little pretense.

Faced now with the woman who has consumed his thoughts over the past year, he cannot summon a single suitable topic of conversation.

"Did you send that letter?" she blurts.

He blinks. "Did I *what?*"

"Because I've thought and thought about it, and it seems to me that the only person who could have written it was *you.*"

"*What* letter?"

She trembles. From some secret pocket inside the bib of her overalls, she produces a creased envelope, still warm from the heat of her body as it reaches his hand.

> I knew you once, long ago. Not for long. But long
> enough to wonder who you might be, who you
> really are, in your heart of hearts. We think time will
> swallow up the secrets. But it doesn't. Secrets grow.
> Just like children grow. You'll hear from me again.

He pushes the paper back at her. "You'll hear from *who*, again? What is this? I wouldn't know anything about it."

"You sure about that?"

"Rose Marie, why would you think *I* wrote this letter?"

A whole rainbow of expressions disrupts the composure of her face, until finally she settles on something sour.

"Well, who else would have known what happened that night? Who else would *talk* like this?"

"Right," he says at last. "Well, you see—" He exhales. "Cabrón." He presses a hand to his face. "Could you refresh my memory?"

The silence she offers him is a brittle one.

"I'd had a lot to drink," he adds.

"You and me both, compadre."

He raises an eyebrow but levels it. "Tell me."

Rose Marie studies the man pressed against her house. She could almost laugh. At herself. Because there is more, and then there is *more*.

"Well for God's sake. Do you even remember the block party?"

"Of course."

"It was . . . a strange night."

Except that wasn't right. It was an ordinary night. An ordinary week. Her ordinary life. The only exceptional fact was that her children were gone—packed up and shipped off for the week to her in-laws' house in Sherman. *Hillbilly summer camp*, she and Huck had joked as the kids turned to wave through the back window of Harold Sr.'s extended cab. It was the first time she'd sent them off anywhere on their own, the first moment in their lives—or so it had seemed to her—that the twins were able to look at her and shrug without feeling the need to consume her entirely. They were eight years old.

She spent the first hours of her solitude pacing the house, unable to relax, gnawed over with an anxiety that was as much about not knowing how to stop moving as it was about how the twins were faring. And then it occurred to her that the house was *empty*. Cause for rejoicing! The moment had arrived for reconnecting, making plans, quality time, goddammit! She turned to her husband.

But Huck only shook his head at her. Waved her away with *Maybe later*. He had things to do. Work he'd brought home. Televised sports. Home-improvement projects, undertaken alone, in dark spaces that were difficult for other humans to access. Okay, whatever. Whatever, whatever. It was no different than the way Huck had ever been, he was just more so post-parenthood. She had some damned things to get done herself. She organized the volunteer committee for the food bank's summer drive and purchased school supplies.

In the quiet of the afternoons, between phone calls and errands, she felt something inside her own body. A tremor. A ripple. The tiniest disturbance at the surface of something vast and dark.

Whatever. The party. Whose idea had it had been anyway, insofar as the neighbors had never been a particularly chummy bunch? Who cared. Two nights before the end of summer camp, music boom-boxed into the street and rattled the windowpanes.

Huck seemed not to notice. Generally speaking, he liked a good shindig, but he was deep into the newspaper this evening and he needed a shave. She wasn't sure she was in the mood herself. If she drew near him, he reached out to pat her hip, not looking. She circled, watching him, doing busy things.

"Are you just going to sit?" she finally spat. "Sit through everything? Sit away your whole life?"

"Will it actually make you happy?" he growled back. "If I get up?"

She allowed him to lead the way into the crowd.

Apparently, people had invited friends. And also friends of friends. She could focus on no particular face. She swayed slightly beside Huck in the street, feeling prickly and lost, until someone put a vodka tonic in her hand. When she tossed it back, another one immediately appeared in its place. A corner of her lip lifted into a smile. The faces before her separated and became distinct. The asphalt radiated warmth at her feet and the porch lights came on and the sun set over them all like a yellow-and-pink apocalypse.

She plunged in. She shook hands with neighbors she'd never met before or had never even seen. She leaned against new walls, petted strange dogs. It was the kind of party that *fed* itself—the farther she penetrated it, the more it seemed to grow, unfolding like an origami paper chain, redolent of the keg-fueled ragers of her college days, and you know what? She was actually having fun. She had another vodka tonic. Somewhere she lost track of Huck, and she wandered in and out of houses, chatting with strangers about no-water days and school districts and local politics, eyeing the quality of their furniture and their family photos, until finally she backed out of the crowd to catch her breath and found herself in an empty backyard.

"Good evening," a surprised voice called out.

It was Jerry Gonzales, sitting on the edge of his flower planter in the moonlight, clutching a bottle of whiskey.

She jumped. Flushed. Apologized. Explained, truthfully, that she'd sort of forgotten where she was.

"Not to worry," he said. "I haven't the faintest idea where I am either. Care to join me?"

She looked over both shoulders, as though to check whether the invitation was meant for someone else. The mood was festive. She shrugged. "Why not?"

He rose to fetch some glasses, but she waved him off and reached for the bottle.

His face registered amusement. "Clearly, the fates have sent me a worthy companion."

She grinned and wiped her mouth with the back of her hand.

The moon was a half disk that lit the tops of their heads. And what had they spoken of? The moon itself, perhaps. Also, landscaping. The heat. Their children. How he'd grown up just a few blocks away—no one had to tell her which neighborhood he was talking about—and had lived his entire life right here in El Paso.

"Ten generations!" he told her. "My family has been here for ten generations!"

She leaned back on her hands. "That's almost beyond my comprehension."

"Indeed, it's quite the ancestral precedent."

"I'm adopted," she said before she could stop herself. "I know nothing about my origins." And when he raised an eyebrow in an interested way, she added, "Have you ever walked across that glass bridge at the Grand Canyon?" He shook his head. "Not knowing where you come from is like stepping out onto that bridge," she said. "Your feet tell you you're touching ground, same as anyone else, but then you look down and there's no bottom. To your life. And you try not to fall to your knees."

He lifted the other eyebrow and allowed for a very long pause.

"I have often found myself wishing," he said, "that my family of origin could be swallowed into a void of that sort."

Their eyes met for a moment. She saw the same vague embarrassment swimming around in his gaze that she herself felt. They both burst out laughing.

"¡Salúd!" he said, toasting her with the bottle before he swigged from it.

She reached for bottle and did the same. "¡Salúd!"

She regarded the moon and thought distantly of Huck until the thought of him sharpened.

"I should say hello to Chavela," she said, suddenly self-conscious.

"Ah," Jerry said, also with a start. "Impossible. She and the boys are visiting her sister in L.A." He cleared his throat and offered a cramped smile. "It's not yet clear when they will return."

She drew a tactful breath. "I see."

"But never fear," he continued with rising cheer. "My brother has offered me his companionship in their stead this evening. And as you can see, Tavo is currently discharging his sense of fraternal duty by crashing the party on his own."

A snort of laughter escaped her.

"Propriety has never been his strong suit," he continued. "I expect I'll see him sometime tomorrow."

"Parties that attract crashers are usually the best kind of parties."

"It's just as well, all things considered," he said, and some part of him seemed to slip back under shadow.

She felt herself slip too. Or rather, it was that her edges were blurring. "Because it isn't all right," she said. "Is it."

He raised an eyebrow at the bottle, as though surprised by its contents, before passing it once again. He said, "It seems you understand what it means to be alone."

They sat in sudden silence, the moon setting behind the hills. It was a moment before she realized her elbow was brushing his elbow, and that she was the one who'd moved closer. She reeled inside her own surprise. The man beside her wasn't exactly an Adonis. He was an ordinary man, mustached, middle aged—in fact, she'd guess he had ten years on her— and he was paunchy, with thinning, dark hair. Camaraderie explained nothing. What she felt when she turned to him was a painful and visceral tug. It was as though the whole of her being had been charged like a powerful magnet, and it could do nothing but insist on drawing in some missing part. To attract whatever might be similar to the immensity of her own loneliness. Jerry reached for her, his fingers threading her hair, and she leaned into him. With him. Into the void.

Her hangover the next day was epic. Huck's wasn't half-bad either. Somehow, they'd each found their way back to bed, groaning and chuckling at each other as they awoke. It wasn't until Huck dragged himself toward the bathroom that she noticed the stinging pinpricks trailing up her arms and scalp. She passed a hand through her hair and retrieved a thorn shaped like a cat's claw. With horror, she remembered. Not every last detail, but enough. A garden bed of rosebushes, for starters.

And Jerry, of course. Talking. Always talking.

In fact, he was still talking even once they had fallen back into the rose bed, still talking through the tangle of their hands and intractable clothing, still talking about she didn't know what, talking maybe only to himself as their bodies made a hollow in the cool dirt until he rolled back, rattling the rosebush behind him, and took a sudden, shocked breath. "Stop?" he'd asked her. "Go?" And she had kissed him hard to shut him up.

His face turns up to hers now.

"I can't believe—" he blurts. He lifts the palms of his hands, then drops them, looking away. "We never spoke of it."

"Well." She locates her boots in the flattened yellow grass. "I tried."

Although she'd hidden from him, at first. Of course. But days melted into weeks, and with the full understanding of what had transpired that night unfolding finally within her like a terrible flower, she forced herself one morning to open her front door. She needed information.

She caught up with him at his mailbox. He'd brightened—looking courteously uncomfortable, or uncomfortably courteous—at her approach.

She couldn't open her mouth.

He chuckled uneasily. "That was some party, wasn't it?"

She nodded and felt the blood drain from her face.

He looked over his shoulder.

"I'll be honest with you," he continued. "I had a lot to drink that night—not that it's my habit—and I have the distinct feeling I made a fool of myself."

She dropped her eyes. "I'm quite sure we all did."

"We . . . conversed for quite a while, no?"

"Oh yes."

"We had a few drinks ourselves."

"Mm-hmm."

He paced in place for a few beats.

"Is there . . . any particularly foolish thing I should apologize for?"

She looked up. What she saw was a man—sheepish, rueful—in whose psyche she had created no real weight. A man who, suspecting himself of wrongdoing, was asking for permission not to feel guilty. A man who was fast closing in on the moment when he would begin to tell himself whatever he needed to believe, in order to face whatever lay ahead.

The approach held a certain appeal. You just tell yourself a story until it becomes more real than the memory that is already dissolving behind you.

Then as now, she understood that it is possible to feel two opposing emotions at the same time. For starters, pain and relief.

She shook her head, shrugged breezily. There was no way she was going to ask anything more of him.

Nor was there any way she could live the rest of her life with a secret as big as the one she was now keeping. She would make the appointment that very afternoon.

She bid her pleasant goodbyes, walked around the block, returned home, and threw up in front of Huck, who snatched back her hair as she flung herself over the toilet and, with a rare canniness, asked, "Good Lord, Rose. Are you pregnant?"

That, as they say, was that.

In the end, of course, it was best no one knew. Rose Marie's own uncertain origins would prove useful as well, as she prepared to explain away any question of who this baby resembled. Yet, as it turned out, she had nothing to worry about. On the morning Jordan was born, the face Rose Marie beheld was her own. Jordan was destined to be her only redhead, redder than Rose Marie ever had been, even before her hair had faded with time to strawberry blond, before her colorist had brightened out what remained.

"Do you remember?" Her voice is hoarse now.

The stucco scrapes Jerry's skin through his shirt as he pushes himself to his feet, his pulse buzzing electrically beneath his skin. "What do you *want* me to remember?"

Rose Marie returns from her distant place to give him a withering look. Then she glances, pointedly, toward the birthday party.

"Do the math, Sherlock. What's ten years plus nine months?"

Something spins at the center of his head. A compass of sorts.

"You can't mean"—the compass swings in a cold, cold wind and then points north—"you're not saying . . ." The sound of applause emanates from the house.

"What am I not saying?" She turns her fierce eyes on him.

"My God." His own voice is a whisper now. "You can't be saying that I'm Jordan's—"

One of his hands sweeps up the air in front of his body. The other floats down over an imaginary head.

She snorts. "*No.*"

The compass needle in his head trembles and swings to one side. "Huck, then, after all," he says in a rush.

"Most likely not."

The compass needle spins. As though there was no true north to begin with. "Then *who?*"

"Who's what?" comes a voice from the end of the hedges. It's a familiar voice to Jerry, of course, gravelly, inappropriate in volume, oddly buoyant.

Stiffening, he turns to it.

"So this is where you've been hiding," Tavo continues, strolling up. "Inez just popped out of a hole in the wall and now she's busting into every room like a one-woman SWAT team, in case you care."

Jerry gives his brother an evil eye. "Could you kindly give us a minute?"

"Give who a minute? Aren't you going to introduce . . . oh! *Hey.*"

The eye is lost on Tavo. He's too busy taking in Rose Marie, a slow grin spreading across his face.

"How you doing, sweetheart?" he adds and widens his grin at his object. "Long time no see."

Jerry huffs, "Rose Marie, I beg your pardon. This, I'm afraid, is my legendary brother, Tavo. Who is leaving."

Rose Marie seems not to hear him. She's gone pale. Now red. She offers his brother a curt, thin-lipped nod.

For it is clear they already know each other.

"Hey, it's cool," Tavo adds, raising his hands in seeming surrender. "No worries, Rosie. I'll just leave you two to . . . whatever."

"Wait a minute." Jerry grabs his brother's arm before he can stroll off. "How do you . . . ?"

Tavo grins. Rose Marie, meeting Jerry's questioning gaze, pins him with another look that, for all its fierceness, conveys an unmistakable sense of *Duh.*

"Oh no," Jerry says, stepping back.

"What?" Tavo responds innocently.

"Do you mean to tell me that *you two* . . . ?"

"Well," Tavo says, slipping his hands into his pockets. "I guess the cat's finally outta the bag."

Jerry moves to his brother. He is clawing through flame, he is drowning in relief. "And you never thought to mention it to me?"

"Pues, mira, hombre, I was trying to keep you from kicking your own ass."

"How is this even possible?" He whirls to Rose Marie. "After what you've told me."

Tavo bursts out laughing. "Anything's possible when your brother's passed out in the flower bed." He tips his head in Rose Marie's direction. "Am I right?"

Rose Marie studies the roofline. She nods.

Because, of course, in the moment after Jerry had given her the choice of whether to go on, in the moment after she'd responded with her silencing kiss, came the moment in which Jerry, groping vaguely as he came up for air, added, "The thing is this." His voice dropped to a slurring mumble. "The thing is, you'll have to excuse me." He faced the sky. "Please excuse me. I'm terribly sorry. It's just that I am . . . so . . . very . . . tired."

His eyes closed then, a faint smile still on his lips even as they were parted by his first snore.

She sat up among the roses, stunned, trembling.

Then came the voice at her back.

"Whoa! What the hell happened to *him?*"

She whipped around, heart pounding.

The man who stood waiting regarded her with undisguised surprise. Or curiosity. Or possibly just amusement.

"Drunk as a skunk," she managed finally, tossing her head in Jerry's direction before he could ask anything more. She was grateful only that she had managed to re-clasp her bra.

He grinned.

"Name's Tavo." He extended a hand, then helped pull her to her feet.

He was like Jerry. Only smirkier and a little taller and more trim and possibly better looking.

"So *you're* the one who likes to have a good time." She swayed on her feet.

He snatched up the bottle that lay near Jerry's left foot. "Don't mind if I do."

And here things grew hazier. Or perhaps a better description was *more watery*. She heard a strange sound, emanating from she wasn't sure where.

"Whoa, whoa," said Tavo, as he caught her in her stumble. "Are you laughing or crying?"

Things were watery. She had already been headed downward. There was a strong undertow.

"Drinking!" she choked out. "And lemme tell you, I don't like drinking alone!" She swiveled toward the house. "Anybody home in there?"

He grinned. "Nobody at all."

Her laughter was a shriek as she pulled him toward the back door.

Now Tavo grins at his brother. "I guess it was just my lucky night." Quite frankly, he's got no regrets. You can't tell him that another dude in his place wouldn't do the same. Maybe Rose Marie wasn't his woman, but she wasn't his brother's either, and man but she was *insistent*. Like a coyote dragging off a carcass. Hadn't she told him—smoldering, almost, with satisfaction—that her parents would be horrified if they knew she'd been messing around with a Mexican? Hadn't she called him "sugar"?

"That's *brown* sugar to you, güerita," he told her, grinning all the while.

"Or something," Rose Marie mutters now. The morning after, when she sat on the edge of the tub and covered her face, cradling her pounding head, the only words she had for herself were *Oh my God*. She knew she was a sorority girl, but she didn't know she was *that* kind of sorority girl.

Jerry, for his part, hears himself emit a strangled chuckle. "So in the end, between you and me, nothing actually . . ." He sweeps the air between them with one hand, back and forth.

"Nope."

"Only Tavo."

"Yup."

Gratitude. It billows from the very core of his being. He turns to his brother.

"Pinche cabrón."

Tavo laughs. "Tranquilo, hermano. It's not like mentioning this now changes our lives or anything."

"Oh," Jerry blurts with a sudden wildness he cannot contain, "al contrario." He whirls back to Rose Marie. "Are you going to tell him?"

She returns her gaze to the roofline. "Feel free to take the first crack at it."

"Tell me what?"

"Let's just say, hermano," Jerry says, and he cannot say whether he means to convey this with kindness or with cruelty, "that you probably left something more than just your pride behind. This is a birthday party, no? Do some math."

Tavo opens his mouth for a retort, but a new cheer erupts from inside the house, and he turns in its direction. There he pauses. He lifts one leg from the ground, then the other. "A la chingada," he muses. Then he inhales audibly and turns to Rose Marie.

"You're not asking me for any money or anything, are you?"

Rose Marie runs her tongue over her teeth. Somewhere in the house, the birthday girl is eating the cake she baked herself. The genetic mysteries, she tells herself, are the deepest mysteries of all. "Definitely not."

"Well." Tavo shrugs. "It's not the worst thing I ever heard about myself."

She represses a snort. Because in the end, she supposes, he's right. Whatever the worst, there's always worse. Isn't there? Rose Marie turns away from the two before her, these brothers who—side by side— resemble the twinned theater masks of comedy and drama; she turns away. She turns.

At the corner of the house, a woman she has never seen before is watching her.

III

Who is this guy in the mirror?

The face Marcus sees looks older than the one he remembers, and it's ashen, puffy, blue around the eyes. He splashes it with cold water from the sink and wipes it away with his sleeve. The eyes reflecting back at him are unforgiving.

He tried. Tried, for the sake of every person he has encountered in this whole night turned into day. Tried and failed and then tried some more. Tried, as ever, to do the right thing—or maybe, more accurately, to fulfill his duty.

His vision blurs. The tap is still running.

He cranks it off. He's going home. He will sleep like a dead man, at a depth where nothing can reach him. It's the only place left to go.

He rounds the corner to the kitchen, to the back door, where he encounters his parents' maid.

She drops her dish towel when she sees him. In fact, he can see the gasp she's stifled, the way it bobs along her throat, top to bottom. He regards her numbly, wondering if she's waiting for him to pick up her towel. Then he realizes he's still wearing his goddamned uniform.

He doesn't belong here. That much, at least, is clear.

But neither does she.

"Lourdes," he says by way of greeting. His voice cracks, but he feels the hard line of his shoulders. "You work here too?"

Lourdes doesn't say a word. There's no need. The guilt is stamped right on her face.

III

"Inez," Jerry hisses. "Please. Not now."

"You're here," his sister croaks. She steps from the house's corner, from the shadows. "You're here."

"How long have you been standing there?" Jerry presses. "Were you eavesdropping? This is a private conversation, in case you were wondering."

"Shit, man," Tavo interrupts. "Let's give it a rest. Personally, I'm done with this pity party."

Inez seems to hear neither of them.

"I've waited so long." Her face is strangely radiant, beatific, shucked of rage and shadow. "Waited and then waited some more. All year long. All the years before that. I tried to give up but I couldn't."

Her gaze is trained fully upon the face of Rose Marie DuPre.

Jerry shakes his head, just one quick twitch, as though this would clear it of all disequilibrium. He slips between the two women.

"Inez, por Dios. If you have ever regarded us as your brothers, as your own flesh and blood, just leave us alone for a few minutes."

"You changed your hair," Inez murmurs, as peaceful as a nun.

Rose Marie hugs her elbows, studying Inez with one eye.

"Ma'am," she manages finally, "do I know you?"

Inez smiles.

"I knew *you*, once. Long, long ago. Long enough to wonder who you are. In your heart of hearts."

Rose Marie's breath catches visibly in her chest.

Jerry freezes. Then he lurches for his sister.

III

"You work for everyone around here, no? Trabaja por todos los vecinos."

Lourdes bends to retrieve her kitchen towel. She can't seem to remember what to do with it, how to fold it, where to put it away. She balls it up and shakes it out and turns to wipe the already clean countertop.

"¿Verdad?" the Gonzales boy presses.

He's actually a young man, of course, at least as old as Rosario's Mateo. A young man whom she has seen eating at the table in his parents' kitchen and pushing buttons on their TV remote. Not a stranger. Not this man in the green uniform with the walkie-talkie and the baton, and now his eyes are ringed with purple, his eyes pin her with a crazy look that burns bright. She doesn't know which person is addressing her.

She forces a faint nod and wipes the countertop.

"I just wonder," he continues, "what goes through my parents' heads. I do. I mean, I know everybody does it, but seriously. I have my job. My dad understands that better than anyone."

She wipes, sensing his shaking head. She sees nothing. She sees only what is not before her—the unfolded laundry in the corner of her own living room, the money in the coffee can by the kitchen, the nearly empty bottle of insulin on the milk crate next to her mother's side of the bed. She imagines her daughters tumbling into the empty house at the end of their day, puzzled looks on their faces.

"Because the thing is," continues the edgy voice at her back, "all I want . . . what I want . . ." The young man releases a jerky breath. "This isn't even what I'm supposed to do. I'm not INS. I can't bust you here. You probably don't even realize that. I could talk to someone and

make something happen, if I wanted to. But I can't take you anywhere."
Another breath. "I just want to see something in black and white."

She bears down on the towel. They've all grown so lazy in the weeks
since her return to work, *she* has grown lazy; she has taken so much for
granted.

She hopes the girls won't send word to her sister, truth be told. For as
long as they can manage. Out of pride.

"What I want to know is . . . ," he says, "are you or aren't you?"

His words make shapes in the air, but they blur before they can
reach her ears, before she can unfold them from one language into
another.

"Let me see your ID, Lourdes."

"Tengo ID," she blurts, louder than she intends. Her blood beats in
her ears. "Lo tengo. I have. In my purse."

"Where?"

It occurs to her to say that she forgot to bring her purse today. But
no. Every day some green uniform looks at her papers, every day some
green uniform stamps them. The quicker he can have a look, the quicker
he will go away. She turns, still clutching her towel, and points to the
open pantry door.

"Stay here," he commands.

He steps inside with one foot. Shuffles and pivots until he finds her
bag. Glances up with his hand hovering over the flaps, wordlessly asking
for permission that he's already given himself. Still, she nods.

"En el sobre amarillo."

The documents slide from the envelope into his hand. He flips the
passport under his thumb. His face shows no emotion. There is only the
crazy light in his eyes. He sees nothing. He sees nothing.

And then he puffs some air out of his nose.

"Why?" he asks. He rattles her birth certificate. "Why get a fake
Mexican one? Are you actually from Honduras or somewhere?"

At first, she holds herself perfectly still. Then she folds her towel and
sets it squarely on the stove top. For the young man has forgotten himself. He faces into the pantry now, his back turned. The door yawns
beside him. The door with its metal latch, dangling.

III

"Did you get my note?" Inez persists.

Her gaze—piercing, radiant, spiraling like the gaze of the insane—is still fixed on Rose Marie.

Jerry tightens his grip on her arm. "Inez, what in the name of—"

"*You* sent that note?" Rose Marie pulls the hem of her jacket. "Who the hell are *you*?"

"My sister," Jerry hisses, turning to the woman in his grip. "And maybe she'll kindly explain now why she would send a note like that to my neighbor."

"Like what?"

"Ominous. Threatening. Crazy."

"Threatening?" Inez lifts an eyebrow. "I was just breaking the ice, hombre." She yanks out of his grasp and turns back to Rose Marie. "If I'd been able to send you another letter, as I'd been planning—well. Let's just say I was trying to ease into your life. To let you know that there don't have to be any more secrets."

"Remind me what the hell this is about." Rose Marie's voice wobbles.

"Isn't it obvious, by now?" Inez offers a tenuous half smile. "You haven't any clue who I am? Maybe you don't know who *you* are." She turns up the palms of her hands. They, too, offer the faintest tremble. "I'm your mother."

Jerry can only liken the endless, silent moment that follows to the moments before a tidal wave hits shore. He has read about this. Everything recedes. There is no time. No space. How to breathe in this vacuum? How to speak? Who could possibly begin?

"Holy shit," Tavo hoots. "You mean that baby you had when you were, like, fourteen?"

Inez assumes a dry expression. "That's the one."

"Why should we even believe this?" Jerry blurts.

Inez lifts her chin. "I've got documents, hermano. Friends in low places. I've been searching for years."

"That doesn't mean it's not preposterous!"

"Totally," pipes Tavo. "I mean, come on. They're neighbors. Nobody gets odds like that."

"Al contrario, hermanos," Inez responds, her voice darkening. "Don't you know that nature abhors a vacuum? Divide the whole and still it will converge. Imagine how blown *my* mind was."

Jerry whirls to Rose Marie. "There's no possible way you—"

Rose Marie doesn't so much as glance at him. Her eyes are locked with Inez's, and she clutches her braid.

"Your hair," Inez says suddenly, and her tone soothes and marvels all at once. She glides to her. "Your hair was red when you were born. Just like your great-grandmother's. And, from what I'm told, her mother before that."

"You got the first part of that right," calls a deep voice. Its owner waits at the corner of the house, hat lowered, as though preparing to charge.

III

Now what?

Quinn squints into distance. No precipitation, no trace of the clouds that brought it. The sky over the city is pure blue, scoured of its perpetual brown cloud. His feet make muddy shapes in the sand. No silence in his footfalls—the melting hail crunches wherever he steps. The vegetation bows around him, battered, both shriveled and swollen.

Around him lie the things he's made. The things taken and half-built and left behind, things scorched and now drowned. Hubcaps, forgotten scarves, cracked toys, weathered tricycles, empty bottles, tin cans, floating pool dividers, unattended tools, lawn statuary. More. Arranged and rearranged into something that had once seemed beautiful in its ugliness to him, something more than the sum of its parts. Except that it's junk. It amounts to nothing. He sees that now.

It's so stinking bright out here.

He comes down. Down from the mountain. Where else could he possibly go? As though there were any escaping this town. Swallow enough dust and you become part of the desert. Just ask his mother.

His boots sink and slide as he walks. Does he even want to know where she's been? A more interesting question might be whether she would stay if he asked her to stay. Whether she would go if he asked her to go. Whether anything he wants makes any difference at all. The hail makes a crackling sound as it melts. He can imagine nothing more than looking his mother in the eye, asking nothing. Just looking her in the eye.

The sun is a huge eye above him that doesn't blink.

He opens the back door to find Lourdes—gasping, weeping, pressing with all her weight and might against the door of the pantry as someone else pounds and curses and hurls his own weight against the other side.

She freezes before him, wide eyed. The door shudders again—something splinters—and she gasps and shoves back.

"Goddammit!" bellows the voice on the other side.

Quinn feels something rise up in his chest. It reabsorbs itself before it can escape. He's not sure if it's a giggle.

"Who . . . ?" he manages finally, eyeing the pantry.

"La migra," she chokes out in a whisper, and she looks up imploringly—or possibly with embarrassment—toward heaven. The pantry door shudders again. She winces, her hands whitening. Her face glistens with tears and snot.

Holy crap. He snatches up a chair from the kitchen table, nudges her aside, braces his own shoulder against the door, and before the next crash, wedges the chairback under the doorknob.

The response on the other side of the door is an inhuman roar.

He releases his shoulder, hands hovering over the doorknob until it is clear that the chair will hold. Then he leaps for the low metal filing cabinet beneath the wall-mounted phone. It screeches against the tiles as he pushes it up to the chair. He snatches up Lourdes's mop next and shoves its handle through the rungs on the chairback at an angle to the doorjamb. Her broom he inserts from the opposite angle, crisscross.

He steps back, appraising his work, breathing hard. Lourdes crouches beside the door.

"Go," he blurts. "Fly! Be free! While you still can!" His hands make a shooing motion.

She pauses for only an instant before she nods once and is gone.

And then he is alone before the pantry.

The thud of a single fist-pound punctuates the new silence. "You have *no* idea how much trouble you're going to be in if you don't let me out of here."

The voice strikes Quinn as familiar. He drags up a stool from the breakfast bar and seats himself before the pantry door. "Probably not."

"Why? Why are you doing this?"

"I don't know." Quinn laces his hands behind his head and leans back.

"Let me the fuck out."

"Nope." Quinn stretches his legs. "So." He cracks his knuckles. "How's your day going? Aside from the obvious."

In the background, he can hear the "Mah-Na Mah-Na" song Jordan has apparently commandeered onto the playlist from her Muppets CD. On the other side of the door, a manic, spiraling silence.

"There's some awesome peanut butter granola bars in there," Quinn adds, "if you're hungry."

The back door slams open. Lourdes sprints past the window. He watches the empty space even after she's gone, the faintest smile tracing his lips.

III

Huck turns to his wife.

If someone had told him it was going to come to this in his marriage, in his life, would he have believed them? All he can summon now as he regards the woman before him in worn, baggy overalls, whose skin has reddened and freckled twice over, who tugs now at her scraggly braid, is a wondrous, contemptuous pity.

A scrabbling comes from behind the back gate. Then comes Lourdes, a wild-eyed, hiccupping cannonball, apron swinging around her neck. She gallops across the street to some point unseen.

Huck looks after her with bafflement, then turns back to those present.

"Before I chase you all off and try to have a conversation with this woman," he begins, indicating Rose Marie, "let me get this straight. Are you saying that *she's*"—he looks to Inez—"that *you're*"—he looks to Jerry. "You're saying you're all somehow related to my *wife?*"

No one speaks. Instead, they glare at each other, beaming invisible messages of desperation and hate. Huck once again faces his neighbor, who surely can't remain silent on any topic for long.

But something is wrong with the guy. The porch light behind Jerry's eyes clicks on, and it's as though he's tracking something that circles him. Some crazed thing with wings that comes in the night, that sees only doom as it spirals into the glare but can't stop itself, can't.

"*Wait* a minute," says the guy at Jerry's shoulder, presumably another relation, whose expression also indicates a dawning awareness. "If Inez is Rosie's mom, that would mean that we're . . ."

"Her uncles," Jerry says crisply, just before his face purples, before his knees buckle, before he turns away and vomits.

III

Miguel jumps in his seat as a fist connects with his windshield.

He spins to the blurred figure standing at the passenger's-side window and scrabbles for his glasses. Then he heaves open the door.

"Prima! ¿Que pasó?"

Lourdes wipes her damp face on her apron.

Start the engine! Go! Please!

"Ándale pues." The tailpipe backfires once before the truck lurches forward. Where do you need to go?

The bridge, she answers miserably.

He glances sideways as he rounds the corner, veering toward the stop sign but pulling away in time.

Did something happen?

I don't have my purse. Or my papers.

I've got some change, he says, nodding at the ashtray. What happened to your things?

They're locked up in the pantry with la migra.

He gives her a sidelong glance. Her hands cover her face now; her shoulders jerk and heave. He reaches to pat her hand but draws back. "Prima," he begins again, but stops short. The better gift, it occurs to him, might be silence.

He plows through a trough of standing water. If he took Lourdes to his apartment, it would give her a chance to think. He would seat her at the kitchen table, offer her a Coke. Luz would watch them silently from the metal folding chair against the kitchen wall, looking like a gray moon with her nausea and puffy eyes.

What had he seen in la señora's eyes on the other side of the window?

I could take you to my mom's house, he offers.

She shakes her head.

I need to get to my family. Right away.

He nods. Only nods. The water sloshes in the gutters.

She gasps, her eyes bright with new terror.

Will they even let me go home?

He veers back into his lane. For this question, at least, he has an answer. He pats her shoulder, despite himself.

Don't worry, prima. Nobody is going to try to keep you out of Mexico.

III

Jordan sucks the chocolate frosting from her fingernails. "Where's Mom?"

Beside her, Skyler licks her fork and shrugs.

Jordan adjusts her pointy hat. In the living room, the unwrapped gifts lie heaped in the plastic swimming pool that has been airlifted, cinder block–weighted balloons and all, to the rug. The coffee table is missing. Though the crowd has thinned, the music still thumps—Quinn put it back on techno again—and a few people are still dancing.

"She said she'd watch me blow out the candles."

"Maybe she did."

Jordan rises from the dining room table. "Where is she? Why isn't she here?"

"Maybe she's arguing with Dad." Skyler tugs on the hat elastic under her chin. "What do you want to do now?"

Inside of Jordan, something noisy is happening. An alarm. She whirls to her sister, rips off her hat.

"*Find* her." She shoves Skyler hard with both hands. "*Duh.*"

And she's off.

III

"Pues sí," spits the woman beside the juniper bushes, "it's a whole family reunion." She flashes a look of disgust at Jerry. Her look softens as she turns back to Rose Marie. "I'd planned for our first meeting to be in private."

Rose Marie is here but not here. She treads just beneath some kind of surface.

"It was my plan," the woman says, stepping closer, "to bring you into my life years ago."

Huck meets the woman with a step of his own. "A better plan would be for you to take a rain check on this topic."

She brushes past him. "But it took so long to find you. So *long*. And then to find you here, of all places!" She shakes her head. "Except, of course, that when I finally got here, you'd gone."

"Feel free to book an appointment with each other," Huck continues. "I'm sure there's one hell of a backstory. But I don't give a damn about any of it, and now I'm gonna ask you to leave."

The woman tips up her weathered brown face to look Huck in the eye. Braid dangling. Chest rising. "I've *waited*. Waited and waited. Nobody's going to take this moment from me, and that includes *you*."

"And *I'm* saying," says Huck, his voice growing louder, "that you're in the middle of something that isn't your business and that you don't know a goddamned thing about."

"Is that so, cowboy?" Inez's voice is low and deadly. "You think you've got all the answers? You think I should go?"

Huck adjusts his hat's brim. "Yep."

"*Make* me."

She widens her stance.

"Huck," Jerry croaks. "Don't. You won't want to. Trust me on this one."

Huck's eyes are flaming spirals. But he tears away.

"Well, you sure don't *look* Mexican," he tells Rose Marie.

"I'm outta here," announces Tavo, and then he is gone.

"Inez." Jerry pulls himself upright. "You too. Just go. Leave. Go away and stay away, from all of us, for once and for all. 'Gone' is your most natural state. You've got no right—"

The woman's face cracks apart, as though there were someone else beneath her, clawing free, as though she were a clay vessel containing a terrible light.

"*I've* got no right? They took her from me!" She turns to Rose Marie. "They took you and they made me keep you a secret, and I fought them,

I've been fighting my whole life, but you were mine, you were *always* mine!"

At the center of Rose Marie's head is a great pressure.

"Ma'am, I do not know you," she says. Her voice is the size of a gasp.

"You can," the woman answers fiercely. "You will."

"Right now—" Rose Marie swallows, shakes her head.

The woman lifts her hands, inching closer. "Don't you think you could at least give me a chance? What I want, more than anything, is to get to know *you*."

Rose Marie steps back.

"Don't you understand?" The woman steps forward. "Everything would have been different in my life if we had been together. Everything would have been different in yours."

Her cold fingers slip around Rose Marie's arm.

Rose Marie doesn't breathe. Every part of her is numb, unreachable.

And here, with the smash of the screen door flung open, comes Jordan, bellowing.

Rose Marie jerks free as Jordan crashes against her.

Jordan pounds. Rose Marie catches the fists. She traps the small body in her arms and they thrash together, Jordan howling and smelling of chocolate, until their limbs quiet. Until their breath slows.

She lifts her eyes to the woman who waits.

"It's time for me to go," she says quietly. She rises, and the girl in her arms rises with her.

The woman cries out, "Wait!"

Rose Marie sways on her feet. She had wanted this. Maybe not this moment, but this knowledge. The beginning of this story. This pain.

The woman says, "*Please.*"

From the house comes that old Zeppelin song with the mandolin. The light bends around her. Through her. She closes her eyes. There is who she was once and who she is now.

When she opens her eyes, the words spill from her before she even knows what they are.

"I can choose the past or I can choose the future. But I can't live inside both at the same time anymore. I can't."

She can feel the wildness on her own face.

The woman steps toward them again but stops. Eyes uncertain. Voice seemingly caught in her throat.

Rose Marie finds Jordan's hand. Together they take a step backward. Then another. And another.

The woman's eyes widen with understanding, with something that crackles and sears.

Rose Marie can't look away. She can only step back and step back, toward the house, toward the chatter and buzz of the crowd. A pair of children do cartwheels at the edge of the lawn. The early-evening light splays over the roof in blinding, golden rays, and the figure before her grows hazy, indistinct; the mandolin chugs onward beneath the singer's moan and wail, a queen is taking her bow, he says, somebody else waits for angels.

"I'm sorry," she says, whispering now, though she can no longer see the woman's face through the glare. She can only see the slight shoulders slumping and then firming, the dark braid flung like a whip as she turns.

Rose Marie clutches the hand in hers, trying to fix her gaze on the hazy shape before her, as though seeking something she might recognize. But she hears a firm footfall on the grass behind her, and so she looks away. The frenzy lies ahead, and she hurries to it.

24

DAY BREAKS

INEZ, ALONE, AT THE BANKS of the river.

She sits against a barbwire-crowned chain-link fence in which a human-sized hole has been cut. She did not make the hole. Neither has she any use for it. Another five miles or so into the wilds, the fence merely ends, as though it had forgotten its own purpose, but she's already five miles from nowhere. The stars are cold pinpricks in a sky that is only beginning to turn faintly navy. No moon. The crickets still saw at their songs. She swallows the last of her whiskey, savoring the burn in her throat, then hurls the bottle into the water. It makes a faint *ploop* before the current hustles it away.

The river is massive this night, fat with melted hail. When she was a girl, she used to scoff that this río had ever been named Grande. Not when, on the outskirts of town, you could walk in your bare feet through the slow water to the nearest sandbar and wave to some cholo pedaling an ice-cream cart on the other side. Now its depth is incalculable. The meager greenery lining the banks droops greedily against the surface. The current hisses.

The headlights appear from nowhere, the beams swaying in the ruts of the land before she can even hear the crunch of the tires. She leans back on an elbow and waits.

"¿Que hace aquí, señora?" says the first agent who hoofs up over the slippery sand. His accent is laughable, appalling.

She squints into the truck's spotlight and finds his blond crew cut, the gym-sculpted muscles beneath the green uniform. "Nada mucho."

He pulls back his chin. "¿Tiene identificación?"

"No."

He exchanges a glance with his partner, a tall, light-skinned black man who lopes up beside him, and beckons her upright. "Levántese. Con manos arriba."

She looks back to the river. "No, gracias."

The agent looks again at his partner, then with a pointed glance at his handcuffs, back at her. "¿Perdón?"

"Listen, *fellows*," she says, clipping the word British-style, and the agent twitches with surprise. "I'll show you my ID when you show me your high school diploma. Until then, I will lay any bet on the fact that I speak English with more facility and complexity than you do, and with a far superior grasp of the etymology of Latinate words."

Her words are without heat, mere statements of fact.

"No, *you* listen, bitch," the crew cut sputters, stepping toward her, but his partner stays his arm, muttering close to his ear. The partner faces her with his hands on his hips.

"Are you a U.S. citizen?"

"Of course."

"Why didn't you just speak English?"

She shrugs. "You addressed me in Spanish."

"Ma'am, I suggest you move on before the next patrol comes. You've got no proof of anything, and they might not be as willing to take this shit."

She manages to infuse her gaze with a faintly hateful glimmer.

"And for God's sake, woman," he adds, bending near enough to get a whiff of the whiskey, "don't fall asleep out here."

She swats a hand at him. It's chilly out, but she's used to it. How many parks has she made her bed in, over the years of her life? How many doorways, alleys, porches, floors? She's tougher than most. *Tougher than you*, she almost tells the crew cut as he gives her a final mad-dog look.

The truck bounces back the way it came, the headlights fading to black. The sky has lightened to indigo.

She stands. Stretches. Alone again.

She takes a languid step toward the water. It laps against her sneakers, dampening them. But still she feels nothing. It's the whiskey, of course.

But also more. She steps in past her ankles. Her knees. The cold seizes her at last, shooting up her legs, into the marrow. She shimmies in farther. Thigh, waist, nipples. Each new submersion makes her gasp. She tips her head back, her braid tugging sideways in the current, the cold electrifying her brain. There once was a child. She never held her in her arms. She tries to speak her name. The cold current only steals away the wail in her throat, her silence rising past her outstretched hands to the fading stars, again and again, before it rains back down upon her. Before she pushes off from the river's sticky bottom. Before she lifts her legs and drops.

EL TIEMPO NOS DESENGAÑARÁ

TIME WILL ENLIGHTEN US

25

HERE AND NOW

THE FENCE IS COMING. THAT'S been the word for the past three months, on the ground. People still swat their hands and say it will never happen; they argue the same arguments over whether it should be allowed; they shrug, the film already forming over their eyes. The news follows the cha-cha dance of the Senate and House, and in a far-away land of white buildings and cherry trees, the president himself knocks on a door marked Homeland Security and says, "Bam." Here ya go: the Secure Fence Act of 2006.

Brownsville to San Diego. All seven hundred miles.

The Mexican government condemns the act as diplomatically alien-ating. Pro–immigration reform groups are livid. Conservative politicians and militia groups tap-dance with glee. In Texas? Protest. Mayors in bor-der towns like Laredo—40 percent of the economy there depends on Mexican labor, they say—refuse to cooperate with authorities. Uproar in Brownsville, where the planned expansion of the lonely stretch of fence that has stood at the edge of town for years will split the commu-nity college campus in two. Landowners whose families have held title to their land for eight, nine, ten generations—all the way back to the Spanish land grants—freak out as the Feds declare eminent domain, resurvey the border boundaries, and produce maps that will divide their property, their views, the houses of their relatives. Even the governor has said no way. Open the border *more!* he insists. Improve ID technology! Beef up the electronic detection "virtual" fence! Support legal and safe migration—it's the way of the future!

Outside of El Paso, in the distance of desert that runs to the west into New Mexico and the Santa Teresa Port of Entry, between the dome of the sky and the beiges and grays and pale greens of the earth, the fence is already visible, a thick black zipper approaching.

Inside of El Paso, things look the same. On the bridges, the venders still show up in the morning, opening their beach umbrellas near the pedestrian walkways and spreading their wares on blankets. Little Indian girls still creep up on the Mexican side, selling gum or just holding out a cupped hand. But the men, young and old, who trudge back and forth between the cars, hawking newspapers and baseball caps and churros, have a puzzled look on their faces these days. Too much empty space fills the lanes. Whole hours go by when they can count the cars coming through on two hands, and what are you supposed to do when your target is moving instead of gridlocked under a cloud of fumes? Ditto the people approaching on foot. Their numbers have thinned, their pace lacking urgency. Nobody goes to Juárez to get their hair cut or their teeth fixed or to buy cheap booze or vanilla or Viagra anymore. Nobody goes to see Grandma. The drug cartels—the robberies, extortions, kidnappings of Americans—aren't exactly helping to rewrite the travel brochure. The newspaper produces features on the shuttering of the nightclubs of Juárez, fueled since time immemorial by El Paso high school and college students.

The slowdown goes both ways. Word is, it's getting pretty damned hard to find a domestic worker these days, a maid or someone to take care of the yard or fix your roof or pour new cement for your patio—at least, not the kind who can be had for the best deal. It's harder to find construction workers, dishwashers, agricultural help, nannies, assistants for the old and infirm. Those who have made it to this side for good look over their shoulders, buy phone cards, wire money home, circle the Home Depots, disappear farther into the fringe.

The goods of the nations—cars and computers, appliances and electronics—flow freely past them, borne on the swift current of NAFTA.

The fence growing in the distance is a steel structure standing eighteen- to twenty-one-feet tall and running six feet deep into the earth, cemented into a three-foot-wide trench. In places where terrain or security requires it, it has been double or triple layered. When it finally arrives in the city proper, it will replace the old, low, retro chain link and barbwire, and line almost the entire length of the border between Ciudad Juárez and El Paso County with cameras, stadium-style lighting, seismic sensors, and cameras.

Already, the animals know what's coming. They encroach. Coyotes. Foxes. A variety of wild cats. All the things that roam, that follow the language of territory, that follow their own hunger. In some places, the fence will be built to accommodate them; in some places, it won't. Word is, the construction of the fence won't be subject to any laws. The secretary of Homeland Security will waive in entirety—as deemed necessary, depending on the requirements of the locale—the Endangered Species Act, the Migratory Bird Treaty Act, the National Environmental Policy Act, the Coastal Zone Management Act, the Clean Water Act, the Clean Air Act, and the National Historic Preservation Act. Challenges from the Sierra Club and National Audubon Society will be dismissed. The animals circle and pace and go places they don't belong.

At the place where the conquistador Juan de Oñate crossed the Rio Grande into what is now the United States in 1598 on El Camino Real, at the aperture known as El Paso del Norte, the fence will seal the door to the past for once and for all. Protesters liken it to building a fence around Plymouth Rock. Others call it another Berlin Wall.

Some guy in spangled Elvis wear shoots himself out of a cannon right over the top of the fence just outside of Tijuana, in an act of protest performance art. It's hard not to admire that one on the basis of pure style.

Times change. In El Paso, the suburbs push north and east. They sprawl far from water. In the desert outside the city limits, the Octopus and the Yo-Yo of the new Western Playland whirl like fever dreams; El Bandido grins and pulls his pistol once again, though he's overshadowed by a bigger, newer coaster—the Hurricane—right across from the new racetrack and casino. The Speaking Rock Indian casino—victim of crooked East Coast investors—lies silent now at the edge of the Tigua reservation, as shuttered as a Juárez Saturday night. And if a person were able to see into the future, or to at least feel it coming like the rumble of a train—in his ribs, beneath the soles of his feet—he might see a day when Tijuana's Friendship Park is sealed off, not even the passing of a tamale between family members allowed through the fence's bars so as not to violate the regulations of U.S. Customs. He might see the black zippers that will divide the pristine tribal lands of the Cocopah, Tohono O'odham, and Kickapoo nations in California, Arizona, southwest Texas. He might see the mistake the land surveyors eventually will make outside of Columbus, New Mexico, leading to a do-over costing millions when it is discovered that, for a short stretch, the fence has been built six feet into Mexico.

He might see the long-haired dude from the rez outside Tucson— he'll be captured on film on the local evening news as he pushes a toddler around in a stroller, as though he'd been sidetracked from errands— who will heckle a group of anti-immigration protestors: "Go on, you bitches! You're *all* illegal!"

Or maybe the fence is just a fever dream. With every mile that gets completed, the rails that rise out of the Pacific at the start of it all will collapse one by one. Entrepreneurial Mexicans will begin to steal and resell the freshly unrolled razor wire. Maybe the more of the fence that appears, the more the border itself will grow, unfolding hidden crevices like an infinite work of origami.

For sure, a guy can read the future in the memos. Apprehensions plummeting from more than a million every year to just a few hundred. Deportations rising to hundreds of thousands, including—this is more hush hush—those who were brought to the United States as children, deported as adults to a country they do not know, whose language they no longer speak. But nature abhors a vacuum, and already the day is coming when it won't be the Mexicans arriving in the greatest numbers anymore, but the Nicaraguans, Salvadorans, Guatemalans, Hondurans. Word is that Border Patrol is going to be getting some help from the National Guard—if they're ever sent home from Iraq. The future might be hazy, but really, it's like taking in a view of the brown cloud over El Paso from one of those quarter-plugged viewfinders on the flank of Mount Franklin. The line of sight goes on forever.

Times change, but things stay the same. People cross. The heat gets to them, they run out of food, they run out of water, they get robbed, their smugglers abandon them, they get lost. And even if they manage to survive the remotest, wildest parts of the desert (because the middle of nowhere is the only place they can go anymore), even if they dance around the sensors and triggers and hidden cameras, arriving in a magic moment between patrols, even if they find a way to scale a fence with no finger holds for fifteen vertical feet—should anyone be surprised by the abandoned ladders that will start to turn up, or the tunnels that seemingly originate from the center of the earth?—if they're in Texas, eventually they're going to have to cross water. The river. The adjacent canal. Sometimes the beds are dry. Sometimes there's a trickle. Sometimes little green islands poke up from a slow, brown current. And sometimes, when somewhere upstream the weather has passed through hard and without warning, the water runs fast and deep. If you're going to cross over, you'd best know how to swim.

But it seems to Marcus that the majority of these people don't know anything about swimming at all. Maybe it hasn't occurred to them that, like driving a car, it's not something you can manage the first time out, or through sheer will alone.

As with Inez, their bodies wash downstream within hours.

"*Of course* she could swim," his father answered, choking, after the visit to the morgue. "But you'd have to be an Olympic gold medalist to get across the river in those conditions! Where the devil did she think she was going? To Mexico?"

Inez's body sped along the current from some unknown point northwest of the city, through the limbo of downtown—concrete beneath her, the checkpoints above her, the fences of two countries on either side—to the lower valley, where she veered into an arroyo leading to an irrigation ditch beside some pecan groves. When a pair of teenage boys found her, legs pinned against a culvert, she had been there at least three days.

He and Peña are back on day shift now. They still sit in the Bronco and wait. Peña clinks his Zippo. They turn the engine on, for the sake of the air-conditioning, and then off, and rummage through bags of candy chosen for their resistance to melting. The land holds its breath. Not a single leaf of creosote twitches, on some days; not so much as a rodent pokes its head from the dirt. The birds of prey make silent wheels overhead. He thinks. It's easier for him to think in daylight. The mysteries seem greatly reduced. He can think about things like whether or not he wants to join a recreational basketball league. He can think about Laxmi, the woman he's been dating, and how nervously they both laughed when her mother sized him up across her dining room table in her sari, lips pursed, before serving them both a yellow curry.

He can think about the woman and two grade school–aged kids he and Peña nabbed a few mornings ago—as brown as anyone you were likely to meet out here—who turned out to be Hindi-speaking Punjabis. They spoke a fluid, delicately accented English and had paid thirty grand to be smuggled into the United States through Mexico. The others in their group—nine men, Mexicans all—escaped back across the river before he and Peña could rush them. "Jesus, man," Peña quipped later. "Are East Indians the new Hondurans?"

He will not be mentioning any of this to Laxmi's mother.

He has tried to find the other woman, the one he pushed down into the dirt. He pulled the report, asked a few discreet questions, got more than a few *what the hell?* looks. "There are some questions she needs to answer," he responds with his official poker face. Questions number one and two, known only to himself: *How's your wrist? Did you see a doctor?*

He would ask this quietly, most likely through a glass panel. He would take off his hat.

Maybe she would spit.

He would tell her that Cárdenas and the baby made it back into Mexico.

Maybe she would cry.

Did the guy have anything the baby could eat? he would ask next. *Did they have water?*

He would say to her, *Tell me where to find them, and I promise they won't get in trouble. I'll find out if they arrived. Somehow.*

He's been told she's unfindable. Lost somewhere in the purgatory of detention. Maybe in Texas, maybe somewhere else. No one can say; no one is willing to drill down.

Before his father identified her body, no one was sure whether Inez was a Mexican citizen or an American one.

He thinks about bills, grocery lists, about snatching the cigarettes from Peña's lips and crushing them in his fist. He thinks about what it felt like when the youngest DuPre girl unbarricaded her pantry and found him asleep, his head on a bag of dog food.

He thinks about the Mexican federale who drove up in his SUV a week ago and parked fifty feet away, no fence but the virtual one between them. How he'd looked at Peña. Peña looked at him. They looked back at the guy, who stood now beside his vehicle in his black uniform with his rifle over his shoulder, arms folded, watching them.

Peña gave a weird little laugh. "Is this seriously happening?"

The federale tipped his chin at them, beckoned with one hand.

Peña stopped laughing. "Holy crap."

They should have just driven away. At the very least, called it in and sat there. But it was like someone else was giving Marcus's body the orders, telling Peña to stay by the radio.

He'd edged up like he was on his way to the bar for a drink, his heart walloping his ribs, stopping just short of the dotted line he imagined under the sand.

The federale moved forward to meet him—slowly, confidently, hands swinging freely at his side until he stopped. His rifle bumped against his shoulder.

They watched each other across a fifteen-foot gap, until the federale again tipped his chin at him.

"¿Qué tal?" he called out.

Marcus swallowed and tipped his chin in return. "Qué tal."

The federale was a few years older than he and had a nose that had been broken but poorly reset. He was chewing gum.

You need anything? the federale inquired.

Marcus raised an eyebrow.

The federale chewed.

Guns? Weed? Something else? What do you want?

An infinite moment stretched between them, one that could be filled with a million different outcomes.

Nothing today, Marcus chirped. Thanks.

They edged back to their vehicles, facing each other.

Other answers have been harder to come by. For starters, what's the right thing to say to his father, whose eyes these days are blank and hollow? To his mother, who cries. A lot. What he can't say for certain is whether or not they're thinking of Inez, or where she had actually meant to go, which, of course—is he the only one to whom this was obvious?—was nowhere.

He considers the horse, the one Peña found. Out here, in the middle of nowhere. A freaking *horse*. How it was as shriveled and dry as jerky, a leathery eye open to the sky, as though watching for the carrion eaters who had refused to touch it. At the base of its sinewy neck were—what else?—three puncture wounds the size of quarters. He can't explain why he wasn't surprised. Maybe it was the light. The bright, bright desert light. It makes the strangest things look ordinary, makes you consider the possibility that you should stop asking questions.

At night he has dreams. He looks for Inez but can't find her. His feet are wet. His ankles. His knees. He tries to grab a hand clawing up from the surface of a river, tries to pull before the current yanks it from his grasp. He yells but the words are trapped in his mouth; he makes no sound at all.

He sees the whole of the land at once from behind his sunglasses, the brown mountain peaks with their hidden pathways. Maybe he'll take some time off. Maybe he'll send away for his incomplete college transcripts.

Or maybe he won't. Maybe he needs to stay right here, thinking. Until Border Patrol puts them on bikes so they can ride through the residential neighborhoods, the grocery store parking lots, the UTEP campus. Not waiting but seeking. Approaching.

He sees many answers. He sees no answers.

He sees all the way to the mirages on the horizon, so far that the air shimmers in the heat, blurring the line between land and sky. "Freaky," Peña said the other day, squinting. "It's like we could just step right through." Marcus only nodded to the windshield. For sure, it was like a world poking through from some other dimension over there. It was a million miles away but so close, glimmering.

III

Since Rose Marie's return, Huck wakes efficiently, despite the hungover sensation of having wrestled with energetic dreams he cannot remember. He proceeds without delay to toast and coffee. He signs permission forms, pays bills, returns phone calls, often simultaneously. He commutes without daydreaming. He is productive and focused and sometimes returns home from work early.

And yet he still startles when he comes upon Rose Marie—vacuuming, packing Jordan's lunch, drinking directly from the milk jug when she thinks no one is watching. He turns politely away when she conducts phone transactions on the patio or from atop her inflatable mattress. When she descends into darker moods, disappearing into her unreachable places, he ascends a ladder onto the roof to examine the swamp cooler and washes the truck and mows the lawn. Somebody's got to.

The discussion about where she would stay had been brief.

"Office?" she suggested. This was in the moment at the curb beside the Lexus—which, once she'd opened the door, gave off a barnyard aroma that was approximately ten times stronger than the one that was wafting from her own person. "No," he answered. He was unwilling to give any more ground in a territory that already involved too many battles with the junior members of his household over computer gaming.

"I gather Skyler's moving out," she said next.

It was true that he had already put down a damage deposit on a run-down bungalow near the university that Skyler had promised to populate with other rent-bearing girls before the school year started, though if he found The Boyfriend to be living there—rent free, no doubt—he was going to open a can of whoop-ass. Skyler had rolled her eyes at this suggestion, though for once he had the feeling it wasn't at him.

He crossed his arms. "She might end up wanting her room back."

"Where to then?"

He'd looked at her dead on. When had they gotten to the point in the conversation when it was assumed he was actually considering this? She was in bad shape, it was true, and considering the look in her eyes, he didn't like to think of where she'd been or what the true nature of her mental state might be. Yet he could still see the iron at her core, that hard strength he had always known her to rely upon in pressing situations and that would see her through whatever needed to be seen through next. She wasn't his problem anymore.

Her gaze was steady and unflinching. Also, her hands were shaking.

He'd shut his eyes, briefly, then led the way to the hole.

Maybe he was stepping onto to all kinds of slippery slopes these days. Such as his most recent conference call with the board. "For Chrissakes," he'd blurted, "they're a pain in your ass and a pain in mine, but they're not exactly gold digging, just give them the goddamned thirty percent salary increase!" Which had led to a conversation in which he almost argued himself out of a job but instead was authorized to raise the offer from 6 to 12 percent. "It's not enough and it's not fair," he told Yesenia Fernandez over the table. "But it's everything I've got. I hope you'll give me a chance to work on the other stuff."

He restrained himself from clapping an arm around her shoulder when she announced to the lawyers—stiff lipped—that the workers had voted to end the strike.

Meanwhile, Rose Marie gardens. She stuffs her chapped, unmanicured hands into the spider-infested gardening gloves she finds in the garage and plants things, clearance flowers and ornamentals from big-box-store nurseries, muddying the knees of her pants as her hair whips in the hot wind; she trims and snips things into place with pieces of equipment he has never known her to touch—and she might as well, if Miguel was just going to up and disappear; it was a great disappointment to him, he'd taken him for more reliable than that, more loyal—but now, of course, there are further complications.

In the relatively brief interval after Rose Marie dragged in the plastic garbage bags filled with her possessions, before the note and the newspaper clipping were slipped into his mailbox, he wouldn't have been able to say for certain what she thought about the bombshell dropped at Jordan's party. All he knew was that the woman whom he had presumed to be his neighbor's sister was apparently his mother-in-law, and he was having a hard time wrapping his head around it himself; it was the kind of story you told at a bar, to someone you'd had a few too many with, if you didn't mind that person knowing your business. After the note arrived—he'd left it for her on the kitchen counter, still sealed—he watched from the corner of his eye as she unfolded it. He heard her suck in her breath, and then she disappeared into the hole for two days. Jordan brought her chicken legs and toast and bowls of cut pineapple and spent the second night with her. Jordan reported that her mother did not speak, though she wrapped both arms and a leg around Jordan as they slept.

He read the note. Rose Marie had left it open on the kitchen counter. Jerry had signed it formally, first and last name.

It was the beginning of a series of notes. He had watched from a window more than once as she stole up to the Gonzales house—always when no car could be found in the driveway—and pushed some new missive into their mail slot. The responses have arrived in the same fashion, except for the one that arrived in the dead of night: a birth certificate, folded in quarters, its paper shiny and thinned with age. Also a note, in small, neat script, written with a red pen: "I remember this young man, vaguely, but I am very sorry to report that my investigations have revealed he was killed in a car accident in 1963."

Attached, the original note in Rose Marie's hand: "Who's my father?"

The certificate of live birth had been issued by one Hospital Ángeles, Ciudad Juárez.

Nombre: Rosa Maria Gonzales

Fecha de nacimiento: 20/01/1960

Madre: Inez Gonzales
   Edad: 14
   Lugar de nacimiento: El Paso, Texas, Estados Unidos
   País de origen: Estados Unidos

Padre: Desconocido

Added in black ink, in a wild, scratchy hand:

Father: Juan Francisco Aragón Terrazas
   Age: 19
   Place of birth: Ciudad Juárez, Chihuahua, México
   Country of origin: México

Rose Marie left all correspondences out on the kitchen counter, unhidden, as though they were part of a conversation she wasn't having. As though once opened, they could not be shut again.

"No freaking way," Quinn had said, almost laughing as he pushed the note away to look up at Huck, who stood drinking coffee by the kitchen sink. "She's actually *Mexican*? All of us kids are part *Mexican*?"

Huck looked from Quinn to Skyler, who only sat blinking at her own hands with what he might describe as wonder, combined with a sudden lack of direction. Then her face flamed over. "How are we supposed to figure out who to be *now*?" Huck swallowed the last of his coffee. The question—the whole situation—called for a verbal response, but he hadn't managed to find it yet. Nor was he the one from whom explanations should be demanded. He lifted up his hands in something that might have been either irritation or surrender. Then he went to work.

Jordan wrote a note of her own, which he didn't know about until the response arrived, care of her mother.

The question: "How can a Mexican have red hair?"

The answer: "Young lady, I regret that we cannot ask my maternal grandmother, who apparently had red hair as a young woman and was rumored to be Basque. Or possibly French."

He wonders whether Jerry thought Jordan was asking the question of herself—Jerry wouldn't have known Rose Marie as anything other than blond. But there is more than one way in which she is returning to her roots these days, and none of them is blind. Gray streaks the strawberry crown of her hair. As it does his own.

Rose Marie cooks now. She cleans, what with Lourdes gone again too—honestly, he was beginning to think you just couldn't rely on any kind of hired help at all—divvying up the remaining tasks between family members on a chart taped to the fridge. With the used Ford Escort he purchased after the Lexus dropped its rear axle onto the driveway, she does the grocery shopping and shuttles Jordan to school and Quinn to his job at the mall, where he takes the bus to the handful of community college courses for which he has generated a middling interest. To his astonishment, she has picked up a part-time job of her own, copyediting for some kind of trade magazine dealing with hydraulic auto parts; he saw a glossy purple lowrider on the cover of a copy she once accidentally left out on the kitchen table.

She writes, scribbling at midnight into a yellow legal pad. When he catches her at it, she tenses and covers it with a hand. "What's *that*?" he finally asked her one night. "A story, maybe," she said without looking up. "It's not very good." Then she kept writing.

What he wonders now is why he has not yet asked her to vacate. For although they are mostly civil to each other, they have not in any way reconciled. Oh sure, she'd apologized to each of them for the whole disappearing act, her personal problems, blah-blah-blah, but the conversation inevitably petered out somewhere around "Actually, there *was* no other man. No, really," and then she lies down for a nap. And so. Divorce was one thing, and he would get around to it, eventually. Probably. Possibly. But other than the expense and the shifting around on paper of finances and property and the formalizing of child custody issues—not that he has any concerns, anymore—he is uncertain that this potential change in status would change much of anything else. For, as days have turned into weeks and then months, Rose Marie has become a contributing member of his household, both practically and economically, and he's not sure he wants her to leave.

He does not love her. He does not hate her. He doesn't have a word for what he feels.

There is so much he doesn't know.

In the kitchen, just this week, he caught her once again swigging milk from the jug. "If you're going to do that," he snapped at her as she whirled, "get your own carton."

She wiped her upper lip with the back of her hand, and after a moment's pause, stowed the milk back in the fridge.

"There are things I could tell you," she said when she shut the door, "about Jordan."

He didn't move, though he felt a rushing sensation within himself, a powerful current carrying him swiftly.

"I know," he heard himself say at the back of his throat.

Rose Marie's breath caught in her chest.

"Not who," he continued. "But I've always known."

Her lips came together, then apart. Like a fish. "How . . . ?"

He snorted a little, though there wasn't any contempt in it.

"The block party. The one when the twins were at my folks and we both got so smashed? I never mentioned it, but you had a huge hickey on the back of your neck the next morning. I told myself for a long time that I was the one who I gave it to you."

Rose Marie seemed not to be breathing at all.

"Of course, you were gone all night. Who knows where you went? Or who you already might have had plans with. As I recall, it was a time when we weren't entirely getting along. Or rather, you weren't getting along with me."

Rose Marie closed her eyes.

"When Jordan was born," he continued, "it was like you were afraid for me to hold her. To look at her. I told myself you did all the work of taking care of her because, well, there was only one of her. You didn't need me anymore. You could do it better yourself." He shook his head. "I told myself a lot of things. That I didn't know enough about biology to explain how two parents with positive blood types could end up with a kid with a negative one. I remember the nurse giving me a funny look when the labs came back."

He was emptying out, emptying.

"A man can choose what to see or what not to see. And then he makes other choices."

He was reaching an end.

"More than anything, though, the timing was off. Don't know why you think I wouldn't notice *that*. I'm the one who's good at math, remember?"

They stood together in silence.

"I spent a lot of time in that hole," he added, nodding in the direction of the dining room. "Good place to think. Even when you don't know you're thinking."

She opened her eyes. Her bottom lip twitched once. "It was—"

"I don't think Jordan needs to know about this," he said quickly.

She drew a sharp breath. "Agreed."

And he saw a whole new sequence in her eyes, how much she wanted to apologize for a far older slew of mistakes and betrayals and things that were possibly even worse—who knew what?—but that would mean apologizing for Jordan.

He knew this woman too well. He had never known this woman at all.

He didn't want to touch her elbow, but he did. He grasped it, in fact, felt her quick, hot pulse in his fingertips. She remained silent as she locked eyes with him, but didn't move away.

In the meantime, he isn't above listening to her talk to someone else. She stands at the stove now, beside the open kitchen window. Quinn doodles through his homework at the table. If Huck lifts his head, he can see them both as he tinkers with the lawn mower on the patio. He notes the way Quinn looks up from his book to study his mother without her knowing it, sees the pensive and possibly sad look that passes over his face. He could have easily done his homework in his room.

"Did you know where you were going when you left?" he asks suddenly, trying to sound as casual as possible. It had been close to two months before he'd spoken to her at all.

Rose Marie stills the wooden spoon in her hand, then taps it against the edge of the pot, as though she's finished with its contents. But after a moment, she plunges back in.

"No," she says, stirring. "I was hoping I'd find out when I got there." She turns down the heat and gazes out the opposite window, into the unseen distance. "I'm just a traveler, Son. Like you."

III

Life is not a path scattered with roses. If the sky throws limes at you, make limeade. In bad times, a good face. The sun still rises every day, spring becomes summer, summer becomes fall, eat your dinner, right now, I don't care what you're tired of eating, not another word. If you lack bread, eat tortillas.

In fact, Lourdes reminds the girls, what they can all be happy about at this point is a routine. No more collecting glass bottles and cans for deposit after school; no more trash can scavenging of newspapers for the want ads; no more circling at the doors of the reopened maquilas and any business that would let her in the door if she slipped a small peso note under her application. Let the money orders come. Or not. She will not hover at the post office. They have managed on their own. They can hold their heads high.

And yet, as she sweeps under her bed one late afternoon, the broom catches on her old notebook. She wipes the dust from its cover as she sits with it on the floor. Inside she finds smudged penciled words that she has already begun to forget.

As though one day soon it would be like they had never existed.

She slips a sheet of paper and a pencil from Pilar's book bag.

Dear Mateo, she begins.

> I remember la Inez tell me to start it like this. I never want to becaus I did not write a letter before, why I will need to, why in English. She say, ¿quien sabe? Be prepare. I hope you are understand me. It is me, Lourdes, la mamá de la Rosario. This is the start of my letter.
>
> Rosario is gone now one year three month. I don't hear nothing, so San Judas y San Antonio is who I pray and pray. You are no Catholic, I know. But I write you y no a la Rosario because she don't want me to finding her.
>
> My girl. Hair long shiney brown, skin como té con leche, chichis like oranges. ¿Verdad?
>
> Rosario friend Martina, she say she know a address, if you want I give a letter, all I want is grab la Martina arm, shake, say, Where? Where is she? But I can shake forever, nobody tell nothing.
>
> I write it in English becaus you say you understanding it more better. Mejor que español.
>
> I can't go back to El Paso. Long story but something happen and I am in trouble and do you know, can somebody go to jail for lock up la migra in the pantry?
>
> Never mine. I take care the toilets now en el nuevo Walmart Juárez. I am the queen of the toilets.

I sit by the door, I make everything smell como
Pine-Sol y Clorox, I give the two paper squares
to everybody coming in, a los mexicanos no se
importan, but when los gringos come, they give me
la mala cara, they hold out their hand for more. I
don't say nothing. I pay for my supplies. I wait for
my tip. En el Walmart, I watch all the peoples buy
vitaminas y desodorante y Kotex y litros y litros de
Coca-Cola y Fanta, I chase out the ugly dogs with
itches that come through the front doors, I listen
a las cumbias in the speakers up in the high, high
ceiling.
      I miss my headphones.
         ¿Y tú? Aquí viene el Mateo we sayed when we
see you in the street, and the little childrens in the
neighborhood grab on you when you walk and you
pick them up, you putted them down, you laughed.
You, big güero wearing your shiney watch, a man
and you come in my house of womens and you never
stop smiling. Ecsept that one time we drink beer. You
say, I think I am sick for home. Then Rosario come
in to say, ¡Vámonos! She pull you up fast by the hand,
like always. I am the only one seeing that sad look of
your eye before you smile at her again and walk out.
      Mira, Mateo—when Rosario is a little girl, I find
her with her doll. She is sticking it with pencils, she
is pulling out the eye. I say, what are you doing. She
say, I am a doctor, Mami, see? La Rosario, she is the
pretty one in my girls but not the smart one, not the
one who can take care to things without breaking
them.
      Híjole, qué epidemico. Es como la señora DuPre
that I use to clean. It is very hard to be marry. My
husband, I think he in este Kansas. ¿Quién sabe?
      This is why you can understand. I try to explain
it. I try to explain, pero me lleva, I don't know the

words, nobody tell me the words, no time for words anyways. I work six days, morning to night. Araceli bring the money from her job en la maquila, next month she have fourteen year but she already look like sixteen, she put the dial in the stereos, la Chelita wear her old school uniform but she stay home if la Pilar sick or my mother can't walk today. The bad boys in the neighborhood, they notice when Chelita home, my mother tell me. Chelita notice them.

If I coud cross the bridge one more time, all of us together, with new papers we can't pay and my mother with a walker we don't have and nothing but purses and the clothes in our backs and our smiles like we are go to visit the relatives, if we coud cross in the daytime como mujeres humanas y no como animales hambrientas, I woud find a place to live. I woud get more English. Then I can work again in El Paso, a new neighborhood, nobody know me, my English good enof nobody sure I come from este lado o el otro, nobody notis me at all.

My girls in school, talking English. Not clean the rich lady toilets, the store toilets, the bus toilets, their knees on the floor like they pray. I think sometimes, one of them—a secretary, a teacher, a nurse? ¿Es possible? When all I can do is worry when will they get pregnant?

Rosario always use to say, Ay, Mamá, I want clothes, I want to go out, it's boring here.

I still want to shake her.

Where you going with my girl, Mateo? How far? You can come see her, you can come in my house of womens, but you got the yellow hair and the smile with so many teeths so you take her. I am thinking for months and months, how do I say to you, bring her. Bring her back. I don't care qué dice mi mamá, a girl shoud go to the school. A girl shoud stay to her

family. How do a family live at all if everybody go
away? ¡Dios, Mateo! I want to shake you. I want to
shake the whole world like a ugly bucket with water
at the bottom. I can call and call my girl's name, I
can pray, I can clean the toilet forever and the rich
ladys talk me in a loud voice, they think I am def, and
maybe things get better and maybe they don't.

Marry her. Marry her now and give her you
babies with the yellow hair. Porque ¡me lleva la
chingada! I love her more than you do, sincerely from
Lourdes.

III

In the night, Jerry wakes to Speedy Gonzales pitching a fit.

He turns over, stuffing the sheet into his ear because the dog's yapping has worked its way into a dream in which a tiny old woman is scolding him. When he rouses enough to realize the neighbors are going to
complain, he folds his pillow into a taco around his head, angry that a
creature so small thinks it can make a difference—against airplanes, box
turtles, other distant dogs. Maybe the little cabrón is calling room service, impatient for high-calorie treats.

Maybe he himself will never sleep right again. Hour after hour he has
stared at the plaster ceiling above him; night after night he has hoisted
himself from bed and deposited himself at his desk. Here, he preps for
classes with the reptilian portion of his brain. He organizes the research
he's been collecting for a new paper on the historical and cultural influ-
ences of the German military presence in El Paso—if he ever finds someone who has contacts, perhaps it will turn into a book. And when he can
work no longer, he retires to the rear deck, to the railing. To the night.

His electric fence hums. Beyond, the land waits. The view still cups
the crescent light of two cities, shot through with the highway's bright
vein; the smokestacks of Asarco point to the sky like two robot fingers
making a peace sign. But the news has come that the stacks are coming down. For real. And when the wrecking ball has its day, the one dis-
tinguishing man-made feature of his life's horizon will settle to dust.

Perhaps the fence that encroaches in the distance will keep the sky from ripping loose from the earth, its visual presence orienting him sufficiently to keep him from taking the wrong freeway exits. It matters not. Beyond, the creosote still shadows the land, the graffitied peaks make purple shadows in the distance, the mountain hulks at his shoulder. The river still runs, nearly invisible in the dark. So smooth and shallow and composed. Unruffled even when it consumes someone whole.

For that is what he has grasped at last, at his railing in the dark—the immensity of the land's indifference. A person could fall into the wide-open embrace of the desert and be lost forever. One day, of course, the land will swallow them all. What he wishes he knew in the meantime, when the center of his chest feels so worn and thin that the wind blows right through him, is whether you can you stop anyone from falling into the void. Who can be saved. *What do you think, hermana?* he asks in moments in which he squeezes shut his stinging eyes. *What do you think about that?*

The wind is the one who answers. It is neither hostile nor encouraging. In the ruffling of his hair, the way it takes hold and flaps his pajama collar, it says, *Here I am, here I am.*

Once upon a time, dry-eyed but struggling to control his breath, he'd told his sister the story of a mother and her son, separated in the desert dark. His sister did not speak. Neither did she turn to him. She only let out her breath, then stretched her thin arm around his shoulders.

She was the only one he told.

Speedy Gonzales yaps. He sits up in his bed.

The coyote is back.

Chavela mumbles in her sleep and rolls onto her back beside him. On her face is the untroubled expression of a young girl.

He told her. Everything. And when he did, his hands turning up as though to catch something that might fall from the sky, she cried. He cried too. And when news of Inez's end reached them, after the funeral where he and his siblings argued about whether or not it was appropriate that their sister Ofelia had arranged for a rosary, no less with an enlarged black-and-white reproduction of Inez's high school senior photo arranged on an easel before the altar, and Tavo hung beside the punchbowl afterward, never once removing his sunglasses; after the days off from work spent numbly before televised game shows and celebrity interviews, he admitted to himself finally that there was another person who needed to be notified. "I can send the news anonymously," he told Chavela, bracing for fire or freeze. "If you want, I won't speak to her. Ever again."

She looked up from her computer screen. There was no way to measure the depth of the anger he saw there, no way to bridge the distance from where he stood to the bottom. She was already spending more nights in Adam's former bedroom than in their own. But in that moment, something else clicked into place behind her eyes. "Tell her whatever she needs to know," she said quietly, and then she turned back to her screen. As though she understood that, if Inez's death was already a punishment for him, the discovery that she was Rose Marie's mother was a far greater one. As though she understood that telling her has been its own penance.

He's quiet now as he slips down the hallway, quiet in the kitchen and the living room, quiet as he comes upon the burglar who is detaching the DVD player from the entertainment center with his back to him.

An odd thing happens. He is flooded with calm. The room becomes very vivid, sharp around the edges.

"You," he says. His voice is quiet, firm, with just enough of a challenge in it to be recognizable as macho.

The burglar whirls, the DVD player clutched to his chest. He's a young man, about Marcus's age, with a smooth, dark, Indian face, too scared to be much good at what he's doing.

"¿Como entró?" Jerry demands.

He can see the thief's impulse to bolt, but the tone of his voice holds him in place. He has not spoken to anyone this way for a very long time.

Then the little shit laughs. "A través de la puerta, vato."

Marcus—Number One Son, charged with keeping the state of Texas secure, who joined them last night for a mostly silent dinner and then let himself out—has left the front door unlocked.

Seeing Jerry's expression, the thief laughs at him again.

This is when he begins to consider the possibility that this young man is not so harmless. What if he has a knife, a gun? His bare hands. Jerry knows himself to be twenty-five pounds overweight and has thirty years of wear and tear on him, and there's a service revolver upstairs in his sock drawer that he last fired ten years ago at an empty 7UP bottle. Chavela is upstairs. If Adam were home, he would sleep through the end of the world, but soon Chavela will awaken.

"Get out," he says, trying to use the same voice, but he can already feel his grip slipping.

The thief laughs again and steps carefully backward toward the door. Jerry follows as closely as he dares. Before the young man turns to grasp the knob, he launches the DVD player into the air with a grunt. Jerry lurches forward to catch it as the thief springs outside for the street.

He hugs his electronic equipment. Outside, the fence hums, and Speedy Gonzales is dancing in dervish circles.

And here comes Chavela, leaning forward as she tiptoes groggily down the stairs. She who was always on her feet first when the boys were young and called out in the night, who flung open the doors to hidden dinosaurs and retrieved stuffed animals from under the bed while he clawed his way, stupefied, back into the world.

He is alive.

"I thought I heard something," she says.

He's so grateful to see her, rising beautiful and unharmed in the middle of the night in her ridiculous footed pajamas, that he feels a slush of well-being in every part of his body. He sets down the DVD player on the sofa.

Chavela frowns at the sliding glass door. "Why is Kiko going crazy?"

"No reason." A smile cracks onto his numb face. "It's nothing. Everything is all right."

She gives him an incredulous look. "Are you drunk?"

"Of course not."

Her hands rise to her hips. "Now he's stopped."

When she hurls open the door, the only sound that reaches their ears is the squeak of crickets, the scurrying of mice. The fence hums. She calls out to the dog, commandingly at first, then softening, stricken, hopeful like the young woman who used to call out his name from her window to his Pinto at the curb. She goes out, rooting through the shrubs, and stomps back to the threshold.

"He's gone," she reports. The tears are shining in her eyes.

"That's impossible." He joins her outside.

He's wrong. What he discovers, where the telltale turf has been torn away, is that Speedy Gonzales has gone under the gate. Off to hunt down their burglar. Or maybe to join him.

"Why didn't you go see what was the matter?" Her voice sounds like a glass about to be dropped.

He sighs. "I was kind of busy."

"Doing what?"

He pushes the air down with his palms. "Tranquilo."

"Don't tell me to calm down."

"Let me explain something."

"What's wrong with you?"

"Everything is okay."

Her fists clench at her side. "Nothing is okay! Do you understand this? Absolutely *nothing* is okay!"

She leaves him to face their fence alone.

He stands there a moment, breathing quietly. That's when he decides he's going to touch it. In the watery moonlight, it looks no stronger than a mosquito zapper. He's bigger than it is. Stronger. Nothing can or ever will touch him. Nothing will touch what he touches.

His fingers jerk and splay when he connects with the wire, and he trips over himself and falls onto his ass. He's the one who turned it up, he reminds himself as he sprawls in the grass with his eyes twitching.

Then he explodes into a thunderous, multicolored rage, snatching the only thing within reach—a metal garden rake—and lurches onto his feet.

He produces a shower of light as he attacks. It hurts. So he whacks the fence again. He bashes away, lifting the rake above his head and clubbing the wires over and over, sparks popping dazzlingly from the rake's tines until his arms shake and his vision blurs and the fillings in his teeth hum.

Chavela calls him from a doorway. Her voice is sharp and uncertain: "What are you doing?"

The center of the world is the growl building in the deepest part of his lungs. His knees unbending. Rake tight in his grip, whooshing down from above. Then only the sound of his name—*Geronimo!*—as

Chavela, a sprinting blur, throws herself onto him with the dead weight of a skydiver.

They make a fat thump against the ground. "Have you lost your mind?" Her voice is unfamiliar and screechy. "¿Estás loco?"

They lie there like that for a long moment, breathing heavily together. The sky is spinning above him. He has grass in his nose and dirt in his mouth, the grit of it between his teeth. It feels good, eating the earth like that. It's like he's made of dirt, and he's just wormed his way to the surface. The first man. On top of him, crushing him slightly, the first woman, a beetle bumbling through her hair.

Her hands are laced over the top of his head. She rests her forehead on the side of his neck, breathing, letting her tears fall. He lays his hand on her back and kisses the spot behind her ear. "Sí, mi amor," he murmurs. "Sí." Then she rolls off, her hand clamping his, and they look up together, past the silhouette of their house and the shoulder of the mountain, both of them trembling a little. It could be that they're scared. They might be astonished. Maybe they're overcome with beauty. The Texas sky above them is a wheel streaked with stars.

III

Miguel startles himself awake.

He turns over, then over again. He lies flat and lets out his breath. He knew it would be rough pulling out of the old neighborhood. He'd put up flyers five blocks south, started knocking on doors, lowered his hourly, just a little. Luz flipped out, of course. No way could she work, not with the way she'd been throwing up for months now, way more than was normal the doctor said, and how were they supposed to pay the bills? Of course, she also wanted to know why.

"I can make way more over there," he told her. "You should see how big the houses are."

He knows he's not meeting her eyes when he says it. He knows that she notices.

He misses Lourdes. He misses their conversations in the street, the way they would lift their heads at each other across the lawns and plow toward the middle, as though to meet on some island of relief. If he could, he would tell her about this one gabacho he's working for now, he asked Miguel to try to cut his hedges into the shape of a dolphin, he said he had some kind of diagram. Luz said, "Pues, y just try to make a stupid dolphin then," which is pretty much the right answer. Lourdes would have looked down her nose at him, as though to say, *Tell me you're joking.* Then she would have leaned against his truck and laughed until she had to wipe her eyes.

He wouldn't admit it, at least not out loud, but he misses la Jordan too. Kind of like the way you might miss a stray cat that's been sitting for months beside your front door and stares at you every time you leave the house. But also in other ways. She needed him to be something. He isn't sure what.

Sometimes he thinks of how, when he was a kid, he and his dad used to sit on the yellow grass at the lake and toss pieces of old bread for the birds that would come, the pigeons and doves and brown ducks, while the Ferris wheel at Western Playland tumbled over and over itself in the distance. Sometimes he thinks about later, when Papá started dying from the things the needles gave him, how Mamá would come home crying from the wino hotel where he'd parked himself. *He doesn't want to see you,* she tried to explain, even though Miguel knew his father had never spoken these words, *because he'll fall apart if he does.*

"Fuck him," he yelled while she tried to cover his mouth. "Fuck that cabrón."

He said that more than once. He said it so many times, there was no way to take it back, ever.

Now, when he wakes in the night, bumping his wife's soft arm in the dark, he doesn't wake her, though sometimes he wants to. He just watches the shadow of her eyelashes falling on her cheek, and the huge, round curve of her belly, rising and falling with each of her breaths. Sometimes when he thinks of the kid curled up inside her, his heart feels like hot glue. How's he supposed to explain anything with that thing in his chest? He lets her sleep.

He would tell his father about a few things, if he could. Like guess what, Mamá's got a new husband. Did he know there's a drive-through El Pollo Loco where their old apartment used to be? That lady he used to work for, Mrs. DuPre, that good-looking white lady, she came to the door in her slip. Touched him like a blind person given sight, who finally understands *This is an eyelid, this is a cheek*, like the world had cracked open, and she breathed her warm breath in his ear and peeled off his cap.

And he wanted. And he almost. But he snatched the check from her hand and ran.

The question is why. Was it because of Luz, how he couldn't hurt her that way, even if she didn't know she'd been hurt? Or was it because the woman who touched him, smelling of honeysuckle and the first drops of rain on a hot sidewalk, was a güera with money, the check in her hand, and he is who he is? Maybe he was too dumb to know a lucky break when it opened the door to him, not enough of a man to take it without apology because he knew it would never, ever come his way again.

He imagines asking his father, *What should I do now?*

In the dream he has awakened from, a dream he has had for years, he walks with his father. They walk and walk through the old neighborhoods, through the alleys and past the bars and convenience stores, never stopping. They don't speak. The point seems to be only to walk, for Miguel to keep up, for Miguel to watch his father's face. He's about to say something, Miguel can feel it. He's always right on the verge.

Sometimes he wonders why his father doesn't know he's dead, why he wants to keep living over and over when they both know how it's going to turn out.

This time, his father stopped in his tracks and turned to him.

"Here, m'ijo," he said. His hands patted his pockets, and then he had something. A shiny gold coin that didn't say what it was worth. Or no, an old toy—a fancy train car with wheels missing. But wait, not even that. In his palm, glowing as though a candle had been lit under his skin, a handful of smooth pebbles, a white folded handkerchief. "M'ijo, here." Miguel cupped his hands. His father reached into his pockets, over and over, like someone still hoping to find the right thing.

III

Jordan leans out from her bedroom window. The night tastes like faraway rain that won't come.

She rests her elbow against the sill and lets the breeze jiggle her hair. Is she tired? Sort of. Yes. But she likes being awake when no one else is, likes feeling like the only one in the world, except for crickets. A moment ago, there was a brief ruckus down the street, a small barking dog and an electric crackle and then people shouting, but that's not what woke her up. She's brimming with thoughts about her day. This morning she helped her father re-stucco the side of the house. They worked together quietly, not speaking, only the scrape of the trowel and squirt of the caulking gun and the sloshing buckets between them. When, finally, they stood back to appraise their work, his hand found her shoulder and rested there. Then it found her head and tousled her hair. She ducked out from under him and scolded, "Dad, I don't like that." He looked down at her, amused and worn out all at once, and said, "I know." Then he did it again.

Her mother joined her at bedtime. She sat at the foot of the bed, and they talked, lazily, about the things they needed to do this weekend. The science fair project Jordan was considering. How nice it was that the weather was finally starting to cool off a little. The dog grunted and released a deep sigh from his spot on the floor. "Maybe," Jordan said suddenly in the silence that followed, "you should tell me a story." Her mother lifted an eyebrow and said, "A story?" Which also meant, *You're ten years old*. Jordan nodded firmly. "A story." Her mother huffed a little and rubbed her tired-looking eyes. "I think you should tell *me* a story." Jordan went silent. Then she raised herself up on her elbows. "Where should I start it?"

Both her parents watch her these days. She catches them when they think she doesn't know they're watching, as though she were cells in a petri dish and they were waiting for her to divide, and then she stares, and then they act like they were actually looking at something behind her, and they dust something or fold something or pick something invisible up off the floor. Also, they think she doesn't know that this living arrangement they have is weird, but she does. She knows there's a mystery here in her house, more than one, probably, and they think she doesn't notice, they always think she doesn't notice, but she notices everything, notices and notices, and someday, the light bulbs will explode and the missing pieces will all fall at her feet, and before anyone can tell her anything, she'll say, *Guess what, guess what? I knew it all along! You tried to fool me but you couldn't!* And the knowledge will be like a scroll that she brandishes over her head, it will contain the answers to questions they never thought to ask, all the questions they ever will have, and they will beg her forgiveness, they will stand quivering before her in anticipation and awe.

She's just too happy to sleep.

At the foot of her bed, her mother shrugged and said, "Just start anywhere." Jordan peered at the ceiling. "Once there was a girl who lived in a dry city by a river," she said, the air rushing into her lungs. "And?" her mother prodded. Jordan shrugged. "That's it." Her mother shifted on the bed. "What do you mean 'that's it'?" Jordan dropped back on her pillow. "It means I have to think about it. I'll finish it some other time."

She could think about it right now, if she wanted to. She could write it down and go back to bed.

Or she could reach into the wind that tosses her hair, as though she could grab it and stuff it into a jar. She could stretch and sway and drink up the dark until the sky explodes pink and gold at the edges and the birds start to chortle. The wind blows through her fingers. The crickets squeak, squeak, squeak. Tomorrow she'll be cranky. Maybe even the day after that.

But not now. She is awake, and she's not tired at all.

ACKNOWLEDGMENTS

IT TOOK A VERY, VERY (very) long time to write this book—and it would have taken even longer without the help of the many people who had a hand in shaping it during its promising infancy, difficult adolescence, messy young adulthood, and somewhat more dignified middle age. Members past and present of my writing group—Wendy Call, Allison Green, Donna Miscolta, Jennifer D. Munro, Lily Yu—read this book as it was written, piece by piece, year after year, applying their advice with the patience of the saints. Roxane Ramos knew parts of this manuscript back in the day. Suzanne Morrison and Sean Michael Robinson helped push it across the finish line. Jennifer Stierli provided years of moral support. A special shout-out is owed to my high school mentor (and now friend and colleague) B. K. Loren, with whom my true writing journey began—nothing could be sweeter than circling this journey back in her direction. Last but not least, Rick was instrumental in providing his expert knowledge of Border Patrol life and culture. You all have my heartfelt thanks.

I'm grateful, too, for the support I received during the writing of this novel from Artist Trust, 4Culture, the Bread Loaf Writers' Conference, and the Rona Jaffe Foundation, and for the efforts of the literary journals that published early short story versions of some of the material in this book: Boulevard, Passages North, Narrative Magazine (twice), Kweli Journal, and Cutthroat: A Journal of the Arts (in collaboration with the Black Earth Institute), which published an excerpt of the novel proper in the anthology Puro Chicanx Writers of the 21st Century.

Much gratitude goes also to the University of Arizona Press and everyone who works on the Camino del Sol series, including its board, generous peer reviewers, editorial team, and series editor Rigoberto González—all of whom "got" this book from the get-go and shepherded it with enthusiasm and care toward its proper home at last. My agent Stuart Bernstein deserves a special badge of honor for believing in me for so long (so much longer than we ever thought possible), and for being a fine—and tireless—editor in his own right. He's a lovely human being.

And thank you, finally, to all the family members who have ever let me pick their brains, corrected my memory (or my Spanish), or driven me around El Paso in the years since I've been gone. Is it possible to thank a city itself? (Gracias, El Paso.) Of course, it almost goes without saying that this book would never have come to life without the support I've received on the home front from my husband, Mike, whose patience with this quixotic and, at times, all-consuming venture has been epic, and our son, Nico—for I have been writing this book for his entire life. How is it possible that neither of you ever lost hope? In so very many ways, this book is for you.

ABOUT THE AUTHOR

Alma García's short fiction has appeared as an award winner in *Narrative* magazine and, most recently, in *phoebe* and the anthology *Puro Chicanx Writers of the 21st Century*. She is a past recipient of a fellowship from the Rona Jaffe Foundation. Originally from El Paso, Texas, and Albuquerque, New Mexico, she lives with her husband and son in Seattle, where she teaches fiction writing at the Hugo House and is a manuscript consultant. This is her first novel.